Calling all gods,
calling all gods . . .

The creature *landed,* crashing through the flaming trees. The huge clawed hands, the tentacled mouth, dripping slime, all blindly lashing about, searching for the Bard.

Who was sprawled in the smoldering leaves, less than twenty feet away.

Oh God—oh God—it's trashing the Grove, trying to find me. If I run, it'll zero in on me in a few seconds, there isn't anything else I can hide behind. And if I stay here—

Eric brought the flute to his lips, and played for all he was worth.

"Banish Misfortune"—oh, God, please, if there's any resident deity around here, get me out of this!

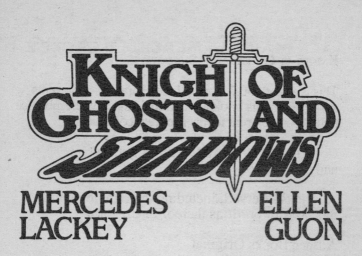

KNIGHT OF GHOSTS AND SHADOWS

MERCEDES LACKEY   ELLEN GUON

AN URBAN
FANTASY

KNIGHT OF GHOSTS AND SHADOWS

Copyright © 1990 by Mercedes Lackey and Ellen Guon

A Baen Books Original

Baen Publishing Enterprises
P.O. Box 1403
Riverdale, NY 10471

ISBN: 0-671-69885-0

Cover art by Tom Kidd

First printing, July 1990
Fourth printing, January 1996

Distributed by
SIMON & SCHUSTER
1230 Avenue of the Americas
New York, NY 10020

Printed in the United States of America

Dedicated to:

Russell Galen, a jewel among agents,
Christy Marx, a true gem among women,
And the musicians, dancers, and players
of the California Renaissance Faires

Long may you wave—

· 1 ·

Tom O'Bedlam

"Selfish, inconsiderate, irresponsible—"

Maureen's voice had been rising all through this tirade; by now she was hitting A above high C, and everyone in the Faire could hear her. Eric Banyon winced, and wished she'd get to the point, since it was pretty clear he wasn't going to be able to patch up *this* fight.

Christ, it would be nice if she'd tell me what it is I'm supposed to have done that was so awful.

She stamped her foot, and got angrier—if that was possible—when she made no impression on the hard-baked adobe. "Shit, Eric, I can't *take* you anymore! You, you, you, that's all you think about! Where *you* want to go, what *you* want to do, when *you* want to screw—now this—this—"

Now wait just a cotton-pickin' minute here— Her accusations bewildered—and angered—him. *What is this shit? I've never asked her to do anything she didn't want to. I've never gotten her into anything she didn't okay first! So I'm doing the Faires for a while—I'm a musician, dammit, and so is she! What's the big deal about my taking a couple of gigs?*

Maureen's long red hair was coming loose from its knot; strands of it flew around her face as she gestured at the messy area back of the Elizabethan Faire mainstage. Eric presumed, however, that she was including the whole of the Faire in her gesture.

"Dammit, I have *had* it with you!" she screamed, com-

1

ing into full operatic voice. "I have *had* it with your selfishness and I have *had* it with this grubby little dump and I have *had* it with *you!*"

"But—" he said weakly, unable to compete with a voice that could fill the Greek *without* even using the push of anger she had behind it now.

"You can just *take* this stupid gig and all the rest of it, and you can . . . can . . . *keep* it!" she shrieked at the top of her range, probably shattering glassware in the taverns and booths out front. "I am *leaving!*"

And with that, she threw down the bodice and skirt he'd talked her into wearing and stormed off in the direction of the parking lot, every visible inch of her pink with rage— and in the scraps of shorts and halter she was wearing, there was a *lot* of her visible.

She nearly collided with one of the Gypsies, who was laden with costumes and couldn't see her. He half expected her to turn on the girl, but she was so angry she didn't even notice the wide-eyed dancer/musician; she just stormed on past, leaving the faint scent of scorched earth— and scorched Eric—in her wake.

He wanted to run after her, but Beth was in the way, and he'd have to bowl her over to get to Maureen in time.

Always assuming Maureen didn't deck him in full view of the "travelers" when he caught up with her.

"What in hell was *that* all about?" The dark-haired, dusty dancer put her armload of clothing where it belonged in the Costumes storage, and gave him an incredulous look. "Who was that madwoman, Banyon?"

Eric sighed, and picked the skirt and bodice up out of the dust, beating the worst of the dirt off them. "That was a . . . personality conflict," he said, choosing his words carefully. "Half of it was my fault, I guess. And the other half of the conflict was Maureen Taylor."

"*That* was your girl? The man-eating soprano herself?"

"Ex-girl," Eric replied bitterly. "At least at the moment. She made that abundantly clear just now. She doesn't like the Faire in particular and my itinerant lifestyle in general."

"But—Eric, *everybody* knows what you're like."

"Maybe she thought that when she moved in with me

I'd change? She never came out and told me that but—maybe she thought I'd settle down. Get a job. Join the Moose Lodge." He ducked behind the burlap curtain and set the costume down in a stack of others. He turned around just in time to catch Beth's sardonic expression through the open door flap. "Well, go ahead, you might as well say whatever it is you've got trying to beat its way through your teeth."

"Do the words 'fat effin' chance' translate properly?" she replied. "You've been a footloose street busker for as long as I've known you, Banyon. You're a darlin' man," she continued, slipping into her Faire dialect, "But I'd ne'er be after chasin' ye if were ye the last stallion in all of Eire. Jaysus, O'Banyon, but ye've got the wanderin' foot an' the rovin' eye, ye do, an' I'd ne'er trust ye wi' a puir maid's heart. Not t'mention the uither fairer portions of meself . . ."

"Give me a break," he said, wincing a little. "I just like my freedom."

"Yeah, and I just like to know where *my* man is once in a while." But she took a closer look at him, and her expression of irony softened to something a little like pity. Not quite—but it was at least more sympathetic. She patted his hand. "Hey, c'mon, Eric, I'm sorry. You just had a rather spectacular breakup. That was a stupid thing to say. I didn't intend to make fun of you."

"It's okay," he said, only *now* beginning to *feel* anything besides confusion and pure embarrassment. The full impact of what had just happened started to hit him. Maureen was *gone*.

Worse than that. Really *gone* this time. She'd never walked out on an argument before. Not ever. He'd always managed to get her cooled down, they'd always talked it out. Not this time. She hadn't given him a chance to get a single word in. He *still* didn't know what he'd done—but he'd sure stepped over the line somehow. And it started here, with the Faire.

Like he'd said to Beth, the Faire in particular and busking in general.

What's wrong with being a traveling musician? he asked

himself angrily. *What's so important about having a mundane job? Shit, I'd rather die. I get by just fine. I did
great before I got to L.A., I'm doing all right now, and I'll
do okay when I move someplace else. If she wanted a CPA,
she should have moved in with one.*

He pummeled his memory, trying to remember *exactly*
when she'd first put up the storm warnings. *Okay, she was
getting zoned, and I showed her the camp—that's when
she just came out and asked me how long I planned on
keeping this gig going. And how long I planned on staying
in L.A. with her.*

So I told her.

*Damn. What did she expect me to do, lie to her? It's not
like I wouldn't be coming back eventually. Why does she
want a leash on me? What would she have that she doesn't
have now?*

He kicked at a corner of the stage, and checked for
"travelers" before venturing out into public pathways. *Just
what I need right now, a bunch of customers wanting to
hear me play "Greensleeves" for the millionth time.*

He ducked through the burlap doorway, and into the
dusty Faire "street."

*I thought she'd figured out I don't like being pinned
down, like the way my parents managed to pin me down
for so many years. I've had my fill of being tied hand and
foot, like a poor little lamb about to get his throat slit.
Sacrificed on the altar of Great Art. Bullshit. No more.*

*I wonder if she's heading straight home to clear out her
half of the apartment? Or are we going through this all
again as soon as I get home? Goddammit, Maureen, you
knew what I was like when you moved in with me! Why
did you have to pull this shit on me now?*

Beth put her armload of costumes away and changed out
to jeans and a T-shirt with "Gentle Ladies of Death and
Destruction ™" embroidered in pink and lavender on
the front.

*Poor Eric. He is going to be in real deep kim chee when
word of this gets back to Admin.* She pulled the shirt over
her head and shook out her hair. *The audience didn't*

know whether to listen to the show or Mademoiselle Mimi. At least he doesn't repeat his mistakes. Traci just went away. Donna married her shrink and left an invite to the wedding on his coffee table. And Kathie—the bitch—drove him out of Texas Faire. Even if that isn't the way the rumor-mill has it.

She hung her mini-ocarina around her neck and mentally slapped her hand. It was itching for her Fender—

We have a gig Wednesday night and rehearsals Monday and Tuesday. Stop thinking heretical thoughts! Guitars alone could get you burned at the stake by the Renaissance Purists at this place, Kentraine. Electric guitars, oh horrors!

She poked her head out into the street, and saw Eric off in the distance, shoulders slouched, head down.

Lawsy. It's hit him. Now we're going to be in for at least twenty-four hours of Gloom, Despair and Agony.

Eric slowly walked down the Tinker's Lane, past the wooden booths, decorated with colorful ribbons and cloth, where the Faire merchants were already closing up shop for the night.

Irish Hill. It's quiet up there this time of night. Nobody to bother, or to bother me. I could play a bit, get my head straight—

A few "travelers" were still wandering the Faire, gently herded towards the exit by the red-tunicked Faire Security. Mostly only the Faire folk were out in the narrow dirt streets, dancers and musicians returning from their last shows, actors carrying their props back to Lockup.

The road continued on in a marginally straight line up to the Hill, his usual post-Faire hangout. But he could see that something was happening up there, a group of Faire folk gathered around a table, the burning candles visible even at this distance. Their bright costumes were now replaced by cowled dark robes. A neo-pagan Wiccan Coven was in session, and it was looking pretty serious.

Tonight is May Eve, Beltane, that's right. I'd almost forgotten. High Holy Day. Lord. If you want to raise an occult ruckus, seems to me this would be the place for it. I wanted to sit on the Hill—naw, they're already in Circle, I'd better not disturb them. I'll find another place to play.

He trudged up the slope to the Traveler's Road, that met the Tinker's Lane just below Irish Hill. He could hear the soft words from the Hill: ". . . Great Goddess, save our Fairesite, keep those who would destroy it at bay. This is all we ask, Great Goddess . . ." The chant faded as Eric walked down Traveler's Road towards the Wood, the dark oaks hiding the last glimpse of red-gold sunlight.

So it's bad enough that they're praying for help. I didn't know it was that grim—sounds like the death knell. Shawna and her bunch are into "the Goddess helps those who help themselves," and if it's gotten to the point that all they can do is pray— He shook his head, stopped, and looked around, the familiar booths and stages of the Faire, the stubby brown grass, ancient oak trees, the shadowed Southern Californian hills rising above it all. *Damn shame. Just because some developer thinks this would be a terrific place for shopping mall . . .*

I wish somebody really could save it. This is the best Faire I've ever seen; it's so alive, always music and laughing— But when a corporation gets something into its collective head, there ain't much you can do about it. Not when they've got all the money, all the pull they need to make whoever owned the land sell it. Possession being nine-tenths . . . and I know I saw surveyors out here Friday.

General depression piled on personal depression.

I don't know if I want to stick around and see this place turn into another shrine to McDonald's and Sears Roebuck. Maybe this is a good time to move on.

Maureen sure wouldn't mind seeing me leave L.A.

Eric sighed and continued walking, dodging three drunken travelers, two guys in shorts and T-shirts, each carrying stacked paper beer cups, at least fifteen each—and keeping their balance despite the added burden of the third member of their party, slung over one guy's shoulder, out cold.

No wonder he's DOA. Their blood must be at least sixty proof. He felt sorry for the Security guy, trying to push the three in the direction of the Faire exit. *Not my idea of a fun job.*

The Wood loomed before him now, oak branches curving overhead to create thick darkness beneath. Dark and forbidding, to anybody who didn't know it.

But it was as familiar as an old friend to Eric, who'd played there for years: on the Wood Stage, and on the streets filled with travelers and Faire folk.

His pace slowed, and he felt a pang, thinking about how this would all go under a bulldozer's blade. *God, but I love this place. It's the only place I've ever really felt at home—even when I want to escape from everything, there's that grove, hidden at the edge of the Fairesite . . .*

It occurred to him that since Irish Hill was occupied, he might want to play there for a while tonight, just get away from everybody and everything and play until he couldn't think or feel anything anymore . . .

Damn it, Maureen, everything was fine! How could you walk out on me like this?

He walked to the edge of the haybale rows that were the seats for the Wood Stage. A group of musicians was seated on the stage, playing. Eric smiled sadly, recognizing the tune even before he saw the players. *"Banish Misfortune"* . . . *yeah, I wish it could.*

The reality of the fight—and what it meant—hit him. He began to feel empty inside, and lost; like he'd lost more than just Maureen. Like he'd lost his way and he'd never find it again. Black despair came down on him, so palpable that he was mildly surprised that he wasn't surrounded by a dark fog like a cartoon character.

God. I don't know where I'm going, what I'm doing. Nothing makes sense anymore . . .

All of the Celtic musicians were on the stage, some still wearing their Faire costumes, others in denim jeans and sweaters. All his friends, his favorite people. Linda and Aaron, fiddling like crazy, with Ross and red-bearded Ian pounding out the fast tempo on their Irish war drums. Judy standing over her dulcimer, the hand-held hammers moving so fast they blurred, with Jay sitting next to her, playing tinwhistle.

And four of the visiting Northerners, two fiddler girls looking like a matched set, one with short curly hair, the other a blonde; off in the back, a serious dark-haired woman concentrating on an intricate rhythm on a dumbek, and that blond bearded fellow playing the bouzouki.

Together they sounded better than any professional group Eric had heard in six years of busking, and the music was magnetic, drawing him to them. He half-reached for his flute, then sighed. *Not tonight. I can't pretend that nothing's happened, pretend to be cheerful and happy. They'll know I'm pretending, they'll hear it in my music. No, they're having fun. Better not to spoil it.*

"Hey, Eric, you crazy whistler, come down here!" Judy called to him.

He forced a laugh and shook his head, calling back to her over the loud music. "Not tonight, sweetheart, I have a previous engagement." He grinned. "Maybe afterwards."

Judy laughed and said something he didn't catch, though from the look on her face it was probably salacious. He just kept his mouth stretched in that phony grin and hurried past them, hoping none of them would decide to follow and haul him back.

"Hey, Eric!" Beth hailed him from behind.

Oh shit. I didn't want to talk to anyone—especially not somebody who saw the fight.

Beth could hear Eric groan, but he stopped, and turned to face her.

"Beth, I'm not in the mood—" he began. She shoved a flask into his long, fine-boned hand before he could finish his statement.

"Have a pull on that," she ordered. "I only heard the tail end of the fight, but I suspect you need it. Besides, we can stay here and talk about it, if you want. I may have to go take care of the rumor-mill after that ruckus."

And I want to know, because you don't usually go around making women screaming mad on purpose, Banyon, she thought wryly. *You may not think about things before you do them, but you don't screw up on purpose. And I don't think you would knowingly hurt a fly.*

Beth remembered Kathie, and how she'd used this lad to get herself into the Texas Faire, then into a pro band, then dropped him like a hot rock.

In your own peculiar way, you're the gentlest man I know. And, in your own peculiar way, the most forgiving. You forgave Kathie, and I never would have. Hell, I still haven't, and I wasn't the one who got it in the teeth.

"I'd almost rather not talk about it," he said plaintively, shaking his shoulder-length chestnut hair out of his eyes.

God, how can anyone be that pretty? He looks like Sophia Loren at sixteen. With the appropriate male accoutrements. Very . . . nice.

Down, girl. He's also as feckless as they come. He's no good to you or himself as he is.

"You want to live till morning?" she retorted, hands on hips. "Look, maybe I can scotch some of the worst rumors. Tongues are already clacking, and they're not being real flattering to you. Besides, you've never hesitated to talk to me before, right?" He gave her an open, vulnerable look that almost made her want to take him in her arms and give him the best kind of comfort for a broken heart.

Almost.

She continued, trying to keep her thoughts where they belonged—*out* of the gutter. "And maybe I can help you figure this thing out, keep you from getting into any more screaming break-up fights behind Mainstage . . . during the five o'clock show, no less."

His eyes widened. "You mean . . . could they hear us out there on the haybales?"

"To the tenth row, m'friend."

"Shit. Somebody from Admin is probably going to toast my tail for breakfast." He uncorked the flask, and took a mouthful. His eyebrows rose, and he took a second.

Well, at least he appreciates my whiskey.

"Thanks," Eric said, pausing long enough to come up for air. "This helps a lot. I think Glenfiddich can cure almost anything, even broken hearts." He took another swallow, and Beth waited until he recorked the flask.

"Okay," she said, "You and Signorina Tosca seemed to be doing all right around noon—what happened after that?"

He shuffled his feet in the dust, and looked sheepish.

Too damn cute for his own good, that's Eric Banyon. He attracts too many women who think that sweet face means he's malleable. They don't look past the face to the eyes, the eyes watching for somebody who might put fetters on him. They look at the generosity, and they think he's theirs for the taking. He'll give you anything, all right; anything but himself. That part of him that he won't let anyone see, or touch . . .

"She was getting hot, I guess, and sweaty, and she wanted to know how much longer I was going to be out here. I told her all weekend. Then she wanted to know where the motel was. I said there wasn't one, and I told her about my campsite."

Oh boy, the operatic soprano hothouse-plant meets reality.

"I can hear the storm brewing already," Beth remarked sagely, since he seemed to be waiting for her to say something.

"Yeah." He took another swig, and his eyes took on their habitual expression of wariness. "Then when I was checking the schedules backstage, she wanted to know how long this was gonna go on. I told her. *Then* I said I was thinking about hitting Northern Faire in the fall, maybe stay up in SanFran after, if the busking was good. I didn't get a chance to tell her I'd be back by Thanksgiving, 'cause that was when the excrement hit the rotating blades."

Beth shook her head, and recaptured her flask. "Eric, Eric, you lovable idiot . . ." *She* took a swig. "If I was planning on setting up a fight between the two of you, I couldn't have managed it better. You probably punched every button she has."

This one is obtuse even for you, sweetie. First you let her think you're planning on a long-term relationship, then start wandering off at odd intervals, then casually tell her you may be cruising on out—without her—this fall. Banyon, you definitely take the prize.

"I don't see why," he said, obviously nettled. "She *knew* I was a street busker, that was how we met! Right at the downtown YMCA. I was playing the street; she was coming back from a rehearsal at the Pavilion. She knew *exactly* the kind of guy I am, from the minute she met me."

"Allow the Great Madame Zarathustra to read the past," Beth intoned in a cheap gypsy accent. "Tell me, in the past several weeks has she, or has she not, been making hints about how you should go do some serious auditions?"

"Well, yeah . . ." The eyes were warier.

"Has she not, in fact, set up a couple of auditions? Like the one you were telling me about a few weeks back, with that chamber orchestra?"

"Well, yeah . . ." He wouldn't look at her.

"Did you not, in fact, *go* to those auditions? *And* get job offers?" *Taking the line of least resistance, you lazy sonuvabitch. Avoiding a confrontation, and inadvertantly leading her on—*

"Well, yeah—but I didn't *take* any of those jobs!"

"Which looked like what? That you weren't interested? Hell no! Like you were waiting for something *better.*" Beth ran her hand through her hair in exasperation. Banyon actually looked perplexed. "Look, dummy, anybody with half an ear knows how good you are. Madame Butterfly has considerably *more* than half an ear. She figured you saw how well those piddly auditions were going, and you were gonna go for something big—and then settle down with her."

"Aw, come *on,* Beth—I never— I mean—*she's* the one that moved in, *she's* the one that started the thing in the first place. It's not my fault, dammit! You know it isn't! Come on, Beth . . ."

He finally wound down, and sighed. "Shit. I did let her think I was planning to stick around and take a serious gig, didn't I?"

No shit, Sherlock. "I think that's a pretty fair assessment."

He looked down at the dirt of the path for a moment, and when he looked back up at her, the haunted expression in his eyes finally made her feel a bit more sympathetic. Maybe more than sympathetic—

Hold on there, girl. Don't let that pretty face and those big brown eyes make you forget. He's the original Love-'em-and-leave-'em. Mister Drifter. He likes having no ties.

*Though I don't think he likes the feeling of having someone
like Maureen walk out on him—they were a pretty tight
little item, and the chemistry sure seemed to be there.*

"I didn't mean to, Beth," he said quietly. "I didn't mean
to string her along. If she'd *said* something, I'd have told
her."

She sighed. "I believe you. I just wish for *once* you'd
look at what you're doing before it gets to scenes like this.
Holy Saints Paddy and Bride, you never do things by
halves, do you, Banyon?"

She shook her head; he hung his.

"All right, now that I know what happened, I can at
least see what I can do to keep your reputation out of the
mud. I'll try to put in a good word for you with the Admin
people, too, convince Caitlin that you couldn't avoid it,
wasn't your fault." He started to turn away. "And by the
way—"

"What?" he replied, lifelessly.

*Come on, bucko. Keep looking down in the dumps, and
I may bed you just to cheer you up. Pure therapy.*

*Sure, Beth, and I've got this beachfront property in
Nevada . . .*

"We've got another gig over in that place on Van Nuys,
and we'll keep a corner of the stage warm for you. You're
welcome to come on by, usual split. It's been a while—
would be nice to have you back, you and that whistle of
yours."

He gave her a miserable attempt at a smile. "Thanks,
Beth. I just may do that. Hey, Spiral Dance is a helluva
lot better than *that* dump deserves—how come you keep
going back there?"

"We have our reasons." *Which I wouldn't tell anyone
unless they're one of us. Not even you, m'friend. 'Sides, I
bet you wouldn't believe it anyway.*

"Oh."

Beth passed him the flask for a last swig, then headed
back the way she had come, towards Woods Stage and the
jam.

But as she walked down to the stage and pulled out her
ocarina, she spared a last, pitying thought for the lonely

figure trudging off into the dusk. *He really doesn't under-stand it at all. He tries, but he doesn't. Banyon, Banyon, when are you ever going to grow up?*

Beth already had her ocarina out, adding the tiny wooden whistle's voice to the jam session's version of "Kesh Jig" before she even reached the stage. Eric watched her join the others, then sighed.

Yeah, dammit, she's right. But what am I supposed to do? I can't lie. I can't. And I don't want to change.

From the stage, Beth glanced up at him, as though asking him if he wanted to join the circle of friends and musicians. He sighed again, and turned away.

No. Not tonight. I just want to be alone.

He headed farther into the Wood, where the gnarled oaks clustered closely. *Far away from everybody, that's where I'll go. The edge of the Wood and beyond. "Ten leagues beyond the wide world's end . . ."*

Most people wouldn't come back this far, past the last palm-reader's booth and the faint lingering chemical reek of the porta-johns. *Dirt and trees and me. Seems real good right now.*

It was in a small grove of oaks, set back against the hillside, where Eric finally set down his flute case on a handy rock. He sat on the ground beside it, opened the case and took out the silver pieces of his flute, carefully fitting them together; as if, by taking especial care with the task, he could put his life back together again. For a moment he just sat there, the chilled metal slowly warm-ing against his fingertips.

This wasn't the first time he'd broken up with a girl, but it had to be one of the worst. Maureen had been—nice. Not pushy. Always there for him—the way he'd tried to be there for her.

Only it was pretty likely she wasn't going to be there anymore. Until this moment, he hadn't realized what that meant in terms of loneliness. He'd gotten used to not being lonely.

God, it hurts inside, it hurts. I can't believe she's left me. I just can't. We were so tight . . . Maureen, Maureen,

I'm so sorry. I didn't mean to hurt you. I didn't want this to happen.

His fingers moved gently on the familiar flute keys; remembered patterns so deep he didn't have to think about them, bringing back other memories, of music, laughter, late evenings with his friends, drinking and playing.

God, it hurts . . .

He brought the flute up to his lips, taking a deep breath and playing a soft note, hesitant. It hung in the air for a moment, followed by another note, quavering, equally uncertain.

Then the notes grew stronger, louder, more confident. He began to play an ancient Irish air, "Brian Boru." It was a melody created a thousand years before he was born, by someone else who was also mourning, hurting. Someone else who had longed after something that had been—or was it something that could never be? The tune seemed to hold all of his heartache.

The last note drifted away, fading into the darkness around him. *Damn. Is this what it always comes to, sitting alone, playing sad music? Trying to say whatever's inside me, when I can't say the words out loud? I always end up in a place like this, alone and lonely, no one in sight. Christ. Is this how I'm gonna end, too? What's the use? When am I ever going to find somebody who can hear what I'm trying to say, instead of hearing what they want me to say?*

His fingers shifted on the flute, as though of their own accord, forming the first notes of "Sheebeg Sheemore." *Yeah, old O'Carolan, now there was a modern bard. Crazy old blind guy, wandering the Irish countryside and writing melodies for his friends. Like this one. What a story, you don't even need to know what it's about to feel it. The elves of Eire, two rival groups of Faerie—kind against kind, kin against kin. Maybe even once-love against once-love, love gone sour and turned into hate.*

But it's a pretty melody, not like "Boys of Ballysadare," where you can almost see the Scottish bodies piling up. I guess elves don't believe in really ripping each other apart, not like us humans. Not like Maureen, anyhow. Yeah, a beautiful song, even if there's no such thing as Faerie.

He could feel the music starting to change as he stopped thinking about it; just playing, trying to take what was aching inside him and transform it into the melody. It was as though something had taken hold of his mind and body, and that something was flowing through him and the music. Like his soul was talking directly through the flute, pure, unambiguous. It was the feeling he had once in a long while, when he was playing and everything was working and it just *clicked.*

And it was happening now, as he played the O'Carolan tune, every note flawless and clear as crystal, every inflection and trill absolute perfection. But not a cold perfection, mechanical—no, this was music straight from his heart, all emotion, with no unhuman intellectualism intervening.

Eric felt a hush, a quietude, as though the grove itself was suddenly still, not a single bird echoing his flute, as though the night itself was holding its breath. As though everything that could hear his playing was *listening* to him, to the music, to what the music was saying; listening with every pore, and watching him. The ancient oak trees, branches gnarled and bent, seemed to draw closer to him, as though concentrating intently.

He closed his eyes, ignoring them. *What an illusion. Oak trees can't move. Too much whiskey, Eric, m'lad.*

He continued playing, adding all the extra trills and ornaments he'd always wanted to, but never dared try. Then he reached the last delicate run, straight down the scale, that was the end of the tune—

—and he kept going. Something inside him, all the pain and sorrow, was suddenly in the music, and he couldn't stop. It was a different melody now, his own, original. And the music was flowing through him, wild and fey, relentlessly pulling him onward.

It built to an impossible climax, a last fiercely defiant high note that seemed to shatter the still air, then—

—silence. Profound and absolute. As though the world was waiting, watching for something to happen. Nothing marred it; it was the kind of silence born of anticipation, as though a door was opening, and everything paused for a moment, expecting Someone to step through—

Eric took a deep breath, hearing a quivering echo from the trees as the last notes faded away. His heart was pounding, his fingers clenched tight upon the flute, trembling. *Damn. Was that really me?*

God, I should have some lady break my heart more often, if that's what it does to my music!

Something startled him, and he sat up suddenly. For a moment, Eric thought he heard something, an answering song from the grove, not just the last echoing notes of his melody.

Then the wind kicked up, sending swirls of dust and dead leaves scattering around him. Eric's eyes began to sting from the dust—as he blinked to clear them, he saw something glinting across the grove, a brief flicker of green light.

Green light?

He felt a chill run down his back; a thrill of wonder and expectation—then his good sense kicked in and brought him right down to earth again. *Probably some Faire kids playing Jedi Knight with lightsticks on the hillside. And scaring the local rattlesnakes half to death, I'm sure. Don't they know that no one is supposed to go up into the hills? B'Jaysus. Where in hell are their parents?*

He looked down at the flute, still cradled in his hands. *I wish I had a tape of that. Damn. I'll probably never play like that, ever again.*

Eric took the flute apart, moving carefully in the dark, replacing each piece in the case by feel. There were times when he loved that instrument more than *any* human. He wouldn't play any better than that tonight, and he wasn't going to try.

He stood up, dusting off his jeans. *Might as well call it a night. I've got that bottle of Irish back at camp, and I think this is a good time to start on it. A real good time.*

Eric felt his way to the edge of the grove, walking with care to avoid tripping over anything, then glanced back. Something gleamed among the oak trees, another glistening trace of pale green light, as verdant and alive as spring leaves. It swirled right where he'd been sitting for a moment, then vanished. It reappeared a heartbeat later, half-hidden behind a sprawling oak tree, then faded again.

Kids. I wonder if they're playing at saving the universe? Must be too young to realize that you can't.

He headed down the dirt road towards his campsite.

Eric managed to avoid meeting anyone by carefully planning his route, but it took a lot of detours. He was tired and footsore by the time he reached the camping area, and feeling the effects of the long and stressful day inside *and* outside.

An hour later, Eric was tumbled in his sleeping bag in a faded blue tent that had seen too many Faires, groping for his bottle in the darkness.

If I make a light, they'll know I'm here. No, not tonight. Not tonight.

His hands closed on the cool neck of the bottle, and he set himself for a bit of serious drinking.

A half hour later he was falling asleep—or passing into unconsciousness—with the better part of a fifth of Bushmills becoming one with his bloodstream.

And since he was the only one with a vantage point—and the only one not engaged in nocturnal activities that precluded idle observations—he was the only one of the Faire folk who noticed the activity over the hill. The verdant green glow that flickered and vanished between the trees, in the hidden oak grove he had left to sing to itself.

Eric would have chalked up the effect to the Bushmills, except that he'd seen it start *before* he took his first drink.

It was still playing its little games among the tree trunks as he passed out, and his last coherent thought was to wonder if it would continue until dawn.

· 2 ·

Echoes From the Forest

"Shit! Quarter till nine, and I can't find my goddamn *socks!*"

"Damnation, Seamus, I'll nc'er be o'er thar in time! Run on wi'out me, laddie!"

Eric Banyon awoke to the absolute cacophony that was the usual "morning song" of Faire. The assorted cries and shouts of the actors and musicians in the campsite mingled with the clanking of pots and pans. The gabble of voices in a dozen conversations nearby echoed vilely in an unholy concert with the pounding in his head. He opened one eye warily, felt the bright sunlight kick him in the face, and closed the eye again.

God, I'm going to die. Please God, let me die. I think I drank too much. No, strike that—I know I drank too much.

If I'm going to die, I sure hope it happens soon . . .

He reached a hand out without opening his eyes, and felt around the floor of the tent; when his hand encountered the coolness of glass, he picked up the whiskey bottle, shaking it slightly.

No, strike that again—I couldn't have drunk too much. There's some still left in the bottle.

He opened his eyes long enough to take a healthy swallow from the half-empty whiskey bottle. *Mmm, good old Irish Breakfast. I'll bet this is the only reason they never conquered the world.*

He swigged again, and sighed.

19

I think I'm going to live. Which means I'd better get on 'site.

He pried both eyes open again and crawled out of the sleeping bag, blinking blearily. Eric found his faded brown breeches on the other side of the tent, where he had discarded them last night, then rummaged through his backpack. A fresh Faire shirt, one that used to be white but now was a shade between gray and brown, replaced the one he had slept in last night. He pulled breeches and shirt on, and scratched his head, trying to remember what came next.

Feet. First, find your feet. Then find what you put on your feet. New socks came out of the bottom of the pack; he pulled his moccasin boots on over them without jarring his skull *too* much. After a brief moment of panic, he found his belt beneath the jumble of assorted props and costumes on the floor in the "storage" corner of his tent.

Eric fastened the money pouch, wooden comb, and flask on the belt, took another swig of whiskey, and he was ready to face the world again.

Well, maybe not, but I'll give it a try . . .

Taking a deep breath, he unzipped the door to the tent, stepping outside. As he expected, it was a beautiful morning, clear blue skies over the green-brown hills, with almost everyone in sight already in costume and heading into the Fairesite.

He staggered to the large water tank at the edge of campsite, and braced himself.

Here goes—

He stuck his head beneath the faucet and turned it on. The water, cold as a mother-in-law's heart, hit him like a hammer on the back of the skull, and froze him all the way down to his toenails. He was shivering when he straightened up again.

Much better. I think.

He used the metal side of the water tank as a mirror as he combed his hair, trying without success to make the shoulder-length brown mop look presentable.

Some day I'll shave it all off, honest to God. Hell, it worked for Yul Brynner, didn't it?

"Good morning, Eric!" one of the dancers from the Irish show called to him from across the sink.

Some people are just too damn *awake in the morning.*

"Bah, humbug," he replied, somehow managing to sound cheerful enough.

Brigid, that's her Faire name, if I'm remembering correctly. Don't remember her Mundane name. He gave her a long, appraising look as she sauntered away from him with a definite swing to her hips. *Scenic. Very scenic. Lovely from the front, lovely behind, terrific dancer's legs. Well, now that I'm a bachelor again . . .*

Oh, hell. Maureen, that should be you wiggling your hips at me . . .

He watched the dark-haired dancer start towards the Main Gate with morose appreciation for a moment, then returned to his tent for his flute.

Besides, Brigid's a morning person. I could never cope with somebody who's that happy *at nine in the morning, never.*

He slipped the flute case into his embroidered gig bag (gift of Kathie, late of the Texas Faire, two girlfriends before Maureen) and started down the hill towards the Main Gate.

I've had my Irish Breakfast; I'd better get a real one before I fall on my nose.

Eric expertly dodged through the thickening Faire crowds, a tankard of coffee and a stack of hot sticky cinnamon buns balanced precariously in his hands. He found a quiet haybale near one of the smaller stages, and sat down to break his fast.

Three Commedia dell'Arte actors were on the stage, wearing the brightly-painted leather masks of the legendary Italian comedians.

". . . Isabella, don'tcha know you're a-breakin' my heart?"

"An' that isn't all I'll break, Harlequino!"

Eric laughed with the travelers seated around him as dainty Isabella chased Harlequino around the stage, waving a rolling pin with wild enthusiasm.

Except Isabella's hair was long and vivid red, and her voice was a little too strident.

Almost operatic.

A piece of cinnamon bun stuck in his throat.

Eric stood up abruptly, leaving the show even as Harlequino protested his innocence to the furious Isabella.

He walked through the Faire, eyes mostly on the dirt road littered with pieces of hay and sawdust. "Boothies" were briskly doing business with the crowd of travelers, haggling over handmade jewelry, leather pouches, intricately-decorated costumes. Hawkers were already calling to potential customers: "Ice cold milk and hot fruit pies!" "Turkey legs!" "Beef ribs, two hundred pence!"

I don't have anywhere to go, anything in particular that I have to do, at least not until the 11:30 show. Christ. Nothing to do at all . . . except brood.

Well, if I'm going to brood, I might as well do it melodically.

He took his gig bag off his shoulder, removing the flute case. He fitted the flute together, slinging the bag back to its comfortable place at his side.

The travelers looked at him peculiarly. It wasn't all that odd to see a costumed musician walking the Faire, but a flautist was a rarity, and the morose melodies he chose were *definitely* out of keeping with the "merrye spirit of Olde England" that everyone else was projecting.

Eric finished a rendition of "Coleraine"—*Funny, you never think of how an Irish jig could be so depressing*—and began another slower, even sadder tune. He was so lost to the melody and his own depression, that he really didn't notice the two step-dancers that smoothly moved in and escorted him around the corner.

Until they each grabbed an elbow.

"Hey, wait a—"

"Och, don't ye be frettin', Master Eric," one of the dancers said with a wicked grin. "We've been sent to fetch you, we have."

"But—"

"No arguments, sar, we shan't listen to them!"

"But—"

One of them carefully took the flute from his hand, replacing it in his gig bag before they hurried him through the crowded "streets."

Suddenly he realized where they were taking him. Eric's eyes widened.

"No, not the washing well!" He tried to pull free, but the two young women had him past escaping—unless he wanted to take this out of the realm of a street bit and practical joke and into a serious scuffle.

"We've brought him, Mistress Althea!"

The heavyset woman, her dark hair tucked up into a clean muffin cap, looked him over with a practiced eye. "Well, then, he does seem truly the scruffiest of minstrels. We can't have this. Before we take 'im over, first we'll need to give 'em a bath . . ."

No, not a bath! Not in the godforsaken filthy washing well!

Mistress Althea took him firmly by the ear, pulling him over to the washing well to the vast amusement of the onlookers. "I'll get even with you for this, Susie," he whispered, too low to be heard by the mundanes.

"But not till after I've had a good chance to wash your ears," she whispered back, barely able to keep a straight face. "This'll teach you to clean up your act before you come on 'site."

Eric suffered through having a scrap of cloth, dipped in the well, rubbed over every inch of his face.

Finally, Mistress Althea pronounced him cleansed, and fit for human company. "Now, girls," she said sonorously, "do take him onward to his next stop."

My next stop? All right, who's playing games, here?

Eric let the two girls drag him onward, down the dusty road to the stage where Sunday Mass was in progress.

Father Bob, wearing a Roman collar over his Elizabethan costume, dutifully blessed Eric as the girls paraded him up to the front of Mass. "In the name of the Father, the Son, and the Holy Ghost, Lord, who watches over fools and children, wilt Thou see that somebody please keeps an eye on this minstrel boy? Thank you very much, God."

Eric stared backwards at Father Bob as the dancers pulled him away again. The priest was trying not to break into laughter. *Yes, something definitely strange is going on here* . . .

The two girls—Eric realized he didn't even know their names—pulled him down the lane, past the glassblower's booth and the stall hanging with dozens of bota bags, directly towards the Kissing Bridge . . .

Now wait just a second—

Before he could react, they were halfway across the bridge, beneath the colorful garlands and ribbons that festooned the wooden archway. They stopped, keeping him trapped between them, and the two dancers kissed him expertly, one after the other.

More than a bit bemused, Eric let them. After his initial surprise, he *helped* them.

Well, this is definitely an unusual *experience* . . .

Then they tugged his hands to draw him onward, across the bridge and down the lane to the Laughing Fool Tavern. And there was Beth, waiting with the other musicians by the gate.

Oh, now *this is all starting to make sense* . . .

The two dancers delivered him to the tavern gate, bobbing a quick curtsy to Beth. "An' here he is, mistress, clean and blessed. And warmed up. As 'twere."

"Why, thank you, my dears," Beth said, her eyes never leaving Eric's. "I do truly appreciate your efforts." She took Eric's arm, leading him into the tavern.

"Beth . . ." he muttered, "I'll get you for this."

She let go of his hand and stepped up onto one of the rough-hewn tavern tables, calling out for silence in a clear voice. "M'lords and ladies, we have here a lad who has been well and truly heartbroken, who spent last night all alone with only a bottle for comfort . . . and we all know that a bottle is a rather cold and miserable bedmate, not like a saucy wench!"

Eric felt himself blushing as the crowd of travelers outside the tavern cheered rowdily.

Beth smiled. "Seems he needs a hand. So, what shall we do for this poor lad, I ask you?"

"Give him to the German mercenary wenches!"

"Sell him to the gypsies!"

"Make him play us dancing music!"

Beth turned to him, her voice slightly softer. "Well, sirrah, what shall it be?" She looked him up and down. "I dare say we shouldn't get much for you from the gypsies. Too skinny, methinks. So, it's the girls, or the tunes. A spritely dancing tune, or the meaty paws of the German wenches?" Beth grinned evilly, and added in an undertone, "I'd play the tune if I were you, Eric. Karen Wolfsdottir has been yearning to get her mitts on you all season."

Eric was already reaching into his gig bag for his flute.

The first tune he played was "Banish Misfortune," as lively and cheerful a melody as he could think of. The Faire folk, seated at the wooden trestle tables, began to clap and pound the table with their tankards in rhythm with the tune, and then he saw Ian and Linda sneaking up from the back of the tavern, drum and fiddle already in their hands. *Oh, Bethie planned this one in advance, methinks! Okay, then, let's do it right!*

He leaped up on the table without missing a beat, startling the two peasants playing a game of Cathedral next to him. With Ian holding the beat steady on his bodhran drum, and Linda deftly carrying the melody for him, Eric continued to play the flute, but also began to hop and skip down the long table, to the raucous cheers of the onlooking travelers. Beth clapped her hands in glee, watching him from a precarious perch atop the tavern fence and laughing wildly.

Winded, he jumped off the edge of the table, landing in the straw next to the two giggling dancer girls who had brought him there. He stopped the tune in mid-note and grabbed the older of the two girls, the one with the long red-gold hair and wicked green eyes, and kissed her soundly before letting her go. She landed on her posterior in the thick hay, still laughing.

Eric doffed his cap at her and her companion. "I thank ye both for bringing me here," he said in his finest Elizabethan accent. "You're both lovely lasses, and I implore you to dance for us all!"

The two girls looked at each other uncertainly.

Beth called from her position on the rickety tavern fence. "Oh, and come on with you now, lasses! Show us what ye can do!"

And they did.

Eric applauded and cheered with the travelers and Faire folk as the red-haired girl helped her companion up onto the table. Then they moved into proper stepdancer position, arms linked, one foot raised with the toes delicately pointed forward.

Linda and Ian were watching him for the signal. "Athol Highlander's!" he called, then hit the first note of the rollicking Scottish jig straight on, Linda joining in a moment later with as sweet a bit of fiddling as he'd ever heard her play, then Ian tossing off a few clicks on the rim of his bodhran before settling into some serious drumming.

The girls danced down the long table, skipping and pirouetting to the shouts and calls of the audience. Then, as the tune wound to a close, they also leaped off the table, startling Eric so much that he flubbed the last note. They both laughed with him, as he shook his head in disbelief.

It only got better after that.

After several more dances and tunes (including a very bawdy Elizabethan song that sounded almost prim when sung solo, but when you sang it in a round, the words made the most amazing sentences), Eric relaxed at one of the tables. A tankard of the Fool's best was in front of him as he watched the expert belly dancer strutting her stuff to a Scottish strathspey.

Well, it may not be "period," but who cares at this point?

Beth sat down next to him, taking the mug from his hand and draining a long draught. "Is life treatin' you better now, Banyon?"

He sighed and reclaimed the tankard from her hand. "Well, I still think telling Susie to wash me in the well was a rotten trick . . ."

"Agreed. But I couldn't let you in here with dirty ears." She leaned close to nibble on his right ear. "Do you see why?"

He took a moment to recover. "Uh, yeah."

"I'm glad." She stood up, taking his hand. "I think we've caused enough mischief for one morning. Want to take it elsewhere?"

Eric glanced up at the main trestle table, where the two dancer girls had kidnapped two Spaniards and were trying to teach them to stepdance, to the laughter of all onlookers. "Sounds good."

Beth led him behind the tavern, through the back gate and across the lane. Directly towards the Kissing Bridge.

Oh no, not the Kissing Bridge again . . .

She pulled him onto the Bridge, already populated with lingering couples. "There's only one cure for a broken heart, Banyon, and I've taken it upon myself to administer it. Don't take it personally. This is for purely therapeutic reasons only."

"Bethie—"

And she kissed him.

A significant amount of time later, he managed to find his voice again. "Uh, Bethie—"

"Mmmm?" She cuddled even closer.

"You know, I have half of a perfectly good apartment that's free for the taking, anybody could move in. And it could really use someone with a nice feminine touch—"

Beth suddenly stiffened in his arms. "Don't even think it, Banyon. Someday you may find someone who's right for you, but I'm not that lady. Don't get me wrong, I like you a lot, but let's not complicate it past that, all right?"

"Okay." He kissed the tip of her nose, making her giggle. "I just like you a lot, too." His lips moved lower, down her neck. "The offer's there if you want it, all right?"

An apologetic voice, somewhere next to his left ear, interrupted what had been a fascinating progression down the strong line of her shoulder. "Er, ah, Mistress Beth, they're about to start the Mainstage show, and Carl really is wondering if you're planning on joining us today."

"Oh, damn." Beth retrieved herself from Eric's arms,

quickly straightening her costume. She gave him a wry grin. "Well, duty calls, Master O'Banyon. I'll look for you after the show."

Eric watched regretfully as Beth and her showmate disappeared into the crowd of travelers on the street. *I never can manage to hold on to that girl for more than five minutes at a time. That's all she's interested in with me. I guess some guys would like that, a lady who's just a good friend and a willing bedmate. The perfect situation, right?*

Damn.

He walked away from the Bridge, wandering aimlessly. After a while, he realized that he was back on the road above the Laughing Fool. Since he and Beth had left, the tavern had returned to its usual quiet state, a few actors conversing over a mug of ale, some "peasant women" eating lunch at another table.

Eric found himself an empty haybale near the tavern gate, sat down, and took out his flute again. He touched the keys lovingly, as the metal warmed to his hand.

Hello, old friend. Just you and me again. He remembered how he had argued with Admin over playing a metal flute at a "period" Faire. *I don't know what I'd do if they hadn't given in. I can't see doing a gig without you. I think they knew that, and decided they'd rather keep me and be anachronistic than watch me walk out.* He played an experimental run, thinking about how the red-haired dancer had laughed after he had kissed her. *I should write a tune for that lovely, something she and her friend can dance to.* He smiled as a tune began to shape itself in his mind and fingertips, a lively little melody that brought pleasant images, recollections of Faires past; of laughing girls, dainty feet tapping out an intricate highland dance, and of chilled ale on a hot Faire afternoon.

Then his spirits dropped again, and he settled down to some seriously morose music.

"Cliffs of Moher," there's a good one. And "Kid on the Mountain," that's challenging and depressing.

Without his realizing it, Eric's sad fluting brought in a crowd of listeners to the edge of the tavern fence. He looked up to see the travelers listening intently to him, and smiled sadly to himself, thinking: *They don't understand.* He continued to play.

Eric looked up again. Something in that mass of faceless travelers had looked strangely familiar . . .

. . . yeah, that skinny guy, the tall blond, the one with the embroidered cloak . . . wait a minute—his cloak—my cloak!

Eric leaped up from the haybale, diving over the wooden fence like an avenging angel. The young man in the shrouding cloak took one look at Eric's snarling face and ran like hell.

A matronly female customer screamed as Eric catapulted past her, one hand reaching for the trailing edge of the ankle-length cloak. Other travelers scattered out of the way as Eric pursued the young man past the astonished washerwoman at the well and right through a colorful troupe of morris men dancing in the middle of the dirt street. Angry shouts and the sound of clattering leg-bells followed them down the road.

The thief crashed through the bota-bag booth, sending the hanging wineskins flapping wildly at their tethers. Eric followed close on his tail, waving his flute like a deadly weapon. "Stop, you lousy bastard! Thief! *Thief!*"

The cloaked robber dashed under a monger's carefully balanced tray of fresh tripe and crossed the Kissing Bridge in one desperate leap. Eric vaulted after him, thoroughly disrupting the amorous affairs of the kissing couples on the Bridge.

Then he saw the kilted Scottish troop directly ahead of him, carrying their pikes at attention as they marched down the street. Eric skidded to a stop, not wanting to crash into the Scottish warriors—and their six-foot spears.

But the cloaked man kept running.

Right through the formation of marching pikesmen.

Eric stared in disbelief as the nimble thief danced past the warriors and their deadly spears. Somehow he made it look simple and easy as he dodged between them. Then the thief was across, on the other side of the formation without so much as causing a single pikesman to miss a step.

Several of the watching travelers applauded, doubtlessly thinking this was part of a show. Eric just stood there, staring after the escaping thief in amazement.

Nobody should be able to do that. . . .

Eric took a deep breath and ran after him, straight into the pike formation . . . and three seconds later, he found himself sprawled on the dirt with several pikes lying around him, and a half-dozen irate Scotsmen glaring at him in disgust.

Then the dark-bearded Scottish chieftan himself walked over and looked down at Eric.

"Oh, Eric, lad, you've done yerself quite a turn this time, ye have," the Chief said sadly.

"Sorry, Boss," Eric muttered, trying to stand up without much success. His ankle hurt. Not to mention his pride.

After yesterday, there wasn't anything left of his dignity to hurt.

The Chief crouched down in the dust close to Eric. "By the way," he said in a quiet voice entirely devoid of Scottish accent, "Caitlin wanted to see you in Admin. Something about the Mainstage show yesterday."

"Terrific," Eric said morosely. One of the Scots helped him stand, dusting him off. Eric thanked him, then scanned the crowd for any sign of the thief.

Nowhere in sight. Damn.

So much for my favorite Faire cloak. I wonder how that little rat got past Security and into my tent?

The pikesmen lined up into their formation. The Chief gave Eric one last, pitying look, a look Eric caught out of the corner of his eye as the troop of Scotsmen marched off towards their encampment.

Well. Better get it over with.

He headed for Admin Hill and the offices directly behind the large brightly-colored Faire mural.

Caitlin's a good lady; she usually understands these things. I mean, she's the one who got me out of that jam

*last year with the Maypole dancers. They're not going to
can me . . . I hope.*

Eric moved carefully through the thickening traffic on
the dusty lane, past the travelers haggling with the boothies
over their wares. He stepped carefully over three peasants
sprawled out "drunk" in the street and doffed his cap at
the bored Security guard at the office entrance.

Inside the musty, crowded office area, costumed actors
and musicians were relaxing, several smoking some defini-
tively non-period Marlboros, others drinking sodas and
catching up on gossip. Eric crossed to the hanging burlap
flap that was the door to Caitlin's office, and took a deep
breath. "Caitlin?"

A tired female voice answered. "Come in."

Eric walked into the makeshift office. Caitlin looked up
from the stacks of paperwork on the table, her ever-
present can of diet soda in her hand. "Hello, Eric. Is it
Fate or bad luck that you always end up in my office?"

"A bit of both, I think." He sat down on a folding chair
across from her. "Does it help if I tell you that I really try
to avoid this sort of thing?"

"Yes, a little. I was starting to wonder if you got in
trouble just so you could flirt with me in my office." She
leaned back in her chair, wearily running her hand through
her short auburn hair. Her long blond wig, with the floppy
hat she usually wore as part of her costume, was lying on
the table near the papers.

Eric stared at the wig to avoid meeting her gaze.

"So, Eric, you and your girlfriend decided to break up,
right behind the four-thirty Mainstage show yesterday.
Made it quite interesting for the audience. I understand
your ex-girlfriend has quite an operatic voice."

Eric winced. "Yes, she does. Great projection, too."

Caitlin almost cracked a smile. "You're classically trained
too, aren't you? Somebody told me you studied at Juilliard.
Is that true?"

"Yeah, I was at Juilliard. Two years." He shifted uncomfortably, a knot already beginning to tighten in his gut at
the mere thought of those two years. He flashed on his last
recital—

Playing better than he ever had in his life; playing his heart out. Then putting the flute down. Announcing to the panel—"Today was my birthday. Last night somebody threw rocks at my window all night long to keep me awake. This morning somebody else jammed the lock on my door so I had to climb out my window to make it here on time. I can't take this shit anymore. I'm eighteen and my parents can't do a thing about me now. Gentlemen, ladies, you can take your goddamned classical education and shove it."

And the long, absolute silence as he walked out.

Six months before I could bear to touch the flute. Eight before I could play again. Three years before I could even listen to Bach.

Damn. I really wish people wouldn't ask me about that.

Caitlin was watching him with knowing eyes. "Eric, you're a sweetheart, and one of the best musicians we've ever had here, but somehow you're always getting in trouble. I'll clear you on this one, cover you for the people Upstairs, but—try to avoid this kind of thing in the future? Just try, all right? Promise me?"

He sighed. *I don't know whether to be relieved that she let me off easy, or embarrassed because I know she's letting me off just 'cause I'm good. Guess I'd better just count my blessings.*

"Thanks. I'm really sorry about this." He stood up to leave. Caitlin's voice stopped him before he reached the door.

"Eric?"

He turned back to her.

"I know you're going through a rough time, your girlfriend walking out on you and everything. Just don't . . . leave, okay? I heard what happened in Texas, when you had girlfriend problems there. Don't just walk out on us, Eric. I'd really like you to finish out the season with us, okay?"

He nodded, and lifted the burlap flap, walking out of the relative quiet of her office into the overwhelming noise levels of the Admin area.

So. Somebody told Caitlin about my Texas adventure. Shouldn't be surprised, I guess.

Damn it, what's so terrible about just packing up and leaving when things go that wrong? God, if I'd stayed at Texas Faire—between us, Kathie and me, we'd have had the place divided like the Civil War all over again. So I split, and now everybody treats it like some kind of sin. And Caitlin, she's acting like I'm about ready to run from Southern California. She doesn't have any reason to think that. Except—

—except, well, maybe I did think about it last night.

Okay. So maybe I have a tendency to get out while the going's good. It's not like I'm the only musician they've got. Why should I stick around anyhow? Maureen's left me, probably already moved out all her stuff from the apartment. I could leave next week, no one would care. I don't have a steady gig here, they don't need me for the show. Nothing I promised to do, just Bethie and Spiral Dance once in a while, and this Faire, and both of them could keep running fine without me . . .

Caitlin's words echoed in his mind: *"Just don't walk out on us, Eric."*

And Bethie, sure, she'll give me a roll in the hay, but nothing more than that. I may not be Mister Commitment, but I'd like a little more than just that in a relationship, y'know? Maybe not True Love, but—Serious Like? Honest Lust?

He left the Admin building, walking through the crowded streets. *At least Caitlin didn't throw me off the Fairesite. Thank God for that, I guess.*

He sidestepped a group of Faire children playing tag in the middle of the lane; narrowly missed a collision with a black-velveted noblewoman and her retinue.

"Oops, milady," Eric said respectfully, doffing his cap, Lady Anne Millesford (AKA Terri Leiber of Riverside, California) just gave him a disdainful look and flounced onward.

Then he heard them, the exuberant Gaelic shouts and keening and general noise, approaching from twelve o'clock high.

Oh shit, I forgot about the show!

He dashed through the crowd of travelers and Faire

folk, towards the Scottish parade marching past. The double line of Celtic warriors, the Chief and his household walking within the protective row, processed past the washing well as Eric caught up with them. With an expertly-timed move that he had down perfectly after years of always being late for stage shows, he ducked under the closest Scotsman and slipped into his proper position with the other musicians.

He hollered the Gaelic gibberish (that he really didn't understand) along with the rest of the marchers, the ululating cries of the women echoing in his ears. As they marched up to Mainstage, he joined the other musicians on stage right. The Chief began the show patter: We're traveling through England and Donal just up and croaked, so we're holding a party—I mean wake—for 'im.

The frazzle-haired Dancemistress ran through the show order as Eric and the others did a last minute tuning check, ticking off the numbers on her fingers. "Jig set. two-hand reel, slipjig solo, Gaelic song . . ." She turned to one of the other dancers. "Hey, remind everyone that we're doing 'John Ryan's'—you know, 'Boom Boom'—right after the song, so everyone should line up fast." She emphasized the "Boom Boom" with a quick shimmy of her hips, and the dancers laughed. "All right, let's do it!"

The dancers ran out to center stage, grabbing partners by the hands and forming sets.

Looks so impromptu, they never guess we practiced these routines for four weeks.

Linda kicked off the tune, a lively fiddle version of "Top of Cork Road," and Eric joined in with Ian on the fifth measure.

It was a good, solid show, one of their best all season. The audience applauded and laughed at the right places, the music was at the right tempo, no one tripped or missed a step in the strathspey-reel, and—*Thank God*—none of the stepdancers sprained an ankle. *Not like last weekend, two casualties in the Saturday 11:30 show alone, not to mention the three the weekend before.*

And Maureen's comment when he told her about the sprained-ankle victims: "Probably wouldn't have hap-

pened if they did decent warm-ups, like we do at the Chandler . . ."

"Och, and now we'd be after hearing our fine musicians play us a tune, indeed we would!" the Chief called out in a voice that carried to the last row of haybales.

Musicians' solo time. Well, here we go again . . .

Eric and the other minstrels moved to the front of the stage. " 'Banish Misfortune' into 'Drowsy Maggie,' two and three," Linda called.

Eric gazed at the audience, row after row of attentive faces, waiting, watching him . . .

Bright lights, starched collar of my concert shirt scratching my neck, the orchestra ready and waiting behind me, taking a deep breath and beginning to play...

That damned program book: "Eric Banyon, flute prodigy, performing Dances Sacred and Profane" . . .

Then he heard "Banish Misfortune," as wicked and sprightly an Irish jig as he'd ever played, and Eric realized in dismay that the band was already halfway through the A part and he hadn't even noticed that they'd started. He tossed in a quick trill, hoping that it sounded like he had meant to join in in the middle of the tune.

Linda's giving me that "raised eyebrow" look, though, I don't think I fooled her! I'll probably catch hell for this later . . .

Then Aaron gave the signal and they dived into "Drowsy Maggie," half again as fast as "Banish" and twice as lively. They ended in a flurry of wild notes, and the audience applauded enthusiastically.

Oh, that was fun. Maureen, you would have liked that one . . .

That brought a sudden pain to his gut, his throat tightening. *Damn it, Maureen, I thought you'd love the Faire, I thought we'd be terrific together, soprano and flute. You'd actually get to be close to your audience, see their reactions, how much they like your music; three feet right in front of you instead of on the other side of the orchestra pit. I thought you'd be happy here, and understand why I love doing this, playing Faire.*

Why did you have to walk out on me?

He marched with the "Celtic bus" halfway back to the Hill, leaving the parade formation just outside the Turkish coffeehouse. Eric waited in line at the counter, already imagining how the sweet iced coffee would taste. Then he reached for his belt pouch to get out some cash, and—

—and there were only the leather strings dangling from his belt, neatly cut just below the knot.

Oh SHIT!

Somebody stole my money pouch! GODDAMMIT, this isn't FAIR!

He *started* to get angry—but he ran out of energy, halfway through "disgusted."

Flat-lined. Emotional burnout.

Eric left the line, walked slowly to a convenient haybale, stretched out and closed his eyes in numb despair.

What a truly revoltin' development. First Maureen walks out on me, then someone steals my cloak, then I damned near get thrown out of this Faire, then somebody cuts my belt pouch. All the money that I made yesterday, busking with Maureen and the others. Gone.

I can't believe all of this is happening to me.

"But it could be worse."

The low male voice spoke quietly, directly into his left ear. Startled, Eric sat up, looking around.

And realized that no one was within ten feet of him. The closest person was a four-year-old girl who was busily smearing baklava over her face while her mother and a friend were watching the dance show on the small coffee-house stage.

Terrific. Now I'm losing my mind, too. Just what I always wanted.

The little girl held out a sticky hand to Eric, gravely offering a piece of straw-coated baklava. He smiled and shook his head, then stood up.

Maureen's left me, he thought at her, as if she could hear him. *Then someone stole my cloak, I nearly lost this Faire gig, and a cutpurse got my cash pouch. It only had fifteen bucks in it, not the end of the world, but that was all the money I had on me.*

Methinks I need something stronger than Middle East-

*ern pastry, sweetling. But, in the interest of the Faire's
pristine reputation, I'll get out of the way before I look for
it.*

He waited until he was in the hidden grove, far from
the thick dust and crowds, before reaching for the corked
flask at his side.

Then Eric proceeded to become thoroughly, profoundly
drunk, for the second time in twenty-four hours.

*I love the smell of fresh dirt—but I wish my nose didn't
hurt.* He opened his eyes a little, and saw—

Brown.

*Oh. I'm lying facedown in it. That must be why it's a
little difficult to breathe.* Eric tried to roll over onto his
back, and failed. He tried again, then gave it up as hopeless.

*S'okay. I really don't want to go anywhere, anyhow. I've
always wanted to be a worm, anyway. Worms can have a
good time all by themselves and never know the difference. "Oh, you're my tail? I thought you were my
girlfriend."*

He lay there in the dirt and oak leaves, imagining a
beautiful red-haired woman smiling at him. A *particular*
beautiful red-haired woman.

"Eric, I've decided it doesn't matter to me what you do
with your life, all I want is to be with you, always."

Then she leaned forward to kiss him and . . .

Dream on, Banyon.

Oh, Maureen . . .

He managed to get his head turned to one side, and
pillowed his cheek in the crook of his arm. He blinked
back tears and sniffled, startling a bluejay who had been
investigating him curiously, doubtlessly wondering if all
that hair would make a good lining for her nest. *Great. I'm
lying in the dirt, completely wasted. Now I'm going to
start leaking from the eyes. I'm going to make mud to lie
in. A perfect ending to a thoroughly delightful weekend.*

"Bard? Bard? I need to talk to you."

The voice spoke softly, low musical tones, definitely
male. Eric tried to open one eye to look at the guy, but
decided it wasn't worth it. "Go 'way. 'M trying to meditate."

"Please. It's very serious. I would not disturb your meditations, but I must ask some things of you."

"Nothing's *that* serious. Here, have a drink." Eric still had his hip flask in his other hand. He blindly shoved the flask in the direction of the voice. "Feel free to join me, there's plenty of whiskey, plenty of room here on the ground. It's quite comfortable, really. If you don't mind having rocks poking holes in your body."

The voice sounded profoundly puzzled. "No, thank you. But please, I must speak with you. I have many questions, and you are the only one who can tell me the answers."

"Why? Who put me in charge? Go ask Caitlin or somebody."

"Why? You must—you're the one who Awakened me." The voice became desperate. "Please, Bard—please."

Eric tried again to lift his nose from the dirt so he could see whom he was talking to, then gave it up as a lost cause. "S'sorry. I didn't mean to wake you up. I just talk to myself when I'm drinking, can't tell how loud I am, you know, just happens."

The voice wasn't paying any attention to him. "Please, you must answer my questions. Your song Awakened me last night, and I don't know how long it has been. I cannot find any of my own kind here, and . . . I heard disturbing talk, Bard. They are saying that this place will be destroyed soon. You, of all people, must know what that will do to all of us. And the others—are they still Dreaming, or has something worse happened to them?"

Either I'm more drunk than I thought, or this guy is talking about something really and truly bizarre.

Third possibility. Whatever he's doing has sent him into another reality. Bad drugs, Eric. Humor the man. "Is this part of some street bit? I'm not in on it. Maybe you should save it for the travelers, m'friend."

There was a long and profound silence, during which Eric felt his tenuous grip on consciousness slipping even further from his grasp. *Yeah, passing out right now does seem somehow like the appropriate thing to do.*

Oh, Maureen . . . .

He choked on a sob; remembered he wasn't alone, and held it in. All of it.

Stillness, unbroken by so much as the fall of a leaf. Then a single word.

"Oh."

Then someone's hands gently rolled him onto his back, removing the rocks and sharper branches from beneath him, piling leaves to create a comfortable bed for him. He tried to open his eyes and thank the stranger, and couldn't manage either.

"Rest now. Forget a little. I will find you later, when your heart is not in such pain."

Eric smiled as an unseen hand brushed the stray locks of his hair from his face. In the alcohol-confused haze of his mind, the gentle hand could only have belonged to one person.

Mmmm, Maureen, that's nice, feels good . . .

The last he heard was quiet footsteps, crunching through the dry oak leaves as the stranger walked away.

When he awoke several hours later, the sun already fading from the leafy branches above him, Eric was alone in the grove.

· 3 ·

The Unfortunate Rake

Eric managed to pry one of his eyes open, and looked around blearily. *God, I feel awful. This is getting to be a habit.*

He pried open the other eye, and his head reacted with a predictable stab of pain.

Maybe I'd better think about changing my habits.

He sat up. Slowly.

Was there somebody here earlier, or did I dream that?

He succeeded in getting into a sitting position and realized that he'd been nestled in a snug little bed of leaves. *I sure didn't have the sense to do that. No, he was real. Guess he went back to Fairesite.* His stomach lurched, and he lay back down before it could turn rebellious on him.

Wonder who the guy was? I didn't recognize the voice.

He looked up at the darkening sky through oak branches above him. *Sun's setting. I must have been here for hours.*

All right, Eric. Time to return to Reality. Or, at least, the Fairesite. He made a second attempt at mobility, a successful one this time, and staggered to his feet, wincing as he bent down to pick up his abandoned gig bag. *Gods, I ache all over, just like I've been—*

—drunk all weekend.

Yeah.

Well, it seemed like a good idea at the time . . .

He beat the dust out of his breeches, and walked—carefully—back towards the main grounds of the Faire. *I wonder how badly I've managed to screw up. I did make*

41

*my show before I went facedown in the bean dip. I didn't
get drunk in a public place. But I wasn't making the
rounds.* He sighed. *Oh well. The worst they can do is fire
me. Then I* will *have a reason to head north.*

He entered the Faire grounds—cautiously. The boothies
were packing up, carrying boxes to the cars and pickups
parked in the narrow streets.

Andrea and Tom were loading up the last of their hand-
made costumes into Andrea's Honda as Eric walked by.
"See you guys next weekend," he called to them. Andrea
called out a good-bye to him; it got lost in the noise of one
of the water trucks passing by, liberally soaking everything
in its path with fire retardant. Andrea's Honda joined the
line of cars on the dirt road leading out of Fairesite,
kicking up a small cloud of dust as it chugged up the hill.

Eric walked past a small covey of actors carrying their
props, ungainly stuffed hobbyhorses embroidered in bright
colors, then he saw Judy, struggling to carry her large
hammer dulcimer.

"Need a hand?" he asked, catching up with her.

She flashed him a grateful smile. "Thanks, Eric. You're
a sweetheart."

He took the dulcimer stand and her costume bag from
her hands, knowing she'd rather carry the musical instrument herself. "So . . . did you have a good weekend?"

She sighed. "If you don't count that drunken idiot who
tripped over my Pass-the-Hat bowl, then threw up almost
on my feet."

Eric winced.

Judy gave him a very direct look. "But that was the only
bad spot in an otherwise terrific weekend. I heard you
weren't so lucky."

He shook his head ruefully. "Damn, but bad news trav-
els fast around here."

"A lot of people were really concerned about you, Eric.
I remember what happened out at Texas Faire a couple
years back . . ."

He stiffened slightly. "Well, this is different. I'm handling it just fine."

Just fine, half the weekend drunk off my ass, barely

managed to do my shows, didn't even play street at all. Yeah, that's really handling it, Eric.

Judy set down the dulcimer on a haybale outside the Turkish coffeehouse. "I'm meeting some folks here before heading out. Maybe play a few last tunes before returning to Mundania. Want to join us?"

Eric propped the dulcimer stand against the haybale, the costume bag next to it. "No, I think I'm going to wander for a little longer, see who's still hanging around the 'site. I'll probably see you on my way out, though."

He headed back into the main area of the Faire, not certain what he was looking for, or who.

Looks like everyone's packing it up for the weekend. I probably should, too.

Two of the Scotsmen were lifting up stacks of pikes, lashing them down in the bed of a faded Dodge pickup.

Hope they tie those down good. I sure wouldn't want to be driving on the freeway behind them and suddenly see a dozen pikes flying point-first toward my windshield.

I can see the headlines now: Man Skewered by Runaway Medieval Arsenal? Killer Scottish Pike Strike Massacre?

Spear Today, Gone Tomorrow?

But I bet Maureen's land-tank is tough enough to handle a pike assault. I'll wager on a Chrysler any day against a Scottish brigade . . .

Oh, damn. *Maureen's car—she was going to give me a lift home. I'm sure she isn't coming back to get me. I'm stranded out here.*

Terrific. One last lousy touch on a truly wretched weekend.

Maybe if I can catch up to Judy . . .

He hurried back to the coffeehouse. As he approached, he heard the faint sounds of hammered dulcimer, bodhran, and fiddle.

Well, that's a break. I probably can talk Judy into giving me a lift home.

He recognized the tune—"The Butterfly," one of his favorites. Eric quickly pulled his flute case from the gig bag, and was playing along with the melody by the time he reached the jam session at the coffeehouse.

Judy was intent upon her dulcimer, hammers dancing lightly across the strings, but the four other minstrels smiled in welcome as Eric joined them.

The four Northerners, that's right. Damn, but they're really together, really tight. I'd bet my flute that they've done a lot of gigs together.

The dark-haired fiddler girl suddenly grinned impishly at the others and switched into a harmony that Eric had never heard before, beautiful and haunting. As the tune came back around for a second time, Eric smiled to himself and began playing counterpoint.

For a moment, it was almost as good as the melody he'd played in the grove, every note falling perfectly, the counterpoint transforming the music into something more than just a tune.

When it was over, the last note fading away, Judy was the first to speak. "Eric, that was *nice.*"

"Damn good playing," the bearded bouzouki player said. He pulled a flask from his belt, offering it around the circle of musicians. Eric took a draught, smiling as the Irish Mist burned with a heartwarming fire all the way down his throat.

He handed the flask back to the man, then noticed that the drummer girl was gazing at him thoughtfully. "Where do you play? Are you touring with a band, or playing concerts?"

Eric shook his head. "I do Faires, street stuff. Haven't been in a band on a regular basis in years, or played concerts . . ." . . . *since the day I walked out of Juilliard. No more. Life's too short.* "Mostly I just sorta sit in."

"Haven't you ever thought of doing something more with your music than just busking? You're a damn sight better than any flautist I've ever heard on the Faire circuit."

He shrugged. "This is all I want to do. I'm happy. That's all that matters." He turned to Judy. "Listen, I came back because, well, my girlfriend was supposed to give me a lift home, and you know what happened with that . . ."

"You're in Van Nuys, right? No prob, although . . ." Judy glanced up at the sun, barely visible above the hills.

". . . we should start out soon. The traffic's going to be something fierce on 101."

"But one last tune, Judy?" The fiddler's fingers were twitching. "Not a Faire tune, we've been playing them all weekend. How 'bout something a little different . . . ?"

She raised her bow to the strings, and began the opening violin solo from "Danse Macabre."

And stark terror reached out to grab Eric by the throat.

Oh my God, no, please . . .

He tried, but couldn't block the memories rising up in his mind to drown him. He backed up without knowing he was moving; half fell over the haybale behind him, landing on his knees in the straw and dirt, shaking and retching, unable to think or speak.

No, it's just music, it's nothing, it can't happen again . . .

"Eric!"

"What's wrong with him?"

He heard the concerned voices, somehow distant, unreal. The only things that were real were the bright lights of the stage and the shadowy darkness of the concert hall, and the nightmare stepping out of his mind and into reality . . .

It's only a memory, it happened over ten years ago, it's not real. Dammit, it's not real!

But he could hear them, the whispering voices, could feel them closing in, calling to him, reaching for him . . .

Then he felt a *human* hand gripping his shoulder, yanking him back into the present. Judy, staring down at him with eyes that were wide and frightened, her hand clutched tight on his shoulder.

"I'm . . . I'm okay," he said weakly, looking up at her. The others were gathered around him, worried. "Probably just food poisoning from that damn Hungarian pie booth," he said, hoping that his voice sounded calm. That it didn't shake the way he was still shaking inside. "I got sick after eating there opening weekend, shouldn't have done it again today." He took a deep breath, steadying himself.

He managed to stand up, the blond bearded Northerner helping him regain his feet. "Thanks, man. This hasn't been one of my better weekends. I . . . I think maybe I should go home." He tried to grin, but by the looks on their faces, it wasn't convincing. "Is that all right by you, Judy?"

"Yeah, sure." She quickly packed her dulcimer away in its case, slung it over her shoulder. "Let's hit the road."

Judy's tiny car disappeared around the corner, leaving Eric alone on the street, the ominous bulk of his apartment building looming overhead.

Home to the concrete jungle. Maybe Maureen's upstairs, waiting for me to get home, wanting to talk it over, work things out.

Not bloody likely.

He unlocked the security door, and the children playing in the courtyard stopped to look at him curiously as he headed for the stairs. *Yes, kiddies, it's the refugee from the 16th century, home from the wars.*

Eric opened the door and walked into his apartment. He stepped into the living room, took one look, then wearily sat down on the battered couch.

No, I don't think Maureen wants to talk things over . . .

With no more than a glance, he knew she was gone. *The Beethoven statue, the Japanese flower vase, that "Ride of the Valkyries" poster with those funny little Vikings climbing all over it—she's taken all of it. All of her stuff.*

His record collection was neatly stacked on the floor, next to a now-nonexistent record cabinet. He looked through them briefly—she hadn't taken a single record of his, from what he could see, and she'd even left the ones they had bought together, over the last few months.

Like she didn't want anything to remind her of me . . .

He walked into the kitchen, and saw the note on the fridge: "I took the cat. You don't deserve her. Goodbye, Eric."

Great. Terrific. At least that scrawny furball will have a good home. Now there really isn't anything holding me in Los Angeles, not even that damn cat . . .

Maureen, how could you do this to me? Why?

He sank down into a chair, his head in his hands. *Oh, Maureen . . .*

Something clicked behind him, the sound of a door closing. Eric sat up abruptly, looking around.

My God, is someone in here with me?

Eric slid to his feet, quietly moving to the dish rack and palming a large sharp steak knife.

All right. I've been ripped off twice this weekend already, and this is it—if anybody's in the apartment, they're toast!

He slipped off his Faire boots, padding silently across the living room to the closed bedroom door. The knife clenched tightly in his fist, Eric suddenly flung the bedroom door open and leaped inside—

—and tripped on a pile of his clothes. He barely managed to avoid cutting himself with the knife as he landed face-first on the floor. He sat up slowly, gingerly rubbing the new sore spot on his chin.

Oh. That's right, Maureen was the one who bought that standing wardrobe. I guess she decided to take that, too.

The bedroom window was open, the curtains fluttering in the breeze. *That must be what caused that noise. There's no one in here.*

Just to be safe, he checked the closet. As he closed the closet door, Eric had the strangest sensation, as though something was moving just on the edges of his vision. He turned quickly, but there was nothing in the room but scattered clothes and the unmade bed.

My brain is draining—it's turned to yogurt, and it's draining. I'm seeing little green men who aren't there. Bad booze, Eric.

He returned to the kitchen and opened the fridge, wondering if Maureen had cleared out half of the food as well. He reached into the freezer for one of the many identical stacked dinners of genuine frozen food-shaped plastic, and realized that the bottle of iced Stolichnaya was missing.

That was a low blow, Maureen. Sure, it was a Christmas gift from a friend of yours, but it was to both of us, remember?

Eric absently shoved the frozen dinner into the oven, turning on the gas, then leaned back against the cabinet, trying not to feel too much.

He took the carton of milk from the fridge, drinking straight from the container, as he sat down again at the kitchen table. *Well, it's not the End of the World. I've lived through this kind of thing before. I'll live through it this time.*

I always do, whether I like it or not.

His feet were chilled, bare skin against the cold linoleum. Eric reached down for his Faire boots, and—

—and his hand encountered empty air.

He looked down. No boots.

I think I'm losing my mind.

No, Eric, you're not insane, just stupid. Okay, you must have moved them and not thought about it. Absentminded. Pre-Alzheimer's. And you drank too much this weekend . . .

He ate dinner in silence. *No Maureen, to tell me all about the rehearsals at the Pavilion, all the little inside jokes and gossip. No damn cat, even, trying to steal my dinner. This is the most depressing meal I've had in a long time.*

Eric finished the pre-packaged dinner, leaving everything on the table. *I'll clean it up tomorrow. Right now, all I want is a hot shower, and a toke, and crash.*

Half an hour later, drying his hair with a towel and wearing a second one around his waist, Eric returned to the kitchen for a glass of juice.

And the abandoned frozen dinner tray had vanished. The fork and knife were missing, too. After a moment, Eric realized that they were in the dish rack, dripping wet.

This is very, very weird. I don't remember washing the dishes. I hate washing dishes. And why in hell did I wash the tinfoil thingie?

He shook his head, and looked at the dishrack again, but the stuff was still there. *Okay. Too much whiskey, too much stress, and not enough sleep. But, I can cope. Though maybe I'd better just call it a night now before I start*

*speaking in tongues and telling the neighbors to find
Jesus . . .*

He returned to the living room, and sat down on the
couch. On the low table were a carved wooden pipe and a
small plastic bag.

At least she didn't take the stash.

Eric filled the pipe with the fragrant weed, lit it, and
smoked in silence for a few minutes.

*Uncle Dan's cure for heartbroken insomniacs. When I
see him I should thank him for scoring this for me at such
an opportune time.*

He felt his head beginning to fog; the hurt inside started
to seem less important. *He always seems to come up with
things I'm gonna need before I need them. I wonder if he
knew what was going to happen? Wouldn't surprise me—
Beth, Allie, Dan, all those Spiral Dance crazies, they're all
a little strange that way.*

The pipe went out, and he stared at it in mild surprise.
*Amazing how fast it goes. Huh. Just like the Bushmills last
night. Now, say goodnight, Eric. Goodnight Eric.*

He took pipe and bag and tucked them carefully into
the nook under the corner of the couch frame. *Paranoia
never hurt. God. Thank God this weekend's over . . .*

He stood up, slightly unsteadily, and staggered to the
bedroom. He had to wade through the piled clothing to
reach the bed, and had barely enough cognizant thought
left to pull the blanket over him before all of his sorrows
faded away in a deep, dreamless sleep.

Dreamless? Well . . .

There *was* a voice in his head. Just a voice, though, and
a presence that . . . comforted.

*Heal, saddened one. You feel the song? It is yours; you
have only to follow . . .*

A non-dream like ones he'd had, a long, long time ago,
when he was a child and music was spun of equal parts of
melody and magic, and he could hear things in his sleeping mind that slipped maddeningly away when he woke.

Follow, and find healing . . .

Oh God, it's morning again. Eric blinked at the bright

sunlight shining through the open window. He glanced at
the alarm clock on the nightstand. *Well, almost afternoon,
I think. Ten o'clock. I'd better start moving or I'll miss the
lunch crowd downtown.*

He stood up, stretching, and looked around the room.
And found himself smiling. *Amazing. I actually feel* good
this morning. Almost human again. He rummaged through
the piles of clothing on the floor, and found a pair of jeans
and a T-shirt that were relatively clean and unrumpled.

Time to pay the rent, I guess. Energy filled him, and he
discovered he was looking forward to getting out on the
street with anticipation. He hummed as he laced a pair of
ancient tennis shoes on his feet, and sang a little as he
slung his gig bag over his shoulder. Five minutes, and he
was ready to head out.

He grabbed a leftover donut from the fridge on his way
out the door, whistling "Banish Misfortune" as he strolled
down to the bus stop. *This is really a beautiful morning,
blue skies—well, bluish-brown, this is L.A. after all—and
I feel terrific. Surprisingly good. I don't even miss
Maureen—*

A lump in his throat suddenly sprang up and interfered
with the passage of his donut.

Much. He swallowed donut and lump and resolutely
grasped after his earlier cheer. *Dammit, I am* not *going to
let this ruin the rest of my life!*

To his amazement, some of his cheer returned. *Wow.
Instant self-psychotherapy. I wonder if it was Dan's grass?*

He saw the bus approaching the corner and ran for it,
his gig bag bouncing off his side. He caught up to the bus
just as the driver started to close the door, and leaped
inside just in time.

*Maybe this is to make up for the weekend? Reverse
Instant Karma?*

Eric took the last seat at the back of the bus, propping
his feet up and gazing out the window as the bus trundled
down Victory Boulevard. *Another day, another twenty-
seven dollars and thirty-three cents. At least, that's what I
made on Friday. I sure hope this Instant Karma helps with
the busking, too.*

He got off the bus at Broadway over an hour later, with the steep hill ahead of him, the unmarked border between the crowded, dirty downtown area and the classy and immaculate business district.

He found his favorite busking spot and set down his gig bag on the bench. It was a street corner near the YMCA, with a small outdoor cafe and a small lawn area that was terrific for relaxing and wriggling your toes in the thick grass. *Best of all, I've never had a single problem with the cops over here.*

Most of the "suits" walking past didn't even look at him as Eric set up for busking, "salting" the hat with a handful of dollar bills and quarters, positioning his sign just right: *"Yes, this is my real day job. Please support the Arts."* But a few of the businessmen and women recognized him, and smiled or waved hello. Eric smiled in response as he fitted his flute together and played a few quick notes to warm up.

Then he began busking in earnest. Light, lively Celtic tunes, with the occasional phrase of a classical piece thrown in for kicks. The serious-faced suits walking past stopped to listen; when he finished the tune medley, there was a burst of spontaneous applause, and no few of them reached into their pockets for change to toss in the hat.

Hey, not bad for first thing in the morning. And the lunch rush hasn't even hit yet . . .

He began "Irishman's Heart to the Ladies," one of his favorite jigs. Several corporate types, apparently on their way to a meeting, stopped to listen, and one of the silver-haired businessmen kicked up his heels in an impromptu jig step. They moved on, but not before the older man dropped a five-spot in Eric's hat.

Eric doffed his cap, grinning from ear to ear at the departing businessmen. *All* right! *Let's hear it for that kindhearted gent and the Instant Karma!*

An hour later, as the lunch crowd thinned, Eric's energy dropped as well. He began to play slower tunes, trying to find a spot on the corner that wasn't in the bright sunlight.

Too damn hot. He stopped playing in the middle of one

tune to wipe the sweat off his forehead. *L.A. in May, it shouldn't be this hot yet. This is almost as bad as Faire last year. A hundred and ten in the shade, and all of us doing shows on those blacktop stages . . .*

He mustered the strength to play another fast tune, "Fox Hunt," one of the best slipjigs he knew.

"Hey, Misty, listen! He's playing the 'Foxhunter's Jig'!"

Eric looked up in surprise at the three suits gawking at him. He finished the tune with extra energy, adding a last trilling ornament and long, intricate run, then bowed elegantly as they applauded.

The blonde woman was shaking her head in disbelief. "A Celtic musician playing on the street! They'll never believe this back home!"

'Where are you from?" Eric asked, wiping sweat from his brow.

One of the men smiled. "Tulsa, Oklahoma. We're all Celtic music fans, but had no idea that people played Celtic stuff on the streets of L.A. This is quite a surprise."

"Well, there's not many of us," Eric said. Winded by the fast-moving tune, he sat down to catch his breath. "Most everybody plays at the Faire or in bar gigs, but there's a few of us that play street as well. There's one lady, a terrific singer who lives in the South Bay, she sings traditional ballads. And a few others, like a fiddler that I know. There aren't very many buskers in this town, not nearly as many as in San Franciso, but we do all right."

"That's really wonderful." The woman smiled, then asked hesitantly, "Maybe . . . could you play 'Rocky Road to Dublin' for us? It's one of my favorites."

Eric nodded, and took a deep breath. It was one of his favorites, too—a fast slipjig that was difficult, but not impossible. He added in extra ornaments on this tune as well, and was very pleased by the wide smiles on their faces when he finished.

"Thank you, so much. You've made our trip out here something special." The woman knelt down, setting a folded bill in his hat. "I really hope we'll see you again."

The younger man handed him a business card. "If you're ever in Oklahoma, give us a call. Maybe we can help you get some gigs, introduce you to people." He also slipped a bill into the hat.

"Thank you very much," Eric said, pocketing the card. *Well, that'll be handy if I ever move to Oklahoma. God only knows why I'd ever want to do that, though.*

The three walked away, leaving Eric alone on his street corner again.

Eric picked an easy tune to play next, "Fair Jenny's," as sweet as an Irish tune could be. A man in a five-hundred-dollar suit walked by, stopped briefly to listen, reached into his pocket and tossed two pennies into Eric's hat.

Oh, that's cute. Real cute. I bet you think you're really clever, mister, tossing in your two cents' worth. Give me a break. Eric sneered disdainfully at the man's retreating back. *What a twit.*

But those Okies, they were something. I wish there were more folks like that, in L.A. So good-natured and friendly . . .

Still, the local business suit types, they're all pretty much the same. They think the world is theirs. And hell, who knows, they may be right. There isn't much an individual can do against the corporations, the government, and the ones with the bucks. Not when they have the power and the cash to hold on to it.

He finished "Fair Jenny's," and began a fierce, angry rendition of "Tamlin's Reel." *Yeah, look at the Faire, it's going under because some corporation guys decided that the land would be terrific for a shopping mall. Sure, people are trying to stop them, but I'm betting on the corporation. They always win.*

Well, I've got money for groceries, and a good start on next month's rent. Might as well pack it in. Otherwise, this heat will do me in. I can just see the Channel 13 news bulletin: Itinerant musician melts into puddle on downtown L.A. street. News at six, film at eleven.

Eric completed the tune, ending on a mournful, unresolved C sharp. *Yeah, that's how I feel today. Very unresolved. Though not especially sharp . . .* He disassembled the flute, and replaced it in the case. *Tomorrow, maybe I'll try the busking outside Century City, haven't played*

*there in a few weeks. The business crowd around there is
usually pretty good on tips, not like the tourists in
Hollywood.* He smiled, remembering the gawking faces of
the Japanese tourists, doubtlessly trying to figure out *why*
this *gaijin* was playing classical flute next to the Chinese
Theater.

He walked down to the steep hill, toward a crowd of
rookie cops learning how to direct traffic on the corner
below. *I've never seen so many cops in one spot in my life.
But I bet somebody's car could be ripped off fifty feet
away and they'd never even notice.*

Eric strolled past the Chandler Pavilion, with its endless
glass windows and the huge chandeliers just visible inside.
*Maureen's probably in there right now, rehearsing for
"Traviata." And probably listening to that crazy guest
director endlessly scream things in French. I wonder if
he's figured out that none of them can understand him?*

Somehow, though, thinking about her didn't really hurt
at all. He remembered when he first met her, not far from
where he had busked today; a beautiful red-haired woman
who listened to him play, then improvised a harmony to
the old O'Carolan tune. How he joined her and her friends
for lunch the next day at one of the hangouts the Pavilion
people frequented, then went backstage with her, climbing around the high walkways above the stage. *God, we
had fun.* Walking on Venice Beach, laughing as they dodged
the kamikaze rollerskaters. He thought about the late nights
they'd spent talking, singing impromptu duets, making
love.

Eric tested the memories gingerly, like someone worrying at a sore tooth, and was surprised to feel no resulting
heartache. *Just memories, good memories of all the times
we spent together. It doesn't hurt anymore.*

He smiled suddenly, clicking his heels in a quick jig
step, and reverenced to the huge Pavilion building. *Ave
atque vale, m'lady Maureen. I hope you'll find someone
who'll make you happy, I really do. Goodbye and good
luck, my mistress of music.*

The rookie cops looked at him suspiciously as he danced
past, whistling. *They probably think I'm on drugs. But I'm*

not. At least I don't think I am. I just feel good. As though everything is about to change for the better—

He waited at the bus stop, and was surprised to see the RTD bus show up exactly on schedule. *Hot damn, something is right with the universe. These buses are never on time . . .*

He stopped briefly at the supermarket, picking up a sixer of Guinness, two cans of chili, a hunk of plastic-wrapped cheddar cheese, and a package of Hostess cupcakes—*Yeah, I feel like celebrating tonight. A real feast. Today was a great day for busking, and I feel terrific. I think I've even gotten over Maureen.*

But the moment he unlocked his apartment door, he knew something was wrong.

Eric glanced around the living room, and his eyes narrowed suspiciously. *I didn't leave those books lying out on the floor, I know I didn't. And my leather jacket, I know Maureen didn't take that out of the closet. It was hanging there last night . . .*

Moving quietly, Eric set the bag of groceries down by the door, and reached for the baseball bat, propped against the wall. *I thought I was just imagining things last night, but I think there really was somebody in here. And I was too zoned to catch them.*

Oh God. Maybe they're still here now . . .

He glanced into the kitchen, then crossed to the bathroom, looking inside.

Nothing here.

He pushed the bedroom door open with his foot, carefully leaning inside to look around.

The clothes were sorted. By color. And stacked in careful piles along the wall.

But his bed was a mess, and he'd made it before he left.

Oh God—whoever was here—is here—is a serious loony. He tried to remember what drugs did things to your head like that. *PCP? No. Acid, maybe. Acid and THC? Could be—* He swallowed with difficulty, and gripped the bat a little harder. *I could be in for a world of hurt here.*

He backed out of the bedroom and into the kitchen.

The drift of cold air over his feet told him that his

intruder had left the refrigerator door slightly ajar. He edged over to the fridge and opened the door enough to look inside.

There hadn't been much in there in the first place—but now anything that *had* been left was useless. Because everything, *everything* in the refrigerator had had one neat bite taken out of it. Including the apple-shaped candle he kept in there as a joke.

If he'd had any doubts about there being an intruder, they were gone now.

Oh God. Oh God. *I'm dealing with a real, genuine lunatic here.*

He shut the door firmly and crept into the living room—

Where the first thing that met his eyes was his own Faire cloak, draped over a chair. Except it hadn't been there when he came in.

He felt his jaw dropping open; stared at the sweep of wool—

And a red rage swept over him. *Maureen's gone—my purse gets cut—my cloak gets stolen—and then the* bastard *that steals it follows me home and eats my food and sleeps in my bed and makes a* mockery *out of me!*

"*Get out here!*" he screamed, brandishing the bat. "Goddammit, I *know* you're in here—*you get your ass out here, you bastard!*"

Sure, Banyon. Like he's going to— a tiny, cooler corner of his mind thought—just before the young man stepped into the bedroom doorway, smiling shyly.

He was very tall, taller than Eric; he was *very* blond, white-blond, hair that was *too* silken and curled too tightly to be real. He was muscular, but slim—and he was wearing Eric's clothes.

Eric's jeans, *Eric's* favorite Faire shirt and *Eric's* black leather vest—

And my goddamn boots!

That was too much for flesh and blood to take.

Eric charged him, swinging the bat. *You lousy sonuva—*

The young man flung out his hand in a gesture of warding—

And music. Hit. Him.

A wall of music. A chord so pure there were no over-tones or undertones, no pulsings of harmonics. A progression of four notes of blue-white, crystalline clarity. Perfection.

Oh, he thought. *A* major.

And the floor rose up and hit him.

"Bard?" said the soft, frightened voice. "Oh please, Bard, I didn't hurt you, did I? You startled me—"

I'm lying down. On my back.

Cool, slick surface under his right hand, his left lying across his stomach.

Umph. He took inventory without opening his eyes. *Hide of nauga, with a lump just under my left kidney. I know that lump. Maureen complained about it often enough. I'm lying on the couch.*

"Bard?"

With a nut-case bending over me.

Eric cracked his right eye open, cautiously. And was caught in emeralds.

Eyes, he told himself. *Those are just eyes. You can look away—*

Only he couldn't, not until they blinked, and the generously sensuous mouth under them smiled in delight and relief.

They're eyes. They're green. Like a cat's—

Ohmigod.

"Bard?" said the owner of those green, slit-pupiled eyes, touching his face, gently.

Bad drugs, Eric. Really bad drugs. Serious bad drugs. This is a hallucination.

The hallucination bent lower, his face shadowed with concern. Tendrils of that unbelievably white-blond hair fell into his unbelievably green eyes, and he tucked them behind one pointed ear in an unbelievably graceful gesture of annoyance.

He used the same hand to touch Eric's cheek—

Pointed ears?

The figment of his fevered imagination frowned, then bit his lip. "Bard? Can you speak?"

Pointed ears?

Another touch, the concern deepening in the hallucination's eyes. But the almost-caress was no hallucination, though it was the lightest of feather-strokes.

Pointed ears? Like—an elf?

Ohmigod. Eric blinked; then blinked again. *Ohmigod. Either I've gone crazy, or there's an elf coming on to me in my living room.*

He squeezed his eyes shut. *Please God, let it be crazy, and I promise I'll* never *do drugs again . . .*

· 4 ·

The Faerie Reel

Eric opened his eyes, and wished he hadn't.

The elf was still there.

Please, God, don't let this be real. This has to be a drug flashback. It just has to be.

"Bard?" Again, that soft, hesitant voice. It bordered on timid. It was *certainly* diffident. "Please, talk to me, tell me you're all right. Bard?"

It's not real. I'm just seeing things. There isn't an elf in my living room. I'll close my eyes, and when I open them again, he'll be gone, or he'll be a rubber tree, or maybe a unicorn. Eric shivered, his head throbbing, and closed his eyes again. *If he's still there—I won't think that. This isn't happening. If there isn't an elf, if it's all in my head—*

It has to be in my head. If it isn't in my head—those nightmare things—were—

Real. No. Oh God. Please, no. Not again. I can't face them twice.

"Bard?"

I can't even face an elf. Maybe if I don't talk to it, it'll just go away.

The hallucination sighed deeply, and said something that Eric couldn't understand, a brief phrase in a language that was liquid and musical, even if it *did* sound like a muttered curse.

A hand traced a delicate line down Eric's cheek; rested on his shoulder.

He shuddered away from the touch. *Just go away, please . . . don't be real.*

Then an electrical shock slammed into him; he'd gotten hold of a live wire once, helping set up for a gig, and this felt *exactly* like that all-too-unforgettable incident. Eric yelped and somehow managed to leap into the air from a prone position, levitating in midair for a brief moment before landing again in a painful heap on the couch.

He glared accusingly at the hallucination, who was smiling broadly, his grin bright with relief. "Oh, good, you weren't hurt at all! I was . . ."

That was all the elf had time to say. Eric was goaded past being afraid. The creature froze at the rage in Eric's eyes, and then he gurgled as Eric reached over and grabbed him by the throat.

The next exciting thing Eric experienced was the unmistakable sensation of having his face flattened against plaster as he slammed against the far wall of the living room. With a groan, he slid down to the carpeted floor.

He did not want to move. Not at all.

Not for four or five days, anyway.

His head rang with the impact and with a strange polyphonic harmony. *This can't be a hallucination,* he thought dazedly, tasting salty blood where he had bitten the inside of his cheek. *It hurts too much.*

"Bard?"

Oh God, he's still here.

"Please, Bard, you have to stop attacking me. I don't want to hurt you anymore."

Eric turned over—slowly—then blinked a few times, as the room spun wildly around him. "Yeah," he muttered thickly, "I don't want you to hurt me anymore, either."

He pulled himself up into a sitting position, and shook his head to stop the ringing in his ears, then looked at his unwelcome house guest.

Eric stared in fascination as several identically-blond elves moved towards him from across the room, then slowly reformed into a single figure that knelt down beside him.

"Let me see," the figure said, and lightly touched Eric's

forehead. Eric winced at the sudden pain that lanced through his head, front to back.

"This is my doing. I shall take care of it," his imaginary visitor said quietly. To Eric's surprise, the pain began to recede as a soft melody (somehow as close as the wall, and as distant as the moon, simultaneously) echoed lightly in his mind.

If anybody ever puts that in a bottle— he thought; then he wasn't thinking, just listening. Listening to music that seemed to be becoming a part of him. Like the very first time he'd ever listened to anything on a really good pair of stereo headphones, only better. Enchantingly better.

It's like Bach, all the layers of voice, building together.

Finally, the music faded. Eric sat up with a pang of regret, feeling as though he had just awakened from a long restful night's sleep. The elf was looking at him with those large, emerald cat's eyes, eyes that were darkened with concern.

This cannot be real. Scratch that. It can't be what it looks like. So what would it be if it wasn't what it looks . . .

Maureen. She's getting even with me. And she must know a bizillion people over in the studios.

Those ears—

The delicate ears, curving to a graceful point— *They have to be fakes, like what those Faire kids all dressed up in wolfskins were wearing last season.* Eric wondered if the tips would come off if he pulled on them . . .

"Try it," the creature said in a voice suddenly cold and steel-hard, "and I'll knock you on your backside again, Bard or not."

How did he know— "No thanks, I think I've had enough of that," Eric said hastily. He carefully stood up, gingerly touching the side of his face that had impacted so resoundingly with the wall. To his surprise, it was slightly sore, but didn't hurt. Much.

The elf helped him walk back to the couch, and Eric sank down onto the squeaky cushions with an audible sigh. The elf sat beside him.

"This is not going as I had planned," the elf said, looking at him out of the corners of his eyes. "You are not cooperating, Bard."

Take a different angle. Yeah. It's not "real" because this has to be some kind of trick. "My name's *not* Bard," Eric snapped. "Who the hell are you, when you aren't breaking into people's apartments and bashing them into walls?"

The elf straightened, pride written in his stance and expression. Eric's blue jeans and Faire shirt looked incongruous on him, like a polyester business suit on King Arthur.

Okay, so he's an actor, at least. Pretty good one, too.

"I am Korendil, warrior and mage, second to Prince Terenil, leader of the elves of this region."

"Uh huh," Eric replied dryly. "I'm Eric Banyon, street busker. What the hell are you doing in my apartment?"

The hair could be his, could be a wig. Ears are latex. Eyes—contact lenses. You could even do the funny pupils that way; that's what they did in "Thriller." Korendil, Terenil, they sound like somebody lifted those names right out of Tolkien. And—yeah. He didn't read my mind, he read my eyes. I looked at his ears—he's gotta know that the first thing anybody would think is, "Are they real?" And he's too smart not to figure I'd try to yank on them.

"I followed you here," Korendil said, some of the pride draining out of his stance. "I followed you from the place-of-festival."

Cute. "Place-of-festival" instead of "Fairesite." Oh, you're good, fella. But I'm not that stoned, no matter what Maureen told you about my habits.

"You followed me, huh?" Eric sat back and rubbed the sore side of his face. "Why?"

"I was trapped in the Node-Grove, the magic nexus at the place-of-festival, trapped by our enemy, Terenil's and mine, the traitor we once harbored in our midst."

"You expect me to believe elves have traitors?" Eric laughed. "Come *on!* You'll have to do better than that."

Korendil glared. "You, who play 'Sheebeg Sheemore' with such feeling, how can you be such a great fool as *that?*"

"Watch **who** you're calling a fool, buddy," Eric growled.

He's got the script down good, that's for sure. "Just what is this guy supposed to have done to you?"

"He caught me unawares and bound me in sleep in the oaken grove. Until *you* Awakened me."

"Say what?" *Whoever wrote this script sure has a weird imagination. And Maureen sure gave him a lot to work with.*

Korendil leaned forward, earnestly. "You Awakened me, Bard. With your song, two nights ago. And you freed me from imprisonment in the grove."

Music, wild and fey, the trees bending closer to listen, then that moment when everything had clicked, *that moment . . .*

And how the hell did he know that? Maureen wasn't there. There's no way he could know what happened Saturday night.

Okay, wait a minute. He was *at the Fairesite, he stole my cloak. He probably talked to people who know me, knew I tend to slink off to that grove to be alone. Hell, he probably was hiding in the trees and* listening *to me!*

Bastard. You almost had *me falling for it.*

But I didn't hear or *see anyone, and I would have. Wouldn't I?*

"You're stoned, mister," Eric said slowly. "Yeah, I played in that grove on Saturday night, but I didn't do any more than that."

"But you are a Bard—and Bards are the greatest of mages. Bards control the magic of creation, the magic only the most skillful of High Adepts can use. Even untutored, you are a greater mage than I or even the Prince. Untutored, you can break the spells of lock and ward simply by wishing for freedom as you play."

I wanted freedom—and—

Damn, he's good. He almost suckered me in. I wonder where Maureen found this guy? The annual Screen Actors Guild Christmas party? "You still haven't said why you followed me home."

"It is a long tale—" Korendil looked at him doubtfully.

Eric spread his hands wide. "I've got nothing but time. Humor me."

The elf cleared his throat, and took on that proud posture again. "Once we lived freely in this land," he said, his words sounding as if he was reciting some chronicle. "We came here from across the sea, seeking freedom from fear even as your kind sought it. We spread farther and faster than your kind, and were well settled by the time they came upon us again. We welcomed them. Our groves were scattered among the humans' dwellings, and we lived in peace with them. That changed; in the way of humans, so swiftly that we were taken unawares. You humans began to build with cold iron in this valley, more and more as the years went past, and slowly our people were cut off from each other."

Eric shrugged. "So? What's that got to do with anything?" *Logic; let's have some logic here. How'd he do what he did to me? How would you fake magic?*

"We have been cut off from the Node-Grove, the nexus, the source of all our magic, by the walls of cold iron you humans have built. That has weakened our power, and—"

"So move," Eric interrupted. "Do what everybody else does. Head for the suburbs." *He's SAG, I bet. Using some kind of special effects. Bet Maureen can just wiggle her hips and have forty techies begging to do her favors.*

"We are *tied* to our groves," Korendil explained, as if to a particularly stupid child.

Eric bristled a little, and Korendil continued, apparently not noticing. "Without the magic of the Node-Grove, most of us are bound to the groves where we anchored ourselves in your world. We cannot travel far from the home-trees without much pain and further weakening. Only those of the High Court, who need no anchoring to dwell on this side of the Hill, remained free to move. They could not, and *would* not, leave the others."

Eric was only half-listening, sizing the guy up. *He could be a martial artist. He's got the build for it. That would sure account for him being able to toss me across the room. And if Maureen gave him her key, he could have been in and out of here all he wanted.*

"Uh huh," Eric said vaguely, shifting his weight so that

the couch creaked. "So, they're stuck. What's so bad about that?"

"What's 'so bad,' " Korendil said acidly, "is that when elves are cut off from each other and the source of their magic, they fall into Dreaming."

The capital "D" was as plain as if Korendil had written the word.

"Dreaming what?" Eric replied, interested in spite of his anger at the trick being played on him. *Whoever came up with this should write a book. It's better than half the fantasy schlock I've picked up lately—like telepathic horses, or ancient Aztec gods invading Dallas.*

"Dreaming . . . it is a—" Korendil groped for words.

This part must not have been in the script.

"It is a state," he said, finally. "A state in which only 'now' is important. There is no memory of the past, or thought of the future. All that matters is existence and amusement."

"Sounds like half the kids hanging out at the malls," Eric replied, uncomfortably aware that Korendil was describing something very like his own life.

"And that *is* where you find them," Korendil said, nodding. "In the malls. What little magic they have left to them, they use to help steal what they want. Things of amusement, entertainment, and clothing that catches their fancy. *Surely* you have seen them, and yet never noticed them, nor noticed that they are not to be seen outside of your malls."

God, what a concept! Eric suppressed the urge to laugh. *Mall-elves! Tolkien invades Southern California! Christ, it's as hokey as a Saturday-morning cartoon show! Like that one I saw a while back—what was it called? Jewel?*

Damn, but this guy should really *write a book!*

"Even the Prince has been lost to the weakening of magic," Korendil continued sadly. "Even he has begun to give up all hope. So—I turn to you, Bard Eric, and I offer you your heart's desire."

Eric crossed his arms over his chest, and put his feet up on the scarred coffee table. *Okay, this is too clever and too consistent to be some lunatic's private fantasy. So let's hear the pitch I'm supposed to fall for.* "And just what is that?" he asked.

If he has a Taser up his sleeve, that would account for the electric shock too. I think I've got you figured out, fella. I'm willing to play the game through before I throw you out. Make you work for your money.

"I offer you," the elf said, proudly, "a cause to fight for."

"What?" Eric laughed aloud. "Go around playing reveille for all your little mall-elves?" He shook his head. "I'm a flautist, not a trumpeter."

Korendil's eyes darkened and narrowed. "No," he said coldly. "Have you heard *nothing* in the past three days? The place-of-festival is *doomed*—and all magic for this Valley originates there at the Node-Grove. Bad enough that my people are lost in Dreaming, but if the nexus is destroyed, all magic here will *die*. My people, unable to flee to a new source, will fade and die. And you mortals stand to lose as well—mark you. The Node-Grove is the *reason* for Hollywood and all that is associated with it being located here. If the Node-Grove is destroyed, *your* connection to magic and creativity will be lost, and the dreams and hopes that make your short lives worth living will be destroyed as well."

You slipped up, fella. One minute you're talking forsoothly, the next, about the Industry. Uh huh. Gotcha.

Eric laughed in the impostor's face.

"Sure," he said, deliberately sneering at him. "And I'm the only person in the whole of L.A. who can help you. Right. Where'd you get this idea, anyway? Some script you couldn't sell? Well, you can't sell it to me, either."

"You mean—" Korendil looked aghast. "You mean you don't believe me?"

Still playing the part. He's good, I'll give him that. Wonder why I never saw him at Faire before this?

"Damn straight I don't believe you—and even if I did, I don't see anything in it for me." He shrugged. "And you can tell Maureen I said she's not gonna be playing any games with *my* head anymore."

"But—the magic here is one of the reasons you play so well," Korendil cried, his face twisted with anguish. "You respond to it, and it responds to you, don't you see? You're a true Bard, like Merlin, like Taliesen—"

"Like bullshit," Eric interrupted. "You can tell Maureen that I didn't find her little trick very funny, and I didn't fall for it. I hope she paid you a bundle—you earned it, that's for sure. But, no matter what she told you, I'm usually in pretty good control of my reality. And I don't like this kind of practical joke, mister. So you can just pack your act up and get the hell out of my life."

"But I'm not—" the phony elf started to say.

"Bye," Eric said, wriggling his fingers. "You'll pardon me if I don't get up. I've had kind of a strenuous day."

Korendil rose from the couch—

Probably a dancer, too. Maybe he's in ballet. Too tall to get a lead part, though; he must be six-five if he's an inch. Wonder if he's gay? It sure seemed like he was coming on to me for a while.

I wonder if that was part of Maureen's little game, too? Would it make her feel better about the breakup if she found out I was into guys?

"I will be back," the elf-actor said, making the words a promise. "I *will* be back. I will convince you somehow, Eric Banyon. That, I swear!"

Eric shrugged. "Just don't expect Maureen's key to work again. I'm having the locks changed."

The elf wrapped anger and frustration around him like a cloak, and glided out the door, which—despite Eric's assumptions—did *not* slam shut behind him.

Christ. What kind of an idiot did she take me for, anyway? A few special effects and a fairy tale, and I'm supposed to fall for it. Hell, he wasn't even dressed like an elf, he—

He was wearing my clothes!

Shit! And he took them with him!

Bastard!

Eric sat up slowly, feeling a residual ache in too many places. *Christ, Maureen, why did you have to do this to me? I never thought you'd stoop so low—*

—or that you hated me this much.

The elation he'd had earlier was gone.

What did I do to make you hate me like this?

He looked around the living room, seeing only the empty places that used to be filled with Maureen's posters, her Beethoven, all the other reminders that someone else lived here. *Funny. Most of the things that made this place look like a home instead of Howard Johnson's were hers. Everything I care about you could put in a couple of backpacks.*

If I died tomorrow, nobody'd miss me until the rent was late.

Helluva note.

From the high of the afternoon he slid abruptly into one of the lowest lows he'd had in a long time. He rubbed his eyes, as the silence around him oppressed him further still.

I can't stay here alone tonight. I can't. If I do, I'll go crazy, or drink everything in the apartment, or do something equally stupid. Maybe I should call some people, set up a jam.

Wait a minute—

There's Spiral Dance, they're playing in Studio City tonight. Beth wanted me to join them, the usual split. Hell, the money would be good, and I sure don't want to stay here tonight, staring at the ceiling, listening to the water pipes play percussion solos.

His throat felt tight, and he shivered.

Maureen is probably in Westwood tonight with her Pavilion friends, drinking wine and laughing about that idiot flautist she walked out on.

Eric closed his eyes tightly, fighting off the impulse to bury his face in the couch pillows.

Dammit, I am not going to cry. I'm going to get off my ass and play a gig tonight, make some cash, drink a few with Beth and the Spiral Dance folks. And have a good time. I sure did the last time I did a gig with them.

He thought back to his last gig with Beth Kentraine and her wild crew of folk-rock musicians—which had climaxed with Beth launching herself, Fender and all, from the stage and landing on one of the tables, much to the surprise of the customer, sitting there.

She didn't even make the table rock. God, she's crazed.

He began to smile, and his depression slowly lightened. *Yeah, I'm up for that. Old Celtic melodies with electric guitar and trap set. Black leather and studs, and Bethie's dark velvet voice, singing an ancient, gentle Irish air.*

Oh, they're crazy, but fun-crazy, terrific to play a gig with. Now they might have taken that pointy-eared joker seriously.

That's a good reason not to get tied up too closely with them, though. There's something kind of weird about them—like how they cancel a gig if someone has a bad feeling about it. All that weird shit. Like too many people at Faire, acting like their characters are real. Caught up in some reality I don't understand.

Hell. They got a right. Beth and the Spirallers are good people, damn fine musicians. Even if they are a little weird.

That's it. I'll go gig with them tonight.

He pried himself off the couch, and headed into the bedroom to look for his gig clothing. His black leather boots, his least-faded pair of jeans, a dressy shirt, bright red with little fake-pearl buttons. *Yeah, that's me: Eric Banyon, the hottest rock-flute player in L.A., and a snappy dresser too.*

I really wish that SAG guy hadn't walked off with my leather vest, though. That was pretty cheesy, taking off with my clothes. And my Faire boots.

Damn it, Maureen, that was a low trick! But I'm not going to let your stupid games spoil my life, or even one night.

Eric retrieved his cloak from where the actor had left it, draped over one of the chairs. He fastened the brass clasp at his throat, then walked over to where his gig bag was lying on the chair.

And stopped at a tug on his throat. *Something isn't right—*

He looked down. The cloak was six inches longer than it had been the last time he wore it.

But it used to fit me perfectly, exactly ankle length. I don't—wait, that pointy-eared actor was at least six-two,

*closer to six-five, and I'm five-ten. Could he have had
somebody add more material to my cloak, make it longer
so it would fit him right?*

Eric examined the hem of the cloak, and shook his head
in disbelief.

*Nope. No sign of anything added. Not even that the hem
got let out. It's just longer. Besides, how in the hell could
he have matched the plaid lining?*

*Okay, okay. It's wool. Wool stretches. He got it wet,
and it stretched. Let's get real about this.*

He let the cloak fall, trying to ignore the fact that it was
dragging on the floor with every step he took. *I'm not
going crazy, it's just that somebody is playing mind-games
with me, messing with my head, and dammit, Maureen, it
isn't funny!*

Screw that. I'm going to play a gig and enjoy myself.

Eric slung the gig bag over his shoulder, and stopped,
one hand on the doorknob.

*Okay, the cloak got stretched—but how in hell did that
guy fit in my jeans?*

Don't ask, Banyon. Just—don't ask.

Deliberately whistling a jazzed-up version of "Banish
Misfortune" with determination, he locked the apartment
door behind him.

The RTD bus bounced and swayed along Van Nuys
Boulevard, the driver honking angrily at someone who was
blocking the street in rush-hour traffic.

Eric added that snycopated rhythm to the tune he was
composing. He smiled at the elderly woman in the seat
across from him, who was glaring silently at him as he
whistled another brief snatch of melody then quickly scrib-
bled the sequence in his notebook.

*That's what I like about L.A., everybody is so
friendly . . .*

Eric leaned against the grimy window. His depression
was gone, just as quickly as it had descended. Everything
seemed somehow brighter, touched by the red-gold of the
sunset, the wisps of multicolored clouds overhead. The
Hollywood hills were a reassuring presence on the right.

All those rich Industry people, just waiting to discover a talented musician like meself—

Ahead, Burbank and Pasadena vanished into the thickening brown-blueness of the sky, the last glint of sunlight reflecting off the distant antenna towers capping Mount Wilson, high above the Valley.

Looking down at the street, Eric watched the moving crowd: the shoppers, weighed down by packages; the high school kids walking in clusters, like some modern kind of herd animal. A policewoman directed cars as a broken traffic signal flashed its single red light forlornly.

I don't know what it is, but I like this city. Of all the places I've lived, or just wandered through, I really like L.A. the best. Sure, it's crowded, and smoggy, and dirty, but there's such a feeling of life to it. Maybe it's the dreams—all the hopes and dreams of all the people who live here make this place come alive.

The little old lady on the opposite seat suddenly gasped with surprise. Eric stood up quickly and looked out the window as two motorcyclists, both wearing skintight red-and-white racing leathers, arced past the bus, barely avoiding the cars ahead of them. One motorcyclist dropped down on one foot, the bike banking sharply, then gunned the engine and followed his friend down the boulevard.

The elderly woman muttered something about hooligans and reckless drivers, and transfixed Eric with a dark, accusing look, as though all of this were his fault. But Eric barely noticed, watching as the bikers disappeared into the late afternoon traffic.

They're crazy. But beautiful. I wish I could do things like that with a motorcycle. Though that's not too likely, not unless I could find a bike that somehow drives itself! But they really are beautiful to watch. Like dancers.

Eric sat back down in his seat, looking out the bus window. Even through the glass, he could hear the pounding beat of a rap song.

A group of kids were breakdancing on the sidewalk. Eric watched in disbelief as one boy moonwalked backwards, flipped over into a handstand, then rolled to the concrete in a tight backspin. The kid vaulted back up onto his feet, moving aside so one of his friends could take his turn on the pavement.

Damn. Another thing I wish I could do! He laughed silently at himself. *"If wishes were fishes we'd walk on the sea." They make it look so easy, but I'd probably kill myself if I tried any of those stunts.*

A white limousine pulled in between Eric and the sidewalk, blocking his view of the street dancers. Eric tried to peer over the top of the car—

But his gaze was caught by a movement inside, and he saw a man in the back of the limo, gazing out the open window. An older man, silver hair, strong features—

I've seen someone like him before, somewhere. I know I have. The curve of his jaw, the high cheekbones—God, he looks familiar . . .

Then the man looked up, and saw that Eric watching him. Their eyes met; Eric was unable to look away, trapped by the intensity of the man's gaze.

Green eyes, clouded emerald—falling into a bottomless pool of water. Jade mirrors reflecting the shadowed night sky. Something watching, wanting, reaching out and reaching in—taking hold—taking possession—

Eric turned away from the window with an effort, shaking his head. *What in the hell is wrong with me?*, he thought desperately. *I know what it is. He has the same eyes as that actor, Korendil, that so-called "elf," the same leaf-green eyes. No. I'm seeing things. Or else they've both got the same optometrist.*

Against his will, Eric slid back to the window, and stared down at the man in the limo again. The man, gazing up at the bus window, smiled—but it was a smile edged in frost. The emerald eyes caught him, drew him in close, and refused to let him go.

Eyes—

Reaching up and through, touching intimately, examining everything, no matter how secret—echoes of scornful laughter—something foul and slimy where no one should ever be able to go—shame—violation—stripping everything away, all the illusions, all the delusions, leaving a rag of self for all the world to see . . .

A wave of dizziness hit Eric like a wall, blocking out everything except the feeling that the world was spinning around him, and there was nothing he could hold onto, nothing that was still *him*. He clung to the window, his mouth dry, bile in his throat, and clutched for *anything* that was real.

Nothing I've ever done has made any difference to anyone; nothing I do is ever going to make any difference. I could throw myself in front of a semi, and no one would care. I wouldn't even rate more than three words in the obit column.

This was more than depression, this was despair, bleak, cold, hopeless.

Nobody would ever miss me. Maureen wouldn't. My landlord wouldn't. The Faire wouldn't. Beth might wonder where I vanished to—for about five minutes. Then she'd forget about me. They'd all forget about me. I might as well never have lived.

Despondency weighed heavily upon his soul, and sent his heart plummeting downwards.

Nobody gives a damn about me, and nobody ever will. I've never done anything worthwhile. I've never done anything right. I might just as well take that dive and get it over with—

When he looked out the window again, unable to keep from shaking, the white limo was gone. Nauseated and sweating, Eric closed his eyes and leaned against the cool glass, breathing unsteadily.

Christ. What's happening to me?

I think I'm losing my mind. God, I'm better off dead . . .

He concentrated on the feeling of the glass against his forehead and closed his eyes until the nausea passed. When he opened his eyes again, everything had changed.

The breakdancers were still lounging on the sidewalk, but now they were gathered around an elderly man like hyenas around a helpless gazelle. Eric stared in horror as one of the youths shoved the old man hard against the wall, sending him sprawling facedown on the pavement, where they proceeded to strip his pockets, riffling through the fallen bag of groceries spilling out onto the sidewalk. A gray-haired shopkeeper watched in silence from behind the dubious safety of his glass storefront, then turned away. Even the pedestrians on the street carefully looked the other way as they walked past.

What in the hell is going on here?

Everything is so gray, so unreal . . .

Even the Hollywood Hills, instead of their usual green-brown dotted with houses, seemed to have faded. The sky had darkened to a sullen gray. No one on the street laughed, or smiled, or even looked as though they were enjoying life, or were glad to be alive.

They looked more as if they were enduring the last few moments before their own executions.

Eric trembled and closed his eyes, turning away from the window. *God, what's happening to me?*

A burst of laughter and applause drew his attention back to the window. Eric saw the breakdancer bow to the gathered crowd, as the elderly man, still carrying his bag of groceries, bent down to put a dollar bill in the cardboard box next to the dancers' tape player.

The bus lurched into movement again, slowly rumbling down the boulevard, as Eric stared at the receding sidewalk and the breakdancers. *But I know what I saw—*

The despair was fading, almost tangibly.

It's the drugs, Eric. Serious drugs. Definitely too much in one weekend.

He shook his head, hoping to clear it. *First a gay elf, then Svengali in a limo, then a remake of 1984. Shit. I hope I can get my act together for the gig tonight, or Beth Kentraine is going to kill me.*

· 5 ·

Parcel of Rogues

The club's name was "Diverse Pleasures," but Beth and the band just called it the Dive. *Not to the manager's face, of course, but then even the manager must have a hard time justifying this place. Cheap and pretentious, that's this joint.*

Eric edged his way past the noisy crowd at the bar, trying not to inhale the overly-redolent aroma of cigarette smoke, cheap whiskey, and cheaper perfume—*No wonder this place doesn't have roaches; they have too much self-respect to hang out here*—and narrowly avoided colliding with a barmaid carrying an overloaded tray of drinks. Eric smiled apologetically at her, but the bleached-blonde just sighed, casually sidestepping the drunk reaching for her thigh from the closest table.

Sure wouldn't want her job, either . . .

Eric quickly escaped to the relative quiet of the back-stage area, and the small offices that served as warmup rooms for the bands that played the Dive.

Beth was tuning the Fender, the guitar propped care-fully on her knee. She looked up, surprised, as Eric walked into the cluttered room, then grinned. "Hey, you made it! I was hoping you'd show tonight." The smile faded. "Dan's got the flu, so we're down on electric bass tonight. Allie can try to cover with the DX7, and Jim says he'll just pound the hell out of the drums, but three people isn't much on stage, y'know?"

75

"Yeah, I know." Eric sat down on a packing crate next to her. "How much time till we're on?"

"Twenty, twenty-five. It's a good crowd out there, for a Monday night. Bo promised to turn down the TV when we go on."

"That's nice of him. Not that anybody would be able to hear a damn thing once we start playing, anyhow." Eric fished his flute case out of the gig bag, quickly fitted the pieces together. He played a practice run, and Beth grinned, echoing the line on the guitar. Even in the relative quiet of the back room, he could barely hear the trill of the unamplified electric guitar, but caught the touch of bluesy ornamentation that Beth tossed in with the run.

"Even without Uncle Dan, it should be a good gig tonight," she said, setting the guitar down. "We'll do a sound check in fifteen, okay?"

"Okay." Eric stood up, his fingers moving absently on the flute keys, then set the flute back down on its open case. "I'm getting a drink, I'll be back in a few."

"Sounds good." He started towards the door, and Beth called after him. "Hey, Banyon!"

He turned. "Yeah?"

"Thanks for showing up tonight. I *really* appreciate it. Honest to God."

He nodded, a little embarrassed by the look on her face.

Beth Kentraine, looking grateful, like she actually needs *me. I've never seen Beth look like that at anyone ever before. She's always in control of the situation, always knows what she's doing. Probably the most "together" person I know. One helluva lady . . .*

A real changeling, too. Today, hard-rock lady, yesterday—

Oh yeah, yesterday. Standing on the Kissing Bridge with Beth Kentraine in my arms, now that was the one nice sideline to the afternoon. I wouldn't mind it if that kind of afternoon became a permanent part of my life.

He felt a twinge of pain. *I liked that. I liked that a lot. But that's all she wants. A casual fling. That, and another permanent person in her band. Not necessarily another permanent person in her life.*

And I could never go to bed with someone who only feels sorry for me.

At least tonight, I feel useful. Eric flagged down one of the barmaids, requested a Scotch and water, watched as the brunette shimmied back toward the bar. *It feels right. And I'm glad I came. This should be a good gig tonight.*

When the barmaid returned with his drink, Eric found a quiet corner of the club, sat back, and took a look around at the crowd. The Scotch burned a comfortable path down his throat, relaxing him, wiping away the last vestiges of stage fright.

I always feel nervous before a gig, don't know why. God knows I've only done a few hundred performances, so far. But I don't think that'll ever go away.

Someone walked past him, laughing lightly at her companion's words. Eric caught a glimpse of bright eyes, iridescent green beneath a tangle of black curls, before the young woman vanished onto the crowded dance floor with her friend.

Eyes, glowing; like a cat's, emerald green—

No way. It can't be.

How many people in this town are going to the same damned optometrist?

Eric stood up, moving towards the dance floor. The rock rhythm held them all in thrall. Even as he pushed past the swaying bodies of the dancers, no one even glanced at him. He moved in closer to one of them, a slender woman with a riotous mane of black hair, lost in the beat, trance-dancing with an inhuman grace.

Her ears . . .

Just visible through the dark curls. Delicate, curving, *pointed* ears.

What in hell is this, anyway? Some kind of fad?

He looked around the crowded club, the gathered circles of dancers on the floor, the tables with clusters of drinkers, laughing and talking. He began to count them, the different ones—

The clothing, wild and costumey; the hair done in more styles than he could count, like off the set of a sci-fi movie. The glitter of jewelry: incredible jewelry, rings, belts, necklaces, and things he couldn't define, like the dragon, with emerald eyes just like its wearer's, that perched on one dancer's shoulder, wings wrapping over her neck and shoulder and tail down her arm. Or the necklace that turned into a breastplate of chains that turned into a belt studded with thumbnail-sized gems.

This was *not* the Dive's usual Monday-night crowd. Oh, they got some flashy customers, maybe as many as half a dozen—but *half the club?*

My God. They're real. Or I'm nuts. Or both.

He stopped looking *for* them and began looking *at* them.

They move very gracefully, that's for sure. Terrific dancers.

He noticed something else. *You can spot them by the faces, too. Oval faces, fine cheekbones, sharp chin, and those eyes . . .*

He stared at one table after another, silently tallying up the numbers.

Half the people in this club look like Korendil. Elves. Maureen couldn't have gotten to this many people. One, but not dozens. Oh God. They're real.

This club has been taken over by elves.

I wonder if the management knows that they're catering to non-humans? He shook his head, afraid to believe what he was seeing.

That's it; I'm going crazy. I'm losing my mind. Instead of pink elephants, I'm starting to see green-eyed elves.

But there's a shopping mall here in Van Nuys, only a block away from this club. One of those older malls, where they decided not to cut down the trees but left them standing, a whole grove of old trees—oak trees—

What if I'm not crazy? What if that guy was telling the truth?

What if there really are elves, living in Los Angeles?

What if I'm completely, utterly insane, and all this is my delusion?

I think I'd rather be insane. I think.

But—they're so . . . beautiful—

He started shaking, and had to hold onto a support

pillar for a moment to keep his knees from giving out under him.

Beth is going to kill me. I'm supposed to play the gig tonight, not have a nervous breakdown. Shit.

Eric found an empty chair, and sat down heavily, draining his Scotch in a single swallow.

Okay, so what if the club is filled with refugees from Middle Earth? I have to play a show. Right, Banyon. The show must go on. Afterwards, *you can go crazy. Offstage, preferably.*

He set the empty glass down on the table and headed backstage.

Another thrilling night at the Dive. Beth adjusted the Fender's strap, wishing that the band could find a better weekly gig than this club. *It helps pay the rent, and we can use the practice, but I really wish we could find a better gig.*

Maybe there'll be a rich promoter sitting out there tonight, scouting for talent.

She sighed. *Might as well wish for Eric Banyon to permanently join the band. That's about as likely.*

I shouldn't think that way about him. Oh hell, I shouldn't, but it's true. He doesn't seem to think twice about getting involved with any of his lady loves, but try convincing him to take on any other commitment, and he runs like hell.

He's a damn fine flute player. I just wish he'd get his act together.

If he ever did—

No. Beth, you'd be crazy to get involved with a man like him. Give him your heart, and he'll probably leave town the next day.

But, if he ever did get his act together—

She glanced at her watch. *Strike that. I just wish he'd get in here!* "Sound check!" she called to Allie and Jim, who were carrying the DX7 out from the practice room. She followed them out onto the stage, the Fender's pickup line coiled in her hand. *Dammit, Banyon, where are you?*

She saw his face, the mop of unruly shoulder-length brown hair backlit by the dance-floor lights. He was walk-

ing quickly through the crowd toward the backstage door.
For one moment, it looked as if he was glowing.

Right, Beth. Saint Eric. Fer sure.

She blinked again, and the glow was gone. She shook
her head, made a mental note *not* to try the house brand
of Scotch again—

Probably has diesel oil in it—

—and headed for the stage.

The Dive's overworked electrician/sound engineer was
checking a mike cable as Beth stepped up onto the stage.
"Bo, we've got our flute player with us tonight, we're
using the AKG mike for him. I think I wrote down the
board settings last time," she said, plugging the Fender's
cable into the appropriate socket. Bo nodded, jumping off
the edge of the stage and heading for the sound board
controls.

Beyond the darkened stage, the crowd was only a blur,
lit by the colored glow of the dance floor and the occasional flash of a cigarette lighter. The noise of Spiral Dance
setting up their equipment was lost beneath the pounding
beat of whatever Top Forty dance-rock song was currently
playing over the speakers. No one even glanced up at the
stage.

*Well, let's see if you can still ignore us when we start
playing, hey?*

*At least there's a good crowd tonight. I don't know what
pulled them in, but it's almost twice our usual Monday
night crowd. And they're all dancing.*

This should be a terrific *gig . . .*

Eric hurried onto the stage, flashing a quick smile at
Beth. "Are we ready?" he asked, moving in front of the
fourth mike, where Dan usually stood.

What the hell. Let's see what the crowd really wants.

She glanced up at Bo, half-hidden in the shadows, and
he gave her the thumbs-up signal. The Top Forty song
ended, and the dance-floor lights faded away. The stage
was still unlit, leaving most of the club virtually pitch
black, completely dark.

Now, let's have some fun . . .

Beth moved close to the microphone. "Ladies and gentlemen . . . we *are* Spiral Dance."

Behind her, Jim began the drum line to "Missing You," starting softly, then gaining in intensity. Allie followed him on the synth, minor chords building up to an impossible climax.

Beth hit the first notes on the Fender, just as the lights came up on the stage, blindingly bright. A moment later, Eric dived in with the descant, leading right into the first verse.

Lovely bit of work there, Banyon—

Then she leaned in close to the mike, and let the song pour through her. Hard rock, her voice nearly breaking on the high notes, but strong, the strongest she'd sung in a long time.

"Too long, too many nights, no reason left to try,
Too far to go to see a glimpse of light.
Don't tell me you don't know, don't give me reasons
   why,
I don't care, 'cause I'm missing you tonight . . ."

Beth could hear Allie and Jim, their voices blending perfectly with hers on the chorus. Then she glanced up at Eric, who nodded. *All yours, bucko—*

Second verse, and Eric took the solo.

Eat your heart out, Ian Anderson! Beth couldn't help but grin as the flute solo, first low and breathy, then building to a wailing intensity as Eric caught the melody line, caught the audience and took them with him, high with the music.

The shouts and whistles after the solo almost drowned out the words of the chorus. Beth caught a glimpse of Eric, grinning like crazy, as the crowd cheered wildly.

Damn, but that was good!

The floor was overflowing with people dancing, some just standing by their tables instead of fighting for space by the stage. And one young man, very tall with flowing silver-blond hair, just standing near the edge of the stage, not dancing. Just staring at Eric.

It's hard to see with the stage lights, but it almost looks as though his eyes are glowing green—no, that's impossible, must be a trick of the lighting. Ye gods, I'm seeing everything in fireworks tonight.

She shifted position just a little, and caught a glimpse of something in his expression before the crowd swirled between them.

Need.

She started. *Ye gods—was he— No, scratch that. It wasn't sexual. Or at least, it mostly wasn't sexual. Not that Banyon isn't a honey by anybody's standards—*

But this was something—desperate. What has our whistler been up to?

The song finished with a sudden chord, and the lights cut abruptly.

The applause was deafening, and she dismissed the question from her mind.

This is definitely turning out to be a fantastic *gig . . .*

As the lights came back up, Beth gestured to Allie, who began the first notes of "Come by the Hills," an old traditional air.

**"Come by the hills, to the land
where fancy is free . . ."**

This song was as gentle as the first rock song had been wild. Eric joined her on the first chorus, the flute weaving a bittersweet counterpoint around her voice. Then he took the solo again, a delicate melody line, beautiful and fey, and aching with unspoken longing.

It was hard for her to see the crowd, past the blinding lights, but something was happening out there—

They're not dancing, they're not walking away to the bar, they're just standing there. Standing, and listening, and swaying with the music. Some of them holding hands, and all of them looking up at the stage, at us, at Eric. Like they're in some kind of a trance.

This is definitely the weirdest *crowd we've played to in a long time.*

Then a flash of movement out on the dance floor; a pair

of gracefully dancing figures whirled elegantly across the floor, and the crowd moved back to give them room. *Looks like some kind of waltz, but not quite—not ballet, either, but it's close. Damn, but they're good! I wish I could find out who they are—I'd love to see them dance when I don't have to concentrate on the music. They're truly lovely.*

Slowly, other dancers joined the pair on the floor, until all Beth could see was the beautiful swirling patterns of color and movement, strange and wonderful. Something about their flowing clothing caught her attention for a moment.

God and Goddess—you don't buy that stuff off the rack! At least not at J. C. Penney's. This is not our usual draw. Not by a long shot. What in hell happened tonight? Did we just get discovered by the Rodeo Drive crowd?

What's happening to us tonight? We're so hot, the energy is so damn good, it's incredible. It's more than just having Eric jamming with us—it's something else, something that I don't quite understand—

Four songs later, though, she didn't care about understanding anything. *All I want to do is sit down. Just for a few minutes.* She glanced around, and saw that Allie and Jim were also looking faded, though Eric looked like he could keep going on all night.

One corner of her mouth quirked up in a lopsided grin when she picked up on that.

Damn him, he probably could!

She signalled Bo, then spoke clearly into the mike. "We'll be back after a break." Then the stage lights darkened mercifully.

The break room seemed like an oasis of calm after the set onstage. Beth propped the Fender against one of the packing crates.

"I think I'm going to die," Allie moaned, and slumped down on a wooden chair. "That far left stage light has been shining right in my eyes all night. I can't see anything except purple and blue spots."

"I'll tell Bo," Jim said, leaving the room.

"How are you holding up, Bethie?" Eric asked, sprawled on the floor.

"They're really a demanding crowd tonight," Beth replied thoughtfully. "Really alive. I feel like they're taking everything we can give them and then a little bit more."

And they seem to be focusing on you, my friend, though you're too modest and unassuming to notice it. I really wish that you would join Spiral Dance for more than an occasional gig. Especially if all the gigs could be like this one.

"I think I'm going to die," Allie said, staring at her hands. "There's spots crawling all over my skin."

Beth reached over and mussed Allie's hair good-naturedly. "Close your eyes, hon, you'll live. I played an all-night gig once, with bright green lights shining right in my eyes. I thought everyone in the audience was an H.P. Lovecraft Cthulhuoid after that."

"I'll get you a wet paper towel," Eric offered. "You can lay that over your eyes, maybe that'll help."

"Anything," Allie said mournfully. "But I won't guarantee that I'll still be alive by the time you get back."

Eric opened the door, admitting a blast of noise and cigarette smoke, then closed it behind him, shutting out the bedlam outside.

Beth eased herself to her feet. "I'm going after a beer, Allie. Want anything from the bar?"

"Some Guinness to pour over this poor musician's grave," the keyboardist said solemnly.

Beth couldn't help but laugh. "All right, I'll snag you a Guinness. I'll be right back."

She stepped into the hallway, waiting a moment as her eyes adjusted to the dim light. *And my lungs adjust to whatever in the hell is in the air tonight. Smells like weed—God, I sure hope the cops don't bust this place while we're playing! That's all we need. A police record would be a real boost to our careers.*

Someone was standing near the entrance to the hallway, silhouetted by the flickering light from the dance floor. He caught at her wrist as she walked past.

"Excuse me," Beth said, trying to be polite as she disengaged her arm from the stranger's grasp.

"Hey, pretty lady," the man said, his voice low and hoarse. "You sing real nice."

"Gee, thanks," Beth said, attempting to move around him. "You'll hear some more in a few minutes." *Who is this guy? Jeans, boots, leather jacket—one of the usual bar crowd, and drunker than hell.*

Wonderful. This is just what I need right now—

His hand tightened on her shoulder, refusing to let go even as she pried at his fingers. "Hey, we can go out back, have some fun, smoke a little. I've got some fine stuff, nice and dusted. You'll like it."

Smoke? With this guy? And pigs fly, my friend . . .

. . . dusted? Shit, he can't mean—oh God, get me out of this! He's talking about PCP!

"I don't think so," Beth said carefully. *This guy's eyes are so dilated, he probably shouldn't be able to walk.* "That's really not my scene. Listen, I've only got a few minutes before we're starting again . . ."

She glanced down the hallway. *No one in sight. Shit. And this guy is dusted, I could break his arm and he'd never feel it. I can't handle this alone—*

Before she could move, the man suddenly shoved her away from him, knocking her off-balance into the wall. "Whaddaya mean, not your scene? You don't like me or something?"

Oh shit.

The man moved closer, blocking Beth's line of escape. She pressed back against the wall, looking for anything she could use as a weapon. *Nothing in sight. Terrific. What now, Kentraine? If I break his instep with my heel he won't even blink. If I give 'im a knee, he might get angry.*

"Come on outside with me. We're going to party, right? Have some fun." The man's fingers gripped her upper arm tightly, digging in. Beth knew she'd have bruises from that by tomorrow morning.

If I get to see tomorrow morning. If I live that long. He's drugged out of his mind! If I shout for help, who

*knows what he'll do? And if I give in, go outside with
him—*

Lord and Lady, get me out of this!

Eric moved quickly through the crowd, trying not to
drip water from the paper towel in his hand, and trying
not to look intently at the people around him as he walked
past.

Yeah, don't stare at the elves, Eric, it isn't polite.

I know I'm going crazy, now.

*Well, everybody thinks that musicians are crazy any-
how, right?*

He dodged a drink-laden customer, staggering in the
direction of the johns, and saw a vivacious redhead, eyes
made up like a pair of iridescent butterfly wings, laughing
merrily with some of her friends. Green-eyed, of course.

*Damn, but there's a lot of green-eyed people in the club
tonight . . .*

"Bard?"

Eric froze in mid-step. *I know that voice.*

No. It can't be him again. It can't. I can't deal with this.

"Bard? I must speak with you."

Eric steeled himself, and turned to face Korendil. The
elf-actor was staring at him beseechingly, that impossibly
blond hair cascading over his shoulders . . . *and my leather
vest! Damn it, he's still wearing my clothes!*

*Be nice to the man, Eric. Or he'll probably knock you
into another wall.*

"Uh, hi," Eric said eloquently, very aware of the water
dripping from the paper towel onto his jeans. "The name's
Eric, by the way. Remember?"

The blond man nodded quite seriously. "I know, Bard. I
heard your name at the place-of-festival, when the beautiful witch was trying to aid you. And you told me again this
evening."

*Beautiful witch? Do I know any beautiful witches? Who
is this guy?*

"Please, listen to me, Bard. I know you did not wish to
see me again, but you must hear my words." *The—elf. He*

is. He's an elf—spoke earnestly, his green eyes pleading with Eric's, reaching out to him . . .

Green eyes—can't look away—that man in the limo—

Eric broke away from Korendil's gaze with an effort, shuddering at the memory.

What's happening to me? I thought nobody could be hypnotized against his will!

"Look," he said, trying to think of a way to get out of this conversation. "I'm in the middle of a show, I can't talk right now."

Korendil gestured at the hallway to the break room, and the back door beyond, where Beth was standing, talking to some guy. "Bard Eric, can we go outside to speak? Just for a few minutes?"

Eric shook his head. "Not 'Bard Eric.' Just Eric. And no, I don't want to go outside, I have to be back onstage in a few minutes."

And if I have to talk to you, I want to do it where there's witnesses. In case you decide to slam me into a wall again.

The elf—*no, dammit, he's as human as I am, it's just makeup and F/X*—looked at him in shock. "Do you think I would purposefully hurt you? I would never do so, I promise. But I need your help. We all need your help."

He really means it. "You're serious about this, aren't you? You're an elf, and somebody's trying to kill your people, and you need *me* to help you?"

Korendil nodded, gravely earnest. "Will you help us? Even as we speak, our enemy is marshalling his forces, preparing to destroy that which gives us life itself . . ."

Eric tried to keep a straight face. *Come on, Eric, you've got a few friends with—unusual—realities. This guy's no worse than any of them. Besides, he's trying to be nice, and you should be nice right back to him. Instead of laughing in his face, and then calling the cops.*

"I don't know, I need some time to think about all of this, really." *Yeah, just get away from him, that's the first step in dealing with a loon—*

Something doesn't feel right. A ripple of honest-to-God

fear—fear with no cause—rolled down his spine. *Something is very,* very *wrong*—

Eric glanced over the elf's shoulder, and suddenly what he had seen a moment before registered: Beth, cornered by a man near the back door, glint of shiny metal—*oh shit, he's got a knife! He's holding a knife on Bethie!*

Korendil's eyes widened just as Eric gathered a breath to shout for help, and the blond man whirled—stared—

Less than a microsecond, Eric would have sworn to that. *Surely* not enough to have seen what was happening, much less think of anything to do. Yet suddenly he was crossing the distance between them and the hallway in a few quick leaps.

Eric dashed after him, pushing people out of his way. *How in the hell did he get through the crowd so fast?*

He skidded into the hallway, just as the blond actor—*elf?*—dived between Beth and the stranger, shoving the man away from her. Eric caught a glimpse of her frightened eyes, then the man with the knife was on his feet again, facing Korendil, hissing words almost too low to hear.

". . . mess with me, mister, you don't . . ."

The words suddenly faded away, as the man stared up into Korendil's eyes. They seemed momentarily frozen, all of them: Beth, crouching back against the wall; Korendil, gazing in the man's eyes; and the stranger, the knife only inches from Korendil's face, not moving . . .

What in the hell is going on here? That guy's still holding the knife, but he's not moving, just standing there, staring into Korendil's eyes. My God, isn't he going to do something before the guy goes for his neck?

Then the man dropped the knife suddenly, the blade clattering on the floor. He staggered backwards, hitting the wall and sliding down into a sitting position, blank-eyed and shuddering.

Eric stared at the man, who was clutching his hand and wimpering, as Korendil moved to Beth, his voice quiet and concerned. "Are you all right, Lady? Did he harm you?"

Beth was shaking her head, wiping tears from her eyes.

Bethie, crying? I've never—oh shit, that guy's about to—
Eric shouted a warning as the man on the floor suddenly
moved for the knife. "Korendil, look out!"

The elf turned just as the man lunged with the knife.

Freeze-frame.

A flash of fire—no, a rope of fire—

Next frame.

Fire coiling, lashing out at the man's wrist—

Music up.

*A burst of melody, a discordant B-flat minor that could
break your eardrums—*

Resume speed.

*—as Korendil's fist slams into the man's face, and the
surprised look on his face as he falls—*

And the thought, lingering in Eric's mind: *That can't be
real. But it wasn't a special effect. That was real.*

*I've gone crazy, the whole world is crazy. I've com-
pletely lost it.*

The stranger twitched once and then was still, sprawled
unconscious on the floor.

Eric was suddenly aware of the dripping paper towel,
forgotten in his hand. The blond actor—*actor?*—held Beth
gently in his arms, murmuring something as he brushed
away her tears. Beth was trembling, her hands shaking
uncontrollably.

The break-room door opened suddenly, and Allie looked
out blearily, blinking at the dim light. "What in the hell?"

Her eyes widened as Beth, half-carried by Korendil,
staggered unsteadily into the break room. "Beth?" She
focused on Eric as he walked past her. "Eric, what—"

"I don't know, some guy attacked Beth," Eric said,
watching as Beth, with Korendil's help, sat down on a
packing crate. "He's out cold on the floor. This guy decked
him."

Beth, her face in her hands, tried to push Korendil away
from her. The blond man shook his head, said something
too low for Eric to hear, and rested his hand on her
shoulder again.

For a moment, Eric thought he could hear a faint
melody, echoing from somewhere in the room.

Very classical, sounds maybe like a variation on the third Brandenburg Concerto—

Why am I thinking about music at a time like this?

"Beth?" Eric asked hesitantly, sitting on his heels at her feet, and looking up at her anxiously. "Are you okay?"

She nodded without looking up.

Then Beth took several deep breaths, and spoke quietly. "It's all right, I'm okay," she said. A moment later, her voice was stronger. "Allie, could you tell management that there's an unconscious sonuvabitch lying in the hallway? They'll probably want to call the cops."

She's starting to sound like herself again. Eric tried to banish the image of Beth Kentraine, crying, barely able to walk. *She's Bethie again, she's okay now. Thank God.*

Allie nodded silently, and walked out of the room. Eric shifted uncomfortably, looking at the way Korendil's hand was still resting on Beth's shoulder. "Listen, uh, Korendil, I, uh—" *Might as well spit it out.* "Look, Korendil, I still think you're crazy, but—thanks for being here."

He wanted to say something more, but the look in Korendil's eyes stopped him short. Eric left the room quickly, but he could feel Beth's and Korendil's eyes intent upon him as he closed the door.

The L.A.P.D. officers hauled the man away, slumped between them. Eric watched from the edge of the hallway. *Damn, but whatever that guy Korendil is, he sure knows how to deck somebody in one punch.*

And whatever he did to disarm the guy—

No. That wasn't real. You can't hit somebody that way, not with fire and music. It didn't happen.

Doesn't matter what I thought I saw. It wasn't real. It didn't happen. It's a drug flashback or something.

Or something.

Eric glanced at the half-empty dance floor, and noted the cluster of people over by the club's restrooms.

Amazing, how many people suddenly had to go to the bathroom when the cops showed up. Eric snickered to himself. *Sure hope they didn't clog up the toilets with all the stuff they were flushing down 'em—*

He walked towards the break room at the end of the
hall. He stopped outside the closed door, hearing quiet
conversation within.

". . . what I can't understand is how anyone could profit
from something like that. I mean, they'd lose the magic,
too, right?"

Beth's voice.

She's talking to that loon about— Oh, terrific. He's
probably telling her how I have to be the Great Savior of
Middle Earth. What did I do to deserve this?

He opened the door. Beth and Korendil looked up.
"Hi," Eric said awkwardly, wishing he had knocked first.
Beth and Korendil were sitting very close together on the
packing crates.

Too close.

"Bo thinks we should start up real soon," Eric continued, noting the way the elf's—*actor's!*—arm was around
Beth's shoulders. "Take everybody's mind off all of the
cops that just came through the club."

Beth disengaged from Korendil and stood up, dusting
off her black pants. "Sounds good." She smiled at Korendil.
"I'd like to talk some more, Korendil. Maybe after the
show?"

Eric felt something tighten in his throat, at the warm
way Beth and Korendil were looking at each other, so
intense and intimate.

Damn it, it's her life, none of my business—

But he's an elf! Not even human!

No, he's an actor, with good makeup, contact lenses, all
of that. He's just another guy. Another six-foot-five guy,
blond, built like a dancer, and handsome. Even if I don't
swing that way, he's damn handsome. I can see why she
likes him.

It's none of my business who Beth Kentraine gets in-
volved with—it's her life, not mine.

Maybe it's just that I'm on the rebound, but it hurts,
the way she's looking at him—

"Eric, perhaps you could join us?" Korendil ventured,
gazing at him with an intent, worried expression. "I would
speak with both of you, if possible."

Oh, great. Now the loon wants to flirt with Beth and drive me nuts at the same time. Very economical.

I can't handle this.

"Maybe later," Eric said, wishing he was anywhere else but here. *Even Juilliard. At least when I was there, I had reasons for thinking I was crazy.* "But we have to do the show now." He started towards the door, not looking back.

Maybe if I wish for it hard enough, this guy'll go back to Oz or the North Pole or Santa Monica wherever he came from. It's worth a try.

I just don't want to think that I've gone completely, utterly insane, that's all—

—and I don't want this to be real . . .

· 6 ·

Give Me Your Hand

"Wait a minute, Banyon."

Eric turned slowly, unwillingly. *I don't think I'm going to like what's coming.* "Yeah, Beth?"

She pushed her dark, ragged bangs back out from her eyes with a tired gesture. She looked wrung out.

Not surprising.

And preoccupied.

Which doesn't bode real well, either.

"I want to talk something out with you. Now. Just for a couple of minutes. I have this bad feeling that you're going to vanish the minute we finish the show."

Eric warily glanced at Korendil, then sat down on a crate. "What did you want to talk about?"

Beth sighed, giving Korendil a sidelong look. "What do you think?"

They've been talking about the elves, and that "Eric the Bard" bullshit. Damn it, Beth, how did you let him sucker you in so fast? I thought you were smarter than that!

"Uh, I don't know what he's been telling you, but—"

"You don't?" Her lips tightened. "Than you're dumber than I thought, Banyon."

He bristled. "Oh come on! You don't really believe this guy, do you, Bethie? I mean, look at him! He has to be an actor. And those ears are fake, I know it—"

Eric reached out his hand towards the tip of one of Kory's ears, showing through the blond curls.

The fake elf held up his right hand in a graceful, but

93

dangerous gesture of warning. There was a steely glint in his green eyes, a definite challenge, as clear as if he'd spoken aloud.

Touch my ears and you die, white boy.

Eric hesitated, suddenly remembering the pain he'd felt earlier this afternoon as his face met the wall at high speed.

He coughed, and turned his own gesture into a shrug.

Well, maybe I won't *demonstrate how the ears are just a latex special effect . . .*

He turned to the only other—marginally—sane person in the room. "Beth—listen to me. You're not a ten-year-old, or a member of Hobbits Anonymous. You can't really *believe* what he's saying. There's no such thing as elves. Or magic. Or any of that crap."

Beth leaned back, crossing her legs and surveying him with a faint smile on her lips. "Really? Then how do you explain what Korendil did to that creep in the hallway? How do you account for three-quarters of the people out there in the audience tonight? Have you taken a *good* look at some of those outfits? At the way they look?"

So she's seen them, too. "I don't know, maybe they all just showed up from a cast party on the Universal lot. It's a helluva lot more believable than a nightclub full of dancing elves." Eric shook his head, trying stubbornly to break through Beth's conviction. "I just don't believe in Santa Claus, the tooth fairy, *or* elves. As far as I'm concerned, this guy is playing a practical joke on all of us. I think Maureen paid him to do it; she's got enough connections. And she's always been a bit jealous of you. She'd be perfectly happy to get *both* of us with her prank."

"I told you he'd be difficult to convince, Lady Beth." *That* was from Korendil.

Eric gave him a dirty look.

The elf sighed, ignoring it. "For a Bard, he has a very closed mind."

That's it! *I am sick of hearing that word!*

"Goddammit, I am *not* a Bard!"

The actor turned to face him. His voice was very soft, yet it demanded attention. "Then what are you?" he asked simply.

Eric was silent for a moment before speaking. "I don't know. I'm a musician. A reasonably-talented street musician. Sometimes I'm a composer. I don't know if I'm any good at it. And besides that?" He shrugged. "Not much else."

"No." Korendil shook his head solemnly, but with stubborn conviction. "You *are* a Bard. You must feel it, the magic that flows when you play your music. Everyone else can."

Midnight, alone in the grove, playing "Sheebeg Sheemore," then the music taking over, a melody strange and wild, as the trees bend down to listen—

Korendil continued relentlessly. "You can heal, and harm, and create with your magic. Glimpse the distant past, or—" His voice suddenly took on a tone of desolation. "—touch the future . . ."

The bleakness of the last three words threw Eric into the waking nightmare of that moment on the bus—

Los Angeles, grayness everywhere, no life, no joy, only misery like a living thing, dragging everything down, destroying all hope—

He shook off the clinging weariness, shook off the despair. *How can he know this? How can he reach into my thoughts and know exactly who I am and what's happened to me? That's not possible. Nobody can do that. That's—*

—magic.

Fear made him clench his jaw; made him try to deny that last thought.

No. This can't be real.

But—

The rope of fire—the music—

I wasn't stoned. I saw it, back there in the hallway. I wasn't stoned on the bus, or this afternoon at the apartment. It was magic. And it was real.

I can't keep pretending that it's all fake. There's too many things that have happened, too much to disbelieve. It's real, as real as I am.

And if it's real—

Then so are my nightmares.

Oh shit.

Eric sat down slowly, before his knees went. "Okay," he said weakly. "You know. I don't know how you know, but—yeah, I saw the future. At least, I think it was the future. It was horrible."

Korendil nodded sadly. "You probably saw what would happen if the magic nexus was destroyed. Now do you see why that must not happen? *That* is what this city will become."

Eric shuddered, thinking of the desolation on the faces of the people in his vision. "When I saw that—there was a man, watching me from a limo. An older guy, with silver hair, and green eyes like yours—"

Green eyes, reaching inside where no one should see, violation, a hand that fouls all it touches—

"Perenor." The elf's voice was a whisper of apprehension, threaded with pain.

Eric looked up at Korendil, startled. "What?"

Korendil's eyes were clouded, his face as still and pale as a death mask. "His name is Perenor. He was one of us, and now is our greatest enemy. Where did you see him? When?"

Perenor. I won't forget that name.

Eric shivered, remembering the despair, the hopelessness that had *almost* pushed him over the edge. "I saw him on Van Nuys Boulevard, this afternoon. It was weird—it was like he recognized me, somehow he *knew* me."

Knew me, and tried to take me apart at the seams—and he knew every button to push. Every twitch. Whatever else is going on, I wasn't imagining that—it was real! What that bastard did to me, it was real!

Korendil's green eyes were troubled with things Eric couldn't read. "I did not realize that Perenor knew of your existence. Perhaps he felt the magic in the place-of-festival when you awakened me, and decided to seek you out. Perhaps it was an accident—but I cannot believe that. If Perenor knows of you, then you are in great danger, Bard. He will hunt for you, knowing that you are the only one who can stop him."

The only—hey, wait a second— His horse sense reared and snorted in alarm. "What do you mean, the only one?

You've got other people who are going to help you, right?
I mean, you're pretty flashy with the magic, mister—"

"Not compared to Perenor," the elf said, resignedly.
"My power is nothing to his. Believe me, Bard Eric, the
little power I have is insignificant beside even your own,
untutored as you are. That is why we need you so very
much."

Beth gave him a *look*.

*Like—"Turn him down, and I just may decide never to
speak to you again." Thanks, Beth.*

"Even if I *do* help you," he said, trying to keep from
sounding like he was ready to dive under one of the
crates, "you don't expect me to take on this guy by myself,
do you?"

Korendil gazed at him with rising hope and eagerness.
"Then you will help us?"

He froze. *Oh shit. I just said that, didn't I? Me and my
big mouth.*

*Well, if I'm going to back out of this one, better do it
quick.*

He started to open his mouth, started to search for
words to extricate himself without Beth disowning him—
then stopped again, struck by something he wasn't certain
he understood. A feeling that whatever he chose or said at
this moment was incredibly important. And a feeling of
conviction.

*What if I am a Bard, like this guy says? What if I really
do have some kind of power that his people need?*

What if I'm the only one who can help them?

*If that's true, and I walk away from this guy, I'll be
doing the worst, lowest thing I've ever done in my life.*

I can't live with that.

Eric looked away from those too-bright eyes for a moment. "I—I don't know," he replied, haltingly. "I mean,
I'm just Eric Banyon. I'm not some great hero out of the
legends, here to save your ass. I'm just a busker, a wandering musician . . . God, it's hard enough for me to stick
around one place long enough to finish a run of Faire, let
alone fight a Crusade! Aren't there any other bards around
who can help you?"

Korendil shook his head, wearily. "No. Not one. Either they do not believe, or they do not have the power to aid us. And most of the elves are Dreaming, trapped in despair and apathy. Even the great Prince, our leader, is lost to Dreaming. It may be too late to save them, I don't know. But if *you* will help me . . ."

He gazed at Eric now with pleading, and something akin to worship.

Or awe. Great. Now I've got an elf who's convinced that I'm the Second Coming of Christ. In addition to whatever it is that he wants me to do.

This really is too weird for words. Even if I really do believe him, I'm still not certain I can deal with this . . .

"So, what are we going to do?"

Eric and Korendil both glanced up in surprise.

Beth Kentraine stretched, standing up slowly. She looked at them questioningly, hands on her hips. "Well? What are we going to do about this?"

"We?" Eric repeated.

"Yeah, bucko. *We.* Did you think I wasn't going to get involved in this? Get real, Banyon."

She smiled, but her eyes were distant, looking off at someone, something that wasn't in the Here and Now. "When I was a kid, a friend of mine told me about elves, how they were real. How he'd seen them, talked with them, how there were maybe even a few of them living in California. I believed him; he'd never told me anything else that wasn't true, no matter how strange it had sounded. I used to dream about them—but I never really thought I'd see one."

She turned her gaze back to the present; looked from Eric to Korendil and back again. "Now, I *have* seen them. Now I *know* they're real—hell, there's one sitting right here in front of me—and I hear that they're in real trouble. What the hell do you expect me to do? Of *course* I'm going to help." She grinned. "Just try and *stop* me, Banyon."

Before Eric could speak, there was a sharp knock at the door. "Hey, guys, are you in there?" They could hear Bo's anxious voice through the thin plywood. "We've got a crowd waiting out here, and they're getting tired of the canned stuff. Are you going to start up soon?'"

"Just a sec, Bo!" Beth called to him. She turned back to Eric and the elf. "We'll talk more after the gig, right?"

"Right," Korendil said, glancing at Eric.

Yeah, right. Terrific. Now Beth's involved in this lunacy, too. I don't know if this is going to be dangerous or not—I don't want her to get hurt—

He followed her out the door, heading for the stage, thinking furiously.

I've got no idea what this is all going to cost. Or even what or who we're going to have to face—like that Perenor guy. He really did mess with my mind; a little more and I would have been playing tag on the Ventura Freeway. What could he do to Bethie?

This could be worse than dangerous. I don't want to think of him doing something like that to her.

But as she took her place in front of her mike, he looked at the straight line of her back, and sighed with resignation.

I know her. There is nobody in the world that can out-stubborn Beth Kentraine. Once she's made up her mind, she won't budge. There's no way I'll be able to convince her to stay out of this.

Terrific. Three of us committed to this idiocy: me, an elf, and a rock singer. Against God knows what. Shit. We should be committed.

Maybe we should get some cards made up: The Unholy Trinity. Weddings, Bar Mitzvahs and Parties. Worlds saved, only a modest additional fee—

The Porsche banked sharply around the curve, barely touching the dividing yellow line, then swerved back for the next turn. A professional race-car driver might have taken that curve at a tighter angle, but no one else.

The engine purred as the driver downshifted for the canyon hills that rose stark and shadowed above the accelerating car. The lights of the city reflected off the glistening black paint, glittering against the windshield's glass, brighter than the stars in the night sky above Mulholland Drive.

Another turn, at a speed that most would consider reckless. A policeman would have called it illegal. But for the driver, it was only skill, reaching for the edge. Perfectly controlled. Flawless.

A test of excellence.

Ria Llewellyn clenched black-gloved hands on the steering wheel, ignoring the strands of blonde hair flying haphazardly in the wind from the Porsche's half-open window, concentrating on the road, and driving at the limits of her abilities.

Damn him!

The Porsche banked around another tight curve. For a moment, the sports car skidded towards the edge of the canyon, the steep stone wall blurring past, only inches away from the Porsche. Then Ria tightened her grip on the steering wheel, expertly bringing the car back to the center of the twisting canyon road.

Right in the middle of the goddamn board meeting. "Ria, I need to see you. The Japanese restaurant in Studio City, one hour."

And when I ask him what in the hell is so important that I need to leave a critical strategy session at ten o'clock at night, all he says is "Korendil has escaped . . ."

She sighed, brushing long blonde hair back from her face with a gesture of annoyance. *As if one person—even a warrior of the Old Blood—could make a difference in this. I told him we've secured the land, it's already signed for, nothing and no one is going to stop it now. Definitely not a fool who's spent the last ten years asleep under an oak tree . . .*

Like the rest of those fools. Unable to see the real world around them. Living in Dreaming—hell, living in shopping malls! When everything they could possibly desire is so close, within their reach—

Like Mother, in that commune somewhere—Mendocino? Marin? I don't remember. Not that it matters, I never see her anyway. How could she give up everything that Father could offer her—for that? What a sham she is, to preach about caring, then walk out on us before I was even in kindergarten. And what did she get? Tie-dyed

T-shirts, drugs and "love." "Love," what a joke, what hypocrisy.

It's all escapism, hiding from reality. That's all these fools are doing. Like Mother.

Except now, it's too late for that. They're going to lose everything. Even if Korendil is free, it's too late for him to do anything.

A wailing siren interrupted Ria's thoughts. She glanced into the rearview mirror, and saw the flashing red-blue lights of the police motorcycle, close behind her.

A motorcycle cop, on Mulholland at night? Unusual. A bit of bad luck that he spotted me. But it doesn't really matter; it'll take only a moment to be corrected—

She pulled over to the side of the road, waiting for the helmeted policeman to dismount from the white police-model Kawasaki. His boots made sharp crunching noises on the rough gravel as he walked towards the black Porsche.

"Good evening, officer." Ria smiled at him through the open window.

How pleasant. A handsome motorcycle cop. That curly brown hair would be quite attractive if he let it grow out a little longer and got rid of that mustache. Why do all the policemen in L.A. have mustaches?

"You driving license and car registration, ma'am. I'm writing you up for reckless and exhibitionist driving—"

"Here's my license." She reached down to the black purse on the seat beside her, removed the license from her wallet and handed it to him.

"This says your name is"—he glanced up at her over the edge of the laminated piece of paper—"Arianrhod Llewellyn? Is that correct?"

She smiled, gazing into his eyes. "Absolutely correct."

Brown eyes, ordinary, very human. But reach beyond, brushing past surprise and disbelief, and you can touch, and take control, and change—

Brief struggles, like a small bird fluttering in my hand, trying to escape. They always try to escape, never realizing that it's already over . . .

The cop stared at her blankly, unable to look away, Ria's

driving license trembling slightly in his hands. His right hand edged towards the .38 holstered at his hip.

No. You are mine, now. Be still.

Ria surveyed the man standing beside her, motionless. *Unfortunately, I do not have time for you tonight, even if you are a handsome, obviously virile man. But, if I ever see you again—*

She released him, breaking the spell. The officer shook his head slowly, dazed. "I—I, uh, I'm just going to give you a warning, miss. Please drive more carefully."

"Thank you, officer." Ria smiled to herself as the cop walked unsteadily towards his parked motorcycle.

Remember me. Dream that one day I will call you.

A pity that Father needs to speak with me tonight. That man could have proved to be an interesting . . . diversion.

She waited until the cop had left, then started the Porsche, driving through the shadowed canyon. At Laurel Canyon, she turned left, and a moment later the lights of the Valley were visible before her, scintillating jewels against the darkness.

Beautiful, but I would rather be back in Century City, finishing up the contract for the meeting tomorrow—

Dammit, Father, why tonight?

Ten minutes later, she parked the Porsche in front of the entrance to the restaurant. The valet opened the door for her. His eyes brightened when he saw the folded bill she handed him with the keys. "Make sure nobody scratches the paint."

"Yes, ma'am." His eyes followed her, hungrily, as she strode to the restaurant door. She smiled to herself and gave her hips a little extra twitch, just for his benefit. She could feel the heat of his eyes upon her as she reached for the lacquered black door handle.

Dream on, little man. Only—this dream costs more than you'd ever want to pay.

She stepped inside, glancing around the entrance. A distinguished older man rose from his seat near the koi pond, and moved gracefully towards her.

"Good evening, dear," the silver-haired man said, and

she leaned close so he could kiss her cheek. "You're looking especially lovely tonight."

She offered him a hint of icy smile. Enough so that he
could read her annoyance—not enough so that he could
read how *very* annoyed she was.

He took her arm to lead her towards the back of the
restaurant. "Kyoshi's holding a table for us. Have you had
any dinner yet?"

"Not really."

*Damn him, he really wants something from me, I can
tell. Of course, he'll never just come out and say it. We'll
have to go through this whole dinner routine first.* "Some
sushi, maybe. And hot sake would be wonderful. It's been
a rough day."

"You'll have to tell me about it." He maneuvered them
to the table, isolated behind a colorful paper screen and a
small stand of potted bamboo.

"Sake, Kyoshi," he instructed the waiter standing patiently beside the table, "and a tray of sushi to start with."

Ria sat back in the chair as the waiter hurried away, and
surveyed her father thoughtfully. Was it her imagination,
or were there faint lines at the edges of his eyes? Probably
not—he was never less than perfect.

As always, his silver hair was immaculately barbered,
carefully masking the tips of his long, slightly-pointed ears.
But nothing could disguise his eyes, the cold emerald-
green, slitted black pupils.

*At least my eyes are human. I suppose I should thank
Mother for that.*

A twinge of something, not quite concern, touched her
briefly. *He looks tired. This Korendil affair must be worrying him more than I thought. Unless it's something else
that he wants—*

I suppose I might as well start the game myself.

"As much as I enjoy seeing you, Father, I must admit
that tonight isn't the best night for this. Did I tell you that
we're about to sign the investment deal? Twelve million in
paper, tomorrow at noon. My execs are still at the office,
hammering out the details. And I'm sure they're wonder-

ing just what was so important that their boss had to disappear immediately."

To see her father—

His green eyes glinted with hidden amusement. "I'm sure they have faith in you, my dear. They probably just think you're closing another deal, right now."

"Am I?"

Her father smiled. "Perhaps."

You bastard. Games within games, even with your own daughter.

I know what he sees. His beautiful little girl. A corporate executive. Half of the Old Blood, half human. Not quite his equal in power, but damn close. Someone he can manipulate and control, and use in his games.

But you taught me not to trust others, Father. To believe only in myself, and what I can do, and never let anyone past my guard. So of course as I grew older, I realized that included you *as well. You never put that variable in your equation, did you?*

Now you think you can snap your fingers and I'll come running to help you—

It'll snow in hell first.

The sushi arrived, with two small ceramic containers of hot rice wine. Ria and her father were silent as the wine was poured, a brief respite in the verbal fencing match. Parry, riposte. Feint and feint again.

Ria sipped the steaming-hot wine, then dipped a piece of octopus sushi in the small bowl of soy sauce beside her, savoring the unusual texture.

And waited for her father to make the next move.

Which, of course, he isn't going to do.

Perenor sampled another piece of sushi, then mixed more green wasanabe horseradish into his soy dipping bowl. "Try the crab, my dear, it's really quite excellent tonight."

He's trying to bait me. And, damn him, he's succeeding. I don't want to spend all night sitting here, making polite conversation, trying to figure out what he wants from me. Not when I've got twelve mil in paperwork sitting back at the office.

She heaved an obvious sigh, and gave her head a little shake. "All right, Father. Why are you so concerned about Korendil? What does it matter if he's free? He's just one person, and he isn't going to awaken the Dreamers, or desert them to rouse the High Court; he can't do anything against us. He isn't even one-tenth of the mage that you are."

The silver-haired man was silent for a long moment. There was an indefinable expression in his emerald-ice eyes. "Ria, what would you say if I told you that there was a Bard in Los Angeles? A true Bard, with *all* the abilities of the ancient Bards?"

"I'd say that you've been drinking too much sake," Ria said flatly. "There are no more true Bards. Taliesen was the last one, and he died a thousand years ago." She pondered that a moment. "Well, *perhaps* O'Carolan. But he was a drunkard, and he never used his magic."

Her father picked up another piece of sushi, a pale-orange fantailed shrimp, and gazed at it thoughtfully. "You shouldn't discount what I say so quickly, Arianrhod."

Ria stared in silence at her father.

It's true, then.

A Bard, in Los Angeles. A true Bard.

But that's impossible—

"All right, you've found a Bard." She shrugged. "And Korendil is free. That still doesn't add up to any danger that *I* can see."

"You still don't understand, do you?" Perenor said tersely. "Korendil is the one who *found* this Bard, somehow—or the Bard found him. This one has great potential—too great. I saw that when I encountered him, recognized his power, and touched the boy's mind. I've taken steps to neutralize him, but I want to be rid of Korendil before he brings any other players into this game. And for that, I need your help."

Ria almost laughed aloud. *Why, father mine, you're not feeling inadequate now, are you? A little bit of self-doubt, here? Is that why you needed my help so many years ago, to trap Korendil in that grove?*

You are getting older, even for one of the Old Blood—

you wouldn't happen to be getting weaker, *as well? Your power fading, even as mine grows in strength? Now,* that *would be an amusing thought—*

"I imagine I could help you with this, Father," she purred. "Of course, I *would* like to know what's in this for me . . ."

Perenor's first slammed down on the table, rattling the sake bottles. The young couple at the table across from them glanced up at them in surprise, then carefully looked away.

He leaned forward, speaking in a low whisper. "Don't play games with me; and don't forget, *daughter,* exactly what is at stake here. This is our chance to finally rid ourselves of any who might thwart us. To avenge ourselves on those who cast me out, who refused to acknowledge you. And to gain such power, power as you've never dreamed of it—"

"I have power," Ria said, cutting through his words. "Power in the humans' world, true, but it's good enough for me. I have my business, and money, and control in this city. Why should I help you? What does it matter to me what happens to any of the Old Blood? They're fading now; they're no threat to anyone, least of all to me. I see no reason to exert myself, to involve myself, just because *you* want to amuse yourself with another game."

He leaned back a little, his eyes glittering, and toyed with another piece of sushi. "Even if, with a little 'exertion,' you could win immortality?"

Breath failed her momentarily. "What are you talking about?"

Perenor shrugged. "I thought you knew. You . . . inherited . . . certain gifts from me, Ria, but you *are* half-human, after all. Eventually, you'll grow old and die."

An unpleasant smile passed briefly across his lips.

"I'm sure," he continued, "that I'll still be alive to see it. That, of course, is one of the reasons I suggested that we purchase the Elizabethan Faire land. I was thinking primarily of you, my dear, though, of course, I will gain a few benefits from this as well. Once we have control of the nexus, you'll never have to worry about this again. The power itself will hold time at bay and keep you young."

He reached out, touching a strand of her pale blonde hair with mocking tenderness. "You're so lovely, such a remarkable child. I truly would hate to see you grow old, see your beauty wither away."

She tasted the bitterness of being outmanuevered. *I'm sure you would, Father. I know I'd feel just the same way, if you were the one who was aging and dying.*

Very well; for now, our goals are the same. But, when this is over . . .

She laughed lightly. "Father, of *course* I'll help you. I, I just thought this was part of your fight against the Old Blood, and that was why you wanted control of the magic nexus. To avenge what they did to you, so many years ago. I never dreamed it was more than that . . ."

Perenor leaned back in his chair, a faint and satisfied half-smile flickering across his handsome features. "Well, now you know." He glanced at his watch. "There's time enough to deal with this tonight. I know where Korendil is—this shouldn't take very long."

The silver-haired man tossed several bills onto the table, then stood, extending his arm to his daughter. "Shall we?"

"Of course."

But I won't forget this evening. And, once we control the nexus—

—we'll talk again of power and promises, Father.

· 7 ·

Beware, Oh Take Care

Korendil, Knight of Elfhame Sun-Descending, squire of
the High Court, Magus Minor, and Child of Danann—
Fine titles, but will any of that aid me now?

Korendil sighed, gathered borrowed hope about him like
his borrowed finery, and stepped out into the crowded
hall of the place called "Diverse Pleasures." Hope was
such a fragile thing—and it rested upon such fragile mortal shoulders.

He watched the young Bard, Eric, follow the lovely
witch to their places on the stage. *Such frighteningly
fragile mortal shoulders . . .*

The Bard hardly looked his part. Taliesen—or so
Korendil's elders had told him—had been as skilled with
blade and bow as with his harp. Eric was small and thin,
with a face that would have been sweet, had it not been so
wary, so marked with distrust. A very attractive young man—

But *not* a warrior, nor anything like one. And just now,
a hesitant man, one uncertain about what he had just
agreed to.

A very *young* man.

Korendil knew exactly how he felt. Korendil was a very
young elf; scarcely two hundred years old as the mortals
counted time. There was only one younger than he in all
of the High *or* Low Courts of Elfhame Sun-Descending
and Elfhame Misthold, and that was his cousin to the north.
There were too many times when he was uncertain; too
many times when he felt a fool. Especially of late.

But I cannot just give up. I cannot allow this to happen—

He glanced about at the Dreaming elves, scattered through the crowd like so many exotic butterflies. *I could conjure my own garments,* he thought absently, while counting the number of elvenkind who had somehow gathered *here,* and marking those who seemed by their eyes to be the least lost in Dreaming. *I would not look so out of place in them here. Then I could give Bard Eric his property back* . . . He recalled the Bard's resentful stare when the young man thought that Korendil was not aware of his glances. *They take possessions so seriously, these mortals—*

But if I did that, I should only need them again before I left—and besides, I have already altered them to my own use. Would that I knew them well enough to conjure duplicates. I suppose I could try kenning *them now, so that I could duplicate them later.*

He took stock of himself, first, and decided against the idea.

A distinctly foolish notion. I am no kind of a mage, not really. Subduing that madman expended enough of my magic as it was. I have little power to waste on kenning. *Not if I am going to have any hope of Awakening any of the others.*

Perhaps the Bard's music will help. That is surely what drew them all here this evening. Although he scarcely seems to believe it himself.

Korendil smiled to himself, remembering Eric's shocked expression when he had first seen the warrior-elf in his place-of-dwelling. *So young, so eager to disbelieve. Would that this Bard was a Taliesen, older and powerful, ready and willing to do battle with our Enemy. But if Bard Eric was as skilled as Taliesen, Perenor would have learned of his existence before this, learned of him and taken steps to dispose of him* . . .

No. Better this way. At least now, I can have hope that he will quickly learn what he must do to save us. And perhaps, if we are very careful, Perenor will not be able to find us.

He moved out of the little space by the hallway and into the milling crowd. His goal was a table near one wall, with three brilliantly-costumed elfmaids on tall stools about it, like three bright tropical birds upon their perches. Two of the three he knew, both of the High Court: Variel and Mayanir, sisters; and both—at least ten years ago—Awake enough to *know* what was happening to them.

Awake enough to have begun to fear.

And that was before *the danger to the nexus,* he thought soberly, easing between two chattering groups of mortals who seemed as oblivious to the presence of elvenkind as the elves were to them. *If there are any that I can Wake—surely it will be Val and Mai.*

Loud, discordant laughter made him wince as he passed the bar. His sensitive hearing was suffering in this place.

I cannot see how the Bard can tolerate it. The mortals' world seems to have changed so very much in ten years— but then, that is the way of their world. He sighed. *And the world of Elvenkin is different as well. I cannot say that either of them have changed for the better.*

He politely declined the advances of a very drunk mortal woman, one with too much flesh crammed into too little clothing. Moments later he declined again—with more grace, and a touch of sympathy—the advances of a shy and bespectacled young mortal man. *He* was equally drunk, but Kory could Read in him that he had so indulged out of unhappiness, and in an attempt to bolster his nerve.

These mortals were all so rawly open. It was hard to move among them and feel their thoughts and emotions jostling his mind as their bodies jostled his.

And so few of them were here out of joy. *That* was the saddest of all.

The elves were still, deep pools of silence in this jungle. Too silent—but a relief from the screeching of the mortals. Unless you needed, as Korendil needed, to rouse them.

Finally he reached his goal, the three elfmaids poised beneath an overhead spotlight. *In other times they would have been lit softly by their own magic. But that was before the magic was choked off by so much cold iron about us.* He stood beside the table, patient in the shadow, waiting for one of them to notice him.

None of them did.

Their eyes were bright but vacant, like all the others he'd seen here this night. They sipped at drinks, listened with half an ear to the music playing, and giggled conversationally to one another, weaving a circle of attention that closed them inside and Kory out.

He decided to violate protocol. "Val—" he said, touching her blue-silk-clad arm, sending a little tingle of carefully hoarded power from himself to her. "*Val—*"

She blinked, turned very slowly, and looked into his eyes. She blinked again, and licked her lips. "Hi," she said, uncertainly. "Hi. I know you—don't I?"

"It's *Korendil*, Val," he replied with emphasis, trying to get her to focus on him. "Kory. You certainly *do* know me."

"Oh, yeah," she said, blinking again. "Hi, Kory. You haven't been around for a while. Have you been away somewhere?"

He reined in his temper, and refrained from swearing. *Is this the depth to which we've sunk?*

"Perenor and that half-Blooded daughter of his trapped me in the nexus grove," he said as forcefully as he could. "It's been *ten years*, Val."

"Oh, wow," she said, a little more interest stirring in the back of her eyes, focusing a little better on him. "Ten years? Gods. That long? Like—you were trapped?"

"Yes," he replied fiercely, fighting with Dreaming for her attention, spinning out his feeble magic to try and pull her back to something like the maid he had known. "That long. Val, listen—" she started to gaze off past his shoulder and he touched her arm again to bring her back. "*Listen.* This is important. The nexus grove is in danger. Someone is going to destroy it un—"

"*Ladies and Gentlemen,*" Beth Kentraine's voice called over the babble of the crowd. "*We* are *Spiral Dance. We're back and ready to rock!*"

Kory cursed in every language he knew. The moment the first note resounded, he lost Val completely. She was off her stool and onto the dance floor; every word, and even his existence, completely forgotten.

He tried again, with another elf he recognized. Eldenor, a warrior of the High Court, who currently sported a purple mohawk and a black leather jumpsuit so tight he must have magicked it on.

Eldenor was alone, sitting in a two-person booth near the bandstand; his eyes fastened on the Bard, drinking in every note the young man played. When Beth began singing a traditional Celtic tune, and Eric built a foundation for her voice to soar over, Eldenor's eyes began to take on a glow of *here-ness*. A sense that he was at least focusing on *something*. Kory slipped into the other side of the booth.

"Eldenor?" he said, when the other took no note of his presence.

"Yeah?" The eyes didn't waver from the bandstand.

"Eldenor, don't you remember me?"

"Shit no, man."

Kory closed his eyes, asked for patience, and tried again. "Eldenor, it's Kory. Korendil. *You helped train me.* To be a warrior. Remember?"

The eyes flickered briefly from the stage to him, returning to the stage. "Oh, yeah. Kory. You went away."

Kory reached out and seized the other by the elbows, sending power in the kind of shock he'd used to rouse the Bard this afternoon. "Eldenor, I *didn't go away.* I was *imprisoned.* By Perenor and his daughter—" The shock brought only the barest of responses, and Kory lost his temper. "*Damn* you, Eldenor," he cried, shaking the other. "This is important! The power nexus is going to be destroyed!"

As if to underscore his words, the lights flickered briefly. Kory sensed that a storm had begun outside.

Eldenor shook is head, and looked at Kory, a faint hint of puzzlement in his expression. "Hey man, chill out," he said. "Nothing's all that important—"

Then Eric began playing a solo, and Kory lost him completely.

He tried several more, but all with the same lack of result, and all the power he used to try and shock them back into an understanding of their peril vanished without a sign of any reaction. They were *so* drained of magic that it just trickled into them without making an impression. Any glimmer of hope began to fade before despair, and the depression that failure after failure left him with. *How can this be, that they are so completely lost? What has happened to them in the ten years since I was imprisoned?*

The lights flickered again just as the band finished the Celtic song, and flickered a third time as they began a rock number. And in the moment between those flickers of light, Kory caught a familiar lift of a head, a high, proud profile—and his heart raced.

Blessed Danann. He's here. My Prince—

He shoved his way through the crowd, paying scant heed to those who swore at him or cast angry glances in his wake. He fought to reach the table at the rear where he'd seen that glimpse of majesty—

Only he reached it to find just how ruined the majesty had become.

Kory could feel something dreadfully wrong as he forced his way between packed chairs to the table at the back where the Prince was sitting alone. He *knew* that the wrongness went deep when he saw the way the Prince was sitting, slouched down in his chair, with his eyes blank, and his hand wavering a little as he reached for his drink.

But when he recognized just what it was that Prince Terenil was drinking he froze in horror. Dark brown, effervescent—

Coca-Cola.

There was a pitcher of the stuff on the table, and it was three-fourths empty.

An elf could drink any five mortals under the table. An elf could shrug off the effects of most of the drugs that left mortals paralyzed or insane. But *this*—this stuff that mortals imbibed with such careless ease—*this* was another thing altogether.

Caffeine. Soft drinks, coffee, tea.

To the Old Blood it was deadly.

It enhanced Dreaming; induced hallucinations. Destroyed will, and removed the elf that indulged in it from any semblance of reality.

And Prince Terenil, the pride of the High Court on this side of the Hill, was sitting in a mortal nightclub, his eyes glazed, his hands shaking, and most of a pitcher of cola plainly inside him.

Kory was not even certain that he could hear the Bard's music, much less Feel his magic as the others so clearly did.

He had thought he had seen despair at its worst when he had first awakened, and heard the talk of the place-of-festival. How at the festival's end the place would be leveled, the groves of oaks destroyed—including the one that anchored the magic nexus to this side of the Hill. He had thought that there was nothing that could possibly be worse—

Until now.

He looked at the ruin of his liege and lord, and wanted to howl his despair to the four winds.

Instead, he sat himself carefully by Terenil's side, and used most of the last of his magic to *try* to touch the Prince's mind.

By Danann, I don't know if I can even find it, much less touch it!

He could only imagine one reason for Terenil falling to this state. The Prince had given up any hope of Awakening his people. It must have happened soon after Kory, his friend and closest advisor, had fallen prey to that traitor Perenor, and vanished from the ken of the elves. Perhaps that vanishment itself had triggered the Prince's fall.

"My lord?" he prompted verbally, holding his despair at arm's length.

The Prince gave no sign that he had heard.

Blessed Danann—is there anything left of the warrior that once held us all in awe? And if he has sunk so low—what hope is there of saving the rest?

"My lord, it is Kory. I've returned to you, my lord."

The Prince stared at his hand, and slowly raised the glass of sparkling poison to his lips.

And drank.

Kory restrained himself from slapping the foul stuff out of his hand, and spoke again, as gently as he could.

"My lord, I have news. I have found a Bard, a human Bard. A true Bard, and one of such power as I have never seen. He has agreed to be our Champion, my lord. He has said he will help me Awaken the Dreamers and save our magic."

Still no sign that Terenil even knew he was not alone.

"My lord, I did not leave you willingly. The traitor Perenor imprisoned me in the Grove, after his daughter had lured me there and struck me down with trickery. This Bard that I have found—he loosed the spells of lock and ward, and woke me out of my spell of slumber. He freed me from Perenor's power, and he is untutored! Just think, my lord, when I have taught him to use his Gift—"

Terenil made no response, none at all.

If Kory had been alone, he would have put his head down on the table and wept.

I still may, he thought, swallowing hard. *Only let me be by myself—and I shall weep and not be ashamed. Oh my lord, my beloved lord—*

"We have a chance, my lord. With the help of this Bard, we have at least a chance."

He stood, as Terenil continued to stare at his hand, the one holding the glass. Blinking slowly, but showing no other sign that he was still conscious.

I cannot stay here, and still remain sane, he whispered to himself. *Perhaps I should go and wait for the Bard to complete his work—*

He began to make his way back across the room, when he felt eyes upon him. Eyes with power behind them, watching him with scarcely-concealed venom and contempt.

He stopped, as the lights flickered once again; stopped and turned, scanning the room with all his senses, looking for the one who radiated such power and menace.

The enemy obligingly displayed himself, moving from the shadows to the edge of the dance floor. The light fell clearly on him, flickering blues and greens illuminating his malicious smile.

Kory's despair was quickly forgotten in a wash of something far more personal.

Fear.

Just as there was no mistaking the Prince, no matter how low he had sunk, there was no mistaking *this* face. Carefully arranged silver hair, hooded, brilliantly green eyes, high cheekbones—and power coiled within, power that showed Kory's magics to be the amateur efforts that they were.

Perenor.

Exiled traitor from Elfhame Sun-Descending. Showing himself arrogantly to the young elf who had been his prisoner for so many years, and now was the only functional Champion in the mortals' world.

The supremely powerful, saturnine elf had avoided elvenkind since his banishment. Perenor hadn't even gone after Kory himself; he had sent his daughter, Arianrhod, to lure him into his hands.

But here he was—and there could only be one reason that he showed himself so plainly.

He *knew* that Kory had escaped from his imprisonment.

And he was hunting for him.

Kory stood silent, staring at Perenor, unable to look away.

And he knows I'm here. He's searching for me. He knows that I escaped, he knows about the Bard, and he's here, searching for both of us—

As he stared at Perenor, the older elf's eyes continued to scan across the crowd, until they rested upon the object of their hunt.

Perenor smiled at Kory.

:Good evening, Korendil. What a pleasant surprise to find you here.:

Kory froze; and found a single phrase echoing frantically around in his head, a phrase borrowed from mortals—

Oh shit—

Eric stood silently on the stage, the flute held lightly in his hands, listening to Beth Kentraine's warm, rich voice, singing the lyrics to an old Gaelic song. To his annoyance, the lights flickered again, briefly plunging the Dive into darkness, cutting off a half-second of the music as the PA system blinked off and on again.

*Great. The thunderstorm must be playing games with
the electrical grid. I sure hope we don't have a blackout
in this club. That's all we need—ten million drunken
idiots trying to run for the doors. And who knows how
many drunken elves doing whatever it is drunken elves
do in the dark.*

The dancers on the floor didn't even seem to notice.

*Hell, don't worry about it, Eric. Worry about the solo
coming up next verse instead. Bethie's already given me
The Look.*

*This is the next-to-last song. Thank God. Just a little
more, then we'll be done for the night, I can crash—*

*—go home, drink a few, and think about all of this.
About Korendil. An elf, for Chrissake, asking me to save
his people.*

*I'm still not certain whether I really believe all of this or
not. Maybe I'll just wake up tomorrow morning, and all of
this will have been a dream . . .*

Yeah, right. Not bloody likely.

Eric lifted the flute to his lips, a quick breath before the
phrase. *It's a beautiful song, needs some nice ornamentation. I'll just play with it, see where it takes me . . .* He
closed his eyes and began to play.

The notes were pure and clear, a delicate line slowly
growing stronger, like a kite tugging at the string, trying
to break free. *A little more, holding that high C for just an
instant longer, then letting go, falling away, fading. Good.
Now Beth is taking the vocal line again—*

He opened his eyes, blinking at the sudden brightness
of the stage lights. *I like that song. We've been doing a lot
of the old trad tunes tonight, more than Spiral Dance
usually does. Last gig, we only did two slow ballads, the
rest was hard rock. Tonight, it's almost half and half.
Very strange.*

He looked out over the audience, seeing the colorful
costumes past the glare, the dancers moving in swirling,
regal patterns amid the colored lights. *No, not strange at
all, not for tonight. The whole evening has been like this,
mysterious and—and magical. Well, I guess that when
half your audience is non-human—*

—strange things are bound to happen.

I wonder where Korendil is? I can't see him out there in the crowd.

Thinking of the elf made him flush slightly, uncomfortably. *Maybe I should apologize to him. I've been a real bastard to everybody, these last few days. And I took a lot of that out on him. Sure, I thought he was a nut case, but still, I could have been more polite about it. Of course, he did steal my clothes and he did knock me into a wall, but still—*

Then he heard it. A soft whisper, a strange female voice, low and breathy, barely audible.

:Bard. Look at me.:

Eric immediately glanced up at Beth, singing with her eyes closed, intent upon the last verse of the song. *Bethie? No, she's not even looking my way. Must have been somebody else—*

A faint whisper, lightly pulling at him, like—*Like a kite on a string—*

:Look at me, look at me . . .:

He looked out at the crowd, too far away for a low whisper to carry that distance. *What in the hell? Who said that?*

God, no. I'm starting to go crazy again—

Then he saw her, at the edge of the stage. Watching him. *Oh my.*

Red silk. Tailored, expensive, and very tight around the right curves. Blond hair, slightly curly, perfectly framing that face, those vivid blue eyes.

What is someone like her doing at The Dive? She looks like a fashion model, the kind of lady you see in Westwood or Beverly Hills, escorted by some handsome guy wearing a five-hundred-dollar suit. Not the kind of lady you see alone in a sleazy nightclub in Van Nuys!

She's beautiful. Very beautiful.

And she's staring right at me.

Oh my God.

Eric forced himself to look away, trying to remember what song he was supposed to be playing. *Oh yeah, the Gaelic song. Right. Shit, where are we? Last verse?*

He saw Beth looking at him, puzzled. Then her eyes moved past him, to the woman standing in the shadows.

Beth's eyes narrowed.

The song ended, just as Eric remembered what key it was in, and was about to start playing again. He stopped himself, just in time.

Terrific. What's happened to my brain? I think it's turned to guacamole. Thank God, we've only got one more song in the show. I don't think I could deal with anything else tonight.

A moment of applause, then Jim started the intro for the last song, a subtle, light pattern on the rim of the snare drum. Beth joined in a moment later: rough, resounding chords on the Fender. Then Allie on synth, a quick run, leading into the melody. Eric smiled at the intensity of the music, fierce and demanding, building with each moment. *Damn, but I like this one.*

Then Beth's voice, breaking through, taking over . . .

> "Starlight and shadow, end to begin,
> Balancing, changing, losing to win.
> Make the choice, take the chance,
> Reach for dreams and more.
> And in that moment you will know
> The spiral dance won't ever let you go!"

First solo was Allie on synth, starting quiet, then letting it rip into a jazz run, her fingers moving almost too fast to see over the DX7's keyboard. The audience roared as Jim took the next solo, pounding on the drums like a wild man, his hair flying, looking like it was glowing in the glare of the stage lights.

He's wrapping it, about to hand it to me—now!

Eric hit a high D, a rasping trill, wailing descant down the scale. A moment later, he heard Beth echoing the flute line on the Fender, following him down. He smiled to himself, starting a fast jazz break, which she caught and held. Then they went into a counterpoint, the electric guitar and flute fighting each other, each striving to hit harder, higher, then finally blending on the last note, harmonizing, matching each other perfectly. Eric tossed in a final trill, unresolved, a ringing defiant cry.

The last note faded into silence.

The lights suddenly cut out, leaving them standing in shadow. A moment later, the screams and cheers of the audience began reverberating around them.

Now that was a nice bit of work . . .

The lights came back up. From across the stage, Beth grinned at Eric, then leaned closer to the mike. "Thank you, and good night."

The stage lights faded down again, to be replaced by the normal club lights. Eric wiped the sweat off his forehead, glancing back to see Beth hugging Allie and Jim, then starting to help them disassemble the stage gear.

A terrific gig. I should play with Bethie and the Spirallers more often. This was a fun night. Definitely weird, definitely wired, but fun.

Eric looked out at the crowded club, the emptying dance floor.

I wonder where Korendil is? I thought he'd be here, waiting for us at the end of the gig.

Oh, what the hell. I'm too tired to deal with all of that "Save the Universe" stuff tonight, anyhow. Might as well pack it up and head home. Maybe I can hitch a ride with Bethie—

A soft murmur, insinuating into his thoughts.

:*Yes. You are the one.*:

Eric looked around in surprise. *Say what?*

Shit. I'm hearing voices again. Dammit, I had myself convinced that I'm not crazy. This isn't fair.

:*No. It isn't. Look at me.*:

Slowly, he turned to the side of the stage, to the blonde woman that he somehow *knew* was still standing there.

He dazedly shook his head. *Who is she? I wonder if—if she—she looks like she might want to meet me. Talk to me. Maybe—maybe she does . . .*

Eric walked several steps towards her, then hesitated. *I'm imagining things again. This time, instead of an elf, it's a beautiful blonde, making eyes at me from across the stage. Reality check, Eric. You are not her type.*

But her eyes—blue eyes—it's like she's calling to me—

He took another step, and another, moving towards the blonde woman, unable to look away from that electric blue gaze.

Blue eyes—reaching out to me—drawing me to her—

Something was wrong. Eric tried to remember what it was. *Something about being on the bus, looking out the window, and—something—trying to remember—this has happened before. Hasn't it? I—can't remember—*

Then the woman smiled, and held out her hand to him.

:Look at me, Bard. Look at me, and dream . . .:

Eric stepped off the stage, his eyes never leaving hers for a moment. He took her hand in his, and touched her fingertips to his lips. He was not certain if it was his thought, or hers, that echoed through his mind, low and seductive, beckoning.

:Yes—you are the one—:

Kory glanced around the shadowed alley, the rain misting down on the dark asphalt, turning everything before him to gray.

I must lead the traitor away from here, away from the Bard. If he realizes that Eric is here—if he realizes that Terenil is here—

Eric undefended, Terenil completely lost in Dreaming. Blessed Danann, how did everything go so wrong so quickly?

The alley was dark, even to elven eyes, but promised a path to safe retreat.

If I can lead him off, then lose him, I can come back to this club and spirit the Bard away to safety.

He could feel the traitor behind him, the menace, the carefully controlled anger—and above all, the power.

How is it that he has such power when the rest have been magic-starved into Dreaming? How—

Oh. Fool. He was High Court, and not tied to the groves. And he has his daughter. She must be keeping him very . . . prosperous. I wonder if she even realizes that he's using her—using all of us—

Anger surged in him, and lent speed to his feet. The heavy rain flattened his hair into his eyes, and soaked him to the skin in a few moments. He ignored the clammy, clinging fabric, ignored the chill.

I have fought in worse circumstances. I have fled in far worse.

He stumbled against something he hadn't seen in the darkness, and went to his hands and knees. He picked himself up immediately, but the power that was Perenor behind him had gained a few precious yards.

If he catches me, that will leave Eric open to him. He uses the mortals, that was the whole centerpiece of his defiance of Terenil; uses them, and discards them. He would take Eric and twist him—turn him into something foul and shadowed, as evil as himself—

Gods. Not the Bard. Anything but that.

The icy rain slashed at him, and he stumbled again on the slippery pavement. Then a flash of lightning from above showed him the end of the alley.

The *end* of the alley.

A *dead* end. All too literally, a dead end.

The passage ended in enormous loading-dock doors set into the otherwise blank wall of a two-storied building. To Kory's right, another blank wall. To his left, a building with some few windows set too high above the street to reach from the ground, and a few feet of tall privacy fence.

If I had a minute, I could climb that fence, vanish into the maze of this city.

I don't have that minute.

Kory whirled, just as he heard the slow, deliberate footsteps behind him, putting his back against the wall of the building.

Perenor had brought his own light with him. It illuminated him softly, and Kory saw that he hadn't so much as a single drop of rain marring the careful arrangement of his hair or the expensive gray suit. He was making it quite clear that he had power to spare. Power to *waste*, if he chose.

He extended a finger, and lit Kory in merciless detail as well. Kory was all too clearly aware of how *he* looked: hair straggling in soaked, tangled strands dripping into his face and down his back, clothing plastered to his body. He drew himself up proudly, anyway—

Pride is all I have left.

"Well, it *is* young Korendil, after all," Perenor said, his voice subtly mocking. "You used to have better manners, youngling. Aren't you going to offer me a civil greeting?"

He is going to kill me—and destroy everything with me. Unless I can keep him occupied long enough for Eric to finish the show and leave—and when he leaves, the others will follow. Perhaps. But "perhaps" is all I have . . .

I must give Perenor something to amuse him, to delay him long enough for Eric to escape.

"We did not have a civil parting, Lord Perenor," he replied as coldly, and dispassionately, as he could.

He may kill me now, but I won't let him take Eric and the others as well.

Perenor shook his head. "Ten years asleep, and no wisdom learned in all that time. Korendil, you disappoint me."

I am not going to answer that—except with this—

He used the last of his power to Call his sword. In an instant, the shimmering weapon was in his hand, ready for battle.

Perenor laughed. "Korendil, that is exceptionally foolish even for *you—*"

And the elf-mage extended his hand again—and the sword vanished in a shower of sparks from Kory's hands, leaving him staring stupidly at the air where it had been. Then Kory moved, drawing light and power from the air, condensing it into a weapon and hurling it at the traitor.

The older elf easily warded off the attack with a single gesture, a snap of his fingers. The magic dissipated harmlessly, leaving Kory and Perenor in the glimmer of witchlight, staring at each other.

Perenor's smile faded, and his face darkened, a moment of calm before the fury.

Kory swallowed. *I think that maybe I don't amuse him any more . . .*

· 8 ·

Smash the Windows

"Enough of this, Korendil."

Perenor's voice was icy. When he spoke again, it was not aloud, but in the silent speech of the elvenkin. *:Korendil, don't be too much of a fool. You know you cannot fight me. Give up now, and I will make this painless and quick.:*

Kory flung his response at the traitor's mind, ringing and defiant. *:Never! May you rot in the humans' hell first, betrayer of our people—:*

Perenor shook his head in mock-sadness. *:As you wish. You know, Korendil, you would have been wiser to stay in the Grove, lost in your dreams.:* He raised his hand slowly, his green eyes incandescent with resonating power.

Kory edged along the wall, knowing there was no escape, but unable to simply stand motionless like a frozen rabbit waiting for the strike that would kill him. His foot slipped on the wet asphalt, and he fell backwards over a garbage can, landing on his knees in the spilling refuse. The lid of the can clattered loudly in the silence.

No! I cannot die on the ground like an animal! Is there nothing that I can use as a weapon, enough time to—

Kory sensed the burst of magic an instant before the blinding light and heat surged towards him.

Oh Gods, NO!

He groped for anything to shield himself, anything, and recoiled at the touch of Cold Iron. Then, disregarding the soul-scorching pain that lanced through his hands,

125

he grabbed the metal object and desperately hurled it towards Perenor.

A silent explosion . . .

. . . as the trash can lid shattered into a million shards of light, impacting with the force of Perenor's magic.

Kory blinked, then looked up to see Perenor warding his eyes with his hand, trying to see past the glittering snowfall of multicolored light-specks. *Oh, thank Danann, I'm still alive—for at least another ten seconds—*

He scrambled to his feet and picked up an abandoned piece of wood, not as long as his elven sword, or as balanced, but embedded with several short, blood-colored spikes on one end. By the icy twinge through his trembling hands, he knew that the pointed metal prongs were iron, possibly the only thing that Perenor might fear.

:I will not be easy prey for you, Perenor.: With a weapon in his grip, he felt the warrior's fury rising within him as he cast the challenge at the elf-lord. *:Come and fight me, if you dare.:*

Perenor smiled, as if approvingly, and conjured his own blade, the bright elf-metal reflecting the lightning ripping through the skies above. *:I am pleased, Korendil. At least you will give me a bit of sport before you die . . .:*

Without warning, he struck at Kory, the sword arcing down towards him.

Kory rolled under the edge of the blade, somersaulting up onto his feet. *I can't let him touch this stick—that sword will cut through it instantly, and then I'll be unarmed again—*

He countered, slashing at Perenor's face with the filthy board. The elf-mage dodged back, and Kory kicked the fallen trash can into his opponent's path. Perenor tripped, falling hard on the wet ground.

Now—while I have a chance—

Kory ducked in close, bringing the spiked wood down sharply. But Perenor reacted instantly, his sword moving up to block.

The blade sliced through the wooden board like paper, then the stroke continued, across Kory's exposed leg—

Kory's scream echoed in the silent alley as he stumbled back, half-blinded by the pain. *Oh gods—oh gods—* he felt the slick hardness of the wall against his back, the warm wetness coursing down his leg. He tried to fight off the dizziness and overwhelming pain, but it was all he could do to stay on his feet.

He shook his wet hair out of his eyes, frantically tried to make them focus on where his foe had been. Perenor was lying on the ground, the elven sword beside him.

He's not moving. Please, Danann, let him be dead! If one of those pieces of Cold Iron—

Then Kory saw his enemy stand up and reach for the killing sword on the ground next to him. Perenor limped slightly as he shifted towards Kory, and he was no longer immaculate.

At least I did that much . . .

Perenor's clothing was filthy and he was dripping wet. His face was a mask of fury as he turned towards Korendil.

Kory tried to muster anything, a last burst of magic, *anything*; but all he could do was stand there, fear coiling in his gut, watching his death approaching, one slow step after another.

Perenor smiled, and raised the sword for the fatal blow.

:No! Korendil—:

Fire, green and gold, blossomed around them.

Kory shielded his eyes against the blinding brilliance. When he could see again, Perenor was sprawled on the pavement again, but this time he was looking up with sudden uncertainty and fear visible—for a brief moment—in his eyes.

Kory followed Perenor's gaze to the far end of the alley, where another figure stood, vibrant green light still flickering around his hands.

"Leave the boy alone, Perenor."

The newcomer stepped out of the shadows, the witchlight reflecting off his golden hair and pale features.

Prince Terenil.

Awakened, alert, ready for battle—

—by all the Gods, it's him!

The Prince smiled at Perenor, who was staring at him in

stunned surprise. "I'm the one you want—right? The one who named you outcast, who banished you from the Elfhame and the High Court." He drew the blade sheathed at his side. "Now is your chance to avenge yourself. Fight me."

He's Awake, he was only pretending to be lost to Dreaming, and now he's going to fight Perenor! He lured Perenor into this, he must have!

Perenor nodded slowly, painfully picking himself up off the gravel. Kory watched silently as the two elven lords moved to face each other across the dimly-lit alley, swords at ready.

Another wave of dizziness washed over him. He glanced down, and saw the blood dripping from the long gash in his thigh. He quickly ripped away part of his shirt and bound it tightly around the wound, clenching his teeth against the throbbing pain.

When he looked up again, Perenor and the Prince were circling each other, each waiting for an opening, a chance to strike.

Even Perenor is no match for the Prince. He never was, which is why he fled into exile rather than face him the last time they met. Another minute, and Terenil will finally defeat the Traitor—

Then fear and dread tightened a fist around Kory's heart.

The Prince's hands were shaking.

No—

As he watched, Perenor feinted lightly, and the Prince responded clumsily, leaving his own side wide open to a killing thrust.

Oh no—no—

But Perenor did not take the opening, only smiled and feinted again.

This—it can't be happening! My lord, my liege—

He's—he's falling to pieces. And Perenor's playing with him! Oh Gods—he's going to kill the Prince!

In that instant, Terenil slipped on the wet pavement, and Perenor lunged, swinging the flat of his blade against the Prince's head.

Prince Terenil collapsed, crumpling on the ground;

Perenor kicked the Prince's fallen sword away from him.
As Kory choked on a sob, Perenor reached down and took
Terenil by the hair, and forcibly turned his former liege
over onto his back.

The Prince stared blankly upwards, unseeing, his body
shaking uncontrollably, convulsively—

—like a man caught in the throes of drug withdrawal.

Tears joined the rain on Kory's face.

Perenor set the edge of his sword against the Prince's
throat. "What an amusing evening," he remarked conversationally. "I've wanted to kill you for some time, Terenil,
but I never thought it would be this easy."

:NO!:

The weak burst of magic that hit Perenor was scarcely
more than a flicker of light, but the elf-lord looked up
nevertheless.

At Kory, standing against the wall, his hands trembling.

:No. You can't kill him. I won't let you.:

"Really?" Perenor smiled humorlessly. The renegade elf
raised his sword, pointing the weapon at Kory. "And do
you really think you can stop me?" His eyes narrowed,
bright with eldritch power.

He's going to—

Oh SHIT!

Kory dived for the fence as the wall exploded outward
in the spot where he had stood; hauled himself over the
top, and tumbled down again on the opposite side. He
gasped in pain, feeling something snap inside his chest as
he landed hard on the ground.

Just run—keep running—

The backyard of someone's house, shadows of trees, a
low hedge. Kory vaulted over the bushes and out onto the
darkened street, the pain blinding him to anything but the
need to run, keep going—

Sweat was stinging in the small cuts on his face and
hands, where he had fallen and hurt himself before and
not realized it, and he could barely breathe against the
stabbing pain in his chest.

Something's broken inside—a rib—can't catch my breath!

Just . . . keep running—

At the corner, he glanced back once, and saw Perenor close behind him, running at a light, steady pace.

If I can keep him after me, maybe the Prince will be able to get away. If I can keep running . . .

Oh Gods, it hurts!

Another alley, the glimmer of streetlights, far ahead. *I can't lose him by running, he'll just track me down with his magic. And I won't be able to run much longer.*

He'll chase me until I fall, and then he'll kill me. And he'll go back and finish off Prince Terenil, and then he'll find Eric, and—

—no! I won't *let him win!*

Cold Iron. That would block his magic. He wouldn't be able to find me, but he'd waste a lot of time trying. Perhaps even enough time for the Prince and Eric to get away.

A glimpse of movement on the street ahead, a large vehicle that Kory could smell even at this distance. He doubled his speed, running desperately, and gathered the last of his strength, channelled it inward, reaching inside, changing—

A small silvery cat, running painfully on three legs, suddenly leaped up at the passing garbage truck, landing in the back among the reeking trash.

The searing touch of Cold Iron, burning through his fur, his skin—

Oh Gods! I can't—the pain!

He clenched his teeth on the feline scream trying to escape from his throat. *This is far better than what Perenor intends to do to me—*

The silver-haired cat shrank away from the side of the truck, and found a large plastic bag among the refuse. Moaning faintly, the cat collapsed upon the plastic, barely moving.

But it watched with large, frightened green eyes as Lord Perenor stood alone on the corner, staring in silent fury at the empty street before him.

This sure has been one helluva night. Beth Kentraine flipped down the clasps of the Fender's case, then lugged it toward the open back door to the club, and the waiting Jeep beyond. Allie and Jim were already standing in the rain next to Jim's pickup, quickly loading the last of the trap set into the back.

"Beth, we're heading out," Allie said, seeing her walking across the wet asphalt towards them. The keyboardist looked intently into Beth's eyes. "Are you—are you going to be all right, Beth? Bo said you told the police you didn't want to press charges against that guy."

"No, I don't." Beth managed to keep her voice level. "They booked him on public drunkenness and felony possession"—*God, the man was carrying a virtual pharmaceutical business around in his jacket pockets*—"And I really don't want to get involved in a court case. He didn't hurt me, Allie. Really, he didn't."

Just scared the living daylights out of me, that's all. And he would have done a lot more, except Kory came to the rescue.

Kory—I've never met anyone like him before. Never seen anyone who could do what he did, fighting off that bastard.

And he's gone. He left without even saying good-bye . . .

Is it just bad luck, or do I always fall for the flakes? The Eric Banyons and Korys of this world, the guys that vanish at the first possible opportunity. Leaving me standing out in the rain, literally.

And Eric—

It's hard to believe what Kory said. Eric Banyon, a Bard? Sure, he's a terrific musician, but Eric's so feckless, such a . . . a twit. He can't even balance his own checkbook. How in the hell is he supposed to save the L.A. elves?

And, speaking of Banyon . . .

"Allie, are you and Jim giving Eric a lift home? It's almost midnight, and I think he's missed the last bus across Van Nuys."

Allie shook her head. "I haven't talked to Eric since we finished the gig. I think he's back inside the club."

Figures. He's probably expecting me to remember that

he's stranded. "All right, I'll check on him. And I'll see both of you at practice on Wednesday, okay?"

Jim grinned. "You bet. This was a *wild* gig tonight, hey?"

"Yeah." *And stranger than you know, m'friend.*

Beth walked back inside the building, shaking the icy droplets of rain from her short hair. *Rain in May. Terrific. If this doesn't dry out in the next couple days, the Faire is going to look like a mud-wrestling competition. Not to mention the fact that I'm going to have a helluva time getting home tonight if I don't leave soon . . .*

She walked into the break room and picked up Eric's gig bag, still lying on one of the packing crates. A moment later, she found his flute, abandoned on one of the stage speakers.

What in the hell? Eric never leaves this flute alone for a minute, never. What's going on here?

She put the flute in the gig bag, slinging it over her shoulder, and looked out at the shadowy, smoky club. Most of the crowd had left soon after the band finished their show, but a few were still on the floor, dancing to the beat of the canned music.

Banyon shouldn't be too hard to spot in all of this. He's probably soaking up a last free beer, knowing him. I still can't believe he left his flute onstage. She moved along the edge of the stage, scanning the crowd.

Then she saw him, standing on the far side of the room, talking with someone, a woman she didn't recognize.

Who in the hell is that lady? And what is Banyon doing with her?

Beth stared at the vision of blonde, tailored perfection, laughing at something Eric apparently had just said, her hand resting on his with obvious familiarity. And Beth felt a peculiar emotion rising within her. *He's making time with Miss America, that's what he's doing.*

Jesus C. Frog, I'm not getting jealous of Eric Banyon, am I?

No, not of him. Of her, maybe. She looks like everything I could never be—beautiful, rich, poised, and elegant. I probably shouldn't even bother to ask him about a lift home. She looks like she'd be more than willing to take him anywhere.

No. I should ask, just in case. Maybe he's trapped in a conversation with this woman, waiting for someone to bail him out. Expecting me to show up any minute to rescue him.

Yeah, right. Sure he is, Kentraine. And you're Princess Di.

Well, I should ask him, anyhow . . .

She walked around the dance floor, sidestepped the gyrating bodies of the two mohawked dancers, wove a path around several others merrily rolling across the floor. As she moved closer, she realized that the woman was even more beautiful than Beth had originally thought. *Lady, you sure know how to make every woman in the room feel real insignificant, don't you?*

Even her voice is lovely, Beth realized, now close enough to hear the blonde's low contralto.

And to see the way her fingers were tracing little patterns on Eric's hand.

I can't be jealous. That's Eric Banyon, Eric "I'm a twit" Banyon. It's not like there's anything between us, more than just friendship—

—so why do I want to kill the bitch?

Beth walked uncertainly towards the pair, and stopped a few feet away. Neither Eric nor the blonde woman noticed her. *What in the hell, am I invisible or something?*

"—No, I've never been to the Elizabethan Faire, Eric, but I think that's really a marvelous idea—"

"Hey, Eric," Beth said uncomfortably.

Eric glanced at her. For a stunned moment, Beth thought he didn't recognize her. Then he smiled. "Oh, Beth, hi. I thought you'd left already."

"I wanted to make sure you have a ride home first." *Something is really strange here. He's not quite looking at me, or her, or anything. If I didn't know better, I'd say he's had too much to drink. But Eric's not like this when he's drunk—he never gets this strange, distant look in his eyes—*

*He gets silly, that's what he gets. Or he gets morose.
And he can't be stoned, either, or he'd be snoring at her
feet, or panting at them like a cocker spaniel in heat. You
can set your watch by the fifteen minutes it takes Eric
Banyon to pass out after he gets stoned.*

*There's definitely something weird going on in the three
brain cells residing underneath all that hair.*

"Thanks, Beth, but I'll just catch the bus."

Beth's voice tightened with annoyance. "Eric, the last
bus went by half an hour ago!" *You fool, don't you ever
look at your watch?*

*No. That's not it. There's something else going on here.
I don't know what it is, but . . . something about this lady
is making the back of my neck prickle. That predatory
little smile, the greedy way she's looking at Eric. Something is very wrong—*

"Oh, I didn't realize it was that late." Eric said after a
moment, and smiled vaguely at her. "I guess we should
go, then." He turned to the woman beside him. "I—uh,
I'm leaving now. It's really been nice talking to you,
Ria—"

The vixen gave him a warm, seductive look. "I've enjoyed talking with you as well, Eric. If you'd like, I—"
Her lips curved invitingly. "*I* could give you a lift
home . . ."

Like hell you will, lady!

The blonde looked up suddenly, as though she had
heard Beth's thoughts. Her eyes met Beth's, intense and
calculating.

*Where did Eric find this wench, anyhow? God, but he
looks wasted. Too many drugs, Banyon. I'd better get you
out of here.*

Beth took Eric's hand firmly, and was startled at the
chill of his flesh, the way his hand seemed nerveless
against hers. "Come on, Banyon, we're leaving."

:*Do you really want to fight me for him, little sister?*:

Beth blinked, not certain if she'd heard the woman
speak, or had just imagined the words. *No, she didn't say*

it, I didn't see her lips moving at all. She didn't say anything.

Then—who did?

I didn't take any drugs!

"Banyon?"

Eric had a remarkably stupid look on his face, one that Beth recognized from too many evenings of seeing him passed out drunk at Fairesite.

Banyon, what in the hell have you been drinking? Sterno?

Well, you can sleep it off. Assuming we don't get caught on the road. Woodley Park is probably already flooded from this storm—

"Nice meeting you," Beth called over her shoulder, starting to walk away with Eric in tow.

A delicate hand descended on her shoulder. Beth felt the elegantly lacquered fingernails digging in, even through the thickness of her leather jacket.

"I think you've interrupted a private conversation," the blonde said softly, her contralto voice rich with barely concealed menace.

"No, I think that Eric and I are leaving now," Beth retorted, with just a hint of steel in *her* voice. *Get your mitts off me or you're going to lose them, Blondie.*

"Are you?" the bitch smiled, her fingers tightening on Beth's shoulder. "And what makes you think that he wants to go with you?"

Beth glanced at Eric, who was staring off into space, completely oblivious to everything and anything going on around him. *Banyon, what is wrong with you? And why in the hell am I defending your virtue?*

No. I know why I'm doing this. I know what this "lady" is, I can read her loud and clear. Man-eater. She wants to take the Banyon-boy under her wing, amuse herself for a while, suck him dry, then spit him out again. And laugh as he falls apart.

I won't let her do that to him. He may be a real schmuck sometimes, but he's my friend.

"Because I'm his friend," Beth said, surprised at the way Blondie was gazing intently at her. *Like she's trying to*

*burn a hole though me with those eyes. If she stared at me
any harder, she'd probably go cross-eyed.* "Besides, he
thinks I'm cute."

"Does he? So, tell me, dear, just how do you get that
particular kind of hacked-off-with-a-knife look with your
hair? I've never seen anything like it before, even at my
coiffeur's in Beverly Hills. I'm sure Eric finds it very
attractive."

Why, you bitch!

"Try hacking your hair off with a knife," Beth retorted.
"And, you know, I really do like your remarkable color
of blonde, while we're on the subject on hair styles. Do
you use Clorox to get that effect, or just hair coloring?
It's really *you.*"

The woman's eyes darkened. "My dear, you're treading
on very dangerous ground."

"So are you, lady." Beth smiled, showing teeth.

The woman shrugged. "Be that as it may, I *do* think
Eric enjoys my company more than yours. Don't you,
Eric?" She favored the flute player with a winning smile.

"Uh, yeah, sure," Eric said dazedly, staring at the flickering colored lights of the dance floor.

What in the hell is going on here? Beth gave the bitch a
stiletto glare. "Listen, Blondie, we're leaving, and I'm
taking Banyon here with me. I won't let you take advantage of my friend, who's obviously too drunk off his ass to
fend for himself. You've struck out, so why don't you go
find some other happy hunting ground? Like, in another
county?" She bared her teeth again. "Maybe you'd find
somebody more your type on Hollywood Boulevard. Or
do you prefer to work in Santa Monica?"

For a moment, Beth thought that Blondie was about to
haul off and swing at her. *Just try it, and you won't know
what hit you, lady. I'd love an excuse to knock you flat on
your derriere.*

Then the woman's eyes narrowed.

*:No. Not that. I'm going to do something very, very
special instead—something you'll never forget, you little
bitch—:*

And she smiled, her eyes locking with Beth's.

Blue eyes—icy blue, so cold, so . . . murderous. As if she's trying to reach out somehow—trying to do something—

Beth felt a chill run down the back of her neck, a warning tingle. *Those eyes, so cruel, reaching—*

She gave herself a mental shake, and glared right back.

Well. I hope the silly bitch gets a migraine, staring at me that way.

Beth broke eye contact first, shrugged, and saw a visible ripple of surprise run through the other woman.

What the hell? Did she expect me to run away screaming just because she gave me a dirty look? Honey, I've had nastier looks from my landlady.

"Come on, Banyon, we're leaving. It's been a long night, and you need to get some sleep before heading off to work tomorrow, right?"

"Work?" he repeated dully, looking from her to the other woman.

"Yeah, your day job, remember?" She glanced at the bitch, still staring at her in shock. "Buenos nachos, Blondie. I hope you enjoyed the show."

The woman's astonished expression faded into something else: a thoughtful speculative gaze. Then her eyes widened, looking at something beyond Beth.

Beth turned to look, and stopped short.

There was a man standing on the other side of the dance floor, a silver-haired man wearing an expensive, stylish business suit.

Well, it *had* been an expensive suit. Now the trousers and jacket were stained and torn, dark with mud. Blood trickled from a small cut on his cheek, mixing with the water dripping from his hair, plastered against his face and ears.

His *pointed* ears.

Equally unmistakable was the burning fury in his green eyes, seething as he stared at Beth and Eric. *Especially* as his gaze rested upon Eric Banyon.

Green eyes, like Kory's. He's an elf, one of them—

No, that look in his eyes, such hatred and fury—I've never seen anything like that before. He's not like Kory,

*not like the dancers, there's something about him that just
feels* wrong. *I don't know what it is, but—*

—Jesus H. Christ, I think I'm in trouble—

The blonde started and crossed the dance floor, hurrying towards the bedraggled silver-haired man. "Father!
What happened to you? Are you all right?"

*Her dad? That figures. They definitely look like two of a
kind. Like a couple of exotic snakes.*

She turned to Eric standing openmouthed next to her,
and punched him lightly on the arm. "C'mon, Banyon, I'm
taking you home."

He looked at her as though seeing her for the first time.
When he spoke, his voice sounded distinctly puzzled.
"Bethie? I thought—"

"That's the problem with you, Eric. You don't think.
Look, I want to get home before dawn. Let's go."

"Yeah." He shook his head. "I just—I just feel funny—"

*Terrific. With my luck, he's going to end the evening by
throwing up all over the inside of my jeep. Wonderful.*

Why in the hell do I bother with him, anyhow?

*Because—because he's my friend. And it was hard enough
watching that bitch Maureen tear him apart, let alone
standing by while somebody else repeats the performance.
I wish Banyon had common sense. Or better taste in
women.*

*Though I have to admit that on looks alone, Blondie
really is a class act—*

"C'mon, Eric, let's go." She gave him a push in the
direction of the door, then glanced back at the two across
the room. And froze.

They were watching her. And Eric.

*I've never seen such hatred in anyone's eyes before,
such venomous hatred. And menace, like all they want to
do is see our blood leaking out all over the floor.*

Sudden fear crawled up Beth's back.

*He's an elf. I don't know what she is, but she's obviously
with him.*

Maybe they do *want to see our blood all over the
floor . . .*

Kory told us about his enemies. No, his Enemy—an

exiled elven lord, by the name of Perenor. An older elf, silver-haired.

Silver-haired.

Like this guy, staring at me from across the room. Who looks like he wants to vivisect me and Banyon.

Oh shit.

What—what if Blondie wasn't just trying to lure Banyon into her bed? What if she was trying for something else?

And—

And where in the hell is Kory? I haven't seen him since—

Everything clicked in her mind at once.

Oh holy shit!

Beth grabbed Eric's hand and pulled him bodily towards the front exit. She looked back over her shoulder, and saw the two start across the dance floor. Heading towards her, towards *them*, striding purposefully through the last of the Monday-night crowd.

Beth signaled frantically at Bo, who was standing at the bar, talking with the barkeep, and pointed at the pair coming up behind them. Bo raised an eyebrow curiously, but nodded and said something quietly to the bartender who stepped out from behind the counter, wiping his hands on a cloth.

At the front door of the club, she took a moment to glance back. Bo, with the barkeep right behind him, had stopped the bitch and her dad and was speaking with them, the words lost in the noise of the blaring Top Forty dance music.

Thank you, Bo. You'll keep 'em busy for a few minutes, at least . . .

She shoved Eric out the door, steering him around the corner to the jeep, parked in the side alley.

"Bethie?" Eric looked at her, very bewildered, the rain dripping down his too-handsome face.

"Just shut up and get in the car, Banyon!" She pushed him headfirst into the jeep, tossed his gig bag in after him, slammed the door shut, and dashed to the other side of the vehicle. *Christ, this can't be happening to me.*

No. It's real. That guy is after Eric, maybe after me,

*and he's definitely after Kory—who has vanished. I have a
real bad feeling about this—*

She turned the key in the ignition, and the Jeep's engine rumbled into life. *Thank God, the Beast is actually
running this week. I want out of here, right now!*

Someone stepped out from the edge of the building,
silhouetted by the jeep's glaring headlights.

Oh shit, it's him!

Beth slammed the jeep into gear and shoved the emergency brake off. *Baby Beast, don't fail me now!*

And a blinding flash of light hit her right in the eyes.

The world vanished into white, images searing into her
retinas, impossible colors and shapes. Beside her, she
heard Eric Banyon moan softly, incoherently. *Something
about D minor . . . What in the hell, Banyon?*

She cursed and rubbed at her tearing, aching eyes with
one hand. *Can't see, can't drive—God, I can't believe this
is happening to me!*

Then she heard the quiet footsteps on the gravel, moving towards the parked jeep.

*Christ! I am not staying around to see if he can do
something besides fireworks!*

She hit the gas, unable to see, but praying. *Oh Lady,
take pity on us. Whatever happens, I'm not going to stop.
Either we're going to get away, or Eric and I will be
splattered all over Burbank Boulevard, but I'm not going
to stop. Gods, get us out of this—*

She tightened her grip on the steering wheel, expecting
to feel the bone-crushing impact at any moment—

A split-second later, her vision cleared. Beth glimpsed a
gray-suited figure diving to the side of the alley, barely
managing to get out of the way of the accelerating vehicle,
just as the jeep bounced off the edge of the sidewalk and
onto the street.

Hah! Almost, but not quite, you bastard!

A red sports car screamed to a stop only inches from
her, and Beth yanked the wheel hard, the jeep spinning
wildly in a half circle across the wide street. Then she had
control of the vehicle again, and floored the gas pedal.

She glanced at her passenger, white-faced and shaking

in the seat next to her. His fingers, clenched tightly to the dashboard, looked like they would need to be pried off with a crowbar.

The Noble Bard gulped audibly as Beth took another turn at a reckless speed, putting all the distance she could between them and the Dive.

And the Elf-lord that tried to kill us.

Beth laughed, and Eric looked at her like she was crazy.

Maybe I am. But, by the Gods, we're alive!

· 9 ·

The Pleasures of Hope

"—and I still don't understand why you were talking to her in the first place. Anyone, even someone as dense as you are, Banyon, could have figured out that bitch was pure trouble—"

Bitch?

Eric blinked, looking around his apartment in bewilderment.

Beth locked the door behind them, then tossed him the key. He caught it unthinkingly and replaced it in his pocket.

How did we get home? It seems like five seconds ago, I was standing onstage at the Dive—

Beth peeled off her dripping jacket and hung it in the closet next to the front door. "—and of course, *I'm* the one who has to bail you out. Jesus, Banyon, don't you ever think before you get into these situations?"

Bail me out? What is she talking about?

"I've never been in such a shitty situation in all my life, and it's all *your* fault. What was that bitch's name, anyhow?"

Eric realized that Beth was looking at him, apparently expecting an answer. "Uh, who?" he asked uncertainly.

"The bitch. You know, the ravishing blonde. The one who cornered you after the show." She glared at him. "*The man-eater*, Banyon. What was her name?"

Eric shook his head. "I don't know who you're talking about."

Why do I feel so—wet? He glanced down at himself, and did a double-take, startled.

143

His boots were completely soaked, his jeans wet to the knees.

When he looked back at Beth, she was sitting on the floor, pulling off her boots and socks, then dropping them in a damp pile on the carpet. He averted his eyes as her pants quickly followed.

Beth stood up, rubbing her hands together. "Christ, I think I froze my patooties off. Can I borrow some sweats for the night, Eric? A blanket would be great, too. I expect that couch gets rather cold at night."

For the night?

What in the hell *is going on here?*

"Uh, yeah, sure," Eric said, more than a little confused. "There's a stack of clothing in the bedroom, on the dresser. Help yourself."

As Beth vanished into his bedroom, Eric looked down at his drenched clothes, then around at the familiar apartment. Slowly, methodically, he hung his Faire cloak on the hook on the back of the door to dry.

What in hell happened to me? What happened to my mind? *I've never blanked out like this before, no matter* what *drugs I'd been doing. The worst I've ever done was fall asleep in the middle of the bagpipe practice.*

He sat down, prying off his boots and socks. After a moment's consideration, he peeled off the wet jeans as well. Beth emerged from the bedroom, wearing a blue pair of sweatpants and a worn Faire shirt that were both several sizes too large for her.

"Hey, Banyon, I thought you might want these." She tossed an armful of dry clothing to him. He caught it— jeans and shirt—and pulled the pants on, fastening them quickly.

"Thanks, Bethie." Eric picked up the wet clothing, draping it over the kitchen chairs.

How the hell did we get soaked? Where have we been?

A few feet away, Beth sprawled out on the living room couch, closing her eyes wearily. "I'm glad we managed to get here. For a while there, I wasn't certain if we could get down Hayvenhurst Street. I still can't believe how fast the streets over here flood during a storm. A foot of water in less than an hour. Christ." She opened one eye to look at him, and smiled tiredly. "Thanks for the offer of crashspace, Eric—I'd never have made it back to Tarzana."

"You're welcome," he said. *I really don't remember inviting her to stay over. Not that I don't want Beth here, it's just I don't remember inviting her. And—*

And I don't remember how we got home, either.

He sat down in one of the armchairs, trying to think.

Okay, we finished the show. I was standing on stage, and then—

—and then, here we are, in my apartment. In Van Nuys.

Half an hour's drive from the Dive.

And I don't even remember walking out of the club.

What was I drinking tonight?

God, just thinking about this is making my head ache—

"So, what was her name, Banyon?" Beth asked again.

He looked up in surprise. "Whose name?"

"Don't tell me you've forgotten her already?" Beth's eyes were intent upon him. "The Blonde Bombshell. The one who was crawling all over you after the show. Christ, I thought she was going to devour you without ketchup, right there on the dance floor."

"Bethie," Eric said slowly. "I don't know if you're going to believe this, but I don't remember a damn thing about any blonde woman."

No, I do remember something—blue eyes, icy blue, smiling at me. A voice. A voice in my head. "Dream of me, Bard . . ."

Who did those eyes belong to? The same person as the voice?

And why can't I remember what happened tonight?

This is definitely too weird for words.

Beth was staring at him, sober and very thoughtful. "What do you remember, Eric?"

He thought about it for a moment. "I remember playing the gig," he said carefully. "That bastard that attacked you during the break, and then talking with you and Korendil. And—you buying into Korendil's little war. Me too. Then we played the second half of the show, did the last song, and—and that's it. I don't even remember unlocking the apartment door just now. Honestly, I don't. Bethie, I think I just lost an hour of my life. And—and I know I didn't drink anything, not even during the break. Well, one Scotch, before the gig. That's *all*. I didn't do anything, uh . . . recreational. And I'm not drunk now. Just . . . very, very confused."

Beth spoke quietly. "You know, this is starting to make sense, if those two were working from some kind of a plan. First, they do something to get Kory out of the way. I don't know what, but he disappears. Then they come after you, messing with your mind, trying to get you to leave with La Chic Bitch. Then, when I interfere and they think we're going to escape, they try to kill us both—"

"Somebody tried to *kill* us?" Eric's voice squeaked on the word. "Holy shit, Beth, what happened tonight?"

She ignored his words, apparently lost in thought. "Or, at least, I think they were trying to kill us. Probably they were after you. I suspect I was just an afterthought."

"Oh, that's *terrific*. That's just *wonderful!* Christ, Beth, what have we gotten ourselves involved in?"

Beth didn't answer for a long moment. "I don't know, Eric. When Kory told us about this whole thing, how he needs us to help save the elves, I never thought—I never thought somebody would try to *kill* me."

She sighed. "Eric, I guess you don't remember this, not if that woman was screwing magically with your mind, but this elven guy—I think it was the Lord Perenor that Kory told us about—he did something, and I'm pretty certain it was magic. He threw light at me; blinded me, and I nearly crashed the Jeep." She was shrinking in on herself with each word. "It was . . . real scary, Eric. Scarier even than when mom and dad and I were grabbed by accident by the Greek cops."

Why, she's trembling. Oh, Bethie—

He moved closer to her, gently taking her hand. "Listen, you must have done something right. I mean, we're alive, aren't we? You got us out of there alive and in one piece." He grinned weakly. "You know, that's pretty impressive, come to think of it. I wish I could remember it."

She smiled tremulously, but it faded. "And I'm also real worried about Kory. He never came back after the show—".

"Hey, I wouldn't worry too much about Korendil," Eric said, giving Beth's hand a reassuring little squeeze. "He seems like a pretty tough guy. Hell, he took care of that drunken idiot that came on to you, and knocked *me* all over the room this afternoon, too. I think he can take care of himself all right."

Beth snuggled closer to him. "I know. It's just I've— I've never had anybody try to kill me with magic before. When it was happening, I didn't have time to think about it, or be scared, I just reacted—but now, thinking about it, I feel kinda . . . spooked."

"Hey, it's okay." He smiled. "I'd probably be scared shitless, if I could remember what happened."

"Yeah." She rested her head against his shoulder. "Eric— you're not going to back out on Kory, are you? I know, we didn't expect anybody to try to kill us, but he's counting on you to help him."

"No. I gave my word that I would help him."

And I will. I know that now. Whatever's going to happen, I won't walk away from him. Especially *after this.*

Beth smiled up at him. "Have I ever told you you're one helluva guy, Eric Banyon?"

"No, not that I can recall—"

"Well, you are. And—and I might as well tell you the truth now. You should know this. I'm a practicing witch, Eric."

He looked at her in disbelief. "You're practicing to be a witch?"

"No, I *am* a witch, silly. All of us in Spiral dance are. That's part of why we're together in the band—we're trying to combine our music with magic, reach out to people, make a difference. Music gets to a helluva lot more people than rhetoric."

Bethie? A witch. Makes sense, actually. And explains a lot of stuff about her. Well, it explains the things she never would explain, or talk about. The other witches I've met, like that group out at the Texas Faire, there were a lot of subjects they just wouldn't talk about, either. "Well, if you know witchcraft, Bethie, couldn't you have just done something back to Perenor when he attacked us?"

"I wish I could've. But witchcraft doesn't work that way. It's a—oh, shit, it's a pattern, a way you start thinking. Like Zen or something." She crossed her eyes, and waved her hands languidly. "Like, man, you *go* with the *flow*—" When he laughed she continued, a little more seriously. "It's not fireworks and special effects. I've never seen anything like what that guy did to us before tonight. I can't do that kind of stuff—and, to be honest, I don't know exactly *what* he did. But I sure don't ever want to be on the receiving end of *that* ever again."

"I hate to say it," Eric said, shifting slightly to put his arm around Beth's shoulders, "but if we continue helping Korendil, and try to save the L.A. elves, we're probably gonna see a lot more of that kind of fireworks."

"Yeah, don't remind me, I've already thought about it." Beth sighed, leaning back. "All I can say about it is, well, that Perenor guy may be real flashy with the magic, but I'd like to see how he'd feel about getting bonked by a good old-fashioned baseball bat. 'Cause that's what I'd like to do to him, next time I see him."

"Yeah, me too." Eric smiled, his fingers toying with Beth's punk tail, a single long curl of dark hair. "Though I wish I could remember that blonde woman. I mean, she sounds like she was real interesting—"

Beth swatted at him. "She must've been. I practically had to drag you away from her."

"Hey, I wasn't the one making eyes at Korendil earlier in the evening—" Eric waited for Beth to laugh, then he saw the way she was looking away and biting her lip pensively. "You really like him, don't you?" he asked quietly, obscurely disturbed.

"He's . . . really something. I've never met anyone like him before. It's not just that he's cute—which he is, he's one of the handsomest men I've ever seen—but there's also an intensity to him, and such openness, honesty—"

He swallowed, trying to sound more easygoing about this. "Yeah, I understand that. He's a really special guy—

tall, blond, and with pointed ears. Who could resist him? Especially the ears!"

Did that come out as bitter as I think it did?

"Eric—" She pressed her fingertips to his lips, trying to get him to shut up, but he shook his head and continued.

"Beth, you know I'd rather see you get involved with someone who's more your type—like, a human being—but if you really want Korendil, that's fine." He took a deep breath. "Really, it is. Besides, I hate to be tied down anyway, right? I hope you'll be happy. I know I won't stand in the way. In fact, you'll probably never see me—*mmmph!*"

Eric had to shut up then, because Beth was kissing him. A very serious kind of kiss that nearly knocked him off the couch, both from imbalance and the surprise of having a double armful of Beth Kentraine in his arms.

"Uh, Bethie—" he managed, when she pulled away long enough for him to catch his breath. "I didn't invite you over for this. I mean, I don't want you to think that I—"

She only smiled and kissed him again. "Methinks the gentleman doth protest too much," she said teasingly, running her fingers through his damp and still-tangled hair.

"It's just—mmmf," he said eloquently, as Beth kissed the corners of his mouth, working her way over to his right ear.

He sighed, then gave up any pretense of resistance as her deft fingers began undoing the buttons of his shirt. *Oh well, when have I ever been able to deter Beth Kentraine from whatever she wanted to do?*

Not that I'm objecting too much to this.

Not that I'm objecting at all . . .

He carefully unfastened the laces of her Faire shirt. Then he moved his hands lightly over her skin, pausing lingeringly at the ticklish spot over her ribs.

Beth, resting her cheek against his shoulder, toying with his shirt buttons, suddenly stiffened in shock, realizing where his hands had stopped. "Eric Banyon, you wouldn't—"

"AAAAAR! There's no mercy for you, wench!" he growled in his best bad pirate imitation, and began tickling her unmercifully.

She laughed, twisting and trying to get away from him. "Eric, no, don't—let me go—ack!" Beth tried to pull free, but he wouldn't let her go, holding her closely in his arms, tickling and kissing her until he couldn't keep from laughing either.

The laughter faded to silence, and a calm expectation that Eric had never felt before. *It's as if I knew we'd reach this point, someday. Like I've known that all along, since the day I met Beth. It's just—I never realized it until now.*

Beth's dark eyes met his. She was smiling gently. He wondered if perhaps she was thinking similar thoughts. *Her eyes are so serious, and . . . somehow open, defenseless. That's how I feel—as if there aren't any facades or masks between us, no more lies or half-truths. Just Eric and Beth . . .*

She leaned forward to kiss him, a light kiss, barely brushing his lips, but somehow that made the kiss more intense, more intimate and passionate, than anything before. *It's like that kiss is a promise—a pledge—*

Eric called upon the last bit of rational thought left to him, wrapped his arms around Beth and lifted her up. She laughed softly as he carried her to the bedroom, and carefully closed the door behind them.

"Mmmm, Beth?" Eric reached out, gently touching her bare shoulder. "Beth, you awake?"

"Ummf," she muttered, turning slightly in his arms.

No, guess not.

He sat up slowly, looking around the shadowed bedroom. Pale sunlight filtered through the blinds, and he could hear the beginnings of rush hour traffic on the street below.

Beside him, Beth Kentraine was still asleep, curled up against him with one arm outflung across the sheets.

She's so lovely when she's asleep. That little smile on her lips, as if she's dreaming of something wicked. She's beautiful when she's awake, too. When she's happy or sad, frightened or spitting like an angry kitten . . . she's still beautiful. I think I could fall in love with her, given half a chance. I wonder if she knows that? And I wonder if she feels the same way about me . . .

Eric moved closer to Beth, wanting to kiss her, then shook his head. *No, she had one helluva day yesterday, between that scum who attacked her during the break, and Perenor coming after us later. I should let her sleep.*

He smiled to himself, thinking about last night. *I could get very used to this, real easy. Playing street by day, Faire on the weekends, evening gigs with Spiral Dance, and nights with Bethie—*

Except she said she doesn't want to get involved with me, when we were talking at Faire. She doesn't want anything serious.

Well, maybe after last night, she'll change her mind.

It's just—I feel that she's a part of my life, now. With everything that's happened to us, I think that if she said, "Well, it's been fun, Eric, see ya around sometime," I'd just want to die. I've never felt that I needed someone so much before.

He sighed, and smoothed Beth's short mane with his fingers.

I need Bethie. I can't just let her walk away from me. I can't—

He stopped in midthought, hearing something from the living room.

What was that?

Eric listened, at first hearing nothing but the distant traffic noises. Then he heard it again, a faint, low scratching noise, coming from the front room.

What in the hell could that be? Giant mutated Angeleno mice?

He stood up quietly, trying not to awaken Beth, and reached for a pair of jeans, folded on the dresser. Eric padded out to the living room, and looked around, trying to pinpoint the source of the sound.

Then he saw the small cat crouched upon the widow ledge, peering at him through the dirty glass. The cat's pale silvery fur was stained with blood, it's green eyes shadowed with pain.

Oh, you poor thing. What could have happened to you? You look like you were hit by a Mack truck—

Eric opened the window, and the cat half-fell into the

room, crawling a few feet before it collapsed on the carpet, shivering and panting.

I'll wake Beth up, then call the vet. There's one on Sherman Way, we can take this little guy over there right now.

The cat looked up at him with large, pain-filled eyes, and then—

And then—

Blur of chords, sounded on an out-of-tune organ by a musician pushed so far past exhaustion that he no longer heard what he was doing, no longer cared, no longer really knew—

Eric blinked.

There *had* been a mutilated tomcat on the floor.

Not now.

He stared, not able to really understand what he was seeing. It had been a cat. Now it was Korendil, lying at his feet.

Korendil, looking very different from the confident warrior who had rescued Beth from her attacker, or the eloquent speaker who had tried to persuade Eric that his story about L.A. elves was no trick. Even different from the shy, diffident creature who, in the end, had pleaded with Eric to help his people.

This was a Kory who had been through a meat-grinder.

He lay in a twisted, bleeding heap on the carpet of the bedroom, and panted, like the tomcat had panted; and his green eyes were glazed with pain. Not surprising, since his leg was slashed from crotch to knee, at least an inch deep. He was bruised and burned, and cut in a dozen places, and he shook like an aspen leaf.

"Holy shit. Korendil?" Eric's voice sounded incredibly loud in the sudden silence.

At Eric's words, Kory raised his head. He looked up blankly, then focused on Eric. "Blessed Danann—" he gasped in a horse whisper, his expression warring between relief and pain. "You're *safe*"

As if he hadn't dared hope for that.

"Oh my God!"

Eric glanced back to see Beth standing in the bedroom

doorway, wearing nothing but a startled and horrified expression. "Christ! What happened to him?"

"Perenor—" Kory's words were barely audible. "He knew that Eric awakened me—knew that we were at the place-of-music. I had to draw him away from you, from both of you, he was going to kill you—"

He started to rise—tried to—and cried out in agony. Both of them reached toward him involuntarily. Kory stared at them, his eyes wildly dilated with pain, his hand outstretched, like a drowning man reaching for a lifeline.

"*Help me*—" he whispered, with what sounded like his last breath.

Eric and Beth touched his hand at the same moment.

Music.

Broken music. Music wounded; music dying.

Eric shuddered as the room faded from around him, to be replaced by something else, an aching pain, a silent scream of agony, and music—

Once, in his first year at Juilliard, one of Eric's teachers had described Johann Sebastian Bach's works as "building cathedrals with melody."

This was a cathedral that had been shattered by an earthquake, or the ravages of a bomb. The soaring arches— cracked. The upreaching vaults—crumbling. The flying buttresses—falling.

Dissonance. Broken chords. Savaged counterpoint. More of it fading with every moment.

More of it trailing off into nothing, into dissolution.

Dying.

No!

He reached out, reached in, plunged into the midst of it, and began trying to hold it together somehow. He saw, then, how the music was trying to repair itself; how the threads of melody reached for the broken lines, trying to patch them into some kind of a whole again.

But I can do that—

He eased himself into the consort; gave the fading music a strong foundation to rest on, solid chords, the way he played a foundation for Bethie's voice to soar—

He heard her singing at that moment, wordlessly, but

*outside the whole. She was lending her support to the
music, but from outside. It would be much better if she
could weave herself into the melody from within—*

*He reached out without really thinking about it, and
caught her up and brought her in. There was a gasp of
surprise that might have been his own, then she was with
them, singing strongly, confidently.*

*Three of them now; three songs that were part of a
greater whole. The two songs that were himself and Beth
moved to bracket the wounded one, lending it power,
keeping it from fading, from faltering, filling in the places
it couldn't—quite—reach.*

*It was like . . . like doing a gig, with one member
having an abysmally bad day. Picking up for him, filling
in for him, supporting him.*

*The third song gathered strength from them, began to
join with them—closer—stronger—*

*Like playing a gig? No, not anymore. This was like the
Pachelbel Canon, with three voices interweaving, braiding
in and out of each other, taking joy from one other and
giving it back again, until Eric could no longer tell where
his song ended and the others began.*

Until they were one song—

*And suddenly the music took fire, and now it was Bach
again, in the Toscanini transcriptions—no, Beethoven, the
Ninth, all the counterpoints fusing into the one harmony
—no, Dvořák, Mannheim Steamroller, Mahler, Clannad,
Rachmaninoff—*

*Emerson, Lake and Palmer. Tchaikovsky. Vangelis.
Prokofiev. Kitaro. Everything and everyone and none of
them at all. It was Eric setting the melody, and the others
following with variations of their own. He couldn't tell
where it was going, only it was glorious beyond anything
he'd ever heard before—*

*—pure, untainted, unalloyed song—a melodic joy that
raised him to a height he'd never dreamed of—*

And then threw him back into reality.

Oh my God, what was that?

Eric shook his head slowly. He blinked, seeing nothing
but pinwheels and blobs of light, like he'd seen staring

into spotlights too long. His eyes couldn't focus, and he couldn't seem to catch his breath, either.

"Holy shit," he said, after a long moment of silence. "What the hell was *that* all about?"

"I'm . . . not sure," he heard Beth say faintly, from beside him.

He blinked again, and finally some of the light-show effects cleared away. *Thank God. I can't deal with that when I'm tripping on a liquid dose—I sure as hell can't deal with it when I haven't even had a cup of coffee yet.*

Eric heard the faint sound of something breathing raggedly, and looked down. Kory was lying beside him, sprawled on the floor, his eyes closed and his face gray with exhaustion. He still looked like he'd been through a major war, and come out the loser.

There was a dark, scarlet stain under his leg, soaking into the cheap puce carpet.

The landlady's gonna love that. So much for my cleaning deposit . . .

God, how can I think about something like that when Kory's bleeding to death in front of me?

Get your brain together, Eric. First, a bandage, something to turniquet that wound—

Beth reacted first. She snatched at an old T-shirt, lying on the floor, went for Kory's leg—and stopped short, looking at the slash in the elf's jeans in disbelief.

The long, hideous slash in his leg was closed. Still nasty-looking, but closed as neatly as if it had been sutured and healing for about a week.

A week, not a few minutes.

But I saw that wound. He was bleeding like a stuck pig, his leg cut halfway open. Something like that just can't vanish!

Eric stared at Kory's leg.

It's impossible.

Finally he looked up, and Beth's eyes met his across the sprawled body of the elf.

"Eric—" she whispered in tones of awe. "Eric—we *healed* him."

"Excuse me," he said, hearing his own voice shaking, "but he doesn't look healed, he looks like hell—"

"It doesn't happen all at once, idiot," she retorted, already sounding more like herself, with a touch of good-natured annoyance in her voice.

"But—"

"Look at his leg, Banyon! Look at all that blood—and tell me that we *didn't* heal him!"

He looked at the blood soaking into the tacky carpeting and felt himself pale. He swallowed.

"Look," he temporized, "let's just get him patched up and in bed, okay?"

Beth gave him a sharp look. "What, don't you like the idea that you could have healed somebody, Eric?"

The curious tone of her voice made the words come out that he had been thinking—not words he'd have spoken under other conditions.

"Yeah," he said slowly. "That's the problem. Maybe I like it too much."

Beth caught his thoughtful gaze, and nodded. "Yeah. I know what you mean." She bent down, and carefully got a grip on Kory's shoulders. "You get his feet. We'd better get him into the bedroom."

Eric sat gingerly on the edge of the bed, looking down at Korendil.

The elf. My elf. The one who practically got himself killed, saving my worthless hide.

Why would anybody do something like that for me?

Kory seemed to be peacefully asleep. There were dark blue smudges under his eyes, bruises and cuts still visible on face and neck. He was so pale, he looked transparent.

My God, this is real. He got trashed bigtime. He can get hurt. He can die . . .

Kory's golden curls spilled over his pillow and half over his face. He tossed his head and murmured something in that liquid language of his. Eric reached forward and stroked his forehead, automatically trying to sooth him back into pleasanter dreams—

And froze, fingers still tangled in Kory's silky mane.

What am I doing?

Before he could pull away, Kory opened his eyes, and

Eric felt as if he was trapped in that emerald gaze. He only shook himself free when Kory touched his hand.

"Bard?"

"Just seeing if you were all right," Eric replied. *I'm trying to be nice to a friend, that's what I'm doing. A friend who damn near got himself killed to protect me. That's all.* "Korendil, please don't keep calling me 'Bard.' It doesn't seem right." Deliberately, he finished the motion he'd begun, smoothing Kory's hair out of his eyes.

God, Kory has great hair. I know chicks that would kill for a head of hair like that.

"Would you call me 'Kory,' as you do in your thoughts?" The elf smiled hesitantly. "My friends call me that."

Eric smiled back. "Sure, if it makes you happy. I'd rather be your friend, anyway, than have you treat me like some jerk up on a pedestal." *I would, too,* he thought, resting his hand on Kory's shoulder. *Jesus H. This guy almost died to keep me safe. What did I ever do to deserve that?*

Eric patted the shoulder awkwardly. "You just get some rest, Kory. You aren't in any shape to rescue a cockroach in distress right now."

"And what will you be doing?" Kory's eyes followed him as he got up and moved toward the door.

"Well, Beth thinks she's got a way to keep the bad guys from sniffing you out, so she's gonna do her thing when she gets back with her stuff. Then we're gonna go talk to a friend of hers who might know something. We're kind of short on information. It seems that the Bad Guys know everything about us, and we don't know jack about them."

Kory sighed, shifted a little, and tried to suppress a wince of pain. Eric saw it in his eyes anyway, and moved back beside him.

"Are you sure you're gonna be okay?" He reached toward Kory's shoulder again. "You want one of us to stay with you?"

The elf lifted his own hand with a visible effort, and took Eric's. "No. I shall be well enough. Truly, Eric, I will. What I need now is to sleep. But—thank you. Thank you for everything."

For what? "Hey, you tried to keep those guys from killing me last night, and now you're thanking *me*?"

"You saved my life this morning," Kory replied simply. "Without being bound to do so, by anything but your word to help save my people. Yes—"

Eric shivered, caught in the grip of emotions he didn't recognize and didn't understand. *He's right, I guess. It's just, well, I couldn't let him lie there and bleed to death. I couldn't.*

It's funny, though—the way he's looking at me right now, it's more than a little embarrassing. Like I'm everything in the world to him. God, if he was a girl, I'd want to kiss him—

Hell, I'd do more than just kiss him. I'd—oh God—why am I thinking these things? About a guy?

"—yes, Eric. I *do* thank you."

Kory let his hand go, and the moment passed. Eric hesitated, then brushed Kory's hair out of his eyes again. "Okay, guy," he said, gently. "Your thank-you is accepted. And I'm thanking *you*, too, for trying to save my ass last night. Now, just get some sleep, okay? You leave the fighting to us for a while."

Kory smiled, and closed his eyes. Eric patted his shoulder once more, and retreated from the bedroom before something else he didn't understand could happen to him.

He sat down on the living room couch, his head in his hands.

I don't understand this at all. What's going on in my head? Why am I feeling this way about him? He's an elf, for Chrissakes, not even a human being!

God, I think I need a drink.

Or several.

Or maybe I'll just finish the whole bottle—

· 10 ·

*F*ighting *for* *S*trangers

"Three parts coffee, two teaspoons sugar, one part Bushmills . . ."

Eric measured out the whiskey, then threw another splash of it in the mug for good measure.

After everything that's happened in the last twenty-four hours, I definitely need a little Irish Breakfast—

"Isn't it a little early in the morning for that?"

Eric looked up at Beth, standing in the kitchen doorway. He shrugged. "Not all that early, by my standards."

"Methinks you drink too much, Banyon," Beth said, settling a grocery bag down on the counter. She gave him a thoughtful, measuring look; then in a lightning-quick change of mood, tweaked his nose playfully, and kissed him—a warm "hello" kiss.

For a moment, Eric hoped that the kiss might progress into something more than that, but Beth pulled away and shook her head, touching his lips with a fingertip. "Duty calls, bucko. First this, then we'll go talk with my friend, then there's the "Save the Faire" rally this afternoon. I'm thinking that we might be able to find out a little more about who's doing what, and where we can throw a wrench into the works." Something intense burned for a moment at the back of her eyes. "I'm sure looking forward to messing up their plans."

"They," of course, is Lord Perenor and the blonde, who I still can't remember. He let go of her reluctantly, and picked up his Irish coffee—which was warm and potent,

159

but a poor substitute for Beth. *Damn, but I wish Beth had less of a sense of responsibility, and more of a sense of, well, timing.*

Beth turned away from Eric, opened the shopping bag, and reached into it as the brown paper rustled.

"What's in there?" he asked, leaning over her shoulder to peer inside. It was quite a jumble.

Looks like a lot of Baggies of herbs, some books, and—a knife? Nasty-looking piece of work, that. Probably street-illegal; it must be at least a foot long.

"My bag of tricks." Beth nudged him out of the way, then rummaged through the bag and tossed Eric a bright red apple. He managed to catch it without dropping the mug of coffee. "And breakfast, too. A better breakfast than *that*." She nodded at the doctored coffee. "How's our patient?"

"Sleeping, last I checked. He's a lot better, amazingly better, really." Eric bit into the apple in his best *Tom Jones*–eating-scene imitation.

Beth took the long-bladed dagger from the shopping bag, and slipped it, still sheathed, under her belt.

He put a little more soul into his next bite.

She ignored him.

He sighed theatrically.

She continued to ignore him, and poured a glass of water from the tap, then carefully shook out three shakerfuls of salt into the water.

He gave up, took a swig of coffee, and returned to the apple without the additions from *The Joy of Sex*.

"What are you doing?" he asked as he sat down at the kitchen table.

She wore a little frown of concentration as she held her hand over the top of the glass. "This is to set up a protecting circle. Then I'll meditate for a while, try to reinforce the idea that nobody's here, not us or Kory."

He accepted that without a blink. A week ago he'd have been snickering into his apple.

But a week ago he hadn't been tossed around the room by magic, or watched a creep get trashed by magic, or—

—or helped heal somebody by magic.

So—I guess I'm getting used to this. This "circle" sounds like a good sort of thing to do. I'm glad Beth knows how to build this kind of stuff. I guess "build" is the right word. I just wish I understood how it works.

Beth unsheathed the long dagger at her belt, stirred the water with the blade of it, then resheathed it and began walking around the living room, flicking drops of water with her fingers at the walls. "This is the actual protection part," she said, as if she had overheard his thought. She flashed him a smile. "Witchcraft 101, Banyon. Salt and water are very strong protection against things you don't want around. You draw the circle with the consecrated salt water, making sure you do the doors and windows—"

"Hey, I've never had a girlfriend who'd do windows before," Eric teased. Beth gave him a look of acute suffering, then continued. "I don't know whether or not you believe this'll work, but figure it's like chicken soup—can't hurt. *I* believe, and I'm the one who's setting it, and that's what counts."

She stopped at the window, sprinkled water on the glass, then drew the dagger again. Eric munched on the apple, watching closely as Beth traced a pentagram over the glass, then moved to the next window, repeating the action.

Definitely looks weird. Huh, I should talk. But—you know, somehow this whole routine is just like Beth. Sharp as a knife, always knows what she wants, and more than a little weird at times. I guess that's part of what makes her so terrific. His mind drifted back to the astonishing events of the previous night—what he could remember of them. *Like she was last night. She's such a complex woman, sometimes so strong and independent, sometimes sweet and cuddly beyond words. Just looking at her makes me think about—*

Eric hid behind the coffee mug, glad that Beth was occupied with the window, and didn't see how he was blushing. *God, that's all I ever think about. I just look at her and want to drag her back off bed again. It's something in the way she smiles, the way she looks at me—*

His thoughts faltered a little as a memory of green eyes superimposed itself over the memory of brown.

What really seems . . . bizarre . . . was that Kory was looking at me the same way. So serious, honest—like he'd never lie to me, never intentionally hurt me. And like he was worried about me. The careful way his hand touched mine—

Eric shook his head, trying to dislodge the uncomfortable memory and the equally uncomfortable feelings it was causing. *I don't understand it. Beth, sure—I've liked her for a long time, and I could see us getting together, that it could work. But—Kory? He's an elf—and a guy. I shouldn't feel that way about him.*

But—

I do feel that way.

God, what's going on in my head? Why am I feeling like this—about another guy?

"Hey, Eric—"

Eric glanced up. Beth had finished trickling water around the living room, and was standing at the bedroom door. "I'll need some quiet for this last bit," she said. "Don't come into the bedroom, or open any doors. It'll just take a few minutes, okay?"

"Sure," Eric replied, taking another swallow of his Irish coffee. "I'll just stay put out here."

"Thanks." Beth headed into the bedroom, and closed the door behind her.

Too many strange things have been happening lately, that's what's going on with my mind. And what I'm feeling about Kory, that's just part of it. Everything's so completely weird right now. Like that big gap in my memory. Like the woman Bethie was telling me about, the one I can't remember—

He closed his eyes for a minute, as something like a twinge warning of headache-to-come hit his forehead. Unbidden, an image rose in his mind, of a beautiful blonde woman holding out her hands to him.

:Bard—are you thinking of me?:

Eric opened his eyes, startled, and glanced around the

empty room, suddenly disoriented. *What the hell? For a minute there, I thought someone was talking to me.*

But I'm alone. There's no one here but me—

Must be a TV show in the next apartment.

Then he heard the voice again, low and seductive, as if someone was speaking right into his ear.

:*No. I am here, Eric.*:

Eric blinked, and his disorientation grew. *Say what?*

:*Close your eyes and dream of me, Eric, and I will come to you—* :

He closed his eyes obediently, and then saw her clearly.

Blonde hair, cascading over her bare shoulders. Blue eyes, bright as sapphires, and blood-red lips curving in a smile. She was naked, gloriously nude, and the sight of her made his breath catch.

:*I have not forgotten you, Eric. I cannot forget you. You are a longing that I cannot deny, a fire in my blood. Dream of me, think of me for just a moment more, and I will find you. And we will be together—*

She moved closer to him, smiling. From a distance, Eric thought he could hear music, a quiet melody slowly building in strength, and another voice, softly chanting.

> "By salt and water, blade and Will
> None shall harm, or wish ill
> Upon those within this circle round
> That wish with my power, I have bound."

What's going on here?, he thought fuzzily. *Why do I feel so strange?* He tried to focus his eyes, to stand up, but something seemed to be clouding his thoughts and his vision, slowing everything down to a crawl, turning the world into flitting shadows and impenetrable darkness.

:*Do not think, Eric, just feel. Close your eyes, and I will find you—*:

Caught by her words, Eric closed his eyes again. Then he felt the touch of her hands upon him, and forgot everything else. She was running her hands down his chest, her breath warm against his skin—*Beth? No, she isn't Beth, Beth's in the other room. Who—*

The distant chanting voice faded away, barely audible over the pounding of his blood. All that existed was his unseen lover, her body entwining with his, warm flesh like silk beneath his hands. Lips, touching his in the darkness, a kiss that made his heart beat even harder. Coherent thought fled before the rising fever in his blood, the longing and the need—

And the silent voice, whispering in his thoughts.

:*Dream of me, Bard. Just a moment longer, and then I will be with you*—:

:*Yes*—: Eric heard himself answer. :*Yes, I will, I am waiting for you*—:

He could feel her silent laughter, the richness of her thoughts, drawing closer to him, reaching for him.

:*So close—another moment—and*—:

Then Beth's voice, loud and disrupting.

"By the innermost fire, grant me this desire
    As I will it, so shall it be!"

Like a door banging shut, *something* slammed down between Eric and the other. He caught a brief snarl of rage, of frustration and thwarted desire, before the whispering voice faded into silence.

Eric opened his eyes, and blinked.

What in the—did I just doze off, or what?

Christ. That—that was quite a daydream. I haven't had a dream like that since I was a teenager and I swiped Jeff's father's Playboy.

He looked around the living room, and slowly shook his head. *Jesus. You'd think that after last night, I couldn't be thinking about sex, at least for the morning!*

A moment later, Beth walked out of the bedroom, carrying the cup and knife. She glanced at him, then walked over to the table, setting the implements down and looking at him closely. "Are you okay, Eric? You look kinda pale."

"I'm just a little tired." He shrugged, then grinned wickedly at her. "Didn't get enough sleep last night, I think."

She hugged him, and mussed his hair good-naturedly. "I bet. Maybe I'll let you get some sleep tonight." She breathed into his ear. "But don't count on it."

He caught Beth's hands, drawing her to him for a lengthy kiss. "Do we really have to go to that rally? I can think of a better way to spend the afternoon."

"Absolutely," she said. "Besides, our patient is still soundly asleep in the bed. I would't want to disturb him."

"Didn't he wake up when you were chanting?" Eric asked.

Beth looked at him strangely.

"Eric—I didn't say anything out loud," she said after a moment's pause.

Yeah? Then what did I just hear?

Oh no. The universe is getting weird on me again. God, I hate this. Like daydreaming about that blonde, just now. Or how I felt when I was with Kory, earlier this morning. I can't deal with this stuff, really, I just can't—

"Does—does Kory look okay? Is he sleeping all right?'"

"He seems to be fine," Beth said. "I guess these elves are pretty tough. But I'm thinking that maybe we should move him to my place, later—I've put some serious protections on it over the years. A lot more than I can do in a few minutes over here." She glanced at her watch. "Listen, if we head out now, we can catch my friend at home, and still get to the rally in time. I want you to meet this guy—he's the one who first told me about the L.A. elves."

"Sure," Eric said, standing up. "Who is this friend of yours?"

"Oh, you'll like him," Beth assured him, as they walked to the apartment door. "He's as crazy as we are. He has to be—he's an animator."

Phil *always* made Beth smile, no matter how serious the situation was. Today was no exception.

"Beth, sweetling, it's good to see you again." The deceptively frail-looking old man hugged her, then stood back a pace and looked at her intently. "You're looking good, honeybunch—there's a nice glow in your eyes, and jeez, you're in terrific shape. Keeping yourself busy, I hope?" He gave Eric a speculative glance.

Eric, of course, began to blush.

Oh, Banyon, I can't take you anywhere!

"I'm doing fine, Phil," Beth said, kissing his weathered cheek fondly. "This is Eric Banyon, a friend of mine. Eric, Phil Osborn. We're here because of another friend of ours, who isn't doing fine."

"Well, come in, sit down, and tell me about it." Phil ushered them into the small apartment, then vanished briefly into the kitchen, returning a few moments later with three cans of Coke. He handed them each a can, then sat down in his favorite old overstuffed armchair.

Beth saw the way Eric was staring at the living-room walls, decorated with animation cels and original sketches, and smiled to herself. *Well, we've lost Banyon for a while, I think. I know how I was the first time I saw Phil's apartment!*

"Our friend is one of the elves," Beth began, sitting down across from Phil on the couch.

Phil started, then settled back in his chair, a look of speculation on his face. "So you finally got your wish, hmm, honeybunch?" He lowered his voice for a minute. "Should we be talking about this with your young man here?"

She sighed. "He's in on it. In fact, he's further into it than I am."

"Oh." Phil considered that for a moment. "Something tells me your experience wasn't entirely pleasant."

"Most of it wasn't pleasant at all, Uncle Phil." She frowned, and haltingly began detailing the entirely bizarre events of the night before.

And it feels like it was a year ago.

"So things are going pretty badly for all the elves," she concluded. "I guess you must have known some of that. Poor Kory got more than his share of getting dumped on, though."

"Who did for him, honeybunch?" Phil ran his hand thoughtfully through his thatch of gray-white hair. He was taking her story entirely at face value. Hardly surprising;

he was the one who'd told her all about the elves in the L.A. hills when she was a child—and convinced her that they were real when she'd grown up.

"He told us it was an elf called Perenor. He *seems* to be part of the bunch trying to destroy the L.A. Elizabethan Faire site, the magic nexus." She took a swallow of Coke, and leaned forward. "I remembered the stories you used to tell me, and I thought maybe you might know something that would be useful about Perenor, something we can use to stop him, or something we can do to bring the other elves out of Dreaming so they can get out of here before the nexus goes."

Phil frowned unhappily. "I hadn't heard about this until you told it to me—but then, the elves are so locked up in Dreaming right now I couldn't shake most of them loose with dynamite. So, somebody is figuring on destroying the magic nexus? That's serious bad news, Beth. Very, very serious."

"I know, Phil," she said, patiently. "That's why we're here. If there's anything you know that might help us—"

"Beth says that you know a lot of the L.A. elves," Eric said from across the room, where he was looking at a framed cel of Snow White.

Phil raised white eyebrows abruptly, so abruptly it looked as though they'd jumped halfway up his forehead. "So you weren't B.S.-ing your old Uncle Phil. This *is* another Believer. Well, well . . ." He turned slightly to get a better look at Eric. "So, Beth told you that I know something about the elves, hmm? Well, that's very true. A lot of them were my friends. Back in the early days, when I first started working in the Industry—did Beth here tell you that I created Defender Duck? He's still my favorite character. Saving the world from Fascism and duck-hunters everywhere—"

"Phil," Beth interrupted carefully, "You were telling Eric about the elves."

"Oh, that's right. Where was I?" He suddenly smiled, a sly, mischievous smile, like a little boy who's just gotten away with something.

Eric was looking at Phil with the stunned expression of

someone who can't reconcile what's before his eyes with what he knows.

Is he seeing something I don't?

"Why don't you tell Eric everything you've told me? That way we'll have a different perspective on things."

Phil smiled again. Beth began to suspect something. *What*, she wasn't sure, but she began to suspect Phil of trying some kind of complicated game on them. "Well, I started in '38 with Warner, then moved over to Disney."

"Uncle Phil—"

"I'm getting there! It was years later—I was working right here in Burbank on the studio lot—when I saw my first elf. We were watching the dailies for one of the early color features—you know what dailies are, don't you, young man?—and I noticed that someone was sitting a few seats over from me, somebody I'd never seen before. I figured he was one of the execs, dropping in to see what we were working on, but then—"

The old man's eyes brightened, and softened with remembrance. "Then, when they turned the lights back on, I saw him clearly. He was very tall, wearing the strangest clothing, with lots of golden hair, curling all over his shoulders. No one, mind you, especially not an executive, wore long hair in those days. My God, he looked just like Snow White's Prince Charming, the way I *wanted* to do him. Jeez, what a travesty *that* was. See, the Old Man had this *thing* about long hair on guys—he'd've just as soon put crewcuts on the Greek gods!"

"Uncle Phil—"

"Right, the guy. He just sat there, looking up at me and smiling. And the most peculiar thing about it was that no one else seemed to see him. It was like he wasn't there. That's when I saw the ears, and I had it figured: either he was an elf, or I was drunk. And I *wasn't* drunk, at least not that day. He saw me *looking* at him, and he kept smiling at me. And then . . . and then he leaned real close to me, and whispered, like it was a big secret: 'Nice work on that last scene, Phil. But you got something wrong—a unicorn's hooves are supposed to be silver, not gold!' "

Phil's cackling laughter rang through the room, and Eric

smiled, slowly. "Well, that was the first time I saw Prince
Terenil. I wanted to talk with him some more—after all,
I'd never seen an elf before—so I just told him right back,
'Look, whoever heard of pastel unicorns, anyway? It's
artistic license!' He laughed, and said we ought to go talk
about it. I tell you, I was just about to bust out with
excitement. I mean, me and an *elf*! We got some sand-
wiches from the commissary and sat under the trees on
one of the backlots, just talking. Talking about eveything—
animation, art, elves, humans. Turns out he was a real
cartoon fanatic—thought it was amazing how we created
living characters out of nothing but voices and blobs of
paint. We had a lot in common, for an animator and an
elven prince." He shook his head reminiscently. "He really liked the Duck. You know, that Duck was sure my
fav—"

"Uncle Phil—" Beth said warningly, having finally figured out what was going on. "You can put on that senile
act with everybody else, but it isn't going to work with
me."

The old man raised his cola can to her, not looking the
least bit repentant. "Okay, sweetling. Yeah, those were
the days. We used to meet a couple times a week like
that, sitting in a backlot, eating lunch, and talking." Phil's
eyes clouded suddenly. "Until the big layoffs, that is."

He sighed, and leaned back in his chair. "That was a
bad time, for me, for a lot of people in the Industry.
Leila—my wife—she was alive then, and working days in a
department store. We were all right for a while, living off
her salary and our savings, but then money started getting
tight. Just when I thought I was gonna have to go back to
being a security guard, Prince Terenil showed up on the
doorstep, with a leather pouch in his hand. Honeybunch,
did I ever tell you that Leila could see the elves too?
Wonderful woman, Leila. God, I miss her."

He fell silent for a moment, and just stared sadly off into
space, so sadly that Beth didn't have the heart to prompt
him. "Best thing that ever happened to me, was Leila," he
said softly. "She really was. God, I miss her—"

The old man's eyes were so lost, so infinitely lonely,

that Beth finally had to pretend to examine her Coke can, overwhelmed by the feeling that she was intruding on something very private.

Phil cleared his throat, and took another sip of his cola. "Yeah, she could see them; she and Terenil had a real thing about keeping me from not going off into a gloom about the layoffs. So Terenil showed up. He *said* he had a sudden craving for a piece of Leila's pecan pie—but after she'd fed him, he said, 'It's about time I returned a little something for your hospitality.' He opened that leather pouch up over the kitchen table, and then there were all these sparkling stones on the formica. A dozen little gems. I thought my jaw was gonna come off, and Leila—she started crying, and hugging him . . . He would never tell us where he got them, just that he didn't steal them. Leila sold them to a jeweler, and we had enough money to live on until the studios started hiring animators again."

You never told me that *story before, Uncle Phil.*

"It was right after that he took me over to the Elfhame side of . . . whatever. What they call 'under the Hill.' My, now *that* was different." His eyes had lost their sadness, and were focused on something infinitely lovely, but very far away.

"Did you ever meet Perenor?" Beth asked.

The animator nodded, but his cheerful smile faded. "Oh, I definitely did, Beth. That was quite an afternoon. Prince Terenil and I were at the Elfhame Grove, you know, the one where they all used to meet and party. We were eating oranges and taking—that was when most of the San Fernando Valley was still orange orchards, Beth, years before you were even born—and suddenly Terenil stands up. He has this intent look in his eyes, like he's listening to something, even though I can't hear anything but the birds in the trees around us. Then he starts off through the trees. I didn't know what was going on, but I followed him."

Phil's lips thinned to a hard line. "And there, on the edge of the oak trees, is this handsome silver-haired elf, with a human boy. They're just sitting there, not doing anything that I can see; but the boy has this *look* on his face like he's drugged out of his mind. And Terenil starts shouting at this other elf; about how that's forbidden magic, that Perenor's hurting the boy and he doesn't even care. Perenor just shrugged. So Terenil just grabbed the boy and stormed off with him. And Perenor gave me this look, like he wanted to rip Terenil apart, but wouldn't mind killing me instead, so I ran and caught up with Terenil."

The old man stared down into his Coke can, as if searching for an answer that wouldn't come. "That boy was in a real bad way. Like he was lost somewhere inside himself. Like those kids they call 'autistic,' now. I took him home to his parents, didn't tell them about the elves, just that I'd found the kid wandering in the orchards. His parents told me that he'd been a normal child, no, more than normal—really a special kid, a bright little penny, with a singing voice that you couldn't believe. But he couldn't speak, or hear, not after that afternoon with Perenor. And, months later, I came back to see if he was doing better, and found out that the kid had been hit by a car. He was walking across the street and the driver honked and the kid couldn't hear it." Phil paused, taking a long swallow of his soda, as if he was washing away something bitter.

"Later, I heard that Terenil had exiled Perenor from the elven community. All I heard of him after that was a few years later, that he had found himself a human girlfriend, and they had a child, a little blonde girl. Arianrhod, I think that's what her name was. Terenil told me about her, about how she was going to inherit human and elven magic, but I don't remember exactly what he said. It's been a good many years."

A little blonde girl—yes, that makes sense! That's the bitch who was with Perenor last night. His daughter—

Out of the corner of her eye, Beth saw Eric shudder slightly. *Maybe he's figuring it out too, or remembering something of what happened last night in the club—damn, but that Perenor and his daughter are a nasty set of people.*

"You don't know anything else about Perenor, or maybe his daughter? Something about them that might help us?"

Phil suddenly grinned, raising his can of Coke meaningfully. "Sure. Just take 'em out for a glass of cola, and you'll take 'em out, fast enough."

Beth just looked at him. "What do you mean?"

The animator sipped his soda, then looked at the can thoughtfully. "It's something that Terenil told me about, years back. Caffeine. It's just a minor stimulant for us, but for the elves, it's a deadly and addictive drug. In small amounts, it acts like a trank, *sends* the elves into Dreaming, even if they're okay before they down it. Enough of it, and they'll die from overdose."

"Well." Beth thought about that for a moment. "That's useful information, though I don't know how we can hold Perenor down long enough to pour some coffee down his throat." *Though I'd sure love to do that to you, you murderous bastard—*

"Besides, I don't know if it would work on his daughter, since she's half-human." Phil shifted in his chair, glancing at Eric. "You're being very quiet, young man."

"Just thinking," Eric said, obviously subdued. "They're holding all the cards, aren't they? The people who own the Faire site have already sold it to a developer, it's going to be turned into condos, and that'll destroy the nexus. Perenor's masterminding that, somehow. I mean, he may be a powerful elf-lord, but he's got a corporation doing his dirty work for him. How can we stop *that?* You don't stop corporations with magic, I don't care how good you are."

"That's one thing that doesn't make sense to me," Phil mused aloud, "that Perenor wants to destroy the nexus. After all, the loss of magic would hurt him as well as the others. He'd fall into Dreaming, just like them, and then when *his* magic ran out, he'd fade. And then, what the loss of that magic would do to Los Angeles—"

"What would it do?" Eric asked. "I mean, it would just hurt the elves, right?"

Phil shook his head. "Unfortunately, that isn't the case, young man. You don't realize how much we depend on that magic here. That's why the film industry, and most of the music industry, are located here. That magic nexus gives the elves what they need to live, but it also powers

human creativity, the human soul. Without it, we might as
well build cars. Because our films would have all the soul
of a Chrysler, all steel and Fiberglas."

Eric looked at him with a puzzled expression on his
face. Phil turned the can around in his hands, thinking.
"You know, there's already places where the magic has
died—look at downtown Detroit, where the druggies are
stealing the aluminum siding off the walls of houses. Think
of the Jersey Turnpike. If you lived there, your imagination, your *soul*, would wither and die. Think about it."

Beth *did* think about it. *Maybe that's why I'm still living
in L.A. This place has so much potential, so many creative
people, all trying to do something* meaningful. *That's the
magic that means the most, the magic of the human heart.
If that magic dies—*

"Now, what I want to know," Phil continued, "is how
Perenor will benefit by destroying the nexus. I think I'll
go out and do a little research. Most of the elves I know,
like Terenil, are trapped in Dreaming. But maybe one or
two of them are coherent enough to talk to me."

"Meanwhile," he said, glancing at Eric and Beth, "I do
think that you should talk to these corporation people. See
if they understand what they're doing. Without making
yourself sound like loons, of course. I'd really hate to have
to spring you out of a mental institution, Bethie."

"I'll try to stay out of trouble, Uncle Phil." She grinned.
"And we're going to a protest rally at the corporation
headquarters this afternoon. I'm hoping we'll find out
something useful." *And, with any luck, we'll find a way to
stop these bastards—*

Eric looked up at the towering building, the opaque
glass window exterior hiding everything within. *Anything
could be going on in there, and we'd never know*, he
thought, gazing skyward.

*So, this is the home of Llewellyn Investment Corpora-
tion, the guys who bought the Faire land—I wonder if it's
as intimidating on the inside as it is from out here?*

All that stone, that glass—it made him think of . . .

prisons. Buildings like this were meant to trap, to hold, to *clutch*—

He looked resolutely away from the intimidating facade. *Caitlin's inside, talking with some of their execs. She's really doing her damnedest with this. She, of all the Admin people, really cares about what happens to the Faire.*

He glanced around at the rest of the protestors, looking to see if any of them *glowed* in that peculiar, silvery way the old animator did. Was that strange, magical light just something that only people who knew elves had? And why was he beginning to see it around people *now*?

That question triggered another. *I wonder if any of these people know that there's more at stake than just an Elizabethan Faire site? Do any of them know about the magic nexus?*

Near him the motley group of Faire people (some wearing mundane clothing, others in their colorful Faire garb) milled around uneasily. Beth was several feet away, talking with some of the dancers from her Faire show.

It's strange, I know so many of these people, but here I am, feeling as though I'm standing out here all by myself. It's not that anyone's excluding me, or deliberately not talking to me. It's just that I feel like I'm on the outside, looking in.

He felt odd, uncomfortable—and obscurely unhappy. He wanted to get a little distance from the crowd—but he didn't want to leave them, either.

It's funny, I never thought about it, but I guess that's how I am with Faire people in general. The L.A. Elizabethans, the Texas folks, everyone else I've ever played shows with. I know so many people, but they really aren't friends. Not really.

He swallowed, not liking the direction his thoughts were taking. *Maybe this is what Beth was talking about over the weekend, about how I never commit to anything.*

But I don't want to get hurt—

"If I don't let them get close to me, they can't hurt me." Yeah, that's true, but look at where I am now. Standing alone in a crowd.

The building seemed to loom over him, gloating at his unhappiness. He could almost hear it in his mind—

Then he *did* start to hear a strange, slithery voice in the back of his head.

"See," it seemed to say, "*see how utterly insignificant you are? See how utterly meaningless this all is? Why, you can't even call any of these people a friend, not really— and what good are friends, anyway? Will they buy you power like this?*"

Friend . . . The only one I feel close to at all is Beth, and maybe a few of the musicians. Like Aaron, that crazy fiddler, over there on the sidewalk with a few of the other Irish.

But somehow he couldn't bring himself to join them. *Now that I think about it, I guess this is how my life has been for a long time. Years. Always moving on before I can make any friends, get to know anybody real well. What kind of a life is that? No commitments, sure, but no real friends, either. Even my girlfriends, it's always ended with me leaving town, moving away. I don't know why, but that's how it is . . .*

"*And that's the way it will always be,*" the voice said in his ear. The building loomed silently, staring at him with a thousand cold glass eyes.

But *that* hit his stubborn streak. *That's just my own paranoia talking. And hell, maybe I can change that. Right now. I'm needed here, to help Kory with whatever it is he needs me to do. Save the Faire land, save the elves. And, after that? I don't know. But maybe—maybe Beth would want me to stay here. And Kory—*

He shuffled his feet. The very thought of Kory made him uncomfortable in a different sort of way.

I don't know what to think about Kory. Already, I feel like he's a close friend of mine, even though I've only known him for a few days. And, yeah, there's something else going on there, something I don't understand. It feels good, but—I don't know. I like him in a way that definitely is more than "just a friend." I don't know what's going on there, I just don't. How can I feel that way about a frizzy-haired elf?

Eric shook his head, looking out at the gathering crowd. *Better not think of it now. Looks like everything's about to get started here.*

Caitlin walked out from the entrance to the Llewellyn building, with a business-suited man at her elbow. She stopped at the top of the steps. "Okay, everybody, they've agreed to hear our grievances. We're going inside in an *orderly* fashion—*not* like the Noon Parade, youse guys! Go into the conference room on the right side of the lobby and sit down. Some of their executives are going to talk with us there."

Eric joined the throng of Faire people moving toward the large double glass doors.

This place looks normal enough inside. Dozens of suits, but that's to be expected. God, my imagination is working overtime. What did I expect? Sorcerers in gray-flannel robes?

Then he glanced around the busy lobby, and saw *him.*

An older man, tall, distinguished, talking with another businessman by the receptionist's desk. Perfectly normal, except—

Except for the tips of his ears. *Pointed ears,* showing through the immaculately-groomed silver hair.

A flashback of memory hit Eric like a slap in the face.

Sitting on the bus, looking out the window at the limo. And that man, that man with the green eyes—

Green eyes, emerald ice—gazing at me—and reaching—reaching—

Oh shit, it's him! That's Perenor!

Eric ducked back through the crowd, trying to put as many people and as much distance between himself and the Elflord as possible. He tried to signal to Beth, but she was already walking into the conference room with some of the other Rennies.

He looked around quickly, trying to spot anything he could use for cover. *In another minute, everybody will be in the conference room. And I'll be out here in the lobby, with* him *standing less than twenty feet away. Shit!*

God, get me out of this!

· 11 ·

Are You Willing?

The boardroom was silent except for the whisper of turning pages. Ria watched as her executives leafed through the copies of the proposal before them, her face a carefully controlled mask.

This one should be a shock for them. Linette typed it up off my notes only ten minutes before we started this meeting. Right after my little lunch with William Corwin.

They don't realize it yet, but if we can muster the cash to take advantage of it, this'll be the greatest coup I've accomplished yet.

The dark-haired man seated next to her was the first to speak. "This—this is a surprise, Ria. Are you sure we want to go through with this?"

She nodded. "Believe me, Jonathan, this one is worth it."

Jonathan Sterling, Ria's V.P. for Acquisitions, gazed down at the proposal in his hands, a faint frown-line between his eyebrows. "It's just—well, Ria, if we pursue this, we'll be overcommitting on capital. Negative cash flow for at least a month, and some serious interest charges from our creditors. If this doesn't pay off, and pay off big, we'll lose a lot. I just think it's too risky."

Oh, Jonathan, you're the only one who's willing to be honest with me. The rest of them are too scared. But you're not telling me anything I don't know already. Ria Llewellyn shifted in her chair and tapped the papers stacked before her with a lacquered nail. "True. It's risky. I know

177

that. What I need you to tell me is—can we commit the cash right now? Because if we're going to do it, it's absolutely critical that we purchase the Corwin stock before the end of the week."

Jonathan gave her a curious look. "You know something we don't," he said, a flat statement.

From the far end of the table, she heard a low mutter, sotto voce. "Oh great, here we go again, another week of working till midnight."

Ria spoke quietly. "Yes, I do know something you don't. And, you're right, Harkness, it probably is going to mean another week of working late." She raised her voice slightly. "I especially appreciate all of you staying late last night to finish that purchase proposal. Believe me, there'll be a solid bonus for that. And another, when—not 'if,' gentlemen, *when*—we pull this one off."

Ria continued, very aware that every eye in the room was upon her. "The reason we need to invest in Corwin Systems right now is because they're about to be purchased by National Technology, as part of National's bid to take over the West Coast market share. When that happens, Corwin's stock will double, possibly triple. We, *and* our represented clients, stand to make a very, very healthy profit. That is, of course, highly confidential information, gentlemen." She leaned back in her chair, waiting for their reactions.

Her executives—

My little worker bees—

—just stared at her, blinking.

Jonathan was the first to recover. "Ria, how do you know that?"

She smiled. "The usual sources, Jonathan."

"That's amazing," Harkness, Director of Accounting, said in a barely audible voice, "if it's true."

"Of course it's true," she said coolly. "My sources are impeccable, and they're *never* wrong. As you should know by now. And we stand to make a killing on it. Harkness, do you have some good, trustworthy people who can handle the accounting end of this? I'll also need several analysts to run projections for the next couple days. Mitchell, if you don't mind, I'm pulling you and Susan off the stock futures project and onto this. Jonathan, I want you to find them some good assistants from your office."

Ten minutes later, Ria called the meeting to an end. The executives, already talking eagerly among themselves, began to trickle out of the boardroom.

They took it in stride. Good people, my execs. I think they're starting to expect the impossible from me. Which is fine . . .

She began gathering up her paperwork from the table. *This should generate more than enough profit to cover that Faire land purchase. It looks like we will have to take a loss on that. The price was just too high—I still can't believe it, over ten million for seven acres that weren't even good commercial property. But Father insisted that we purchase it; just so we can bulldoze it, 400-year-old oak grove and all.*

Father will be pleased—they should begin construction on the site in another few weeks. She straightened, as a thought occurred to her. *If we use that purchase as a tax loss, I won't even have to take it out of his investment accounts. He'd fight me over that, just to have a fight going, and I don't have the time to waste.*

She slipped her neat stack of notes on the meeting into her leather portfolio. *He should be quite happy, in any case. Everything is going so well. Especially with the company. I wonder if he envisioned this, all those years back, when he suggested that I consider business school?*

She glanced around the silent boardroom—*her* boardroom—and smiled cynically. *He probably knew exactly what would happen, that sneaky old bastard. I imagine he just wanted someone to manage his investments for him, so he wouldn't have to bother. I knew he was well off, but that* was *something of a surprise. Quite a considerable fortune—*

And every penny of it gained by business practices even I would consider questionable. I wonder if that sticks in his craw, knowing I've made more money than he ever did, and I never even had to kill anyone to do it? Just by using my wits, and a little sorcery here and there to . . .

what were the lyrics to that song last night? "Throw the odds in my favor . . ."

She could see the face of the young Bard without even closing her eyes, clear and precise as a photograph. Lips pursed over the mouthpiece of his flute, soft, dreaming eyes half-closed in concentration, stage lights sharply defining the delicate arch of his cheekbones—

Throwing the odds in my favor. Oh, if I had that Bard beside me, I'd do more than just that. I don't know why, just can't stop thinking about him.

She recalled the touch of his hand on hers, the dark depths of his eyes, and shivered with self-indulgent pleasure.

Father can't go beyond seeing the Bard as a pawn, someone he could use and toss away—but there's so much more there, so much potential. And there's something about him that just—I don't know what it is, but it draws me to him. Power calling to Power, perhaps. Perhaps . . .

Her thoughts drifted off for a moment, and she called them to heel sharply.

Besides, if all the legends are true, and I could convince him to join me—with my magics as a half-Blood sorceress, and his Creation magics, working together in tandem, there's nothing we couldn't do. No one could stop us. Not even Father.

She analyzed her memories, paying close attention to the way he had looked at her in that shabby club, and the way he had responded to her this morning when she had tried to pinpoint his location. He had been so immediately . . . overwhelmed.

He finds me attractive. That's no great surprise. But does he feel the same way I do? Does he realize the potential, the power that every touch of our hands creates?

Most of the men I've known are so . . . callow. Especially the humans. I have to agree with Father; I can't see them as anything more than tools. But the Bard—he has such latent power. Even just thinking about him—

She put her hand against her flushed cheek, trying to calm her thoughts.

I can't stop thinking about him. I have to find him somehow. He was thinking of me, earlier. I would have been able to go to him, but something interfered, I don't know what. But he'll think of me again, I know he will. And then—then I'll be able to find him—

Ria replaced the rest of her papers in her leather brief-case, then sensed a whisper against the sigh of the air-conditioning as the door of the boardroom opened, and the presence of someone standing behind her. *Jonathan. I wonder what he wants?*

She turned, giving her veep a warm smile. "Well, Jonathan. You look like you have a question for me."

He glanced around the boardroom, waiting until the last briefcase-toting exec had left. His voice was very quiet. "Ria, do you know what you're doing?"

She shrugged. "Of course."

Jonathan's voice was even lower when he spoke. "Ria, you know what I mean."

"No, I don't know what you mean," she said impatiently, closing and locking her briefcase.

He rested his hand on hers, not letting her walk away. "Insider trading, Ria. That's what I'm talking about. I know you had lunch with William Corwin this afternoon."

She shook her head. "No, Jonathan. It's not what you're thinking. There were five other people at the table besides William and I. We never even talked about his company."

But he thought about it, quite a bit. Poor William, that decision to sell was on his mind all the way through the lunch meeting. I couldn't help but overhear it, feel how it weighed on him so heavily, knowing that there'll be layoffs after the sale. Overhear it, hell—he was broadcasting so loud, it was almost deafening. I do feel for him, so concerned about his employees, so conscientious. An admira-ble businessman, William Corwin.

"Five witnesses?" Jonathan repeated carefully, amazed; then he flashed her a smile. "Well, Ria, if you're involved in something illegal, I have to say that you do this kind of thing very well. And I'm glad I'm working for you, no matter how you find your information."

She patted his hand. "You're the best person I have, Jonathan. But I can't reveal my secrets, not even to you."

"Oh, why not?" He grinned. "If I knew your tricks,

then I could start up my own company from a ten-thousand-dollar investment, and have corporate assets of fifty-five mil in less than five years."

Ria was so startled, she only stared at him for a brief moment. Then she laughed. "Oh, Jonathan, how did you ever manage to find that out? There's no one still working here who was with me in the very beginning."

"I have my secrets, too," he said, smiling. "When I'm working for a sharp cookie like the lovely Ms. Ria Llewellyn, I have to keep on my toes. Or else you'll—"

His words were lost as Ria stiffened suddenly, overwhelmed by a roar of noiseless sound, a silent inner claxon as every magical warning went off simultaneously in her mind.

There's someone near me—someone with such raw power—not Father, it's a different signature—

Gods, he's in the building, moving towards me, closer every second!

"Excuse me, Jonathan," she said breathlessly, picking up her briefcase and hurrying towards the door. "I've got to get back upstairs right away."

Yes, get upstairs to my office. I've used it for sorcery before, the shielding should protect me from whoever this is—God, he's strong! Who in the hell can this be?

She moved past Jonathan, ignoring his startled stare, through the doorway and into the carpeted hallway. Ria stopped for a moment, scanning the building with her inner sight, trying to find the intruder.

He's very close—moving closer every moment—he's only a few feet away from me right now!

She turned, and saw him.

Eric ran blindly down the first corridor he saw.

I have to get out of here before he sees me. I can't let him do . . . that . . . to my mind again. I can't. And if he tried to kill me and Beth last night, God knows what he'll try if he sees me now—

There's a stairway sign at the end of this hallway. Maybe I can hide upstairs for a few minutes, wait until he leaves the lobby, then get out. Maybe—

The door at the end of the hallway opened, and a woman stepped out into the corridor, carrying a briefcase. A stunningly beautiful blonde, dressed impeccably in a black silk dress and heels. Eric thought he saw an expression of sudden fear twisting those features, but couldn't be certain.

Then he recognized her, and his breath caught.

That's her. The woman from my dream—

She looked up and saw him, and her eyes widened with surprise.

Eric stopped, right in the middle of the corridor, staring at the woman in disbelief.

:Eric? Is—is it really you?:

The voice was gentle and low, barely a whisper in his thoughts.

Eric couldn't move; just looked at her, bewildered. *How can this be? I—I only dreamed about her—how can she be real?*

She smiled, and held out her hand to him. *:Eric, you came here to find me, didn't you? You came here for me . . .:*

Eric felt his heart skip a beat, seeing the transformation that smile created in what was already an extraordinarily beautiful woman. Without thinking about it, he moved closer toward her, toward that outstretched hand, the beckoning smile.

She touched his hand, and he felt something akin to an electric shock run through him. *God—what's happening to me? I can't think straight—it's so hard to think at all—*

:You frightened me, Eric. I thought I would have to defend myself from some unknown menace, and it was only you.: The voice in his mind spoke lightly, teasingly. *:Let's go upstairs, to my office.:*

:Yes,: he answered silently, *:that's . . . a good idea—:*

He let her lead him back into the lobby, into the elevator. Upstairs, where their feet trod noiselessly on the thick velvety chocolate carpeting, she drew him towards a closed office door; past a male secretary working at his desk, past a young executive who was staring at both of them in astonishment, and into her office.

Inside, a single lit lamp cast shadows on the dark mahogany desk and bookshelves, the elegant leather-upholstered chair and couch. She held tightly on to his hand, not letting go for an instant, looking at him with such longing in her eyes. :*I never dreamed—I never thought this would happen—oh, Eric—:*

She moved closer—within inches of him—then kissed him. For a moment, Eric couldn't think, with the woman's silk-clad body molded against him as his arms closed around her in a tight embrace.

Then a coherent thought flickered briefly through his mind. *No. That was only a dream. I don't know her, I've never seen her before, I don't know what I'm doing here . . .*

But something was speaking stronger than that last whisper of sanity. And then he couldn't think of anything at all except the woman who was in his arms, in his thoughts, everything fusing and fading into a silent song that only they could hear.

Music—two melodies, interweaving, very different but counterpointing perfectly, rising toward some unknown, impossible resolution—

She broke away from him suddenly. Eric reeled back several steps, thoroughly shaken by both the fierceness of the music and the passion of the kiss.

Wow. 220 volts, definitely. If this is a dream, I don't want to wake up, ever.

He blinked; tried to recapture his breath, his balance. *Maybe—maybe that wasn't a dream. She recognizes me, knows me. What if that daydream was real—what if she really was searching for me—*

The blonde sat down slowly on the leather couch. "The music," she whispered, then looked up at him, her eyes mirroring shock and some indefinable emotion. "What are you doing to me? I don't understand—why can't I let go, why can't I think of anything but you?" Her eyes darkened dangerously. "Is this a game to you? Playing with my mind? Is that why you came here today, to amuse yourself by turning my world upside down?"

He shook his head and spread his hands. "I came here

because of the protest rally. For the Faire site. That's all. I—I'm one of the Faire buskers. I've never—I don't even know your name." His voice faded to an incredulous whisper. "I thought you were only a dream . . ."

She was silent for a long moment. "You didn't come here to find me," she said at last. "You're here because I'm the President of Llewellyn Corporation. Not because of . . . me." Her voice tightened, and her face became an expressionless mask. "You don't have any understanding of this at all, do you? Of the games within games, the chess pieces moving across the board." Now she looked at him sharply. "Or do you? Did you think you could use me?"

Eric blinked again, his mouth dry. *What's she talking about? A chess game Who—or what—does she think I am?*

Well, you're here, Eric, in her office. The office of the President of Llewellyn Investment Corporation. Here's your chance to make a stand, try to do something meaningful for a change. Fight for the Fairesite, and Kory . . .

He cleared his throat awkwardly. "No, I didn't think—I mean, I don't want to *use* you, I didn't know that . . . this . . . would happen." He felt his face warming. *Oh, terrific, now I'm blushing, too. I really wish I could keep from doing that.* He shoved his hands down into his pockets, feeling awkward and very much out of place. "I just wanted—"

Come on, Banyon—don't let her bullshit you into talking mundanities. Hit her with the real *reason why the Site has to be saved.*

"Look," he said, taking his hands out of his pockets. "*I* know why you bought the land. You're planning to destroy the magic nexus. And that'll kill the L.A. elves. You can't do it." He crossed his arms, gazing at her defiantly.

"So you came here to plead for your elves?" She laughed, her voice brittle. "How quaint."

Eric flushed. *She's only laughing at me now. She thinks I'm a fool.*

The blonde woman moved to her feet instantly. She reached out, taking his hand. He let her. "No, Eric, I don't think of you as a fool. Untrained, unknowing, ignorant of your potential, perhaps, but never a fool."

She drew him toward the couch, still holding his hand. "Sit down, Eric, and I'll tell you the truth about all of this."

Hesitantly, he sat down next to her. *The truth? Her truth, or the real one? I don't know if I should trust her or not—*

—but how can I not trust her, when she looks at me with those eyes—blue eyes, calling to me—

He brought himself back to reality with a jolt, realizing that he had been drifting away. *I can't make any sense out of this—everything is so confusing right now—God, it's hard to think straight—*

The blonde woman smiled across at him, her fingers lightly touching his. "I—I don't know where to begin. Who have you been talking to, Eric? Korendil?"

He nodded dumbly.

The woman sighed. "Poor Korendil. He means well, but he really doesn't understand what's going on. But you can, I think." She traced a pattern on the back of his hand with one fingertip. "Eric, I'll tell you my secret. You're the only on who knows this, other than those of the Old Blood. I'm half-elven. My father is of the High Court, a warrior-mage. My mother was a human with magic potential, like yourself. That's why, when I first saw you in the nightclub, I knew we had to be together. I'm sure you could feel it, too. Power calling to Power—"

The woman at the Dive—the one I couldn't remember— it's her . . .

He closed his eyes for a moment, and frowned, trying to bring the memory back. *Standing on the stage, and—and then—*

"Listen to me, Eric. The elves, they're not like us. You can grow into your power, your potential. You can redefine your focus. They *can't* change."

The woman, standing across the room, holding out her hand to me—

Her voice took on an insistence, a weight, that made her words sound like they *had* to be true. "Through the years, they've become more and more isolated, trapped within their groves. The humans have taken their territory, Eric, and molded it into a different world, one in which the elves *cannot* exist."

And everything—everything was so strange, so unreal—like I could reach out and touch reality, brush it aside like a curtain—

"And the nexus—well, because of the prevalence of Cold Iron in the humans' cities, and the way that the elves are only tapping into the nexus now through Dreaming, it's become—polluted. It is going to *die*, Eric; die—or go bad. If it dies, there'll be no magic left here at all, not for you to draw upon when you play your music, not for any of us. If it goes bad—" She shivered. "Nothing, only desolation and despair. So, my father and I devised a plan—to direct the magic through a new nexus."

"A new nexus?" he asked. *If the magic dies, I'll never feel this way again, like I do now, or I did, that night in the grove—as if the world is wide open before me, all the chords and harmonies mine to change, to control—I'll never feel like that again—*

But Kory said that his enemies were going to destroy the nexus. He never talked about anything like moving it.

"Korendil doesn't know anything," she said, as if hearing his thoughts. "He's been asleep for a long time, Eric. He doesn't know what's going on at all. We *have* to create a new nexus, or the magic will die or be lost to us forever. We have to, or watch everything worth having become corrupted."

"But if you do that—the elves will still die, won't they?" he protested, weakly.

Faint scorn colored her voice. "Think about them, Eric. You've seen them, last night, in that nightclub. They're already dead. Lost in Dreaming. Nothing can save them now. What you're seeing is only the last moment before they fade away completely. Even the High Court elves, the ones who do not need the nexus to live, they're all lost to Dreaming as well. The only reason Korendil isn't in Dreaming is because he's been spellbound for so long. They can't be saved, Eric; they're terminal patients in the last days of their illnesses. Korendil won't—can't—admit that. But *I* think it would be kinder to them to pull the

plug, to let them go. Korendil is the only one worth
saving, and Korendil is High Court. He doesn't need the
nexus. When he sees it's hopeless, he can save himself."

Unbidden, the images of the green-eyed people—elves
—in the club last night drifted into his mind. Lovely, yes,
but . . . as mindless as any brain-dead stoners. Maybe she
was right—

"This—" he said faintly, "This sounds like you're doing
the right thing, but you also tried to kill Kory last night.
What you're trying to do doesn't justify something like
that—"

Her face hardened, her eyes turning to blue ice. "You're
right, it doesn't. *That* was my father. He hates Korendil
and Terenil, for reasons that I don't really understand.
And I don't agree with him, or his methods." Her eyes
softened again; the vivid blue of the sky at twilight, on a
perfect spring night. "But—but if you would help me,
Eric, we could accomplish this without my father's inter-
ference. No more harm to anyone, just what we have to
do—change the nexus."

"Change the nexus—" he whispered, caught in her eyes.

"And if you help me now, there's so much more that I
can do for you, Eric. You're a brilliant musician, you
should be playing on better stages than some rundown
dive in the Studio City. I have friends in many places—
you could have the kind of music career most people only
dream of, the recognition and money you deserve. It
would be so easy—"

Her blue eyes, intense and alive, held his gaze.

:*So easy, Eric—all you need do is reach out your hand
and take what you want.*:

He couldn't seem to look away from those eyes. *I—I
don't know what to think. She's . . . so beautiful—and
those eyes, looking right into me . . . All I want to do is
say yes, say I'll never leave her again—*

*But—Kory and Beth—I can't abandon them. I promised
I would help them. I can't go back on that, either.*

I don't know what to do—what to think—

She squeezed his hand gently. "Don't make a decision
now. Just think about it, okay?" She stood up and moved

to the large desk, quickly writing down an address on a notepad. "This is my home address." She handed it to him; for a moment, her expression was suddenly very vulnerable. "I'll—I'll be there; tonight, if you want to come over and talk."

Eric took the piece of paper, and slipped it into his jeans pocket. He smiled shyly. "You know, I—I don't even know your name," he said.

"Ria." She moved closer to him. "Ria Llewellyn."

"I'll, uh, I'll see you later, Ria," Eric said awkwardly, distinctly uncomfortable under the intense gaze of her eyes.

"I'm certain you will," she said, walking with him to the office door.

Ria shut the door, then leaned against the wood, closing her eyes and smiling. She had to exercise every bit of control to keep from laughing aloud. *Oh, what incredible luck! I can't believe it. I thought I'd never see him again, and he walked right into my office! It's almost enough to make me believe in Fate—*

Young, untrained, and very malleable. Not to mention a few other perks, like those wonderful dark, dark eyes. He's really quite handsome. And, ah, definitely interesting enough to hold my attention for a long time . . .

She tingled all over; with excitement, arousal—and Power. *He'll come tonight, I know he will. And when he arrives at the door . . . let's see. I'll greet him myself, doubtlessly give him a warm little hello kiss, which he'll return with interest, and— and then—oh, what the hell, we probably won't even make it all the way to the bedroom. Probably shouldn't even try. I'll introduce him to the jacuzzi and the waterbed afterwards . . .*

Then a chill of doubt froze her. *But—but what if he changes his mind? What if he never shows up?*

She shook her head, stubbornly. *No, that's impossible. He has to be there tonight. No man has ever walked away from me, ever. He'll show up tonight, I know it. He will.*

She smiled to herself and stretched luxuriously. *He is so very delicious. I've never felt such . . . anticipation . . . before. I just can't stop thinking of him—*

A sharp knock at the door interrupted her thoughts. "Come in," she said brusquely, and walked back to her desk and took her place behind it.

The door opened. Ria frowned as her father prowled into the plush office. He crossed to the mahogany cabinet without even glancing at her.

"We need to talk, Ria," Perenor said, removing a bottle of Scotch and a glass from the cabinet.

He always thinks he can just stroll in here and take charge! My own dear, sweet Father— "I just had a very important meeting, Father, and I really don't think this is a good—"

"An important meeting? With the young Bard, perhaps?" Perenor smiled, and raised the glass of Scotch to her in a toast. "You're definitely my daughter, Ria. You never let an opportunity pass by, and you're quick to take . . . advantage of a situation. I'm impressed."

Despite herself, Ria flushed. "It's none of your concern, Father." *None of your damn business, either. I know what you'd do with Eric if you got your hands on him—and that's why I'll never let you near him.*

"Oh, but it is my concern." He took a slow draught from his glass. "When my own daughter consorts with the enemy . . . By the way, Ria," he said, giving her a cursory glance, one tinged with the faintest hint of contempt, "your clothes are in quite a state of disarray. Perhaps you ought to rebutton your blouse. You mustn't allow your employees to see you as anything less than immaculate, true?"

Ria met his gaze squarely, not even glancing down at her attire. *I know what you're doing, you old snake. Trying to unnerve me, take control, as always—*

"And you might want to consider, ah, shielding your activities from those of us who are sensitive to such things," Perenor continued. "It's quite distressing to be interrupted in a business conversation by the realization that my daughter is seducing a Bard several floors above me."

Damn him, he's doing this deliberately! Trying to fluster me, to get me off-balance—I won't let him! Two can play at this, Father. "It's no worse than some of your own . . . amusements," Ria said silkily, allowing no hint of emotion to leak into her words. "I've never complained about your choice of companions, even when some of them are distinctly . . . distasteful. Especially the ones who aren't even human *or* elven—"

Perenor's hand tightened visibly on the whiskey glass.

No—you don't like being reminded of your own perversions, do you? But I think I know where this little game of yours is leading—and no, I won't let you get control of Eric. No matter what you say or do.

"That is not the question here," the elf-lord said coldly. "The fact is that you are playing a very dangerous game, with a young man—a young *human* man—of unknown potential. You're playing with fire—"

Ria shook her head. "I know exactly what I'm doing, Father. Believe me, I do." She smiled, noting the way his eyes had narrowed thoughtfully. "Unlike you, I don't believe in destroying my opponents. Not when there're more . . . satisfying ways of winning."

Her father was silent for a long moment, swirling the Scotch in his glass. Then he spoke, very quietly, "He's dangerous, Ria. So is Korendil. After I find Korendil, I will deal with this Bard of yours, I assure you of that."

Her back stiffened; her head came up. *Like hell you will, Father!*

"Don't touch him," she said in a voice like ice. "If you do— "

Perenor smiled.

She tightened her jaw at the sight of that poisonous smile. *As though he just scored a major victory, that old bastard—*

"Of course, my dear," he said smoothly. "I didn't realize you were so . . . concerned about this Bard of yours. I never thought you would become so attached to him so quickly."

"Attached? Hardly. It's just—he'll be very useful to me," she said, carefully choosing her words. "That much potential is *far* too valuable to be wasted, Father. I didn't make this company what it is by squandering profitable property on mere amusements."

She hid a smile as her own dart scored, and Perenor's

back stiffened. "And he'll be safely under my control, no danger to you or anyone. I'll make sure of that."

Yes, he'll be mine, mine to control, and to use, possibly even against you, Father dear—

"How do you intend to control him?" Perenor asked idly, sipping from his drink. "I would think that controlling a Bard, someone of such unfathomable power, might even be beyond your capabilities, my dear."

She shrugged. "I lied to him."

"What did you tell him?" Perenor glanced at her over the rim of his whiskey glass.

"That we're moving the nexus. That the magic is fading, and if we don't do something, it'll die. Technically, that *is* true—though it won't happen for at least another thousand years. And when that does happen, it's likely that the magic will simply find another weak point in the veil between the worlds through which it can flow easily. Creating a new nexus. Or so *you* instructed me, Father dear."

Perenor smiled. "Not bad. But what if he learns the truth?"

"After tonight, nothing will matter to him but me."

Her father laughed, honey with gall. "You have a lot of confidence in your abilities, daughter."

"I think both of us do. And with good reason." A thought suddenly occurred to her. "What did you mean, Father, after you *find* Korendil? Don't you know where he is?"

Perenor cleared his throat uneasily, not meeting her eyes. "Actually, I don't. For some reason, I can't seem to locate him. It's more than possible that he didn't survive the night, of course. Very likely, in fact. He would have bled to death from those wounds in a few hours."

Oh my. Father dearest, have you, of all people, actually fumbled something? Certainly, Korendil is dead—unless he's alive, and somehow hiding himself from you. Oh, this is amusing. I never thought I'd see the day that you'd admit you were incapable of anything.

"Not that it matters," her father added, a little too hastily. "There really isn't anything Korendil can do against us. My only concern was that young Bard, though if you feel you have that situation well in hand—"

Ria smiled. "Believe me, I do." *In more ways than one, Father.*

Perenor drained the last of his Scotch, setting the glass on the cabinet. "Well. That sounds quite definite." He raised an eyebrow at her. "I may visit you, Ria, after tonight, just to see what you do with this young prodigy."

I'll bet you will. And I bet you'd like to get your hooks into him as well. Believe me, I intend to leave him much more . . . intact than he would be after some time in your tender hands. I have more in mind for this Bard than simply to use him once and cast him aside. My plans are much more . . . permanent.

She realized her father was scrutinizing her with a very speculative gaze. "What if he doesn't show up?" Perenor asked bluntly.

She froze for a moment, *Would he—*

No. No man had ever walked away from me.

"He will. I know he will. He doesn't have any choice in this."

No choice at all, she thought, realizing at that moment that this young man was drawing *her* as much as she was drawing him. Which she hardly dared admit to herself, much less to her father.

No, he has no choice. Not any more than I do. There's something pulling our lives together, binding us—Power calling to Power—

Whatever happens, he's mine. And no one, not even my father, is going to stand between us.

He has to come to me tonight. I know he will. He has to—

· 12 ·

No Irish Need Apply

Eric stared through the grimy window, as the RTD bus chugged painfully up the hill over the Sepulveda Pass to the Valley. Even though it was still early in the afternoon, the traffic was already slowing to a turtle's pace, creeping along the freeway through the smog-shrouded hills.

His mind felt just as smog-shrouded. *Nothing seems to make sense anymore . . .*

He leaned against the glass, gazing down at the cars creeping past the bus.

Only a few days ago, everything seemed so . . . normal. I was busking days, playing different gigs nights, Maureen and I were still together, life was fine. Now, in less than three days—

He sighed, and rubbed the back of his sweaty neck with his hand. *Now there's two women in my life. And one elf.*

How did my life get so complicated so fast?

Eric wedged himself closer to the glass and closed his eyes.

Ria Llewellyn. Even her name is magical. What a combination. What an incredible combination. Corporation president, a half-elf, and one helluva lady. Not to mention staggeringly beautiful. She's like something out of my dreams. It's hard to believe she's real.

But there's something about her—

He recalled the odd light, the predatory chill in her eyes when he'd left her, and shivered involuntarily.

There's a funny intensity there when she looks at me.

Like a cat, a cat that's got a mouse trapped, and is thinking about playing with it instead of eating it. It's damn scary—like I'm nothing to her, only a toy, or a tool—

A car honked right under the window, but the sound seemed to come from another world entirely. As if the world that held traffic jams and the world that held Ria Llewellyn couldn't possibly be the same. He replayed the scene with her over and over in his mind, concentrating on it, trying to sift some kind of meaning out of it, but all he got were contradictions—

—like that other way she looked at me, like she's just a child, only wanting someone to hold onto, someone who'll take the pain away. So lost, so vulnerable. It took everything I had to keep from taking her in my arms right then, trying to comfort her. It's like someone hurt her once, hurt her real bad, and she's never admitted it to anyone; maybe not even herself.

He chewed his lip with frustration. *God, I can't make heads or tails out of it; one minute she's about to take a piece out of me, the next, she's like a little kid—*

And yet another facet of memory focused. *—Then she changes again—she looks at me with that little bedroom smile, those come-hither eyes, teasing—inviting—brushing her hand against mine—*

He blushed, and pillowed his head into the crook of his arm, hoping no one in the bus was watching him. *I don't understand that, either. Sure, I'm always making a fool of myself in front of women, but she—she's really something. All I want to do when she smiles like that is drag her off to a cave somewhere. That's not like me, usually. I try to be a little more . . . dignified about my sex life.*

And everything about the meeting was washed in a kind of glowing fog. The more he tried to concentrate on some memory-fragment, the more the memory slipped into a haze. *It's so hard to think straight when I'm around her. It's like everything is wrapped in gray fuzz, I don't know where I am, what I'm doing, what to think.*

And that led him back around full circle, to last night and this morning. *Those* memories were as clear as crystal,

everything sharp-edged and diamond-cut. *That's sure not
like the way it is with Beth. With Bethie, I always know
what's going on.*

Or, at least, I think I do—

He pondered that, and concluded ruefully that maybe
he *didn't* know what was going on between himself and
Beth.

*She's got me going too, I guess. I mean, I thought we
had something special, something really nice. Maybe even
something permanent. I think she understands me, better
than anybody else. After all, she's kinda like me, she's a
gypsy too. I make my way by playing street and gigs—she
works in TV. A production manager is always between
gigs, moving from studio to studio; or on hiatus, like she is
now. She understands how it is.*

But when he'd looked for her in the lobby, she'd been
gone.

*She didn't even wait for me, back there at the Corpora-
tion. Just left without me.*

*Maybe she thought I'd already taken off—after all, I did
kinda vanish from the protest meeting. But she didn't even
leave a note with the receptionist—*

It had been like the time his mother had forgotten to
pick him up from school. He'd stood on the curb forlornly
for an hour, clutching his flute, watching for the car that
never came—until one of his teachers took pity on him
and took him home.

Another car—or the same one—honked again, and this
time he jumped. *Well, that really doesn't matter, I guess.
What matters now is what I'm going to do. I just don't
know who to believe, Kory or Ria. Which of them is telling
the truth?*

*Korendil—what he'd said—the *elf* believed his own
words, that was the truth, anyway. But how much of the
truth?*

*Kory—I really don't know what to think about Korendil
either. Everything is moving so fast, too fast to figure out.
I like him—he's a friend, like no other friend I've ever
had—*

But there's something about him that makes me feel so

. . . uncomfortable. The way he looks at me, like I'm everything he ever dreamed of, the answer to all of his prayers. It's more than a little embarrassing. And whatever it is that Ria's got—that magnetism, that . . . allure— he's got it too . . .

God, why am I thinking that? Maybe it's just that he got himself so trashed trying to keep Perenor away from me and Bethie, or the fact that we healed him, but—I feel so—

He gave himself a mental shake. *Confused. That's how I feel. All of this is so confusing, Kory, Beth, the magic—Ria—*

He clenched his fingers in his hair. *God. Magic. I can't disbelieve in it anymore. What we did this morning to heal Kory, me and Beth—it happened, it was real, as real as I am. Which means that it all is true, the elves, the magic, everything. It must be true—I am a Bard. Whatever that means. And—and if that's true, then what happened, all those years ago, it was real, too—*

He shivered, huddled close against the window. The memory came back, as clearly as if the living nightmare had occurred just the night before.

He was standing on the stage, the bright lights making everything look so distant, out-of-focus—the orchestra was beginning the first notes of "Danse Macabre."

Then he began the opening solo.

And the music—suddenly it was so strong, so powerful, better than he'd ever played before; everything coming together and clicking into place and perfect—

Then—

Caught in the spell of the music, he began to shiver. The weird melody called up his nightmares, the things of childhood; the things that lurked under the bed, behind the closet door, and waited for the light to be turned off—

He felt unfriendly, hungry eyes on him—looked out of the corner of his eye at the wings—

—and saw them.

The watchers in the darkness of the theater, the creatures detaching from the shadows. Unnoticed by the audience, gliding toward him like cloaks of liquid night, hands outstretched, reaching for him—

He stood there, frozen in place, not believing what was happening—

Then flung the flute away and ran, ran—his throat so choked with fear he couldn't even scream—just whimper—

He opened his eyes, and clenched his hands on his knees to stop their trembling. *I ran all right. Ran like hell. The conductor was horrified by the kid prodigy freaking out backstage; my parents were freaking out almost as bad as me. Two years of psychoanalysis, of everyone telling me that it wasn't real, it didn't happen. I just imagined it. Two damn years being told I was crazy that night. Then the kids at Juilliard found out about it—*

More years of taunting, tricks with things being hidden in his closet, with "practical jokes" and attempts to scare him into another fit of hysterics in public. Notes addressed to "Loony Banyon." Getting on the mailing list of every nuthouse in the country. Good old Chuck Marquand, the second-best flautist at Juilliard, setting up phony appointments for Eric with the local shrinks.

Beginning to doubt his own sanity.

But—if all of this is real, then that was real, too—those things, staring at me with such hunger and need, they were real; creatures that shouldn't exist but did, all because of me.

Because of me—

Because I'm a Bard.

Christ.

He tried to laugh at himself. *You know, I really wish somebody else could've been picked for this honor. How did I get so lucky? Anybody else would be better for this. Like Bethie; she'd be perfect. She's got it all together, knows what she wants to do; she never falters or feels like she can't cope.*

He gritted his teeth to keep from shivering. *I do, all the time. I'm not the right one for this, for whatever it is I'm supposed to do. I feel like I'm being pulled in all these directions, with no idea which way I want to go. Everyone wants so much from me—*

But he needed answers, and the only place he was going to get them—

—was from himself.

I'll figure this out for myself, that's what I'll do. I'll make my own decision, and stick to it. That's it.

He glanced out the window, and leaped to his feet, diving for the rear exit of the bus. *Shit, I missed my stop!*

Eric stumbled down to the street, and looked around sourly. *Oh well. It's only a few blocks back to the apartment. I'll live.*

He trudged across the intersection, sidestepping several kids on skateboards. *With the way my luck has been lately, I'm likely to get run over by a rollerskater in Woodley Park. What else could possibly happen that would complicate my life even more than it is now?*

Strike that. I don't even want to think about anything that might complicate my life!

Eric started down Sherman Way, past the sprawling Post Office building. Ahead of him, he could hear the faint roar of a cargo plane taking off from Van Nuys Airport, only a few blocks away. *Probably one of those big World War II bombers. I think some of those pilots are still living through the war, the way they fly those big clunkers. Not living in reality.*

Hell, who am I to talk about living in reality? Me, the Bard, with my best friends the witch and the elf. Some reality, Eric.

He coughed a bit as a junker growled past, burning more oil than gas. More had happened to him in the past week than had happened in the last year—

And it had taken some of the starch out of him, that was for sure. He was sweating by the time he reached his apartment; hot and tired, and a little gritty.

He'd never noticed quite how much of an eyesore the tacky old pink building was. He couldn't help but contrast this—and the steel and chrome sleekness of the Llewellyn Building. And Ria Llewellyn's office—no plastic couch with a lump in it for *her*. Nothing but the best . . .

So what could she possibly see in *him?* Grubby little busker, no money, no muscles, nothing a woman like *that* couldn't have just by snapping her fingers—

Maybe she saw the same thing that Beth and Kory did. *Whatever that is.*

He unlocked the security door and trudged down the hall to his apartment, suddenly wanting both of them around. Needing them. Badly.

I need a sanity check. I need to find out how much of what she said is true—and why she's so hot on me—

But as he unlocked the door of his apartment, a voice spoke from the shadowy living room before he could call out.

"They are not here, Bard."

A voice like broken music.

He opened the door; slowly, carefully.

There was an elf sitting on his living room couch.

Blond, like Kory, and long-haired; but *his* hair was unkempt and neglected, dulled and brittle. Tall, gaunt, with lines of pain etched around his mouth and eyes. And the eyes themselves—

If Kory's eyes were crystalline emeralds, and Perenor's clouded jade, this elf's eyes were reflections of the sea on a moonless night. Deep gray-green, and haunted, they gave Eric the feeling that something too terrible to think about moved beneath the surface. Ancient eyes; anguished eyes.

Eric tried to speak, and found he couldn't get his mouth to work until the elf looked away. "W-which one are you?" he stammered, as he shut the door behind himself. "And where are they?"

"I do not know," the elf replied, again in that beautiful, ruined voice. "They had departed before I arrived." He raised a wing-like sweep of eyebrow at Eric. "I took the liberty of removing the blood from the carpet. Dangerous, to leave it there, and not just for Korendil."

Eric could feel a thousand unspoken, fear-ridden questions behind the elf's calm facade.

"Yeah, well, we weren't thinking about that—"

"No. I would imagine—from the amount—" The elf's eyes closed briefly, and the pain-lines about them deepened.

"Was the boy badly hurt?" he asked, his voice a harsh whisper.

"Yeah," Eric began. "Perenor really trashed—"

The elf opened his eyes, and sea-fire raged in them.
Eric flinched away from his fury.

"*Danann*—if he is dead, I swear by my honor I will—"

"He's okay—" Eric stammered, interrupting him. "W-w-e
healed him. Me and Beth—"

The elf stopped, frozen. "You. Mortals. You healed him.
And you put no binding upon him?" A darker emotion
lurked in those gray-green eyes, roiling with restrained
violence.

Eric blinked. "Say what?"

"No, I see that you did not." The fire died in the elf's
eyes, and he slumped a little. "No Bard would, I think. It
was not all Dreaming, then, what the boy said of you.
Korendil is wiser than I." He pondered that for a moment,
then placed one hand on his chest and bowed, with a
smile of self-mockery. "Bard Eric Banyon, you see before
you all that is left of Terenil, prince of Elfhame Sun-
Descending. I would ask for your help."

Eric felt his jaw slipping. "*My* help? But—"

The elf rose and walked a little closer, and now Eric
could see that he was dressed, incongruously enough, in
stained, scuffed, deep-scarlet leather. Like Robin Hood,
only in red. Eric's jaw slipped a little more.

"Well . . . that is less than the truth," Terenil admitted.
"I came to search out Korendil; I could not sense him nor
trace him with magic, and I feared—"

Eric felt a chill; if Terenil could find his way to the
apartment, how long would it take Perenor? "How did you
know he was here?"

"The blood," Terenil replied. "Suddenly I could sense
the blood. But when I arrived, he and the witch had
already gone. I was not certain what to think; especially
after I found the blood and . . . those—"

He nodded his head toward the chair next to the door.
On it were the ravaged and bloodstained garments Korendil
had been wearing. Eric eyed them mournfully.

My best Faire shirt—and my boots—

"It was only moments later I heard your footsteps. I still
cannot sense him, therefore she must be shielding him. If
he has been hurt, *that* is just as well—"

"Yeah," Eric said vaguely. *They're not here—so they must be at Beth's place. That means he was in good enough shape to move.* Jealousy cramped his throat. *No wonder she didn't wait around for me. Why should she? What am I, compared to him? What have I got that he hasn't got* more *of? And on top of it all, he's an elf. What'd that old guy say to her? "You've finally got your wish"? She's been looking for an elf like him for years . . .*

"Bard—I still need your help." The elf broke into his unhappy thoughts. "Please—help me."

"Why?" Eric spat, suddenly angry at the whole race of elves. *Yeah, I can guess what Beth is doing, now that she's found her elf. They're probably—*

"Because—" Terenil's shoulders sagged. "Because no one else will," he said raggedly. "Those few of my own who are not lost themselves have given *me* up for lost. Even Korendil. I—I failed him, last night. I failed him . . ."

Eric's anger ran out of him. "Hey," he said awkwardly. "Like, it wasn't your fault. You aren't in real good shape, y'know?"

Oh shit. That's it—that's probably why she had to move Kory in a hurry. He was in lousy shape, and she didn't want to risk Perenor tracking them down. Maybe that blood . . . well, whatever. That's probably why she didn't wait.

Though I really wish she'd left me a note . . .

"And whose *is* the fault, then?" Terenil asked, his voice rough with self-accusation. His eyes caught Eric's for a moment, just as Kory's had—

Thoughts ran wild in his head, with an underscoring of lament, dirge to something lost past recall.

Korendil vanished; more of the Low Court falling into Dreaming by the day. Those of the High Court who had not gone north to Elfhame Misthold or under the Hill, had slipped hopelessly into Dreaming themselves. Without Korendil to rally the High Court remnants, to help him—*it was useless to struggle on against the Dreaming. For he, who should have been able to protect them, who was responsible for protecting them, was helpless, helpless . . .*

Only a Bard could have saved them—and Perenor had seen to it that there would be no Bards here.

So why not give up, give in, let Dreaming take him too? They were all doomed. Better that he would not be capable of witnessing or understanding the end . . .

Despair too profound even to register as pain nearly knocked Eric to his knees. Only *once* had he ever run across anyone who lived with anguish like that. An ex-'Nam vet named Tor, up at the law school at Stanford, who used to let Eric stay with him between Faire weekends, feed him and give him crashspace on the dorm floor when the busking got too thin—

And who used to get drunk with him when the pain was too much, and neither of them wanted to get stoned alone.

Wonder what happened to Tor? It's been years. Did he ever get out to Colorado like he always said he wanted to?

He answered Terenil's despair with Tor's own words. "Sometimes shit happens, no matter what you do. Sometimes all you can do is try and keep yourself in one piece, so you can figure out what happened, and figure out how to keep it from happening again." *Yeah, you had the right idea, old friend—*

He was rewarded by seeing some sanity come back into the Prince's expression.

"I have done poorly at even that," Terenil replied bitterly.

Eric cocked his had to one side, and took a really close look at him. *Well, he looks pretty strung-out, but he doesn't look drugged. And hell, enough people have written me off—too many times—*

I'm damn sure not gonna slam the door in his face.

"It happened," he said. "Not even one of you incredibly powerful magical type elves is going to be able to change the past. So, how can I help you out, your Highness?"

Terenil raised his eyes to meet Eric's, astonishment erasing some of the pain-lines.

"You'll help me?" he said incredulously.

Eric shrugged. "Sure. Why not? I think you deserve help. I don't know that I can help you *much*, but whatever I can do, I will. I told Kory I'd do what I could for the

elves, and last time *I* heard, you hadn't turned in your
union card."

The gratitude in Terenil's expression was as hard to face
as his rage had been. Eric *had* to turn away from it—and
to cover his lapse of manners, picked up the ruined clothing and looked it over, hoping to find some sign it could
be salvaged.

"It is beyond repair, I fear."

The voice was right in his ear, and he jumped, dropping
the shirt. "Y-yeah, it's pretty totaled," he agreed. "I mean,
I don't grudge it, but—how come he had to take *my*
clothes?"

And how the hell *did he ever fit into them?*

"Because, Bard, we cannot *create* with our magic. Alter,
easily. Copy, yes—if we know the article intimately. But
not create. Only a Bard or a very powerful Adept can
create something from naught but power."

"Okay—but why *my* clothes?"

"He would have been rather conspicuous without them,"
the Prince said dryly. "Being as he was bespelled wearing
his armor—and so woke in the same condition."

"Lots of people wear armor on the Faire Site," Eric
objected.

"Armor like *this?*"

The Prince straightened, gaining at least two inches in
the process—and began to glow . . .

Eric closed his eyes; the Prince's outline wavered in a
way that was making him slightly ill—and besides, he was
hearing music again—

*Slow, majestic chords; a massive pipe organ, like the
one in that chapel in the Santa Cruz hills—*

The music faded, and he opened his eyes—and lost his
jaw entirely.

The Prince *looked* like a Prince now; clad head-to-toe in
some fantastic suit of gold and scarlet enamel, chased and
filigreed and articulated so finely Eric had no doubt that
Terenil could *dance* in the stuff. It made the armor in the
movies look modest and restrained. Not to mention bulky
and awkward.

Terenil favored him with an ironic half-smile.

"Yeah, I see." Eric swallowed. "I guess he would have been kind of conspicuous."

"And he was bespelled ten years ago. The only clothing he could replicate—assuming he could spare the mage-power, which I do not think he could—would have been bell-bottomed jeans and leisure suits, Bard Eric; or High Court garb. Equally conspicuous."

The idea of Kory in a polyester leisure suit made Eric splutter with laughter. When he looked up again, Terenil was back in his scarlet leather.

"I guess—I guess I don't mind so much," Eric admitted. "Not when you put it that way. But—" He surveyed the blood-stiffened boot in his hand with regret. "I'll miss my boots. Be a while before I can afford another pair."

"If you will permit?" Terenil took the boots from him, held them in front of his chest, and frowned at them.

A quick, staccato chord—

The mocassin boots were gone. What was in Terenil's hands was something else entirely. Eric had lusted after the famous "Faire boots," tooled and decorated, hand-made, custom-fitted boots, for years. *These* made *those* look like his worn-out moccasins. Brilliant scarlet, and embellished with tiny metallic gold sunbursts—

Like Terenil's armor.

"Not your colors, I do not think," the elf muttered; and as a strange little fluted melody played behind Eric's eyes, he watched the tint deepen to wine, watched the sun-bursts vanish, to be replaced by a simple vine and leaf pattern, all in silver, threading from the sole to the top.

"Here," Terenil said, with a touch of pride, holding the boots out to him. "In simple things, at least, it seems I have not lost my abilities."

Eric took them. *This is it. I have gone around the bend. I am no longer operating in this reality*—

Nevertheless he kicked off his sneakers and pulled the boots on. It was almost with relief that he found them to be miles too big

Thank God. Reality. Next, I find out I'm wearing Baggies on my feet, and that he hypnotized me.

"They're—"

"Indeed, I expected. They are, after all, copies of *mine*."
The elf knelt for a moment, and ran his hands down Eric's
legs—

The feeling of Terenil's hands upon him was disturb-
ingly sensual.

Christ! First Kory—

Then the leather *moved*, tightening around Eric's calves
and feet until the boots might have been painted on him.
He'd have jumped, if Terenil hadn't been holding his
ankles.

Jesus H—

The elf stood and straightened. "Now do they fit well
enough, Bard Eric?"

Eric swallowed hard. "Uh—yeah, sure."

Too weird for words. Definitely.

I'm almost afraid to think what could happen next . . .

The Prince hailed a cab at the curb, directing the driver
to some place in Beverly Hills. Eric was too bemused to
note the address. He kept expecting his boots to turn back
into Baggies, or into his old, ruined pair.

*All this talking about magic—but these are real; I can
touch them. And Kory being healed was real, too. It's not
talk, it's not F/X. It's happening.*

The cab stopped. Terenil produced a fifty from nowhere
(literally), and handed it to the driver, who opened the
door for them. Eric found himself stepping out onto a
driveway that looked like it went on for miles.

The cab pulled away, leaving them standing beside a
wrought-iron gate with more security hookups than Eric
had ever seen in his life.

Terenil idly placed his palm on one of the mysterious
black boxes, and Eric heard a complicated burst of
twelve-tone—

And the gate swung open.

"I have the feeling that this *isn't* your house," he said,
nervously. "Are we going to get arrested for breaking and
entering in the next five minutes?"

Terenil raised his eyebrows again. "Are you more concerned with the impropriety of appropriating someone

else's property, or the possibility of being caught at it?"

"Being caught," Eric said promptly, with a grin.

"You should have been born one of us." The Prince pushed the gate completely open and beckoned to Eric to follow him. "The owner of this manse is an old friend of mine. He is currently in Eire, and will be for some months. He has left only one caretaker, who is surfing, and will not return until sundown. I have convinced the alarms that we hold the proper keys. There will be no police here."

The driveway *did* go on for miles, white and glaring under the afternoon sun. "So why are *we* here?" Eric asked, following the scarlet figure up the hot stretch of concrete. "I have the feeling you've been here before."

"I have," Terenil sighed. "Often—though not for this purpose, precisely. I came here when I . . . needed a place . . . undisturbed."

Eric flashed on a glimpse of one of the elves last night, sitting in a corner stoned out of his wits. He nodded to himself. *Yeah. Being an elf isn't going to keep the cops from hassling you by day if they think you're blitzed.*

"So why are we here now?" Eric persisted.

Terenil moved off the white desert of concrete and onto a path of tastefully arranged stones. "We are here, Bard Eric, because we need a place undisturbed. A place of combat, and this manse has such within it."

Place of combat?

"What's wrong with the park?"

They had reached a portico of rough-hewn redwood beams. Terenil played his trick with the door, and it, too, swung open at a touch. He strode inside as if he knew exactly where he was going.

He said he did.

"This a place where we will not be conspicuous," Terenil said carefully, leading the way through the tiled entry and down a birch-paneled hallway. "My abilities are not . . . what they were. I cannot make us 'invisible,' engage in combat, and hold my memories in your mind, all at once. Two of the three, yes, but not all three. Here."

He touched another door and motioned Eric to precede him, and Eric found himself in a dojo.

Who the hell's house is this, anyway?

"Why do I need your memories?" he asked in confusion, as Terenil shut the door behind them.

"Because, Bard, I need very badly to regain my skills in fighting, both by blade and magic—and to do so, I need an opponent." He tapped Eric's chest with an outstretched finger. "You."

"Me?" Eric's voice squeaked.

"Indeed."

The elf-prince placed his hand on Eric's forehead before Eric could scramble away.

The world vanished with a shout.

· 13 ·

False True Love

"In truth, Terenil, this is indeed schizoid," Eric said dubiously, taking his stance where the elf-Prince pointed. "I don't think I like it. I feel as though I am me *and* you, too. It is quite weird, facing myself like this."

"I would imagine," the elf agreed; he moved to about twenty feet away from Eric, and stood with his legs braced. He shook his hands to loosen them, and flexed his fingers. "But giving you my memories is the only way in which I shall face an opponent of equal strength and skill. I *used* to spar thus with Korendil—"

"Well, he's in no shape to do that right now anyway." Eric shook his head to try and settle all the alien thought-patterns. They kept floating around inside his skull, intruding when he least expected them to. Strange patterns, somehow delicate, yet fraught with an intensity he had never—

Oh shit, first I start talking like him—now I'm starting to think like these pointy-eared jokers, too!

"Am I going to keep this shit in my head forever, or can you get rid of it when you're done?" Eric asked plaintively.

"Without my sustaining the memories, they will fade, and quickly," Terenil assured him with a faint smile. "I am just as pleased to be facing you, in truth—Korendil is no kind of mage, and Perenor is both warrior *and* mage. If I am to confront him again, I shall need my skills at both."

"Well, how'm I supposed to know what to do?"

"You do not," Terenil said, with just a hint of maliciousness. "You simply react—"

211

He pointed his finger at Eric.

And suddenly a there was a burst of trumpet-blare, and a bright glowing ball was hurtling straight for him.

Shit!

Eric yelped and dove for the floor.

"Interesting, though not particularly effective," the Prince observed. "Granted, I would not have thought of that."

"But—" Eric protested from his position on the mat.

"Dodging will not help you a second time, Bard—"

This time two of the orange balls of flame were coming at him. He threw up his hands in a pathetic attempt to ward them off—

And one of those *other* memories stirred. Without understanding what he was doing, he reached for . . . something. And when he had it, he twisted it into a C major arpeggio, strong and resounding.

And a ball of red flame intercepted Terenil's two, consuming them.

"Excellent!" the Prince laughed. "And I would not have thought of *that*, either!"

"What's *that* supposed to mean?" Eric panted, getting to his feet.

"You have my memories of working magic—but you *use* your own powers. Like so—"

Roar of brass. Lightning lashed down where Eric stood—

Except that he wasn't standing there anymore. He'd dodged again, and that something inside him acted. He heard a musical run like a trombone cadenza, saw he was sending a streaming lance of fire—*like a flamethrower*—straight at the Prince.

Who deflected it (*crash of cymbals*) but not easily.

Hey, I'm not doing too bad at this! Eric Banyon, magewarrior, just like something out of Tolkien! Hah, take that, Prince Terenil!

Then Terenil got serious.

After a few moments of being chased around the dojo, Eric began searching—frantically—for those strange memories, calling them up on purpose instead of being used by them. He began fighting back.

The Prince was grinning.

And while Eric wasn't exactly *relaxing*, he was beginning to see what was going on. There was a distant source of energy, of power, that he could touch, use.

The nexus—

And he could do things with this power. After several more exchanges, he began to see the patterns, the relationships between what he *heard* in his mind's ear, and what was actually happening.

"Couldn't you have made yourself a robot or something?" he squeaked, when a lash of fire came a little too close and he realized that Terenil was *not* holding back.

"A simulacrum would not have free will, Bard," Terenil replied, dodging Eric's return volley. "It would be like fighting a mirror. Not good enough. I *do* like your evasive maneuvers, by the way. Perenor will never expect me to drop to the ground to avoid a flamestrike."

"Hey, whatever works, y'know?" Eric yelped again, as a little tongue of lightning snuck around behind him and connected with his rump—

I'm gonna charge you for these jeans, you pointy-eared creep!

He fired off a series of things like Roman-candle balls (*staccato bursts of clarinet*), none of which connected. But the attempt forced Terenil to move rather briskly, which at least was *some* comfort.

At least I'm giving him a run for his money—

Then Terenil hit him with the Big One.

A thundering D minor chord from a double orchestra—

A whirling wall of light descended on him.

And the memories momentarily deserted him.

He had *no* idea what to do, how to counter the thing—and there was no place to run from it. He *reached* in desperation, gathering everything he could find and throwing it—

A major.

The wall stopped, not two feet away from him, held there by the glowing shield he had somehow erected between himself and it.

"Enough," said Terenil, and the light vanished. Eric stumbled backward a few steps, and when he reached the wall, collapsed against it and slid down it.

He was sweating, and exhausted, and panting hard to catch his breath. It was no compensation to see that the Prince was in the same shape.

"You did very well," Terenil said, lowering himself down to the floor beside Eric. "*Very* well. Better than I had anticipated. Forgive me; I forgot that you are *not* a trained sorceror there at the end. I had not intended to use that bit of magery on you; it is far more powerful—even when muted—than I would ever have used in practice against anyone but an experienced magician."

"Oh," Eric replied, feeling somehow deflated. "That's why I sort of lost everything. So *you* stopped it?"

"Why . . . no." The Prince gave him a peculiar look. "*You* did."

Eric had hardly enough time to get his breath back before Terenil had him done up in a copy of his own scarlet-and-gold armor, facing him with sword in hand. The armor turned out to be no more uncomfortable than a set of motorcycle leathers Eric had once tried on. The sword, however, felt very strange, and very alien in his hand.

But the actual sparring proved to be easier than the stuff Terenil had been putting him through up until then. The memories he needed *here* were simpler; physical memories only. He could relax, put his mind in neutral, and let his body take over. It was kind of fun, actually—

Until it got to be work.

Then hard work.

Then *painfully* hard work.

Finally Terenil called a halt, and made the armor go away. There was a low bench at Terenil's side of the dojo; Eric sprawled on the floor with his back braced against it, head thrown back, eyes closed, getting his wind back.

I'm sweating like a horse. I don't think I've ever worked this hard before in my life.

"Here." He felt the familiar chill of a metal can in his hand, and didn't stop to wonder where it came from. Terenil had magicked it up somehow, of course—

I'm beginning to take this magic stuff for granted, like microwaves and telephones.

"Thanks," he said; fumbled for the pop-top, and took a long pull, all without opening his eyes.

Yeah. Nothing like a Coke, sometimes.

"And here." Eric opened his eyes at the tap on his arm. Terenil had done the thing with the fifty-dollar bills again; he held out two to Eric. "I will not leave with you," the Prince said. "And you will need a cab, true? Just be very careful not to spend these in the same place."

Eric took a good look at them, and realized they had exactly the same serial numbers. He raised one eyebrow at the elf.

"As I told you," Terenil said shrugging. "We cannot create, only copy."

And I bet the Treasury Department would love to talk to you about that . . .

"So," Eric said, after his second swallow. "What's with all this? Why did you suddenly decide you wanted to take Perenor on again?"

The bench creaked as Terenil settled beside him. Eric opened his eyes. The Prince looked as completely exhausted as *he* was; hair dripping sweat, the leather tunic gone, muscles trembling with a little weariness. He was slumped over, elbows on his knees, hands wrapped around his own can of soda, looking at a point on the floor between his feet.

"Because I must," the Prince replied. "You know, you came very near to defeating me, Bard. More than once. I am not what I was."

"I'm not Perenor—"

"Precisely." The Prince sighed. "If I were to meet him as I am at the moment, the result would be the same as last night. All that saved me then was Korendil's luring him away from me. If Perenor has a weakness, it is that he prefers a moving target to a defeated one."

Eric couldn't think of anything to say. Except—"But you'll still challenge him anyway?"

"I must," the Prince said simply. "For the sake of the others."

You've seen them, Eric. Lost in Dreaming—I think it's kinder to pull the plug.

Maybe not exactly Ria's words, but certainly the sense of them.

"What makes you think you can do anything for them?" he asked bluntly. "I mean, I've seen them—"

And I saw you. A real brain-dead stoner, last night . . .

Terenil winced, as if he had heard the thought. "I do not know that I can, I only know that I must try."

It was Eric's turn to wince away from the conviction in his words. He covered it by draining his cola—and as soon as he put it down, there was a second, water beading on its sides, on the bench beside him.

Yeah, so maybe he can't handle his drugs. But he's not so gone that he still can't think beyond himself. He wants to do something meaningful, even if he isn't actually capable of carrying it off. And what have you done with your life, Banyon?

Not much.

"What's with this thing between you and Perenor?" he asked.

The Prince tossed down the last of his soda and magicked himself up another can. "Hate," he said. "That is what is between us." He grimaced. "One of the two emotions that we are taught to avoid at all costs . . ."

"Huh?"

Terenil pulled damp hair behind his ear, and turned his head a little to look at Eric. "We are virtually immortal, Bard. Our lives are measured in centuries, not decades. That can be as much curse as blessing. Firstly, we are few in number. Secondly, strong emotional ties bind for *centuries*, not mere decades. Your legends call us light-minded and frivolous in our affections—but think you for a moment. Suppose you have a love that turns to dislike. But you are tied to the place where that love dwells, and there are perhaps a few hundred inhabitants of that place. Try as you will, you must see that love *every day*. For the next *thousand years*. Unless one of you finds a way to leave." He shrugged. "So do we avoid both love and hate, granting either *only* when there is no other choice."

"So, why are you and Perenor—"

"A fundamental difference in the way in which we see

you and your world, Bard. It began when we journeyed with Maddoc of Wales, knowing there was another land at the end of his sail. We left because we were being crowded by humankind. *I* thought, and the Queen, that if we could establish ourselves and put down deeper roots than those we had aforetime, we could coexist with your world. Share it, despite your use of Cold Iron."

"Sounds like a good idea to me," Eric offered tentatively.

"So it has proved, most places. It was only that here, *I* misjudged in placing the nexus. Or perhaps—" He looked up at the wall opposite himself, frowning, then shook his head. "I cannot recall. It may be that Perenor urged the placement there. He may have been working against me even then . . . Well, our Queen took a group north to establish Elfhame Misthold; I remained here with a second, smaller group, mostly of Low Court elvenkind who must be tied to physical *places*. I established Elfhame Sun-Descending. Then Perenor began showing his true motives."

"This was how long ago?" Eric asked.

"Before the Spaniards." Terenil frowned again. "Perhaps . . . ten to fourteen of your centuries. Time does not hold as much meaning for our kind."

Jesus, I guess not! Eric stared at a being who *looked* no more than forty years old, and felt a little stunned.

"So. We had found a place for a nexus; the Queen's Bard—a human, like yourself—opened it and created the anchoring point for it, and the Queen and most of the High Court had gone on up northwards. Then Perenor began spreading his poison. Why, he said, should we be subject to the vagaries of humanity? Why should we allow *their* lives to rule what *we* did? We had magic at our disposal; our lives were infinitely longer—why should *we* not rule *them*?"

Terenil took a swig from his can, and tightened his lips, angrily. "He did not mean only to rule—he meant to enslave. I could see that—and fortunately, so could most of the rest. And that was enough to keep him in his place for many years."

"God." Eric shuddered at the notion of having Perenor as "Master."

Somebody who can read your thoughts, and touch the innermost part of you . . .

"Jesus, Terenil, how the hell did you guys see through him? And—I mean, why didn't you just go along with him?"

Terenil gave him a lopsided grin. "You humans make poor slaves, Bard. Your own history should teach you that. Soon or late, you rise beneath your chains and go for your masters' throats. We had *all* seen enough of history to know that. And . . . there was still another reason. Of all the wondrous things we can do, we cannot *create*. Our 'culture,' if you will, is made up of what we have borrowed from you humans. And a slave generally is very poor at creation. After all, why should he create anything, when it is his masters that have the benefit of it, and not himself? There are deeper reasons, too, but these will suffice."

Enlightened self-interest. It never fails. Eric chuckled to himself.

"So, there was mistrust of Perenor on my part, hatred on his. Your people moved to this valley—and then it all began to fall apart for us. You moved too quickly for us to be aware of what was happening. We learned too late that you were trapping us in mazes of Cold Iron, cutting the groves off, one from another. I and those of the Lesser Court who were mages worked to find a solution—for without an Adept, which we did not number among ourselves, we could not reestablish new ties to the nexus, or move it elsewhere. I was so preoccupied with this that I did not watch Perenor. Finally I learned that he was working forbidden magic against the humans, draining them to his own use. I caught him in the act—"

Terenil stopped, wiped the back of his hand across his eyes, and finished his soda in a single gulp.

"I caught him in the act of draining a child. A child who *would* have been a Bard. I realized then that he had probably been doing this evil for as long as humans had been within his reach—and that he had destroyed our chances of moving the nexus by destroying the children who could have grown to be Bards. That is when I exiled him."

"But he didn't leave—"

"Not so. He did, for a brief while. He found a human woman who *could* have been a great magician if she had chosen to train her powers, and fathered a child upon her—yes, Bard, that *is* possible, although it requires the intervention of magic. He raised that child himself, training her in sorcery and elven magic. Human magic—it is very rare, but it is powerful. Perhaps because it is buttressed by all the potential of your brief lives . . ."

Terenil brooded down at the floor until Eric got tired of waiting for him to pick up the story again.

"Then what happened?"

"Oh. Then he returned to challenge my rule again." He discarded the can he was holding, and magicked up still another. "That was not all that long ago. I fought them for days, with young Korendil at my side. Korendil. He was—is—*my* best hope, you know. He has scarce two centuries, yet there is such wisdom and courage in him—he amazes me. Sometimes he frightens me—he is so like a human—so passionate. I have tried to warn him from passion, from caring so deeply—"

"The fight," Eric prompted.

"Oh, aye. We fought them and drove them out again, though not without cost to both worlds. I was badly exhausted. We roused things across the Barrier that were best left sleeping, and the battle itself started a fire, the one that burned out Bell Canyon." Terenil looked at him, and blinked. "Are you old enough to recall it?"

"I read about it," Eric said, half to himself.

"I thought I had banished them. I thought . . . I don't quite remember. Danann, it all fades, it all blurs . . . Then Korendil vanished, and left me the only one of the High Court still aware, with all the rest of Sun-Descending lost in Dreaming. To try further seemed . . . so futile. Perenor gone, the girl-child gone, Korendil gone. Nothing left—enemies, friends, all gone—"

Too late Eric heard the slurring of his words, the rambling. He had seen the familiar red-and-white cans they were both drinking from—but the *meaning* of those soft drinks had not occurred to him.

Caffeine. Terenil had downed at least three cans of Coke as they'd been sitting there, and was working on the fourth.

"—nothing left," the Prince murmured. He looked up as Eric got to his feet, but didn't seem to recognize him. His eyes were glazed and unfocused, his hands shaking.

"Mortals," Terenil said sadly. " 'Don't open your heart to mortals'—that's an old saw, and I told Korendil that, over and over. They die and they leave you. Leave you alone. Don't you, Bard? You always leave us, no matter what we do—"

The elf's head sank; his hand loosened and the empty can of Coke fell from it, to roll around on the floor. As Eric watched, Terenil slid from the bench to curl up in a drunk—or Dreaming—stupor on the floor.

The cab ride home was very depressing. Sunset was grayed-out by haze tonight; in fact, the whole world seemed grayed-out and lifeless. Eric had never felt so alone.

God. Maybe Ria's right, maybe it's better to pull the plug on them. Even the best of them can't stay straight for a single afternoon.

He rethought everything Ria had said, compared it to what Terenil had told him. He couldn't see any flaws in what she'd told him about *herself*, and she'd admitted that her father was doing things she didn't approve of. And yet—yet it didn't feel quite right, as if she was telling the truth, but not *all* of the truth.

I need Beth, I need Kory. I have got to talk to them.

The cab pulled up outside the tacky pink apartment building, and pulled off as soon as Eric paid the driver. He hadn't asked the cabby to wait, but he had been figuring he'd just duck into his apartment, change his shirt, grab his flute, and warn them he was coming.

He got the first two done inside of a couple minutes— but when he called Beth's apartment, all he got was her answering machine.

"Beth?" he said, when the recording ran out. "Bethie, it's Eric—are you there?"

There was no answering *click* of the phone being picked up.

He went blank for a moment, then took a deep breath and went on. "Beth, some stuff happened back at the demonstration, some pretty heavy stuff, that's why I sort of bugged out on you. Beth, I'm on my way over, I've got to talk to you and Kory real—"

Click. Dial tone.

He hung the phone up carefully, and stood there for a moment with his gig bag dangling from one hand. His mind just wasn't working; he just couldn't picture what could have happened that she wouldn't *be* there.

Oh God—what if they're in trouble, and I was out fooling around with Terenil. What if Beth didn't make it here? What if she got arrested back at the Llewellyn Building—

Strike that. Terenil said she was shielding Kory. So she took him from my place. They were together then, and I'm pretty sure she wouldn't leave him alone. Which means they're still together. In her apartment. And they're not answering the phone.

Which means what, Banyon?

He thought about them, closing his eyes the way he had when Ria had tried to . . . contact him—

He blushed at the memory. But he tried it anyway, reaching out with that *something* he'd been working with, thinking very hard about both of them. It seemed like there was a "Bethness" and a "Koryness" that were both tied into him somehow, a tiny touch, as though they were both resting a hand on his shoulders, and that he could follow that to the real people.

It worked; he started to see very vague images against the blackness of his closed eyes. But not *that* vague. Beth and Kory—together—

Anger flared and banished the images from his mind, and he could not recapture them. He struggled for a moment to calm himself down, but every time he tried, he could see them—

You've been played for a fool, Banyon. All that talk about "commitment," being a team, and the first thing Beth does when she gets Kory alone is jump into bed with him. Damn her!

His hurt and jealousy settled into a burning lump in his throat and the pit of his stomach. He clutched his flute against his chest and struggled to breath slowly.

I ought to—

No, violence never got him anything. Violence wasn't the answer.

I could be wrong. This could be my own lousy imagination. I have a dirty enough mind. I can't stop thinking about how Kory is such a hunk, how Beth must be attracted to him. That's probably all this is—just me and my overactive imagination.

He trembled with suppressed anger and with indecision. *I ought to go over there, and see for myself. I could be wrong. But if I'm right—*

The cab ride into Tarzana was accompanied by a growing rage, and an increasing sense of betrayal. He had taken long enough for a shower and a change of clothing, trying to wash some of his unhappiness and anger away. It hadn't worked, and he spent the ride in silence, his throat aching, his flute case clutched in both hands. By the time he reached Beth's apartment building, he was no longer sure of *anything*.

"You'd better wait," he told the cabby, as he passed him the change from the first of Terenil's fifties. "There's a good chance I'll need you right away."

The cab driver shrugged, pulled out an SF book, and kept the meter running.

He'd been tempted, back there in his own place, to throw the money in the trash and send the boots after.

But Terenil hadn't been the faithless one; the Prince had tried (*noblesse oblige?*) to make up for the damages that had been inflicted on Eric. *He* hadn't strung Eric along; he'd been honest with him.

"Don't open your heart to mortals."

Yeah, guess not. Don't trust them with the real truth, either.

Still, Terenil had been fair to him. So he had put the boots on and stuffed the cash in his pocket and called another cab.

He ran up the clattering wooden stairs, stairs that led up the side of the building to Beth's second-floor apartment. He was so knotted up inside it felt like he was going to have to double over any minute. He knew where to go; he'd been here before. He headed straight along the balcony until he reached the end and the last doorway. He started to pound on the door, but it swung open at his first knock.

"Eric, if that's you, I'm in the kitchen," Beth called from somewhere beyond the half-open wooden door. "If it's not, you're in trouble, whoever you are."

He froze, hand on the door handle. He really didn't *want* a confrontation.

I could go away now, and never know—never have to face what's been going on.

No. I have to know. He pushed the door open, shoving it a little harder where it caught on the carpeting.

Beth's voice floated down the hallway, past the living room, guiding him. "Eric, I'm sorry I didn't pick up the phone when you called, but we were bus—"

He stepped in through the door of the tiny yellow-painted kitchen and stood staring at her from within the frame of the door. She was standing beside the window in a T-shirt and a pair of cutoffs, her hair plastered wetly to her head, as if she had just washed it. He caught a whiff of shampoo-scent as she turned. She took one look at the expression on his face, and froze in mid-word.

He felt his mouth twitch, and shoved his hands angrily down into his pockets. *Busy? Yeah, I'll bet you were busy.*

Before he could get a single word past the hard lump choking his voice, Korendil (wearing nothing more than a towel draped negligently around his waist) strolled in through the other door—

The one leading to the bedroom.

The elf's long blond hair hung in damp, dripping ringlets, and there were beads of water on his shoulders.

Looks like he's sure made a full recovery.

Kory didn't seem aware of Eric's presence at all; he moved easily, gracefully, showing no signs of any of his injuries, and no hint of lingering weakness.

"Beth—" Kory made a caress out of the word, and leaned over, embracing her, to give her a very warm, very sensuous kiss. His mane of hair hid their faces, but Eric had no doubt that she was enjoying it. *She* had both her arms around him, returning the embrace—oblivious to Eric still standing there.

Like I don't mean a thing to her.

He started to turn to go. The gig bag knocked against the doorframe, and Kory broke off the kiss, pivoting quickly to face him, his hands coming up in a gesture of either attack or warding. Eric backed up a pace.

Korendil's wary stance relaxed when he saw who it was—but then he saw Eric's expression, and frowned in puzzlement.

"Yeah," Eric said slowly, ignoring the elf. "It looks like you *were* busy, weren't you? Too busy to even think about me."

"Eric—where were you?" Beth asked, pulling self-consciously away from Korendil. "You just vanished on me. I looked for you, I really did."

"Uh-huh." He sniffed, and swallowed, and couldn't clear the lump from his throat. "Yeah. I had to . . . I saw Perenor, Beth. He was in the building. I was scared shitless, Beth—" He blinked his burning eyes to clear them. "Why didn't you wait for me?"

"I had to move Kory before my protections wore off . . ." Her voice trailed off and she looked away from Eric.

"Sure." Eric shifted his weight uneasily, feeling as if his skin were off and all his nerves were screaming. Korendil began toweling his hair, carefully not looking at Eric.

Eric's insides knotted up. Korendil—God. A hunk by anybody's standards. *Christ, why should they give a shit about me? Beth doesn't need me—not with him around. Okay, he needs this Bardic magic crap. So he's nice to me. Big deal, he's nice to me so he can use me, just like everybody else.*

"So, what happened?" Beth asked, too casually.

"A lot," he replied. "I ran into the lady that runs the corporation. Literally. Her name was Ria. Ria Llewellyn."

Out of the corner of his eye he saw Kory stiffen at the mention of that name.

"A very nice lady, a very *blonde* lady, a very *sensible* lady. She had a lot of things to tell me. Things that made a lot of sense."

More so now than they did then.

"Eric?" Korendil said very softly. Eric wouldn't look at him.

"So, all things considered, I guess I don't need to stick around. You look like you're doing fine without me. Maybe you guys had better find yourselves another Bard, huh? Maybe a girl this time." Now he looked at the elf—or tried to. His eyes burned and blurred and he couldn't really see. "Yeah, that would be kind of nice for you, Kory. I . . . it's been real."

Eric pivoted and ran down the hall, down the stairs and out to the cab. He flung himself into the back seat, and fumbled in his pocket for the piece of paper Ria had given him.

They can find another sucker. It's time I started looking out for myself.

He rubbed the back of his hand across his burning eyes, sniffling, until he could read the address. But he couldn't— the letters and numbers wavered and he couldn't make them out properly.

And he thought he could hear someone calling his name.

"Here—" He shoved the paper and the second fifty at the driver. "Can you get me there?"

"Eric! Eric, wait!"

The driver glanced at the paper. "Hey, no problem. What about your friends?"

He gestured at the apartment building. Beth was pelting down the stairs, Kory behind her, both of them waving frantically at the cab.

"They aren't my friends," Eric said, huddled into the seat cushions, holding his flute to his chest. "Let's go."

· 14 ·

My Darling Asleep

The wind whispered through the trees, ruffling the surface of the swimming pool, rising and falling like a soft melody. Eric touched the cool metal of the flute to his lips, smiling to himself. *It is like a song, a little dancing air. Very Irish, come to think of it . . .*

But although he waited, fingers poised, no melody came to him; only a vague yearning and a sense of indefinable loss. He took the flute away from his lips, and moved his fingers restlessly and soundlessly over the flute keys as he looked out over the garden and the crystalline water of the pool.

He sat down on a marble bench near the water's edge, with the leafy fronds of a palm tree shading him from the bright Southern California sun. To his side was the sprawling expanse of Ria's house—*No, her mansion, definitely a mansion. I've never seen a place like this before. It just proves what Ria says is true, that we can accomplish so much with our magic, working together—nothing we can't do—*

But the silent flute mocked that bold statement.

So why can't I think of any new tunes? It's like there's an emptiness inside me where all the melodies used to be. I haven't been able to write a new song in days.

Eric sat up suddenly.

Days?

How long have I been here, anyhow?

He set the flute down in his lap, trying to figure it out. *I arrived here last night—no, it was two nights ago, last night we went to Maxwell's for dinner. Or was it three nights ago? It's hard to remember.*

The more he tried to remember the signposts of the passing days, the more they eluded him. *I haven't really been doing much of anything, just listening to her CD collection on that fantastic stereo upstairs, exploring the library, and—and sleeping. I don't think we've gone to, uh, sleep, anytime before 5:00 A.M. for the last few nights.*

He blushed, just thinking about it. *Ria, she's—she's really—quite amazing that way. I wonder how she manages to get through the day without falling asleep at her office? I know I couldn't live on the amount of sleep she's getting. Two hours a night? Three? Forget it. I usually need at least seven—*

An inexplicable chill crept down the back of his neck. *That's funny; now that I think about it, I seem to be sleeping more than I usually do. And still feeling tired all the time. Shit, you'd think with all the napping I've been doing, I wouldn't be feeling anything but wired.*

Hell, that doesn't matter. What matters is that tune I wanted to play, the one that keeps slipping away from me. Maybe if I just play something I know, rather than something of my own, it'll come to me by itself.

He brought the flute to his lips again, took a breath, and began to play the old Irish air, "Come to the Hills." He stopped after several bars, and looked down at the flute in consternation.

What in the hell is going on here? I sound awful. It's just . . . notes. Nothing special. Like there's no life to it, no magic. Dead.

I've never sounded like this before in my life . . .

Something more subtle than a recognizable sound distracted him. Eric glanced up, to see the sliding glass door open quietly. Ria stepped out into the garden, wearing a dark blue dress and carrying her high-heeled shoes in her hand.

She glided towards him. "Hi, handsome," she said, leaning down to kiss him. "I couldn't bear the thought of you here all by yourself, so I decided to come home for an hour or so. Want to do something interesting for lunch?"

"What did you have in mind?" he asked, standing up.

She gave him a wicked look. Eric laughed, and pulled her into his arms for a lingering kiss, flute and music totally forgotten.

Ria touched her fingertip to his lips. "Now, now. Behave yourself, love. I have to be back at the office for a one o'clock meeting. Otherwise, I know *exactly* how I'd like to spend the afternoon."

"Better be careful, beautiful," he murmured against her faintly-scented blond hair, kissing her beneath her right ear. "Or you'll wear me out."

She pulled away from him suddenly. "Don't say that, Eric."

Say what? Why is she looking at me like that?

Ria took his hand in hers, her expression changing so quickly he couldn't be sure he'd seen what he *thought* he'd seen. "I was thinking of something else. My father is inside the house. I wanted to know if you'll join us for lunch or not."

"Hey, why not?" He picked up the flute lying on the marble bench. "Let's do lunch with Daddy."

Ria watched her father with veiled suspicion, as Perenor speared a piece of pineapple with his fork, and slowly raised it to his lips. His eyes never left Eric, who was busily sawing the last of the meat off a chicken thigh.

"Delicious, Ria," the older man said, coolly. "I always knew you were talented—a brilliant businesswoman, a gifted Adept; it seems you make an excellent pineapple chicken as well. What more could a man ask for in a daughter?"

I'm sure you could think of something, Father dear. Like a daughter who wouldn't prefer to see her pet Bard carving out your tripes instead of a piece of chicken? "I'm glad you approve, Father. You know how much I enjoy having you visit here."

Eric glanced up, as if hearing something other than the

spoken conversation, then smiled hesitantly. "I like the chicken too, Ria. I didn't know you could cook this well."

She smiled back at him, the adoring look in his dark eyes warming her even from across the table. "Thank you, love."

He bit hungrily into a piece of chicken. "Though I can't figure out when you had the time to cook this. I mean, you've been at the office all day, and I know you didn't do this last night—"

"Don't worry about that, Eric." Ria refilled the wine glasses, then sipped hers thoughtfully. *I still haven't spotted the reason why Father wanted to come over today. He said he was curious about Eric, but it has to be something more than that. If he wants something from me, I'm sure he'll tip his hand soon enough—*

Her eyes narrowed, as she noted the intent way Perenor scrutinized Eric. *I know what he's thinking. But if he so much as touches Eric, I'll Challenge him, right here on the spot. And in my home, I hold the distinct advantage, especially now . . .*

Perenor pushed his plate away from him. "Truly excellent, Ria. I should come by here for meals more often."

"That would be nice, Father," she replied lightly. *Next time, maybe I'll serve some steak with amanita mushroom sauce—or roast beef with aconite instead of horseradish.*

Eric rose and began gathering several dishes in his hands. "I'll just run these into the kitchen—"

She gestured for him to sit down again. "Oh, Eric, leave it be. The servants will take care of it."

"No, it's all right, I don't mind." He balanced several glasses precariously on a plate, then carefully moved toward the kitchen.

Perenor glanced at her speculatively as Eric disappeared through the doorway. "You're doing quite well with him, Ria. I'm impressed."

She leaned back in her chair, giving him a patently false smile. "Why, thank you, Father. I'm rather pleased with how things are going, myself."

He chuckled. "I am, too. What are your plans now?"

"Now, as in the rest of the afternoon, or the indefinite

future?" She drained the last of her wine glass, watching him over the edge of the crystal.

"You know what I mean."

She shrugged. "Business as usual, I suppose. Why do you ask?"

What exactly do you want from me, Father?

"It's just—I was thinking of taking a little vacation, now that everything else is . . . taken care of. A visit to the High Court at Misthold. I was wondering if you and your . . . consort might want to join me."

Curiouser and curiouser. Just what are you planning, Father? "Sounds like it might be fun. We haven't been to Court in years. Is there any particular reason why you want to go now?"

Perenor's eyes were distant, as if looking at something only he could see. "Now that everything is under control here, I thought I might—"

So that's the game you're playing this time, Father! I should've guessed—

"No." Her voice was sharp and icy. "Absolutely not. If you want to do a power play in the High Court, you're doing it without my help, or Eric's. I'm not risking everything I have just so you can amuse yourself."

He stood up angrily. "You don't understand, Ria. It's the only thing that matters to me. *You* have influence and power over the mortals—that's all very well, but it's meaningless. They're nothing but pawns. It's only winning over those with *power* that matters."

She firmed her chin stubbornly. "I told you no, Father. I mean it. I helped you with the Faire purchase because there was something for *me* to gain. I have no interest in the High Court, or my full-blooded elven cousins. You can pursue this on your own, if you're determined to do it. I won't risk myself or Eric."

"It's not *your* help that I need," Perenor said quietly, but with implicit threat. "Just your pet Bard. I don't need your help, or your permission . . ."

Oh, really?

She called a small amount of Power, and raised a careful shield; not quite a Challenge, but something to let him know she wasn't to be trifled with. "I won't let you use Eric. Not for this, or *anything*. He's mine." She calmly met his furious gaze, the first hot tendrils of Power writhing around her hands, clenched beneath the table. *Push me any further, Father, and we'll see what happens next—*

"I found some cookies—" Eric stopped dead in the doorway, a plate of cookies forgotten in his hands, staring at Perenor and his daughter. She registered his presence, then dismissed him, ignoring the Bard for the moment, keeping her senses trained on her father.

There was a moment of tense expectation. Ria's eyes held Perenor's, unwavering, waiting. *The instant I sense him drawing Power, I'll strike. He must know that. If he does—*

Perenor's lips curved slightly, a tiny smile, and he bowed ironically to his daughter. "Not now, daughter," he said lightly, then walked to Eric and took a cookie from the plate. "We'll have to continue this discussion at a later date, Ria," he added. "I need to take care of some business. May I borrow some tapes from your video library, my dear?"

"Of course, Father," she said. Her eyes never left him as he walked to the stairway. *Every day, it seems, we come closer and closer to a final confrontation. But, somehow, we avoid it each time. What is going to happen when we can't avoid it any longer?*

I wish I knew what was going on here. Eric set the dirty plates down on the counter and wiped his hands on a nearby dish towel. *For father and daughter, those two argue a lot. Not that I blame Ria, her dad is kinda opinionated. I've never felt quite comfortable around him, either. Something just makes me feel—oh, I don't know— like I don't want to be near him any more than I have to—*

Something nagged at the edge of his memory. Something . . . important. Something he couldn't quite recapture. *Green eyes, like Perenor's— looking up at me with such pain—and blood on my hands, blood on silvery blond hair, on the carpeting—*

He dismissed the image. *That's ridiculous. Must be*

*from one of Ria's videos. I don't know anybody with
silver-blond hair.*

He spent several minutes trying to figure out how to
start the dishwasher, then gave it up as hopeless. *The
servants will take care of it, like Ria said.*

Servants? That was odd. There wasn't anyone here in
the kitchen. *And—I've never see any of them. Not a single
person in this house other than Ria and me. But the house
is always immaculate, spotless; the gardens well-tended,
everything in terrific shape. I wonder if they work late at
night or something? Maybe when we're already in bed.*

That's just one of so many things that I don't understand—

He wiped the counter clean with a sponge, then turned,
hearing a sound behind him.

Perenor stood watching him from the kitchen doorway,
several videocassettes held negligently in one hand. The
older man smiled. "And how are you doing these days,
boy?"

"Just fine," Eric said, his throat strangely dry. "Where's
Ria?"

"Oh, she's already on her way back to the office," Perenor
replied. "I just wanted to talk to you for a few minutes
before I leave, too."

"Uh, sure," Eric nodded. *What is it about this man that
makes me feel like I want to run away, as fast and as far
as I can?*

Perenor walked several steps closer. "We've never really had a chance to talk, you and I. That's a pity—I'd like
to get to know you better."

"Ria—Ria's told me a lot about you." *A lot that I wouldn't
repeat in polite company. She sure doesn't like you very
much, even if you are her father.*

"I'm sure she has," Perenor said, his voice sounding
amused. His eyes met Eric's, brilliant green. "Now, let's—"

*—green eyes, like ice, deep pools of emerald nothing-
ness. Everything fading, disappearing into that void; falling in, consumed, ashes and dying flames.*

He was having trouble breathing—seeing—hearing—

*And music, a strange warped polyphonic sound, rising
up around him. It set claws into him, dragging him in,*

*touching where no one should touch. He could feel it
dismembering him, pulling away pieces in its claws, pieces
of himself. He was losing himself, falling; feeling everything whirling away into nothingness—*

No! Let me go!

*Everything being wrenched out of him, everything he
cared about, everything he loved—*

Eric reacted instinctively, drawing upon a half-forgotten
memory.

*A clear burst of chord, a strident A major thrown up
like a shieldwall, shoving the hungry void away from him;
a flash of light and sound, illuminating the shadows.*

*The warped music shattered into a thousand notes, fall-
ing away into silence.*

He leaned against the counter, panting, his heart
pounding.

Oh God—oh God, what was that?

He blinked several times, completely disoriented; the
room was blurring around him, everything hazy, things
melting into each other.

When he could see again, Perenor was standing very
close to him, but the elf-lord's eyes were wide with astonishment and disbelief. His hand, with its elegantly mani-
cured fingernails, still rested intimately on Eric's shoulder.

He took a deep breath, then another. "Don't—don't
touch me," Eric said unsteadily, shoving Perenor's hand
away from him. *"Don't touch me."*

Perenor stared at him, not speaking. Then he turned,
and strode away. A moment later Eric heard the front
door slamming shut behind him.

Eric collapsed against the counter, trying not to shake.
*God, what's happening to me? I feel like everything is
falling to pieces around me. Nothing to hold on to, nothing
I can understand.*

He staggered into the living room, and sank down onto
the plush couch. *I'm losing it. I'm really losing it. I'm so
tired, it's all so crazy. Nothing makes sense anymore.*

Eric stretched out, closing his eyes, the velvet of the
couch soft against his cheek. *It's easier not to try to think,*

*not to worry about anything. Just let everything drift—
just fall asleep, and it'll all be gone when I wake up—*

*—busking in a New York subway, trying to ignore the
rancid reek of stale urine from the restroom across the
tunnel, looking down at the handful of coins in his flute
case. Sag of despair.*

No, that's not even enough to pay for another night at
the Y, much less a meal and a bunk.

*Out of the echoing tunnel, that hateful, unforgettable
voice, loud above the dull roar of the crowd.*

"Well, if it isn't Loony Banyon—"

*Looking up. That face. Those greedy eyes. Chuck Mar-
quand, the second-best flautist at Juilliard. Looking at
him, and smiling; a smug, self-satisfied smirk.*

"It's been a while, Eric." *A laugh; a braying, trium-
phant laugh.* "You know, you look like hell."

*Eyes that raked over his clothing: the dirty jeans, layers
of plaid flannel shirts against the cold.*

"Poor old Loony. Here. Let me help you out." *He reaches
into the pocket of his thigh-length leather jacket, fishes out
a bill. Drops it in the case.* "For old time's sake, Banyon."

I should take that money and stuff it down his arrogant
throat.

*But it's a twenty, lying there among the dimes and
quarters.*

*He can't reach down to pick it up. He can't move.
Instead, he starts playing again, a fast version of a Mozart
sonata.*

Chuck laughs and walks away.

*The notes fly faster and faster, until the music and the
subway are one blur, invisible behind the veil of tears,
inaudible over the clanging noise of the trains and the
laughter of the pedestrians.*

Twenty dollars means a place to stay for the night. A
hot dinner. A bus ticket that'll get me out of this miserable
city.

I should've rammed it past his teeth.

Oh God, what have I turned into?

Choking on sobs, gasping, the flute sliding from his

hands, that damned twenty burning a hole in his flute case.

Crying . . .

"Eric? Are you all right?"

He opened his eyes. Ria was standing over him, a concerned frown on her beautiful face. Eric sat up slowly, his head aching.

From clenching my teeth in my sleep, yeah.

"I'm—I'm fine."

"No, you're not. You were having a nightmare, weren't you?"

He nodded hesitantly.

She sat beside him, and touched his shoulder gently. "Talk to me, Eric. Tell me about it."

No. No, you wouldn't understand—

"Yes, I would," she said, very softly, and moved over closer on couch next to him. "Eric, I care about you, a lot. If something or someone has hurt you, I want to know."

She does. She cares, I know that. It's just—I can't talk about that, not to her, not to anybody—

:Eric. Please. Talk to me.:

Okay. Okay. I will.

"It was years ago, Ria." He buried his face in his hands. "Not long after I quit Juilliard. I was busking from city to city, barely making enough to live. I was busking the subway. It was November, and cold. I looked up, and there he was. Chuck Marquand, who was second chair back in the orchestra—standing there in his fancy suit, his leather coat, laughing at me. And then—shit, he'd always hated me, I don't know why—he . . . he gave me—" He felt the tears beginning to trickle through his clenched fingers. "He gave me money, and—God, I've never hated myself so much in all my life—I took it, I needed the money so badly—"

He rubbed his eyes fiercely with his knuckles, looked up at her, and managed a wan smile. "Hell, I can't believe a dream is affecting me like this."

She didn't answer; she only looked at him with those wide blue eyes, bright with tears.

"It was one of the most awful times of my life," he continued, after a long silence. "I was starving, but I wouldn't go back to my parents, and I couldn't get even a McDonald's job. And then Chuck, humiliating me like that—I wanted to die, I just wanted to crawl away and die—"

"I—I know how that feels," Ria said, very quietly. "All those times when I was a child, when we would go to the High Court and my father would talk about me like I wasn't even there. His half-blooded daughter, not a *real* elf. The little mongrel. How useful I would be, when I grew into my Power. That was all he cared about, that he'd have a half-human sorceress to use in his little games."

"Ria—"

She's crying. I've never seen her cry before.

As if hearing his thoughts, she dashed away her tears angrily with one hand. "It's all in the past, Eric. You're never going to have to busk on a streetcorner again, ever. And my father—he knows he can't use me now. I won't let him."

"It's not in the past, if it still bothers you," Eric said slowly. "Like that rat, Chuck Marquand. I can't forget him. You can't forget what your father did to you."

When Ria spoke again, her voice was remote, distant. "You know, I used to be scared, when I was a kid, that I'd grow up and be just like him. That I'd enjoy hurting people—" She glanced at him, tears trickling unnoticed down her face. "I don't. I don't like hurting people. But sometimes you don't have any choice—"

"Hey, you've never hurt me," Eric said, carefully brushing the tears from her cheeks, his own tears forgotten. "You've never been anything but wonderful to me, more than I could ever imagine. Even if you do look like a raccoon right now, with all of your makeup dripping down your face."

She hugged him tightly. "Oh Eric. I don't know how I lived before I met you." She smiled, despite the tears. "I'll never hurt you, Eric. I promise, whatever happens, I won't hurt you. I just—I just hope you'll understand someday—why I do what I do. And—and that you'll never leave me."

"I'll won't leave you Ria," he whispered. "I love you."

Eric turned the page; trying to read his novel, but unable to concentrate. *It's like I've forgotten something, and it's nagging at the back of my mind. Something, can't remember what it is—*

:Bard! Bard, can you hear me? Eric?:

He looked across the room to where Ria was seated at her desk, poring over a set of contracts, a pair of wire-rimmed reading glasses delicately perched on her nose.

"Ria?"

She glanced up and smiled. "Yes, love?"

Eric shook his head, slightly bewildered. "—Uh, it's nothing. Sorry I disturbed you." *I could've sworn somebody was talking to me, calling my name—*

He opened the book again, and took another slow sip of Scotch from his glass.

Then an image came to his mind: the moon shining clearly down on the lonely hills, the chitter of crickets, the night air cold and crisp in his lungs, with the faintest scent of the ocean. A perfect night for a walk—

A walk—yeah, that would be nice. I love walking through this neighborhood, all the huge houses, fancy cars in the driveways. That's a terrific idea. I should've thought of it earlier.

He set the book down, finishing the last of the Scotch. "Ria, would you like to go for a walk outside?"

"Not tonight. I have to finish these contracts for tomorrow. But you should go out, if you want to."

"Okay." He stood up, stretching slowly. "I'll be back in a bit."

He left the library, and detoured to the bedroom for his jacket before heading downstairs. *It'll be nice to get outside. I've been spending too much time indoors, the last couple days.*

Eric unlocked the front door, then stopped, just as he was about to step outside.

*There's someone out there. I can't see them, but I know
it—somebody hiding in the shadows.*

Then a figure moved into the pool of light beneath the
driveway lights. A smallish young woman with black hair
cut very short and punk. She just stood there for a long
moment, looking at him.

Like she knows me—

He blinked, then smiled, remembering. *Oh, right, that's
Beth Kentraine. We used to play gigs together, do shows
at Faire, that kind of stuff. I wonder what she's doing here
in Bel Air?*

And then he saw someone standing next to her, a hag-
gard young man with wild blond hair that curled over his
shoulders. *That's funny. He looks familiar, too. That cloak
he's wearing—I've seen that before, too. Kinda like my
boots, in a way.*

"Eric—" Beth said. Her voice cracked. "Eric, what's
happened to you?"

He just looked at her, unable to understand her. "I
don't know what—"

"You don't know?" She walked closer, and he could see
the tear-tracks down her cheeks. *"We* didn't know what
happened to you, whether you were alive or dead. You
abandoned us, Eric. Why didn't you come back?"

Abandoned her? Say what?

"We were worried about you, Eric," the man said,
stepping closer. Eric could see the tips of pointed ears
showing through that mop of hair. *So he's an elf, like
Perenor. Jeez, that's weird—why is Beth Kentraine hanging out with an elf?*

"Look," he said, trying to be patient. "Beth, I don't
know what you're talking about. I haven't even *seen* you
since that last Faire show. And I'm sorry that I missed
the gig at the Dive, but I never promised you I'd show
up—"

She stared at him, her hands curling into fists.

*Whatever shit she's on, I hope I never get talked into
trying it!*

"Beth, take it easy," he said soothingly. "It's okay. I'm

alive, obviously, and I'm doing fine. If that's all you came
here to find out, then I think—"

"No Bard—you do *not* think. You are not thinking at
all," the young man said quietly. "You are caught in your
own kind of Dreaming, and you went into it willingly."

He glared at the interloper.

Just who in the hell do these two think they are?

"Listen, Beth, it's nice to see you and all, but I'm a busy
guy, y'know?" He turned, and glared aggressively at the
strange elf. "And you, mister, I don't even know who you
are, where do you get off talking to me like that?"

They just stared at him. *Like they're seeing a ghost. Or
something that isn't real. What's going on here? Who is
this guy, anyhow?*

"Eric?"

He looked back to see Ria standing in the hallway
directly behind him. 'Yeah, Ria?"

"Who're you talking to?" She walked closer, resting her
hand on his shoulder.

Then she glanced past him, and her eyes narrowed
dangerously.

And he heard something—something deep inside his
mind. In Ria's voice. :*Well, well. Uninvited visitors. I
should've guessed— Korendil and the little witch, both
here to take Eric away from me. Or did he call you here?
Well, that doesn't matter right now—:*

Ria raised one clenched fist, her mouth set in a furious
line, eyes burning with anger.

*Music, a minor descant, starting from absolute silence
and building to a thunderous roar in the space of a single
heartbeat . . .*

The blond elf reacted instantly, grabbing Beth by the
wrist. Before Eric could blink, they vanished, both of
them, as though they had never been there at all.

What in the—

Eric turned back to Ria, and was startled by the venomous look in her eyes. He fumbled for something to say.
"Ria, I don't know what you're thinking, but . . ."

Her voice was icy. "I know exactly what you were

doing, Eric. Don't bother lying to me. I should never have trusted you."

"But I didn't—"

"The first time I turn my back, there you are, consorting with my enemies! I should have guessed you would do something like this, you traitorous bastard! *Damn* you, Eric Banyon!"

She stalked away from him. After a moment, he hurried after her. In the hallway he caught up to her, taking her by the shoulder and turning her towards him. "But Ria, I didn't *do* anything!"

The look in her eyes stopped him in his tracks.

:Traitor. Deceiver. Snake. I bring you into my life, give you everything you could ever want, and this *is how you repay me? I want to throw you to the sharks, drop you out of an airplane at thirty thousand feet, use your guts for clothesline.* Nobody *plays me for a fool, Eric.:*

He backed away from her, into the dining room.

You know, I think she's really mad at me—I'd better do something quick to calm her down—

Before he could speak, the porcelain vase on the table exploded into shards, right before his eyes; closely followed by the table itself, which splintered and burst into silver and red flames.

Maybe it's too late for that—

He backed towards the kitchen, unable to look away from the fury in her eyes, even as the house fire alarm began to wail shrilly.

"Now, Ria, don't do anything hasty . . ."

"Oh, don't worry about that Eric." She gave him a smile that chilled his blood. "I intend to take my *time* with this."

Amidst the roar of flames and the noise of the fire alarm, Eric heard a faint melody, gathering strength and speed with every split second—

Oh SHIT!

He dived to the floor, just as the entire contents of the china cabinet assaulted him from above. Dozens of dishes shattered around him, jagged shards drawing blood from his face and hands. Eric rolled to his feet, sliding through the doorway onto the linoleum floor of the kitchen—

—where every appliance was whirring at high speed. Eric didn't stop to look; he continued his home-run slide toward the living room, bouncing down the three steps and landing in a heap on the ornate Persian rug.

Oh God—she's trying to kill *me!*

He had time for a brief thought—*this can't be happening to me*—before the rug attacked him.

Eric screamed hoarsely as it wrapped around him. He struggled to free himself, feeling the thick rug pressing tighter and tighter against his face, choking him; then he pulled free and kicked the rug away from him, gasping for breath.

Eric glanced back to see Ria, standing in the doorway. "Was this what you were planning all along?" she hissed. "To worm your way into my confidence, then use everything against me?"

"Ria," he gasped, "I don't—you don't—"

"I'll teach you what happens to people who double-cross me, you bastard!" She slammed her hand down, the sound barely audible above the raging cacophony in the house.

Pain hit Eric like a fist, doubling him over, making it impossible to breathe, impossible to do anything.

Music, disharmonic chords, tearing at me—have to stop it, stop her, break free, get away—

HELP ME!

He *reached*— and touched something. Something dark. Something deadly. It wanted to come to him—and he opened a door to it.

The pain vanished instantly, as a darkness moved into the shadows of the room, itself a shadow, gliding from nightmare into reality. He took it all in instantly: the sudden stillness, as though the entire world had stopped moving for a moment; the creature, gaining substance and strength with every moment that passed. The ghost-hands reaching toward Ria, and the look of absolute terror in her eyes.

And he realized that *he* had called this thing—and it wanted Ria.

It's going to—No! Not—not her! Leave her alone!

The creature turned sightless eyes toward Eric, and

suddenly he could feel its not-thoughts, inside him, one with his pulse. Hunger and need, hunger and need, and aching emptiness—

No. Not her, and not me. Go away!

He pushed at it, at the thin fabric of chords that *was* the creature, and felt it unraveling beneath his touch, dissolving into nothingness. When it was gone, he looked up at Ria.

She was still standing in the doorway, clutching onto the door jamb, visibly trembling.

"Ria? Ria, are you okay?"

She shook her head once, not looking at him.

She—she doesn't look like she wants to kill me anymore. That's something, at least.

Eric stood up painfully. His flute case was still on the living room table; he picked it up slowly. He walked past Ria standing silently in the doorway, and out the front door. Outside, the cold air seemed to slap him in the face, a sober awakening.

What now?

I don't have money for a taxi, and I'm sure the buses don't run in this neighborhood.

Eric looked back at the house, wondering if Ria would try to stop him. Plead with him not to leave, maybe. He waited a moment, then sighed.

Not likely, Eric, not after that last bit of fireworks. I think I really scared her.

I sure know that I scared me.

Damn. Helluva way to break up with a lady.

He glanced at the lightless hills around him, and began trudging down the long driveway.

I guess I'm walking home tonight.

· 15 ·

Tamlin's Reel

Well, maybe this wasn't the best route for getting to the Sepulveda Freeway—

Eric looked around at the shadowed hills rising around him, the darkened landscape with only a hint of the moon peering through the clouds for illumination. *I don't think I'm lost. I mean, I kinda know where I am. Somewhere between Bel Air and the San Fernando Valley—*

He snorted. *Yeah. That's most of Southern California. Face it, Eric, you're lost.*

Eric kicked at a rock, and squinted at the sky. *Might as well keep walking. Sooner or later I'll have to hit a street, or a housing tract. The Hollywood Hills don't go on forever, after all.*

But I must be the only guy in the world who's stupid enough to try and hike over them at midnight—

He walked carefully down a dry stream bed, sidestepping the rocks, the wild growths of shrubbery and trees. *A sprained ankle, that's just what I need to make this night the epitome of stupidity.*

He followed the stream bed up the next incline, stewing at himself, and staggered as a wave of disorientation hit him, a feeling like—like everything had been wavering out of focus, and now was back in again. *Yeah, I sure wasn't thinking, when I started on this little hike. Or using my brain earlier tonight, either. That—that thing that I called, when I thought Ria was going to kill me—that could've munched both Ria and me, then gone off to eat the rest*

245

of Bel Air for dessert. Real bright, Eric. I'm just glad Beth and Korendil were far away when I did that cute stunt.

He sighed, and stumbled over an unseen rock. *They're probably real ticked at me, anyhow. I sure didn't give them a warm reception when they showed up.*

I didn't give them much of a reception at all—

He slogged through another stretch of scrub oak, using his flute case to push the low branches out of his way. *I'll call Beth when I get home, and apologize. I don't know what I was doing, treating them like that. They probably think I was stoned off my ass or something, don't know what.*

Or something—

He fought off another sudden wave of dizziness. *That was really strange, how I didn't recognize Kory at first. Must've been the bad light outside. It's like, I was just thinking about that whole little incident just now, and I remembered that it was Kory standing there with Beth. Too weird for words, Eric.*

The scrub oak caught at him, clawed at him. He barely noticed. *Hell, it's been a weird few days, since that scene at Beth's, Tuesday night. I guess it's none of my business who she sleeps with. It's just that, well, it hurt. But then again, I guess I hurt them by running off like I did. And, whatever else is happening between all of us, they're my friends, so they were worried when I didn't surface after a day or two. Good friends, those two. I wonder how they tracked me down so quickly?*

He sighed, glancing up at the pale aurora glow of moon through the clouds. *Must be way past midnight by now. I've been walking for ages, or at least that's how it feels. Damn it, I knew I should've just walked down through the streets, instead of trying to shorten the hike by going through the hills.* Stupid, *Eric.*

A lone owl hooted somewhere off to the side. If he hadn't been so stupid, maybe he could be curled up next to Ria, without a care in the world. *I wonder what Ria's doing right now, back at the house? Is she worrying about me, like Beth and Kory were worried, or is she glad that I'm out of her life?*

Things had been so good with Ria until this evening. *She's—she's really something. But I don't know if I love her or not. There don't seem to be any real connections between us—*

Connections. Ties. Commitments. He'd never wanted them before—and Ria had offered him a life without them. But somehow *now* that seemed an awfully empty way to live.

The way I feel about her—it's not the same way that I feel about Bethie, or—or about Kory, I guess. I do care a lot about those two, it's a little like being really good friends, but more so. Like . . . family. Like we all belong together. *Even with Beth, now that we've well, spent a night together. And Kory—God, but I still don't know what to think about him! But it's not this kind of, uh, fiery emotional stuff that I felt with Ria. Like everything was intense—*

Too intense. Unnaturally so. And the, the sex, too, that was something. But . . . too much, somehow. That was very strange— Ria's very strange, that way.

He shook his head, then cursed under his breath as his hair caught on a branch. Wincing, he tugged it free. *I don't know what to think about that lady, or the last few days. Bizarre. I only walked out a couple hours ago, but already all of it feels so unreal. Like it wasn't really me, it happened to somebody else.*

As if it all was just a dream—

The more he tried to focus on it, the more unreal it seemed. *Maybe it* was *a dream. It sure feels that way. Like I've been completely asleep for the last couple days—*

A pair of clouded jade eyes gazed at him sardonically from memory. *Oh, shit. Maybe I* was *asleep. I know Perenor can play games with people's minds, like what he did to me on the bus—what if Ria was doing the same thing to me? She's one helluva good sorceress, I learned that for a fact. Yeah, that was almost the last fact I ever learned, that's for sure.*

And maybe that's why it's so hard to remember what

I've been doing for the last few days, why it was so hard to think when I was in her house.

A memory of blue eyes interposed itself over the green. Blue eyes, wet with tears. *But she said she loved me—*

Yeah, well, different people show love in different ways. Maybe she didn't realize what she was doing to me. Or maybe she did, but she thought she was doing the best thing for me. I don't know.

He felt as if his mind was going in circles. *No wonder Kory and Beth were so pissed at me, when they saw me at her house. They probably figured it out right away: Eric following Ria around like a lapdog, tongue hanging out, without an original thought in his useless brain. Jesus. I have been acting real brainless lately, haven't I?*

Stupidity runs rampant in the life of Eric Banyon . . .

He swallowed hard. It seemed like all he was doing lately was messing things up. *Well, I hope Beth and Kory will forgive me. I'll definitely call them as soon as I get home.*

A sudden thought made him stop dead in his tracks. *Hey . . . maybe I don't have to wait till then. I'm a Bard, I'm supposed to be able to do all of this magical stuff. The only times anything magical has ever happened, it's been an accident, when I wasn't trying to do anything. Maybe I can do something deliberately, for a change. Intelligently. Use this weird Gift of mine to get in touch with Kory and Beth.*

He had stopped on the edge of a small valley, a tiny ravine with a grove of stunted oak trees visible below him. Eric concentrated hard, thinking of Beth: the sound of her voice, her laughter, the way she looked at him that night on the living room couch. *Trying to reach out to her—* :*Hey, Beth, pick up the phone. It's me, Eric, your crazy Bardic friend, calling you on the Ma Bell cellular brainwave line—come on, Beth, talk to me—:*

Someone else spoke, a low, breathy voice, a whisper in the silent recesses of his mind: :*Who speaks in my dreams? Who awakens me from my slumber?:*

Eric looked around, bewildered. *Excuse me?*

:*Who is it who walks silently through these hills, and*

*calls to one who is far away? Who are you, intruder into
my endless night?:*

He sighed. *Well, this is no weirder than anything else
that's happened to me lately.* Eric carefully constructed a
reply, sending it out blindly to the unseen speaker. *:Yeah,
hi. My name is Eric Banyon. Sorry, I didn't mean to wake
you up, I'm just passing through the neighborhood.:*

:What are you?:

What? Eric looked around in surprise. *What am I?
That's one helluva question.*

He thought about it for a moment before answering.
*:Well, I'm human, of course. And a Bard—at least, every-
one keeps telling me I am. Who are you?:*

The reply came not in words, but in the rustle of leathery wings, high above the valley, spreading to block out
the moon and the stars. *:This is what I am.:*

Eric looked at the monstrous *thing* looming above him,
tattered wings beating soundlessly against the sky, and
gulped.

*Oh shit—I didn't need this, not tonight, not after every-
thing else that's happened—*

The blind moon eyes, pale white, turned towards him.
:You are a Bard, human?:

:Well, yeah,: Eric thought back at it, trying to keep his
mouth closed as he looked up at the bulk of the creature
effortlessly aloft in the air above him, its sinuous neck
craning down towards him.

*I've never seen anything like this guy before, not even in
my worst nightmares—I don't know if I should run like
hell, ask him if he likes to play canasta, or what! What do
you do with somebody who's a hundred feet long, aside
from anything he wants?*

:Good. I am hungry.:

Eric blinked once. Shock and sudden fear coursed through
him as the creature's words registered. *Uh oh—I don't
think he's talking about doing margaritas together at Que
Pasa, here—*

The creature suddenly plummeted toward the ground,
toward him, falling from the sky like a stooping hawk. Eric

didn't stop to think, he just ran; right down toward the only cover in sight: the grove of twisted trees below.

A whisper of foul stench slid past him, a hiss of breath and wings passing directly overhead; then the sound of claws, tearing through the rock where he had stood, until the stones screamed in agony.

Eric dived into the scanty cover of the trees, feeling a strange tingle over his hands as he grabbed on to an aged oak and cowered behind it. *This—this is an Elf Grove, like the place at Fairesite. I can feel the magic, feel the life in the trees themselves. But there's no elves here—* He tried to catch his breath, looking around unsteadily.

:No, there are not,: the oily voice murmured. *:Lord Perenor summoned me here to despoil this Grove, and I have long since devoured the last of the Old Blood that resided here. But I am yet fortunate, for now you have arrived, a young Bard—:*

:Hey, can't we talk about this?: Eric protested, glancing up through the leafy branches at the creature, now hovering a hundred feet above him. *:I mean, I'm not really much of a meal for you. Kinda lean and stringy, y'know? Wouldn't you rather munch out on a horse from the Equestrian Center or something?:*

:I am not interested in simple meat, Bard. I prefer the taste of one with Power, such as the Old Blood. Such as yourself.:

Oh, terrific, Eric thought crazily. *Of all the monsters I could've run into, I get the guy with the gourmet palate, a connoisseur.* He tried again, a different tack. *:Look, you really don't want to do this. I mean, I'm going to put up a fight. It'd be a lot easier just to call it quits, right?:*

He looked up as the huge creature soared past overhead, and ducked back into the shelter of the tree as several droplets of something foul and indefinable sizzled down through the leaves beside him.

:Why should you fight me, Bard? Why should you fight at all?: The voice in his mind was icy, mocking.

:I know you, young Bard. I can see who you are, reflected in the light of your own Power. You have always drifted, letting the winds of Fate direct your life, letting

others make your decisions for you. You have never cared about anything—now, you do not care enough to run from me, do you? You do not care about anything at all, even your own life . . . do you?:

Eric leaned back against the gnarled trunk of the tree, breathing hard. *It's—it's doing something to my mind—it's so hard to think straight—confused—*

:Come out of the Grove, Bard, where I can see you, away from the shrouding wisps of dying Elf-magic. Let me control your life, let me take away the necessity of decisions, the painful choices. All you have to do is step away from the trees . . . :

Eric shook his head slowly, waves of despair and desolation washing over him. *Yes—I should—I should just let everything go. It doesn't matter, I don't matter—I'm never going to do anything meaningful, anything that's going to make a difference. I might as well just let it all go—*

:Yes,: the voice whispered. *:Yes. Abandon all the pain that is your life, let the dark oblivion wash it away. Come to me now, Bard.:*

:Yes—yes, I will—:

Eric began walking toward the edge of the grove, the moonlit hillside beyond. In his mind he could sense a dark exultation, and a dreadful, anticipating hunger.

Then an image flitted across Eric's mind, of Beth Kentraine standing on the driveway, tears wet on her cheeks. "You abandoned us, Eric . . ."

He stopped, one hand resting on a low-hanging branch. "Beth—"

:Come to me, Bard, come to me now—:

Anger raced through him like an electric charge, erasing the haze that the creature's spell had cast upon him. *:Yeah, that's what you want, isn't it? Eric the Bard, your little midnight snack strolling right down your throat? Well, let's try it the other way—how 'bout me having some Cajun-style blackened monster for a change?:* He leaped back into the sheltering trees, just as he felt *and* heard the creature's roar of hatred and frustration.

Then the grove exploded into flames around him.

Holy shit!

Eric rolled to the ground, trying to beat the fire off his jacket. *Oh God—I'm going to fry in here if I don't do something quick—* Gasping for breath, he fumbled desperately with the clasps of his flute case.

He shoved the pieces of the flute together, then glanced up through the burning branches, just in time to see the winged form arcing down toward the grove for another pass.

But the creature *landed* instead, crashing through the flaming trees. The huge clawed hands, the tentacled mouth dripping slime, all blindly lashing about, searching for the Bard.

Who was sprawled in the smoldering leaves, less than twenty feet away.

Oh God—oh God—it's trashing the Grove, trying to find me. If I run, it'll zero in on me in a few seconds. There isn't anything else I can hide behind. And if I stay here . . .

Eric brought the flute to his lips, and played for all he was worth.

"Banish Misfortune." Oh, God, please, if there's any resident deity around here, get me out of this!

The first notes were inaudible against the screaming fury of the monster, the trees shattering in its wake, and the crackling of the raging flames. Then the descanting melody broke through, stilling all to silence; even the crackling fire dimmed down to mere flickers of flame.

It's—it's working, something's happening—

He clambered to his feet, still playing the Irish tune, and moved toward the crouching monster. The pale moon eyes were turned toward him, transfixed.

I'm holding it, somehow. Now what can I do with it?

If I let it go, it'll kill me, just like it killed the elves, and probably every hiker and jogger that's been through these hills in the last few months. I guess—I guess I have to kill it. Now, while I'm holding it trapped.

A memory: he and Prince Terenil in the dojo, and lightning scorching down, barely missing him.

That wouldn't have killed me, though it sure would've

*been worse than sticking my finger in a light socket. If I
do that, but with everything I've got behind it—*

I'm sorry. I wish I didn't have to do this.

He raised his hands, and called the lightning.

Scream of tortured violins. The sizzling roar shook the
ground around him, followed by a reek of stinging ozone.
For a moment, Eric couldn't see, blinded by the smoke
and light—

:FearTerrorPAIN . . . fading, fading . . .:

When he could see again, the winged monster was lying
motionless, its eyes open and staring. Eric covered his
nose and mouth with his hand, overwhelmed by the reek
of burned flesh and smoke.

Is it—is it dead?

:Bard—come closer—:

Involuntarily, he moved forward, caught in the dying
creature's gaze.

*:Yes—if I must to die, trapped here by a hated enemy,
unable to fly from this valley and slain by a mortal, then
at least I will take you with me, into the shadows.:*

*Falling into darkness, falling, dying, everything fading—
NO!*

Eric wrenched free of the creature's dying mind with an
effort, shaking. The monster shuddered once, and was
still.

He stood there for a long moment, clutching his flute
with fingers that were too numb to feel it. *I think it's
really dead, now. Christ.*

Eric staggered away from the huge corpse, away from the
smoldering oak trees, to the open grass. He glanced back—

—to see the monster's body changing, dissolving into
something else.

The wind kicked up, sending the dead ashes swirling
away from the barren trees, scattering the pile of dead
leaves and ragged black plastic sheeting. The plastic crack-
led in the wind, like the snap of leathery wings.

It's—it's really gone. I killed it. God.

He managed another few steps before falling to his
knees, unable to walk; retching his guts out, trembling in
every limb, and covered in ice-cold sweat.

Oh God, oh God—I've never been so scared. But it's dead, it can't come after me again, it's dead, it's dead, it's gone, it's dead . . .

Eric stood on the top of the ridge, the wind running invisible fingers through his long hair. The lights of the San Fernando valley glittered beckoningly before him, the winding road through a sedate tract of houses leading down to civilization.

I'll be home soon. Only a couple more miles to go, thank God; I've never wanted to see my apartment so much in all my life.

I'll get home, wash some of this soot and dead monster slime off of me, and then call Beth and Kory.

Using the telephone, this time.

Christ, I feel like hell . . .

He walked past the darkened houses, down to Ventura Boulevard. Even at this hour of night, there was still traffic on the street, cars passing him by, occasionally slowing down to look at him.

Yeah, I probably look terrific right now. And smell great, too. Eau de fried monster. Really lovely.

After what seemed like an eternity of trudging along the city streets, Eric finally reached his building, and started up the stairway to his apartment.

Then, on the top stair, he hesitated.

Ria—she must've known where I lived, or she could find that out, real easy. I wouldn't put it past her to know exactly where I live, my bank account number, the sock drawer where I keep my cash, everything. What if—

Eric, you're getting paranoid.

Yeah, but I want to stay alive, too.

He gazed at the locked door for a long moment.

Okay. Maybe I'm not going to open the door just yet. Maybe I should drop in on Beth first. I don't think Ria would've figured out where she lives, at least not yet. Especially if Beth's got that magical shielding up around her place—

Damn it, this isn't fair! All I want to do is go inside,

take a shower, and sleep! *Why did my life have to turn out this complicated?*

Eric reached for the door handle, then shook his head. *No. I'm not going to push my luck.*

Then how in the hell am I going to get to Beth's, at this hour of night?

He looked down at his aching feet, and sighed. *Oh well. It can't be more than seven or eight miles away.*

Here I go again . . .

Eric didn't know what time it was when he finally hiked around the last corner and saw Beth's apartment building in front of him. *But it must be getting close to dawn. God, my feet hurt. If Beth isn't here, I'm just going to fall asleep on her doorstep, I don't care if her landlord calls the cops or not. I'm so tired—*

He found a last burst of energy and jogged up the wooden stairs, two at time. He hesitated before knocking on the door.

What if she doesn't let me in? We didn't exactly part on the best terms, earlier this evening.

She has to. I don't have anywhere else I can go.

He rapped sharply on the door, waited, then knocked again. *She's probably asleep. I'd better keep knocking, give her a few minutes to wake up.* He was about to knock a third time, when the door suddenly opened.

She stood, haloed by the hall light behind her, wearing only a long nightshirt, her dark hair tousled, her dark eyes wide with surprise. *Beth, how could I have left you? God, that was stupid. I—I feel so good, just seeing you now— just being here—*

She reached for the door, suddenly, and Eric knew that in another half-second she was going to slam the door in his face.

"Beth!" Eric blocked the door with his foot. She backed away from him, then whirled and—

—and ran. He shoved the door open and stepped into the apartment, seeing her stumbling away towards the living room.

"Beth, don't run away from me!"

She turned, angrily, and he saw the tears on her face. "Me, run away? What in the hell do you think *you* did?"

God, she looks awful. Like she hasn't slept in days. And there's white hairs in that black frizz of hers that I've never seen before. A finger of cold trailed down his backbone. He ignored it, moving towards her.

"Look, I know I was acting stupid earlier," Eric began reasonably, "But I'm back, aren't I?"

"Yeah, you sure are," she said bitterly. "Hooray for you." She sat down on the sofa, reaching for a half-empty bottle of beer, refusing to look at him.

It's Kory. That's what it is, it's Kory. Oh God, I've lost her before I ever had her, and it's my own stupid fault.

"Beth, listen. I—I need to know—are you in love with Kory?" He swallowed painfully. "If you are, it's . . . it's okay, I'll just leave now. I don't have anywhere to go, but that's never mattered before. Are you?"

She stared at him, as though she didn't understand what he had just said, then laughed—only it wasn't much like a laugh; it was more like a cry of pain. "Why should *you* care, after what you did? And why should I tell you?" She clenched her fist, pressing it to her temple, face contorted with pain.

Then, suddenly, she sagged with defeat, and swigged from her bottle. "Not that it matters, anyhow."

She's never talked like this to me before, ever. What's happened since I left? Then something else she had just said sank in, along with a low heavy feeling in his gut. "What do you mean, it doesn't matter?"

Her words were muffled behind the bottle. "Kory's gone, Eric. He—he gave up hope, these last couple months since you left us. He completely lost hope, and now he's left me." She trembled, the beer bottle loose in her hands, close to spilling. "He left me—"

"Why would Kory—" Eric began, then stopped short. "Months? *Months?* What are you talking about?"

She glanced up at him, her dark eyes empty and cold, with something brittle and about to shatter at the bottom of them.

"We spent two months looking for you, Eric," she said

tightly. "Trying to fight Perenor's people without you, to stop them from destroying the nexus. But we couldn't do much, not by ourselves. God, we tried. Kory wore himself away to *nothing*, trying. We *knew* they had you—at least for a while. But he couldn't find any trace of you, nothing. We—we thought they'd killed you."

She choked back a dry sob. "Then one night Kory heard you playing, somehow—so we knew you were alive, and roughly where you were. That's what led us to you, your music. Otherwise we'd never have known what happened to you."

Eric sank down to the couch, his legs refusing to support him. "No. That can't be true. I've only been gone for three days—"

Think, Banyon. All those old Celtic ballads about people being trapped in the land of Faerie, spending a night dancing in an elven circle, then waltzing home to find out that ten years have gone by. That's what happened to you.

Holy shit.

That's *what Ria was doing to me . . .*

He took a deep breath, and another, trying to get his mind back into first gear. *Not in neutral. Wheels spinning, but not going anywhere. That's where I've been for the last* two months.

Two months.

"Okay," he said at last. "Okay. So I lost a bit of time. But why did Kory walk out on you?"

Beth shook her head slowly, her voice ragged with despair, every word tearing at his heart. "You still don't get it, do you?" she said dully. "It's been *months*, Eric. They bulldozed the Fairesite three weeks ago. It's all over."

The bottle fell, a stream of beer cascading into the carpet, as Beth buried her face in her hands, sobbing. "He gave up. We knew, the last day, we knew when it happened. He just sort of . . . folded in on himself when the bulldozers hit the first tree. And he gave up. There's nothing left. No hopes, no dreams. Nothing. It's over, the elves are going to die, Kory's going to die—he knew he was going to die, so he left me, so I wouldn't have to watch him, see him die slowly, fading like all the others—"

Eric moved closer to her, gently putting his arm around her shoulders. "Oh, Beth."

She looked up at him, her face streaked with tears. "But I know he's dying, I can *feel* it; I can feel him dying a little at a time. It hurts, Eric, it hurts so much—" He held her tightly against him, feeling the dampness of her tears soaking through his shirt.

Every word felt like a knife in his heart, but nothing hurt as badly as the knowledge that *he* was the one responsible for the whole disaster.

If I hadn't walked out on them—God, Beth, how could I have done this to you, to Kory? I didn't know—oh God, I'm sorry, I'm so sorry—

She cried until she had no tears left, dry sobs shaking her body. She cried herself into absolute and utter exhaustion.

And all he could do was hold her.

He carried Beth into the bedroom an hour later, after she'd finally cried herself to sleep in his arms. Eric set her down carefully on the mattress and pulled a blanket tenderly over her. From the doorway, he glanced back at her; the gleam from the streetlight outside filtered through the bedroom curtains, casting long shadows on her tear-stained face.

Eric walked back to the living room, his thoughts in chaos. On the living room table was a bottle of Irish whiskey, half-empty; he picked it up, opened it, and took a long draught.

Time for drinking and thinking. In that order. I should probably take a shower, get some of this filth off of me, but I'm too depressed.

He sat down on the sofa, the bottle clenched in his hand. Across the room, the television was on, with the volume turned all the way down. Eric crossed over to the TV, and raised the volume just enough so he could hear and not awaken Beth.

Black and white shadows flickered across the screen. *A '50s science fiction film. Terrific. Something mindless to watch while I get drunk.* He sat back down on the couch, wishing the whiskey would take effect faster. *I want to be really drunk, really soon—*

God. How could this have happened? Why didn't I realize what was happening? I still can't believe it—two months.

Kory's gone, and maybe he's already dead. I don't even know where he is, even if I knew how to help him.

Ria and Perenor—they've won. Last game of the night, all the cards on the table, and they've won.

He drank another swallow of the whiskey, the fiery liquor burning a track down his throat.

It's over. There's nothing Beth and I can do.

A tiny voice spoke into his thoughts, an echo of his own grim thoughts, and the creature he had fought earlier this night: *Yeah. You can wallow in self-pity. Get drunk, get stoned, get trapped under a Faerie hill, wipe the world away. That's what you can do. Like you've been doing for the last two months. You can go on doing absolutely nothing. You're really very good at it.*

Eric stopped, the bottle of whiskey half-raised to his mouth. He hesitated, and his hand wavered, then he slowly set the bottle back down on the table.

No. No more. This time, I'm going to do things right. I don't care if it's hopeless—I'm not going to give up again. I've spent too many years running away from problems and commitments. This one I'm going to face.

There's a beautiful, wonderful lady asleep in that next room, a lady who cares a lot about me. I'm not going to fail her. And somewhere out there is a frizzy-haired elf guy, a guy both of us care about, who depended on me—

And I let him down.

But I won't do that again. We'll find him, and we'll make this work out right.

If we can find him.

If he's still alive.

Something deep inside him refused to give up, revolted at the idea of Kory being gone. *He has to be alive. I won't believe he's dead. If he was, I think . . . I think I'd know, somehow. I don't think anybody, not even Ria, could keep me from knowing that.*

He glanced at the television screen, where a handsome blond hero was blowing away a killer tinfoil robot with some kind of ray gun. *I wish everything was that easy. If I thought it was, I'd pick up a .45 from a neighborhood pawnshop and go hunting for Perenor. But that won't accomplish anything, other than probably getting me killed. I remember real well what he did to Kory.*

The hero-actor posed and gestured like a wooden puppet, somehow more artificial than the tinfoil robot. *God, but that movie is awful. Really bad. Not "so bad it's cute" bad, but just pathetically bad. It's not even funny. Doesn't have any magic to it at all.*

No magic . . .

Is this what all the movies, all the music, are going to be like now? So . . . lifeless? Like the same old stupid plots, replaying over and over again?

That's something terrific to look forward to. If I fail at this, if I can't do something to save Kory and the elves, I'll never be able to sit through a movie, ever again.

Hell, why am I thinking about movies? If I go after Ria and Perenor and blow it, I'll be dead. Perenor would kill me with all the hesitation and moral consideration of somebody swatting a fly. I'd—I'd like to think that Ria wouldn't try to kill me, but I know better than that.

The images on the television changed from scrolling end credits to the early morning news, and a video clip of firemen and police officers clustered outside a burning building. Eric suddenly tuned his ears into what the announcer was saying, curious. ". . . and in Van Nuys, firemen are still battling a blaze that broke out roughly an hour ago . . ."

Eric blinked, looking at the flames rising from the ugly pink apartment building. *I really feel for whoever lives there. That place looks just about totaled.*

Who'd want to live in that ugly—pink—oh my God, that's my apartment building! My home is burning down!

Holy shit!

He stared in shock at the television set, and the green flames rising from the pink apartment building. *Green and pink, really lovely. I think I'm going to be sick—*

Wait a second, here. Green *flames?*

Suddenly he recalled *another* set of green flames. Magic flame. When he and Terenil had dueled—

But Terenil wouldn't have done anything like this—

Even if he *could* have.

Which left—

The only other two creatures in this city capable of wielding that much magic power.

Ria.

And Perenor.

He rose to his feet, so angry he was shaking. *Damn you! Damn you! Haven't you done enough to me? Haven't you got it all? Do you have to turn my apartment into a bonfire? Why in hell can't you leave us alone? I'm no threat to YOU!*

He didn't even realize he was screaming the words at the top of his lungs until somebody began to pound on the wall from the apartment next door.

And he didn't care.

"Damn you, Perenor! Leave us alone!"

· 16 ·

Whirlwinds of Danger

"Damn you, Perenor, leave us ALONE!"

Someone coughed behind him. He turned to see Beth, blinking sleepily, staring at him from the bedroom doorway. "Yo, Eric," she said conversationally, in close to a normal tone of voice. "Could you scream a little quieter? I was asleep for the first time in three days."

Someone pounded on the wall.

"And I think you woke more people up than me." She glanced past him, at the television set, and her eyes widened. "Hey, isn't that—"

"Yes," he said wearily. "Perenor just torched my apartment. Excuse me, I think I'm going into the bathroom to bang my head against the wall and cry."

He started to walk past her, both hands buried in his hair. "Everything's gone to hell. Kory may be dead, the nexus is destroyed, and everything I own except these clothes and my flute just went up in smoke. That's it, I can't take it anymore."

He pivoted and slammed his hand against the wall. "Dammit, they've *won!* Why are they doing this to me?"

A strange expression crept across her face and Beth caught him by the arm. "No. Eric, that's not it. That doesn't make any sense. If those bastards have really won, then they wouldn't have any reason to still come after us, would they?"

He shrugged, and ground his teeth. "I don't know. Maybe they're just bored, and ruining our lives is more entertaining than watching soap operas. Maybe it's just Ria, wanting to get even with me for walking out on her. I don't know." He glanced back at the television set, expecting to see another glimpse of his life going up in smoke, and froze.

It was a different news clip, with a photograph of a pretty dark-haired girl, smiling at the camera. ". . . and in the South Bay, another victim of the 'East Side Slasher' was discovered last night. Octavia—"

Martinez. Octavia Martinez. Eric completed the thought before the announcer was two syllables into the girl's last name. *Octavia, 'Tavy to her friends, a fifteen-year-old who's already a virtuoso on the cello—gifted and bright, lead cello in her school orchestra—*

It was as if he'd known her all his life. The details of *her* short lifespan flooded into him too fast to really comprehend.

How can I know this? What's going on with my head?

But he knew her, he *knew* her. Even though they'd never even matched eyes in a crowd, much less met. *'Tavy, a beautiful young girl, already an incredible talent, so happy, always laughing, loving life so much, her music bringing joy to everyone who heard her—*

". . . and police are intensifying the search for suspects, and now believe that the killer may be using trained attack animals, such as pit bulls, for these murders." A series of photographs flashed onto the screen. "Already the Slasher has claimed seven lives since the first murder in the East Los Angeles area three weeks ago."

The words faded away beneath the images forming in Eric's mind, the still photographs changing to visions of people, alive and vibrant. *Michael, yeah, he was an artist, worked in advertising, with a real gift for making his artwork come to life . . . Sandy Chelsea, solo vocalist with the Master Chorale . . . Danny, only eight years old, but already well-known as an actor, doing voiceovers for cartoons . . .*

All of them people he knew as well as his closest friends— and had never encountered in the flesh. *How can I know all of this? I've never heard of these people in my life, I've never even seen photographs of them before!*

"Eric—Eric, are you all right?"

He opened his eyes and saw Beth watching him with concern. "Beth, all of those victims . . . I *know* them. They were all like *me,* all of them able to do the things that I do . . ."

"Bards?" Beth looked at the television screen, now showing a commercial about vacation homes in the mountains. "All of them were Bards?"

Eric moved to the couch and sat down heavily. "*That* is what's going on. Perenor. He's killing off everyone with the Bardic Gift." He looked up at Beth, who was staring at him, wide-eyed, her sleep-rumpled hair standing up like a cartoon character's. "You were right, there must be some way that we can hurt him still, or he wouldn't have any reason to do this."

"Yeah. If we could just figure out what—" Beth stopped in midsentence, then reacted. "Christ! This means he might try for Uncle Phil, too!"

For a moment, Eric couldn't remember who Beth was talking about, then an image flashed into his mind: the elderly man with the house full of artwork and animation cels, and how his eyes had shone when he looked at Eric—no, not his eyes, but something *behind* them, something that was a part of him; reaching out to Eric like an old friend, speaking to a part of himself that answered in harmony. "Yeah, Phil—Beth, he's got the Bardic Gift, too."

"Of course he does," Beth said tersely, disappearing into her bedroom. Eric could hear the sound of drawers opening and clothing being flung out. Beth's voice drifted to him through the open door. "He's an animator, after all—you just look at his work and you *know* that there's more going on there than just blobs of paint on transparency cels!"

She reappeared a moment later in jeans and sneakers, pulling a sweatshirt down over her torso. "Come on, we're leaving," she said, picking up his flute case from where he had set it down on the table. She gave him an impatient look. "Well?"

"Hang on a sec, Beth—"

He had to close his eyes; the vision overlaying the *real* world of Beth's apartment was too confusing to sort out otherwise. *Images: a sleepy little street in Burbank, the pale yellow house, the first glints of sunlight reflecting off shadowy water, an old convertible parked on the street. And a feeling of cold and calculating intent, of gathering willforce, and—*

"Holy shit, Beth, I think Perenor's doing something there *right now!*"

She didn't say anything, just grabbed him and ran.

What if I'm wrong? What if I'm completely crazy, if all of this is just delusions? What if I'm imagining that Perenor is at Phil's house, planning to do something awful to the old guy?

How do I know if what I'm feeling is real? That I'm not completely crazy?

His mind might doubt, but his gut *knew*. This was for real. The cold feeling in the pit of his stomach intensified, as the jeep careened around another corner. He glanced at Beth, and saw that her knuckles were clenched tight on the steering wheel. *She feels it, too. Something awful is happening—*

Beth floored the brakes. The Jeep skidding to a stop in front of the little yellow house, nearly ramming into the parked convertible. Before Eric even got out of his seat, she had vaulted out of the Jeep and was halfway to the front door. She pounded on it several times, calling out Phil's name, as Eric grabbed his flute and hurried across the lawn to her.

"He's not answering," she said shortly, and reached into a potted plant for a hidden key. Eric followed her as she hurried to the side gate and into a backyard filled with assorted junk and pieces of furniture, past a swimming pool murky with fallen leaves and debris. "Beth, if someone sees us doing this, we could get arrested—" Then Eric stopped, staring at the back of the house.

Or rather, what *used* to be the back. After a giant had reached down and ripped off the wall and roof. Pieces of splintered wood and plaster were scattered everywhere.

I have a real bad feeling about this—

Eric tore his eyes away from the devastation, to see Beth Kentraine already vanishing through the remnants of a sliding glass door. "Beth, wait! You don't know if—"

Shit, she's already gone inside! He glanced at the carnage around him, then swallowed and followed her in.

If possible, the inside of the house was in worse shape than the outside. Eric saw the Snow White cel that he had admired, lying on the floor practically at his feet, shredded. *With all of that slimy black gunk smeared all over it—slimy—like that* thing *that I killed last night—oh shit! Beth! Where in the hell is she?*

He ran into the next room, feeling as though every nightmare he had had as a child was upon him, every screaming terror resonating down his nerves. And he saw Beth, kneeling on the filthy floor, not moving, just staring at—at—

Eric turned away and retched onto the destroyed carpet, falling to his knees, shaking helplessly. *Oh God—oh my God—*

When he could, he looked back at Beth, still motionless on the floor, holding the old animator's hand. He managed to stand and took several unsteady steps towards her, then sank to the filthy carpet beside her, staring down at Phil Osborn's face.

And tried hard not to look at anything other than that wrinkled, surprisingly peaceful face; not at the ruined body, opened like a butterflied shrimp, ripped flesh and exposed internal organs glistening in the dim light, blood spreading slowly into the carpet around him. Eric felt the wetness soaking into the knees of his jeans, and clutched his gut, trying not to throw up again—

—then Phil's eyes opened, looking right up at them, and he nearly lost it one more time. *Christ. He's still alive. They did* that *to him, and he's still alive. Oh my God . . .*

"Beth." The old man's voice was a whispery thread, his eyes glazed and very bright. "Beth, listen to me."

"I'm here, Uncle Phil," Beth said softly, kneeling close to him. She rubbed at her eyes with the back of one hand,

and Eric saw the blood and tears and undescribable filthy smearing together across her face. "I won't leave you."

"Beth, you can stop Perenor. That's why he's—" Phil gasped, his chest heaving. "Stop him, Bethie. I know you can do it."

We can? How in the hell are we supposed to stop somebody who'll do this, turn another person into a piece of sushi?

Then the old man smiled, looking at something beyond Eric and Beth, something only he could see. "Leila . . "

The room faded from around Eric, as a slow rising chord echoed through his mind. *Power, clear and strong as a river, reaching out for something—a brightness, an intensity, shining like a beacon from within—and from far away, the hint of another Power, different, yet the same, reaching toward the first.*

This is what a Bard is, he realized dimly. *This quiet strength and power, the force of creation held by a living being, power shining so bright, almost incandescent.*

—and the distant melody, drawing closer, strengthening the faltering notes of the first. Then the two joining——then fading, fading . . .

And gone.

The aged, agonized eyes focused on nothing, then ceased to focus at all. Beth sobbed quietly, Phil's bloodstained hand still pressed against her cheek.

He's dead.

That—that was him. Phil. A Bard. Is that what I am, too? What I look like to Kory—and Ria?

Eric swallowed, feeling his nausea rising again. *And she and her dad had me in their clutches for* two months. *They could've done this to me at any point, exactly what they did to Phil. Christ.*

He edged closer to Beth, resting his hand on her shoulder, wanting to comfort her, but not really knowing how. *What do you say to someone who's just seen an old friend murdered—hell, taken apart like a laboratory frog! What good are words now?*

"Eric."

Beth's voice was low, it barely penetrated through the

clamor of his thoughts. Then she spoke louder, stronger. "Eric, I don't want to leave him like this. I don't want anyone to see him. Not the cops, not anyone."

He nodded, understanding what she was saying, even though he wasn't certain what she expected him to do. "All right. Stand back a bit, Beth."

She bent low and kissed Phil's bloodless lips briefly, then stood up.

Okay. This time, I'm going to do it right. For Beth. He removed his flute from the case, fitted it together, then brought it to his lips. He closed his eyes, concentrating.

Slow notes, a quiet melody, then building in intensity, filled with aching pain . . . "O'Carolan's Farewell to Music," a fitting tribute to a murdered Bard, someone who held power in his human hands, who created life with ink and paint.

If there's a heaven, this old guy is headed straight for it. Or wherever it is that we Bards go when we die.

Through his closed eyes, Eric saw a bright spark of light, then a burst of green flame. He opened his eyes, watching as the crackling eldritch fire consumed the old man's body. When nothing was left but a fine dusting of ashes on the floor, Eric let the fire die away.

Strange. The floor isn't even scorched. But the fire was hot, hot enough that I could feel it from here. And hear it, the snapping flames—

For a moment, Eric thought he heard something else, a faint slithery sound, like a water hose dragged along concrete. Then there was silence again, except for the sound of Beth crying softly.

He touched her shoulder gently. "Beth, we'd better get out of here. If some neighbor calls the police . . "

She stood up, still gazing down at the small heap of ashes. "Thank you, Eric," she said quietly.

Eric put his arm around her as they walked to the bedroom door. In the ruined living room, Beth bent to pick up a shattered photograph frame. The picture that fell out was a black-and-white of a younger Phil and a lovely dark-haired woman. She caught it before it touched the slimed carpet, rolled it up and slipped it into her jacket pocket.

Outside, the first hints of sunlight were breaking through the clouds overhead. There were only moments left until true dawn. Eric and Beth, walking in silence, picked a careful path through the debris on the swimming pool deck.

"Beth," Eric began hesitantly, "when Phil called out to Leila, did you see—"

He stopped, feeling as if someone was standing just behind him, peering over his shoulder. *Somebody very close, close enough to touch . . .*

Then he screamed as something wet and oily coiled around his ankle, yanked his feet out from under him, and dragged him backwards. He thrashed, trying to free himself, and caught a glimpse of something. Something huge and dark and dripping, topped by a rearing equine head with glittering red eyes and distended fangs. Then the thing slammed him down on the concrete, knocking the breath and wits from him. His flute case went flying in one direction as he was yanked in another.

Toward the pool.

"Beth!" he shrieked, hearing her scream echoing behind him. Then the water closed over him, black and icy cold, as icy as the scaled flesh against his bare skin. He struggled against that inhuman grip, already knowing it was hopeless, trying to reach the surface to breathe, feeling the darkness closing in around him as every second ticked past.

God, please, just let Beth get away, don't let it get her, too—

Then the clawed hand thrust him up into the open air, and Eric gasped for breath gratefully. Then he saw why the creature had surfaced, and his heart stopped beating for an instant.

Beth!

She stood like some fantasy art heroine, her clothing soaking wet and clinging to her, a piece of wood splintered to a sharp point clenched in her hand. He could see where the tip was stained with blood and a foul greenish ichor as she danced closer along the slippery rim of the pool, trying for another stab.

"Beth," he yelled, "get your ass out of here!"

Then Eric screamed again as the piece of wood sailed within inches of his nose to embed itself in the creature's eye. With a shriek that rent the air, it flung Eric onto the concrete and sank beneath the pool's surface.

Eric just lay there for a long moment, choking and gasping, and concentrated on some serious breathing.

Oh God. I'm still alive—

Then he realized Beth was pulling him away from the water's edge. "I'm—I'm okay," he gasped hoarsely, trying to sit up.

She held on to him tightly. For a moment, he thought he could hear her voice, even though her face was pressed too closely against his shoulder for her to speak.

: I thought I'd lost you again, lost you—oh, Eric—:

"I love you too, Beth," he whispered.

She kissed him, then helped him to his feet. "At least you don't reek quite so much now," she said dryly.

A noise behind them made both of them turn. The opaque water of the swimming pool was roiling with darkness, seething as though something was thrashing below. They glanced at each other, then Eric scooped up his flute case and they ran for the gate. And didn't stop until they were in the Jeep. Beth sent it accelerating onto the westbound Ventura Freeway.

It must be dead. How could anything live after getting drilled through the eye like Beth did to it?

Then again, how can anything like that be alive in the first place?

Kory gone, Phil dead, the nexus destroyed—God, I wish this was a bad dream and I could wake up.

Fat chance, Banyon.

He looked across the seat at Beth, and realized that her hands were shaking on the wheel. "Maybe you should pull over for a minute."

She took a deep breath and shook her head. "No. I'm okay. It's just—how long do we have, Eric, before Perenor tracks *us* down and kills us? He obviously hasn't forgotten about you. What can we do against a guy who summons creatures like that swimming-pool thing to take care of his enemies?"

Or that winged monstrosity that tried to eat me last night in the hills— "I don't know. Go on the offensive, maybe?"

"Offensive against *what?* If we go anywhere near him, he'll swat us like flies, Eric!"

He thought about it for a moment. "What about the nexus? Maybe there's still something we can do about that."

"Okay," Beth said after a long pause. "let's go out to Fairesite."

They bulldozed the site three weeks ago.

Even knowing what to expect, Beth was still shocked and horrified by what she saw.

They didn't just destroy it, they devastated it. I've never seen anything like this before, done with such . . . maliciousness. Like they didn't want to leave one single paving stone next to another.

She looked out at the desolation, seeing in her mind's eye what once had stood there . . . *Over there, that was the Mainstage, where now there's only a heap of splintered wood . . . Irish Hill, they practically leveled it completely, there's nothing left except some scattered straw . . . the old Wishing Well, they just left the concrete foundation broken, didn't even bother with removing the pieces.*

There's nothing left here but dirt and chips of wood. Nothing at all.

She reached down, picking up a piece of what had once been a bright green ribbon, now torn and dark with mud. She straightened and saw Eric, moving towards what had been the Wood.

The Wood Grove. That's where Kory said the nexus was, within the circle of ancient oak trees.

Oak trees, torn out of the ground, lying like mutilated corpses on the dusty ground, dead—they've destroyed it completely. There's nothing we can do here.

Uncle Phil murdered, and now Kory is going to die, too, if he isn't already dead—

Pain ripped through Beth, making her clench her eyes closed to keep from crying aloud. Pain like someone stabbing her in the heart—

—or the soul. It's over, Kory must be dead or dying, it's hopeless.

Eric's still picking over the mess, walking through the fallen trees, looking around. Doesn't he realize that there's nothing we can do, nothing at all? Why doesn't he just give up?

Eric disappeared around the edge of the ruined Wood, into the hilly area beyond. Beth followed hesitantly, not certain where Eric was going. *That's what used to be the end of the Wood, there's nothing beyond there, nothing except a few more oak trees—*

Beth climbed carefully over the bulldozed trees, trying to spot Eric. *There's still a few oaks left standing, by the edge of the Wood. And—*

She felt her heart leap with sudden hope, seeing a cloaked figure sprawled beneath one of the oaks' spreading branches. Then she ran forward to where Eric was standing, looking down at the motionless man.

It's him, it's Kory!

Now she could see him clearly, that wild blond hair spilling over his shoulders, mixed with dirt and blood and tears. His slack face streaked with tears and mud, his jeans and Faire shirt the same no-color.

And the six-pack of empty Coke cans on the ground next to him.

Beth slowed to a stop, and stared at the shiny red cans in horror. *But that—that's poison to elves—*

—oh my God, no!

She fell to her knees next to Kory, seized his hands and touched his face, still damp with tears. His hand was icy cold in hers. She moaned, deep in her throat, and began patting his cheeks, trying to get a response. When nothing happened, she searched frantically for a pulse. "Kory, please, no, don't be dead—"

She looked up at Eric, who was staring down at Kory in

stunned silence. "God *damn* you, don't just stand there, *do* something! Use your magic! You're a Bard, this is what you're supposed to do! Help him!"

He swallowed, and stepped back a pace. "Beth, I don't think— "

"I don't give a shit *what* you think, Banyon—you're going to play that fuckin' flute now or I'm gonna ram it down your throat!"

"Beth, I don't know *how!*" he said, shouting to be heard over her rising voice. "The fire—that just came! This is *complicated.*"

She forced herself to calm down, and took a deep breath. "Okay. Let's think this through. I think maybe we need a—a spell of some kind. Maybe what you played to wake him up would work again."

He knelt beside her and opened the flute case. "I think—I think maybe I played 'Sheebeg Sheemore.' That's a spell?"

She took a *very* deep breath and seized his hand, flute and all. "A spell, Eric, is a *process,* and not a *thing.* A spell makes you concentrate your energy on a goal. 'Sheebeg Sheemore' is about elves, isn't it?"

"Yeah, but—"

"It worked last time, didn't it?"

"Yeah, but—"

"If you don't start playing," she said softly, clenching her jaw to keep from screaming at him again, "that flute is going to be shoved where you won't like it."

She turned away from him as the first notes sang out into the sunlight, searching Kory's face for a flicker of life, any sign that he was being drawn back—

Nothing.

The last notes died away, and nothing had changed—except that maybe the pulse beneath her fingers was a little weaker.

She was about to round on the musician and demand that he try something else, when Eric began "Tamlin's Reel." He followed that with "Tom O'Bedlam."

One tune after another poured from the flute, the different melodies filling the stilled air, and now Beth could *feel* the desperation under the notes, the frantic fear that mir-

rored her own so exactly that she trembled beneath the
double burden. And still nothing happened, nothing
changed—except the sun rose a little higher, and the wind
stirred Kory's hair and dried the tears on his face.

Eric could feel Beth's desperation; it was a match for
his. So he *tried*, poured his soul into his playing, tune
after tune, note after note, everything Celtic he knew—
and nothing, *nothing* happened. Finally he ran out of
things to play, and dropped his aching arms.

*He's going to die. Kory's going to die, and there's noth-
ing I can do to stop it—*

Kory's face was as slack and lifeless as before. Eric could
feel the life in him; could *see* it if he looked just right—
flickering, fading . . .

*Dammit, I healed him, there has to be some way to
channel this power right! There just has to be! Maybe—
maybe it's me. I'm not making the right connections. If a
spell is a process, it probably has to convince my subcon-
scious. Which means it has to be simple. And something I
can relate to.*

*Simple—well, the Celtic tunes are sometimes simple
enough, but do I really relate them to what I have to do?
Maybe I'd better get down to my own roots.*

So what do I want to do?

*I want to put Kory back together. To put him back the
way he was. To come out the way he was.*

None of the tunes he'd played so far addressed *that*
need—

Which may be why they didn't work. He frowned,
clenched his hands on the flute. *I need something clear,
something simple. I've got to make this come around right—*

Then it came to him, with those words. It all came
together, making such a perfect pattern that he was blinded
by the clarity of it.

He closed his eyes again, made himself very still inside,
and *reached*—

—and played.

He felt Beth go *still* for a moment, then felt her reaching out to him; heard her begin to sing.

"She danced on the water and the wind—"

He stopped. She sang another word, and faltered. "Eric? What's—"

"That's *wrong*, Beth," he said around the flute mouth-piece. "Not the pagan version—the original. The Shaker hymn. You said we needed a spell; well, that's a spell. It's about returning to balance, to *what you were and what you were meant to be.*"

He heard her swift intake of breath, and began the tune again. She let him play it through once, then joined him on the second round.

" 'Tis a gift to be simple, 'tis a gift to be free,
   'tis a gift to come 'round where we ought to be—"

Yes. That's it. He could feel the power rising now, dancing around him, following the lead of his music—and hers—echoing the simple tune.

"—and when we find ourselves in the place just right,
   'twill be in the valley of love and delight."

Now he could feel the fading flicker that was Kory gaining strength, reaching for the power. He twined it once about the elf, twice, three times, verdant and living, tying him in vines of melody, anchoring him to *here* and *now*.

Beth poured her heart into the song, into the words. Eric could feel *her* strength, a dark fire joining his own power.

"When true simplicity is gained,
   to bow and to bend we shan't be ashamed—
   to turn, turn, will be our delight,
   till by turning, turning, we come 'round right."

But that wasn't enough. Not yet. Kory was *not* a simple creature, a one-dimensional cartoon elf. He had depth and breadth and heights Eric couldn't imagine—

So Eric called to the power and the music, and reached for Kory with it.

Touched.

No doubt; this was the Copland transcription from "Appalachian Spring." Building on the original melody, weaving in and around it, calling in images as well as melody. Thunderstorms in the mountains. A quiet, secret stream. Song of a single bluebird—and the haunting cries of hundreds of skeins of geese. A towering oak. A tiny violet, hidden in fallen leaves. Oboe carrying the melody with him, a second flute making it a round, clarinets laughing a harmony—

—then the strings—

Come back, come home, come round right—

—weaving a braid that turned to a circle that turned, turned, turned—

He couldn't hear Beth anymore, but she was in there too, making the song a prayer, an outpouring of love and passion.

Now the music was returning to what it had been, each part dropping back to join the flute-line, the melody, the simple line; joining it and reinforcing it. "*—till by turning, turning, we come 'round right—*"

When they all were *one,* Eric played it through one last time, slowly, with all the emotion he could muster.

Silence. And he opened his eyes—

—and saw Kory, gazing up at him with those brilliant, leaf-green eyes—

Alive.

· 17 ·

Rocky Road to Dublin

Eric had time for one coherent thought—*He's alive!*—before Kory lunged for him, his mailed hands closing tightly around Eric's throat.

He tried desperately to pry those metal-clad fingers off his neck without success. Kory lifted him right off the ground by the neck and held him dangling with his toes just brushing the dirt.

"Kory—" Eric wheezed, gasping for breath.

"You human bastard," the elven warrior hissed, his green eyes incandescent behind the golden sheen of his helm. "I wasn't hurting anymore, I was beyond that, everything was so peaceful, so painless, and you brought me back! I'm going to rip you apart, mortal!"

Eric was suddenly aware of Beth pulling ineffectually at Kory's arm, trying to get him loose—

And beyond her, a circle of elven observers watching in silence.

Just . . . watching. Just curious, mildly interested. Like it's vaguely entertaining, watching one of their kind strangle a human.

Then he heard the sound of clapping hands, and a few scattered comments.

"A little higher, perhaps . . ."

"His technique is a little sloppy, don't you think?"

"Could be—"

"Well, Korendil is out of practice, after all."

Oh God, Eric thought as everything began to blur and

fade around him. *I'm going to die to a chorus of remarks from an elven peanut gallery, murdered by my best friend. This really isn't fair.*

Kory's not like them, he wouldn't do this, just stand by and watch somebody get killed—

—if he wasn't the guy trying to kill me!

With a last burst of energy, Eric kicked wildly at Kory, connecting with one graves-clad leg; hitting the elf's knee just above the metal plate. Kory's hands loosened from his throat for an instant, and Eric slammed his fist into the side of the elf's helm, connecting with Kory's lower jaw and lip. As Kory staggered back, Eric fell to the ground, choking and gasping for air.

He didn't stop to try and reason with Kory; he just rolled away in the soft dirt and grabbed his flute out of the dust where it had fallen. Somehow he ended up back on his feet, facing the furious elf.

Who still looked like he wanted to rip Eric apart limb from limb.

I could play something, use my Gift against him—but what in the hell would that accomplish? I'm trying to save his miserable life, not kill him myself!

Before either of them could move, Beth Kentraine stepped between them, her hands on her hips. "All right, guys," she said in a voice like ice. "Enough of this. Kory, what in the hell do you think you're doing?"

Kory wiped a trickle of blood away from his mouth. "Stand aside, Beth. I intend to destroy that traitor."

"Wait a second," Eric began to protest. "I was just trying to keep you from killing yourself, you stupid—"

"So you brought me back," Kory finished, glaring at him. "I never should have trusted you, Bard. The first chance you had, you ran away to our greatest enemy, willingly placing yourself in her power. Leaving us to die. *Now,* now that it's too late, you've brought all of us out of Dreaming. Why? So we can die in agony as the last magic of the nexus fades away to nothingness? Did *she* teach you to savor the pleasures of another's pain?"

"Kory—I didn't—I mean, there's got to be something we can do—" Eric stammered, backpedaling before the look of hatred in Kory's eyes. *Maybe this wasn't such a good idea. It isn't just that he was mad that I left. He's not gonna listen to any excuses. He wants to* hurt *me; really, seriously hurt me—*

"There is something that *I'm* going to do," Kory said levelly. "I'm going to kill you, Bard."

Oh my God—

As Kory advanced towards Eric, Beth interposed herself between them again. "Kory, no. Whatever you do to him, you'll have to do to me first. I won't let you touch him." She glanced at the small circle of elves, also garbed in bright metal and peacock-colors. "Eric's *not* with Perenor. He wants to help you. And Eric's the only Bard here, the only one who *can* help you."

"If Korendil believes the human must die, then we will stand beside him," one of the elves said. "It is *you* who should not interfere, mortal woman."

"Oh, fuck off," Eric heard Beth mutter under her breath. From the edge of his vision, Eric saw two of the elves edging closer to her, trying to circle behind her.

I can see exactly where this is going now. Goddammit, Beth, why do you always have to fling yourself into these situations, trying to save my ass?

I thought I was doing the right thing. Maybe I wasn't.

Forget the excuses, Banyon. There aren't any excuses for what you did by walking out on these people. Just because one of them happened to be sleeping with a lady you love—

I guess I'd better face the music.

Eric pushed Beth gently to the side, and moved forward to stand in front of Kory. "Okay, I'll admit it. Running off to Ria was a real stupid idea. And everything that's happened since, it's really my fault, because you were counting on me to be there to help you. Well, I'm here now. And either you can kill me, or we can try to figure out a way to keep you guys alive. It's your choice, Kory." He managed a weak grin. "Though I'm sure you can guess which of the two *I'd* prefer that you chose."

Kory only stared at him, his hands within the gauntlets clenching and unclenching slowly. Eric realized that his own hand, the one that had hit Kory in the face, was throbbing with pain. *That doesn't matter. Nothing may ever matter again, depending on what this guy chooses to do. If he decides he'd rather kill me than let me try to save his skin—well, I'd rather be ripped apart by Perenor's pets. To go into the final darkness, like Phil, but knowing that* Kory *sent me there—wanted* me *dead. And didn't forgive me . . .*

The despair in the back of Korendil's eyes hurt worse than his hand—hurt worse than *anything* ever had before.

He swallowed hard and tried to meet those bleak eyes, and the pure fire of hate in them. *At least, if he kills me, I won't have to watch him die later, when the last of the magic fades away—*

Eric winced inwardly, but did not look away. *That's really a comforting thought, Eric. Sheer brilliance. No wonder Kory has no faith in you at all.*

He tried to find courage in himself—somewhere. *But he should have faith in me. I'm going to get them out of this mess, if—if it kills me. It's mostly my fault that this all has happened. They were counting on me. And I failed them.*

He felt a despair to match Korendil's, chilling his heart. *Right. I failed them. So I shouldn't be surprised if Kory decides to deep-six me after all—*

Then, to Eric's immense relief, Kory nodded. "I do not think you did this out of evil intent, Eric." The elf warrior's voice was weary. "So I will not harm you. Leave us now. Let us fade away in peace." He turned and began to walk away.

"So that's it?" Beth said angrily. She ran after him, grabbing him by the shoulder and forcing him to look at her. "So long, and thanks for the memories? Like hell, Kory!" Eric could hear the pain in her voice as she continued. "I love you, you idiot elf! I won't leave you here to die!"

Eric bit his lip, feeling a different kind of pain tearing through him. *She loves him. I knew that, really I did, but hearing her say it—*

"And Eric may be an idiot, too, but he's a Bard, and I'm sure there's something he can do to *help* you, if you'll just

let him. If you're willing to try something other than
suicide or Bard-murder. God, why are all the men in my
life such fools?"

Kory didn't answer; he only stared deeply into her eyes
for *far* longer than Eric liked. And then he nodded again,
slowly—and leaned forward and kissed her. As the kiss
lengthened, Eric felt the seconds ticking by, each like a
sharp stab into him with every heartbeat. Finally, Beth
moved away from Kory, gasping a little.

The elves were watching with the same detached interest with which they had viewed the fight.

*She loves him. That's obvious. Christ, why did I get
myself involved in this? Saving his life just so Beth—*

He stared down at the dirt at his feet, his throat so
choked he could hardly breathe, and never realized that
Kory was walking towards him until the elf stopped right
beside him. He looked up, startled, and saw Kory was just
standing there, looking at him soberly. Very close. *He
looks like he's going to say something—maybe an apology
for nearly tearing my throat out? That would be kinda
nice, actually. Even if I was a schmuck, it still hurts to
swallow.*

*Or maybe something about Beth, how the best man—elf—
won, but let's still be buddies, hey?*

Oh hell, he's my friend. And if Bethie wants him—

Then Kory placed a gauntleted hand on each of Eric's
shoulders—and kissed *him.*

Eric's startled exclamation was muffled, and his first
reaction was to—

*—to slide his arms around Kory's shoulders, to draw
him even closer, to lean into the kiss, to hold him tightly
and never, ever let him go—*

—then Eric pulled free of Kory's embrace, trembling.

He turned away from the puzzled and hurt look in
Kory's eyes, towards where Beth was standing several feet
away, her expression undecipherable.

"I'm—I'm sorry about abandoning you, Kory," Eric said,
valiantly trying to gather his wits around him. "I—I was a
schmuck. An idiot. I promise, I won't let you down again."
He ventured a look at the elf out of the corner of his eye.

God, no one should look that good.

"I accept your apology," the elf said, faint, courtly formality accenting his tone. Then a ghost of a smile drifted across his face. "And I promise, Bard Eric, that I shall never try to throttle you again." He glanced at the other elves. "Well, if we are to live, I suppose we should start by trying to find a solution to this situation. Shall we?"

For the first time, Eric actually *looked* at the elves around him. And gaped in surprise.

Unimaginably bright colors, glittering armor and sheathed weaponry, thigh-height boots embroidered with fantastical designs, flowing capes over tunics, multicolored skirts and breeches. *Like taking the best of the Faire costumes I've ever seen, then making them a thousand percent better.*

Although some of them were dressed more like the types seen on Melrose Avenue, studded black leather and dyed mohawks forming an unlikely contrast to the ornate garb of the others.

And Kory—

Well, at least he isn't still wearing my clothes— Eric thought, gawking at his friends.

Kory—no, *Korendil*—was garbed like a character out of King Arthur's knights, clad head to toe in golden-hued armor, intricate with blue enamel inlay and gemstones. His blond hair cascaded down over a cloak the color of the sky at midday. There was no mistaking the regal look in his eyes, either: the look of a lord of the High Court of Faerie.

Eric felt terribly shabby. And grubby.

Next to him I look like one of the beggars out of Monty Python. Dirty and rumpled from walking all night, all slimy from fighting monsters, still damp from being dragged into a swimming pool—and he looks terrific.

No wonder Beth has the hots for him.

I could really hate these elves, given half a chance—

A lovely silver-haired elf woman, clad in flowing blue silk with a sheathed sword slung over one shoulder, stepped from the small circle of Faerie still gathered around them. She kissed Kory fondly. "Young Korendil," she said, "we, the mages and warriors of the High Court who remain here, pledge you now that we will follow your guidance and that of this human Bard, though death be the end of it."

"Val," Kory began, looking suddenly awkward and very young. "I don't know what to say—"

Another elf, a broad-shouldered figure in skin-tight black leather, his purple mohawk falling rakishly over one ear, clapped Kory on the shoulder. "Then say nothing, Kory. But you will lead us into battle."

"Eldenor, you're my *teacher!* You should—"

"We are all that is left of Elfhame Sun-Descending," the elf said in his low, resonant voice. "Our enemies have nearly succeeded in destroying us. You and the Prince were the only ones who saw our danger. And now we do not know if Prince Terenil is still alive. But you are here, with the Bard you brought to aid us." Eldenor grinned. "Even if you were ready to kill him a few minutes ago."

"Kory," Eric began hesitantly, "I don't know what I can do, but if you just tell me what, I'll do it."

He does look kinda overwhelmed. But I know he can lead this motley crew, if anyone can. And figure out what we can do to solve all of this. If we can.

He resolutely pushed his doubts away. *No. We have to solve this. There's too much at stake here. Kory, he's my friend. Maybe—maybe he's even a little more than that, I don't know. But I do know that I won't let him die.*

Kory was looking around at the devastated grove. "This is what must be remedied. Unless we do something soon, despite what you have done with your magic, Eric, we shall fall back into Dreaming, and then die. That is why we came here, to the last lingering wisps of magic."

"Wait a minute," Beth said suddenly. "Something just occurred to me . . . if the magic is all dried up, then where is our minstrel boy getting his juice from? Eric?"

Eric shrugged. "I've never thought about it before, but you're right, I must be drawing it from somewhere." He closed his eyes, replaying what had just happened in his mind, how he had reached out . . .

. . . and called the power, called it, drawn it from—

"From Ria's house," he said at last, opening his eyes. "It's coming straight from her place in Bel Air. I guess I can tap into it, just because"—he felt his face warming, and tried to quell his embarrassment before it became *too* obvious—"because, uh, I was so, so close to her, for so long. They must have moved the nexus there somehow."

"That makes sense," Beth said thoughtfully. "That's a terrific way to keep everything under lock and key: kill the old nexus and plant a new one in your backyard."

"She is an accomplished sorceress," Kory acknowledged. "With her father aiding her, I do not doubt that she could redirect the nexus, once its focal point had been destroyed, since of course she would not be able to create a new nexus from nothingness. This must have been Perenor's intent all along, to have all the magic of this region at his disposal."

"But there's one thing I don't understand," Eric said hesitantly. "How can you pick up a nexus and move it around L.A. like this? I mean, what is a nexus, anyhow?"

"The nexus is only a tiny gap in the veil between this world and the world of our kind, Bard," a flame-haired elf woman explained. "It must be small, or it would weaken the veil. To create such a thing is beyond the skill of all, except—"

Except—

Terenil, sitting around the dojo after that workout, drinking and talking. ". . . and the Queen's Bard, a human like yourself, created an anchoring point for the nexus . . ."

A human Bard. Like me.

This is what I can do. This is how I can save Kory and his people.

His mouth suddenly felt very dry. *Except that Perenor and Ria have already taken control of the nexus. Which means I'll have to fight them for it—fight Ria—*

"Kory," he said, slowly, looking at his feet, "*I* can create a nexus. Creative magic—that's what Bards do. That's what the Queen's Bard did when you first came here—"

Only I'll have to fight Ria to do it.

He looked up to see Beth watching him. " 'Bout time

you figured it out, Banyon," she said quietly. "Think you can handle it?"

Eric took a deep breath, then another. Kory and the elves were watching him as he spoke. "I—I don't know. I'm really not very good at this magic stuff, at least not yet. I mean, I don't even *know* what I was doing, I just sort of did it off the cuff. By accident. Improvising. But this is something that, if I screw it up, we probably won't get a second chance—"

"I think you can do it, Eric," Beth said. "But we've got another problem. Even if you can do this whole schtick no sweat, do we want you to put the nexus back here? This place is going to be turned into condos in another couple months. Doesn't seem like the best place for a magic nexus, next to the hot tub and laundry rooms, y'know?"

"She is very right," Val said thoughtfully. "We need another place for the nexus, one which is not close to the humans' dwellings, so rife with Cold Iron. *And* one that is nearer to those of the Lesser Court, trapped in their groves. A place that will be safe for many years to come."

Good luck, finding a place like that in L.A. This place is so overpopulated, even the mosquitoes are having a hard time finding a place to breed. Everything that's not Federal or State land is going to be developed into housing, sooner or later—

—Federal or State land—

That wide, empty valley, with the oak trees growing among the tall grass. Federal land, that no one can touch. An elven grove in the Hollywood Hills. And a dragon, starving to death because no one came near enough to eat—

—that area wouldn't be so great, it's still too close to the city. But maybe if we go a little further east—

"How 'bout Griffith Park, in the Hollywood Hills? There's a lot of land up there where nobody goes except maybe the real compulsive hikers. That might be a safe place for the nexus."

Kory glanced at Beth, who nodded. "That's a real solid idea, Eric. Griffith Park will never be turned into houses or shopping malls, not so long as the city stands. I can't think of any place that would be nearly as good." She gave Eric a wry grin. "Now you just have to do your magic stuff, bucko, and we're back in business."

Eric hesitated as that dark thought reoccurred to him. "What about Ria and Perenor? We know that the opposition isn't going to let us do this without a fight. I don't think I can do all of that, restore the nexus *and* hold off two sorcerers." *Ria and Perenor, they need the nexus, or they wouldn't have gone to all of this trouble. They need it bad enough to kill for it, that's for certain. To kill Phil, and all those other potential Bards—*

Ria. She used me, manipulated me—but there's still part of me that cares about her, that needs her.

If Ria comes at me again, throwing everything she has at me—one of us is going to die. We can't fight like that again, and not *kill each other. But could I really bring myself to kill her?*

Could she kill me?

Eldenor clasped Eric's arm strongly, breaking into his thoughts. "We will guard you, Bard. We will keep any from harming you as you work the Magic. Trust me—as you will fight to save us, we will battle to protect you." The muscular elf glanced down as Eric winced in sudden pain. "Korendil, it seems that your stubborn skull is as thick as ever. Come see what the Bard did to himself, trying to knock some sense into you."

"I think it was the helmet, actually," Eric muttered, as Kory carefully took Eric's hand in his own. Beth moved in closer to look. Eric saw her eyes widen at the sight of his hand, bruised and bloody, two of the fingers already purpling and swollen. Kory tried to bend the fingers, and Eric bit back a yelp.

Damn, but that hurts!

"This is because of my foolishness, Eric," Kory said at last. "The place of magic is nearly drained, but let me see if I can mend what my stubbornness has wrought."

The elf closed his eyes, cradling Eric's broken hand in both of his; and this time, when Eric heard the first stirrings of melody, he *knew* what was happening. The gentle interweaving of melody, somehow touching him;

invisible fingertips tracing over his hand, *through* his hand, knitting together the broken bones, the torn flesh. He was not surprised to hear Beth singing distantly, silently, part of the magic as well.

As the melody faded, Eric looked down at his hand and flexed the fingers lightly, the fingering pattern for "Sheebeg Sheemore."

That's what this is—the two rival groups of elves, just like in the O'Carolan song. Except this time, we're playing for keeps. It's not a song, or a Bard's vision. It's life and death, and not just for them—for me, and for Beth, too.

God. It's so scary that it's almost beautiful.

But I still wish I could wake up, and all of this would just be a dream—

Terenil floated in the vast *nothingness* of Dreaming. No pain, no hunger—just oblivion.

Soon enough he would trade this oblivion for another—when the last of the magic ran out, when his whole being thinned and faded away. He had been in Dreaming longer than any of the others of the High Court; would he be the first to die? He hoped so, when he found the will to hope.

And what would it be like, this ending? A last fading into nothingness? He had only had enough will left to come here, to the place where Elfhame Sun-Descending had been born, and then he had lost himself in his Dreams. No time to wonder, no chance to fear. The humans claimed elvenkind had no souls—if that were so, then there would be no knowing that the end had come. It would simply come, and Terenil would be no more.

No more pain, no more sorrow.

And Perenor would have won at last.

Something in him stirred in rebellion at that thought. Stirred, and struggled to wake, struggled to prod him into action. Spurred him to *listen* when the first thin strand of melody sought him in the darkness.

He listened—and it found him, fastened on him; a melody deep with meaning and rich with magic. Bardic magic, as he had never hoped to hear again.

To turn, turn, will be our delight, till by turning, we come 'round right—

It turned about him, twined about him, fed and nurtured his heart in ways he had never known were possible.

'Tis a gift to be simple, 'tis a gift to be free, 'tis a gift to come 'round where we ought to be—

Without knowing how the magic had reached within him, he found himself recalling his first days in this brave new land, when Maddoc had led them all out to Gwynnedd. How he had stood upon the shore of this western sea and breathed in the salt air, feeling that there was nothing he could not do in this new Elfhame.

The memory was vivid, more clear than it had been for years, decades, centuries.

And when we find ourselves in the place just right, 'twill be in the valley of love and delight—

This *had* been the valley of love and delight, rich with peace and promise. And he had been lord of it all—

And you can be again, the music whispered. *Turn, turn, turn again. Return to what you were—what goes around, comes around, good as well as evil.*

But I can't— he protested weakly.

But you can, it replied. *Turn, turn, return again—*

I'm dying. This is a death-dream. There was no magic left; Korendil's Bard had deserted them, and there was no hope. This was death's final illusion before dissolution—

—*but it was a sweet illusion. So be it. I die in dreams and Dreaming.*

He gave himself over to the music; stopped fighting it. And it turned him, turned him—

Returned him.

Till by turning, turning, we come 'round right.

There was no transition between Dreaming and waking. One moment he was lost in the Dream and the music, the next—

Terenil blinked in the harsh sunlight. He was standing, tree-sheltered, in the shade of a gnarled old native oak on the edge of what had once been the nexus-grove.

I'm not dead. That was his first thought. His second—

I'm—well. Whole. I have not felt like this in—

—in far too many years.

Then he chanced to look down at himself. And stared.

My armor—

His gold and scarlet armor glistened as if new-burnished, new-made. *He* had not been able to conjure it so since the last time he had defeated Perenor. And since that humiliating episode in the alley, in the rain, it had been dull, stained—as if the stains upon his honor had translated themselves into his armoring.

But that was by no means all. For there was none of that *hunger* that had devoured him of late, that craving for the dark poison of the humans' creation. He felt young—strong—

Movement beyond the trees and the glint of sun on burnished gold and azure warned him to hide himself behind the tree-trunk. Shame kept him there, as he overheard young Korendil's converse with the Bard. Not once was there mention of him—

Because they have learned they cannot depend upon me. I failed them once—I, who should have led them. I lost myself in drugged Dreaming; failed their trust, and the vows I made to them.

Bright Danann, what have I made of myself?

Shame kept him trapped, huddled behind the tree-trunk, as the last of the High Court consulted with the humans and planned their next move. He waited, numb and paralyzed, as they separated into two parties—the humans and Korendil going for the girl's vehicle, the rest going to seek out any one of the Lesser Court of Faerie who might yet be awakened.

He watched as they vanished on their two missions.

And a slow tear etched its way down his cheek.

The distant thread of music tugged lightly at her thoughts, barely audible, but slowly gathering in strength and power—

Ria Llewellyn leafed through the thick report and idly jotted down several notes in the margins. She was seated at her desk, relaxed, a cup of fresh-ground coffee at her right hand next to the sheaf of papers. *Jonathan did a good job with this. He always does. If anybody could keep this*

*company running other than myself, it would be him. But
I think his estimate on the interest rates is a little too
optimistic. He'd better check on that before we meet with
the investors on Friday.*

Music, weaving a subtle pattern of words and melody,
speaking deeply without disturbing the surface of her
thoughts: "— *turning, turning, we come 'round right*—"

She quickly scrawled a reminder in her desktop calen-
dar about the meeting with the stockholders next week.

*I'd better make sure Linette has arranged something
with the caterers for this. Lox and bagels, maybe?*

Suddenly, Ria was *aware* of the faint melody, building
into a profound harmony, drawing inexorably towards some
unknown conclusion—

She stopped writing abruptly, listening intently to the
distant music that only she could hear.

Flute, and a woman singing—

Realization hit her like a physical blow.

That's Eric! What in the hell is he doing?

Ria *reached* out, trying to touch something happening
far away, a world away from the glass-windowed office
building overlooking the city.

And drew back quickly, sensing more than just Eric and
the human witch; the presences of other elves, slowly
awakening from their Dreaming stupor.

No! It can't be!

But it was true.

He's doing it. He's awakening the High Court!

She remembered the look on his face as he had left her
last night, vanishing from her house into the hills like a
modern-day Thomas Rhymer. *After nearly killing me. I
can't forget that, either. How he summoned that soul-
devourer, unleashed it upon me*—

I've never been so frightened in all my life.

Ria shivered in spite of herself. *Father told me about
those creatures, but I never thought I'd see one. I still
can't believe that he was able to control it. I was certain
that . . . thing was going to kill both of us.*

But he banished it, somehow. And then he left me.

Left me, and didn't come back.

She bit her lip, truly unhappy for the first time in years. Even worse, there was no remedy.

I should never have let him go. I could've stopped him, by force if need be. Letting him leave was a mistake. We could have worked it out—I know he was happy, living with me.

She twisted her pen in her hands, the cool, matte silver no comfort. *I haven't been able to stop thinking about him. From the moment I saw him, back in that sleazy bar, I knew he was meant to be with me. We were . . . so good together. It's my fault he ran away; I was so angry that I frightened him into summoning that creature.*

Now I don't think he'll ever come back to me; at least not of his own free will.

She closed her eyes in pain. And saw, in her mind's eye, the bulldozed valley, oak trees lying like felled warriors. And Eric, his brow furrowed in concentration, playing the silver flute.

Awakening the Faerie.

Why is he doing this? He must know that Father won't let him save the elves. He's signing his own death warrant, there in the ruined Grove.

Unbidden, another image rose in her mind: Eric, sprawled in an alley, blood staining his white shirt and jeans, his dark eyes empty and lifeless.

And Perenor, walking away and wiping the traces of blood from his blade, walking away without even a backward glance—

She choked. *No! No—I don't want that to happen. Even if he walked out on me, I don't want to see him dead.*

Oh, Eric, how can you be doing something this foolish? I know what you must be planning—once the Faerie are awakened from Dreaming, you'll try to reestablish a nexus. But Father won't let you do that. If you were to succeed, we would lose control of the magic. Father has planned this for too many years, plotting to avenge himself upon the elves and win control of the magic of this area.

And—I can't let you do this either. Because if you succeed, I'll grow old, and die—

A secret thought whispered in the recesses of her mind:

That wouldn't be so terrible, if you have someone like Eric to grow old with, to share everything. Even dying. That's a very . . . human way to live.

But I'm not human.

She clenched her fist, crumpling the papers under her hand.

I can't let him do this. I can't let him take control of the nexus.

But if we fight again, like we did last night, one of us is going to die . . .

The silent music continued to resonate within her mind, the power flowing into Eric, then out, answering *his* unspoken, unconscious will. And calling an answering echo from herself.

We are still touching, Power calling to Power, even though he walked out on me. I wonder if he realizes that? Like it or not, we are bound together by more than just emotions. Killing him would be like killing part of myself.

How could I live with myself, knowing that I've murdered the only man I may ever love?

What am I going to do?

The clock on her desk ticked away the seconds as Ria buried her face in her hands.

I don't want to kill him. There has to be an alternative.

Something occurred to her suddenly, a possible solution. *I can offer to send the elves across the veil, to the Faerie Lands. With the nexus at my disposal, I could do that easily. Then there would be no deaths, no need for Eric to attempt to create a new nexus, no reason why he couldn't stay with me, live with me forever—*

Another voice spoke silently into her thoughts, a voice she recognized instantly. :*Ria?*:

She could see him in her mind, an angel of shadow, infernally handsome—and darkly angry. :*I know, Father. I can hear the Bard's magic. He's probably going to make an attempt on the nexus after he brings them out of Dreaming.*:

There was a brief pause before Perenor spoke, and his words were as cold as the darkness between the stars. :*You know what we have to do, Ria.*:

:*Yes. And I'll help you, but on one condition, Father.*: She took a deep breath. :*You'll let me try to deal with them in my way. Without any killing. I'll make sure that we keep control of the nexus. And—you won't harm the Bard. I want him back.*:

Ria felt her father hesitate, if only for a fraction of a second, before he answered. :*Agreed, daughter. The nexus is what's important; much more than anything else. I'll contact you again as soon as I know where they're going.*:

The light touch of his mind faded. Ria opened her eyes slowly, looking out the window at the hills.

Does he mean that? Or was he only saying that so I would help him?

It doesn't matter. We've been building to this for a long time, Father and I. A final, decisive confrontation. If he tries to harm Eric—

I'll kill him.

I love Eric. And I won't risk losing him again.

· 18 ·

Come Now or Stay

Beth squeezed back against the apartment door and let the other two precede her. Eric first, battered, filthy, and mangled, with bruises darkening his throat—then Kory, looking thoroughly exhausted.

Riding in the Jeep wasn't easy for him. Too much Cold Iron; guess I should have gotten one of those little plastic Korean cars. He was in pain most of the ride. He'd never have managed if he hadn't had his armor to insulate him.

And there's too damned much unfinished business in here.

She closed the door and leaned back against it. "Well?" she said. "Talk, you guys. The tension in here is sharp enough to shave with."

Eric eyed her doubtfully. "Talk?" he faltered. "What about?"

She threw the double lock on the door—the one only *she* had ever been able to juggle open successfully. "You're trapped, guys. No getting out." She leered. "You're in my power."

Eric sagged down on the couch. "Oh come on, Beth— get serious."

"I am." She flopped down in her favorite papasan chair. "We've got the misunderstanding translated. Now—let's get personal things straightened out among the three of us."

Kory started to sit in the recliner—and Beth had a sudden vision of what all that metal would do to the

297

leather upholstery. "Kory!" she yelped, and he froze; half-way between sitting and standing.

"*Without* the hardware. Please."

He flushed, and looked pleadingly at Eric. "Bard?" he said hesitantly.

Eric's head snapped up, his eyes wide and startled.

"Please, Bard—I—" Kory's flush deepened. "I have no magic left."

Now it was *Eric's* turn to blush. "Shit, Kory, I'm sorry— I—oh hell—" He fumbled his flute out of the case, and ran through a quick rendition of "Banish Misfortune." Two verses and a chorus later, Korendil eased down into the recliner clad in nothing more harmful than silk.

High Court garb, Beth was certain of it. *One look at him, and half the producers in the Valley would be on their knees to him offering him contracts.* She grinned to herself. *And the other half of them would be offering him their—ahem. This is* not *the time. We've got a race of people to save, and if we can't get our act together we won't be able to.*

But oh—he looked *wonderful.* Flowing azure silk, velvet, and gold trim, and jewelry of gold and sapphires; his golden curls tumbling into those incredible green eyes . . . and that body under all the finery . . .

Dammit, Kentraine, get your mind on business!

"Guys—"

"Kory—" Eric said, at exactly the same moment. And blushed again.

She bit back a giggle. *Ye gods, he's got a low blush-factor.* He looked at her uncertainly.

"Go on, Eric," she urged.

He blushed even redder and hung his head, staring at his flute. She looked over at Kory out of the corner of her eye. He was collapsed bonelessly in the recliner, eyes half-closed.

"Kory?" Eric said, very softly. "Kory? Listen. Please don't call me 'Bard.' Please?"

"But it's what you are," Kory replied, without looking up at him.

"Yeah, I know that's what I am—I mean, now I do. For

a while there, I didn't seem to know much of anything. But the way you're saying it, it's like we aren't friends anymore." The sadness in his voice penetrated Kory's weariness, and made him open his eyes wide.

Beth held her breath as the elf flowed up out of the recliner and slowly took a single step toward the musician. "Are we friends, Eric?" Korendil asked. "Are you doing this now, finally helping us out of guilt or—"

"Kory," Eric said urgently, finally looking up and meeting the elf's eyes. "Kory, please. *Yes,* I know I've done some really stupid things, how the hell could I *not* feel guilty about that? I nearly killed you—"

Kory took another step toward him, and towered over Eric, his face gone utterly still.

Eric kept his eyes fixed on Kory's. "But it's not just that. I mean, that's not all. I . . . like you, Kory. I thought you liked me, before I messed things up. I want you to like me again. I never had any friends like you and—and Beth before. People who really give a damn about me. And if I screw this one up—" He clenched his jaw against *something.* Beth thought—*tears?*

"Kory, I'm scared. I don't know what I'm doing. I *know* what's going to happen when we try to fix the nexus. It's obvious they're going to try and stop us—and they aren't gonna do it halfway. Any of us could end up—I mean, I don't want to die—but it won't be so bad if—if—I know I've got friends again. If—if it isn't alone—"

Korendil reached down, took Eric's hands in his, and pulled him to his feet.

Oh gods, Kory, don't kiss him again. He doesn't know how to deal with that at all . . . hell, I barely know how to deal with that!

But the elf only put one hand on each of his shoulders, gazed into his eyes, and said, huskily, "You have friends, Eric. Friends who will die beside you, if need be. Two, at least; Beth—and myself. Is that enough?"

And it was Eric who made a strange little sound in the back of his throat and threw his arms around the elf. Kory hugged him back—but carefully, breaking off the embrace when Eric pulled away.

But Eric didn't pull completely away, not like he'd done back at the Faire site. He kept his hands on Kory's shoulders, and his gaze locked with Kory's—and Beth began to feel as if they were reaching some kind of a deep, wordless understanding.

It was a little uncomfortable. *I feel like a Peeping Tom or something*, she thought; she rose to her feet, and began edging toward the kitchen. *Maybe if I go fix some herb tea or some—*

She stopped, because Kory's hand was on her elbow. He drew her towards the two of them.

Then Eric's arm was around her waist, and she was part of a three-way embrace that was *so* warm and intimate that she had to close her eyes and hold her breath.

Oh gods, oh gods—don't ever let this stop—

"Beth," Eric said, slowly, as if he was thinking out every word. "I'm sorry. I screwed things up for you, too. Beth, I never meant to hurt you. I—I'm sorry. I guess I'm saying that a lot. I—I guess I've got a lot to be sorry for."

"I think," Kory replied softly, and very carefully, "that we should all agree to forgive each other and let the past bury itself. We, all three of us, delivered soul-wounds, whether we meant to or no. *I* am as guilty of that as you are, Eric. No matter that I did so out of ignorance—the hurt was there, I saw it, and I did not try to heal the hurt in time."

Beth *saw* the image in Kory's mind, the moment in the kitchen when Kory walked in and kissed her—saw through Kory's eyes the hurt, the betrayal in Eric's expression.

She blinked, and felt a stab of guilt at her own actions— that she had been so angry at Eric for vanishing at the demonstration that she had flaunted Kory in his face.

"Me too," she heard herself saying, her voice gone husky. "I didn't think you would care so much about Kory and me. And—I wanted to hurt you, Eric. It was stupid and childish, and I did it anyway."

"So—can we three find forgiveness in each other's hearts, do you think?" Kory finished.

She looked at Eric—

He was crying, and nodding. So was Kory.

So, she discovered, was she. She squeezed her eyes shut again, and hugged them as hard as she could. Within milliseconds, they had responded.

And . . . *something* stirred.

After years of raising the Cone of Power in Circle, Beth knew the sensation when Power began moving. And this was Power; a Power uniting the three of them, binding them, weaving them into a three-stranded braid of love and faith and strength that nothing would break short of death.

My gods. No. Yes. Jesus Frog on a pogo stick—

This isn't possible. It can't work.

Why not? she asked herself as the power continued to bind them into the whole. *A tripod is the most stable configuration there is. A three-sided column bears more weight per inch of surface than a square one. An equilateral triangle is the prime geometric shape—*

It's crazy, that's why.

She wondered if Eric was hearing the power-flow as music. She cracked her eyes open a little, and saw his beatific expression and figured that he was. *What the hell. So it's crazy. I'm crazy.*

She immersed herself in the binding.

The power faded—as it was inevitable that it should do. Reality intruded itself, and with it, certain discomforts. *Like Kory's damned armor digging into my—* "I hate to break this up," she said, a little hoarse from the emotional overload, "but you're leaving chain-mail imprints on my chest, elf."

Kory chuckled, and let her go. She opened her eyes—and gasped.

Jesus H. Frog—

Her jeans and T-shirt had somehow been transmuted; now she was wearing something like a fabulous cross between Faire garb and her stage gear. Flowing black silk shirt and breeches, tight black leather tunic and thigh-boots and gloves, all trimmed and studded in silver.

Kory, clad again in his armor, was splendid enough—but *Eric*—

He *had* been disheveled, filthy, his hair straggling into

his eyes; bruised, and generally looking as though he'd been through the tumble cycle on a dryer. With rocks and mud and razor blades. The only thing about him that had looked worth saving had been a pair of burgundy-leather Faire boots—and *those* had needed cleaning badly.

That had been a few moments ago. But now—

Now he was clean, as immaculately groomed as Kory, and clad head-to-toe in a elven Court costume of silk, satin, and soft sueded leather, all in a rich wine color trimmed in sliver.

But as Beth looked at him in wonder, she realized that there was something more changed than simply clothing—there was a look in his eyes. A stability. As if he'd finally found himself.

Like . . . he's finally grown up. He's what I never dared hoped he'd be. That's why the power—the binding. There was pain there, and a self-knowledge that wasn't far from pain. Maturity and depth. And not even a hint of bitterness. He looked like a Bard, every inch of him.

Is this what Kory saw in him, all this time?

Kory had switched back out of his Court gear and into his armor, as Beth's chest could attest.

They looked incredible. Beth caught her breath at the realization of how much she loved both of them.

"Jesus," she said, half in awe, half in an attempt at flippancy. "I'm locked in my apartment with the two most gorgeous hunks in the Valley."

She expected some kind of response to that out of Kory—but it was *Eric* who went to one knee; then kissed her hand, and replied, looking to each of them with a grin, "Nay, lass, ye've got it backwards. *I'm* locked in your apartment with"—he dropped the accent—"with the two most wonderful people in the universe."

Kory reached down and brushed his cheek lightly with his fingertips, then held out the hand to help him to his feet again. Eric took it.

She saw that *look* creep into their eyes again, and realized that it would be all too easy for them to mesmerize each other for the rest of the morning.

"Okay, you sexy things, we'd better get our rears in

gear," she said. "Eric—would it help if you had *musical* backup that's equally used to being *magical* backup?"

Eric stood by the apartment window, half-listening to Beth on the phone, half-embroiled in the endless questions that refused to leave him alone.

". . . yeah, Allie, I know, you're supposed to be at work at noon . . . I thought it was hopeless, too, but we've got a chance now. Eric came back last night."

In the street below, the rush-hour traffic was just starting. As Eric watched, an ivory limousine glided past, disappearing into the apartment complex's parking lot.

A white limo? Where have I seen one of those lately?

Those crazy guys from the Mad Hatter booth who showed up last weekend on Fairesite in a limo? No, theirs was a black stretch model, I remember that now.

Besides, that was months ago, remember?

He glanced back at Beth, now dialing another number. And Kory, soundly asleep in the recliner.

He looks so . . . peaceful, sleeping like that. Even with that one silly curl that keeps falling over his eyes, every time he shifts a little.

Eric resisted the impulse to walk over and brush that curl back into place. He glanced back at Beth, and saw her watching him with that familiar, speculative, thoughtful gaze.

Well, at least Kory's getting some rest. I wish I could fall asleep like that. I feel like I haven't slept in days. Which isn't too far off the truth, actually.

It looks like all of this is gonna work. The band and the elves are meeting us at the donut shop, then we'll head up to the hills. And me—I'll do whatever it is that I'm supposed to do.

God, I have never been so scared in all my life.

Beth hung up the phone, and walked back towards Eric and Kory. She bent over the sleeping elf, and kissed him tenderly. "Hey, handsome. Time to go."

Kory's eyes opened instantly, and he gazed up at Beth. She smiled, and lightly pushed that errant curl, the same one that Eric had wanted to fix, away from Kory's eyes.

Then she walked over to the wall, where a guitar case was propped against a cabinet.

Beth picked up the guitar case and cradled it lovingly. "This," she said with the air of a mother showing off her firstborn child, "is my twelve-string acoustic guitar, hand-built by John Mello, a terrific guitar luthier up in Berkeley. It cost more than I'd care to mention—but I'd been earning good money for a while, and I figured it was well-spent on this baby." She patted the case with a fond, possessive smile. "*Now* I'm glad I got her. We're going to need every edge we can get. The others'll be bringing their best stuff as well. Believe me, Eric, you're going to have the finest backups you've ever imagined." She slung her purse over her shoulder, and hefted the guitar case in her other hand. "Well, gentlemen, shall we?"

I'm starting to think this might really work. That maybe we can really make this happen—

"Let's hit the road," he said, turning away from the window.

A faint burst of melody flickered across Eric's thoughts, a brief flutter of distant, discordant music, almost too low to be heard, as he walked back to pick up his flute from the couch.

Then all he could hear was Beth's terrified scream as the living room suddenly exploded into roaring flames.

Jesus H.—

Eric stumbled backward against the wall, one hand flung over his eyes as the fire leaped up before him. Everything around him was burning, green light glowing in weird patterns.

The couch ignited before his eyes, instantly charring and crumbling into gray ash. Eric backed up along the wall, choking in the thickening smoke.

Can't—can't see the others—oh God—

His path to the door was already blocked by green flames, burning even brighter as they encircled him.

Green fire—it's Perenor! He's trying to kill us all!

Eric saw Beth trying to open the closed window through the flames, the frame already buckling from the heat. Then she raised her guitar case and smashed the glass.

The noise was barely audible over the sound of the crackling flames.

At least Beth can get out of here, escape before we all turn into kabobs. And maybe Kory—where in the hell is he? I can't see him through the smoke—

His eyes watering too much for him to see anymore, Eric tried to feel his way along the way—and stopped, sensing the fire, only inches away from him in every direction.

And the malevolence directing the blaze, the intense hatred that fueled the flames.

The hatred, directed at Eric.

:And so it ends, Bard—:

Then someone crashed into Eric with a tackle worthy of a professional football player, slamming him to the floor. He felt himself being physically lifted and hurled through the air, to land in a smoldering heap next to the shattered window.

Kory shoved him through the rough glass, to where Beth was standing on the ledge outside. Beth and Kory both held on to Eric as he choked, trying to catch his breath, wiping the tears from his eyes with a sooty hand.

"I'm—I'm okay," he said at last. Without speaking, Kory and Beth helped him to the corner of the building, where they jumped down safely onto a parked pickup truck.

Eric glanced back at the upstairs apartment, as the windows burst from the heat, the green flames licking hungrily at the walls and roof.

This guy is definitely playing for keeps. That was too close.

He was suddenly aware of Beth's voice, next to his right ear.

". . . that sonuvabitch, that was my books, my records, my art, dammit, all of my costumes, my *Fender* guitar, that bastard just burned up everything I own! Christ, Eric, he did this to *both* of us! God, I am going to *kill* that fucker!" She raised the guitar case like a sword, ready to hack away at anything before her.

Eric glanced at Beth, ranting furiously, filthy with soot, her hair singed at the edges; and Kory, next to her, who for once genuinely looked like hell. *I can't do anything about all of that stuff upstairs, but—but this—just like what Kory did earlier, only more specific—*

He closed his eyes and concentrated on a thin thread of melody, "Oh, the Britches, They Have Stitches," and imagined—

All of us, looking just fine, damn Perenor's eyes.

This time, he could *feel* the music weaving around them, the Power taking shape beneath his hands. A moment later, he opened his eyes—

And looked across the parking lot to where a tall, silver-haired man was standing next to a white limo. Watching them.

Calmly, slowly, Perenor began to walk towards them.

Eric just grabbed both Kory and Beth by the hands and ran for Beth's Jeep parked twenty feet away. Beth vaulted into the driver's seat as Kory and Eric scrambled into the back, Beth shoving the key into the ignition and cranking the engine hard.

Perenor only continued walking towards them. Even from a distance, Eric could see the smile flickering across his lips.

Christ, he's playing with us, he knows he's going to get us, no matter if we try to run—

The Jeep's engine suddenly sputtered into life, and Beth snapped the emergency brake loose, hitting the gas hard. The vehicle virtually leaped forward, heading straight for the parking lot exit.

Maybe we can get out of here before he fries us all—

Then Eric noticed the dark fire burning in Beth's eyes.

Uh oh.

"No, dammit," Beth said from between clenched teeth. "I'm tired of running from this guy. I am *tired* of this guy, period."

"Beth—!" Eric yelped, but she yanked the wheel hard, simultaneously flooring the gas pedal. The Jeep's tires screamed as it accelerated.

Heading straight towards Perenor.

Eric saw Kory's wide-eyed expression of disbelief as the

elf looked back at him in shock, then Perenor was directly ahead of them.

Oh God, she's going to hit him straight on—

Eric winced, expecting the impact at any second. *She's gonna— But this guy deserves it—what he did to Phil, and the others, he deserves to die like an animal, like roadkill—* He forced himself to look up, wanting to see the look on the elf-lord's face, to *see* him die. *To see how you'll react to being cut down, you bastard, just like all the people you've killed—*

And then he saw Perenor *smile*, as with a contemptuous flick of his wrist, he vanished. The Jeep careened directly over the spot where he had stood.

Beth barely slammed on the brakes in time to prevent crashing right into a parked van. The Jeep squealed to a stop, and the three of them just sat there for a moment, staring at each other.

"I knew it couldn't be that easy," Kory said at last. "We had best go to meet the others quickly. I am certain that will not be Perenor's last attempt to thwart us."

Yeah. He's got too much riding on this to let us win. Him and Ria both.

Ria—

What am I gong to do, if she tries to kill me? What if I can't bring myself to fight her?

What if I can't handle the magic, if I can't create the new nexus?

Then Kory will die.

Oh God, please, no.

Yeah, I'm scared. If I blow this, there won't be a second chance.

And what if . . .

At this hour of morning, Whoopie Donuts was virtually deserted, except for the bored man in a dirty white smock wiping the counter with a rag. Eric walked in with Beth and Kory, glancing around to see if any of the others had arrived yet.

Just us, so far.

This was a great place to meet. I wonder if sugar donuts

*can have a positive effect on Bardic magic? A cup of coffee
will probably help, at any rate.*

Eric reached out with his thoughts, touching the small
bit of magic he had created while they were in the Jeep
under Kory's direction. *A disguise spell. To make Kory
look like a normal guy, sans armor and sword. Double-Oh-
Seven, eat your heart out.*

They walked up to the counter, where the proprietor
barely gave them a cursory look before jotting down their
order.

When the man pushed two cups of coffee and an orange
juice across the counter to them, Eric picked up the
Styrofoam cup and sipped gratefully, feeling the strong
drink heating him all the way down.

*Down to that cold lump in my stomach, right next to the
butterflies.*

*Stay cool, Eric. It's okay to be nervous. After all, I've
never saved the elven race before. This is a first.*

The only other patrons were two women, seated at one
of the plastic tables across the room. Eric glanced idly at
them, then realized they were staring at Kory.

As if they could see him as what he was, not a myopic
teenager in a blue T-shirt and jeans.

Oh well. So much for the disguises. Great idea, Kory.

One of the two looked as if she was going to stand up.
Then (amid the squealing of tires that sounded, to Eric's
tired ears, vaguely like horses) the rest of the elves arrived.

Eric peered through the glass door and saw Val: a
beautiful, silver-haired woman wearing a stylish blue linen
dress, stepping out of a white Corvette—

*No, an elf-woman, regal with years beyond counting,
garbed in blue silk, standing beside a white stallion that
butted playfully at her hand as she moved away from it,
striding toward the glass door of the donut shop—*

This is definitely too weird for words.

The man at the counter glanced up as Val and Eldenor
walked into the shop, then went back to polishing the
Formica. But if anything, the two women's eyes were
even wider.

And Eric caught a flicker of light about them. Not

silver, like Phil's had been, but a sweet hint of green. Not
the green of decay, like Perenor's, but playful green, like
sunlight shining through the ocean waves.

With unseen depths, living power welling up from below.

*Sonuva— Hey, maybe it's not the disguises that are the
problem here—*

Eric took a good look at the two, trying to figure out
who—or what—they were.

And why they're in here right now, with us—

The fiftyish, coffee-skinned woman, her silver hair coiled
in an elegant braid, was watching them with a faint, knowing smile. Next to her was a young girl, maybe fifteen,
with short brown hair and a skin-tight black leather jacket
that would make any biker turn green with envy. Eric
winced, seeing the safety pins visible in her ears as the kid
turned her head, eyeing all of them suspiciously. Especially Eric.

*That older lady—I feel almost as if I've met her before.
That calm, quiet way of looking at the world, like she*
understands *people, and knows she can handle anything.*

*But that kid—if I saw her on the street, I think I'd run;
just so she wouldn't have enough time to stick a knife in
me. What are those two* doing *together? They're the
unlikeliest pair I've seen in a long time.*

The kid leaned over and whispered something to the
woman, who nodded.

"Hey, who are you guys?" the girl called from across the
room.

Eric, Beth, and Kory exchanged glances, then Beth
smiled.

"We're in a play," Beth said, absolutely straight-faced.
"It's a remake of *West Side Story.* Set in Tolkien's Middle
Earth."

"Oh, come on, don't give me that shit," the girl said,
with narrowed eyes.

"Kayla," the older woman said reprovingly.

The girl shrugged. "Hey, it's the truth. She's bullshitting
us." The kid looked up at Beth with a wicked grin. "Don't
get me wrong, I sure wouldn't expect you to tell the

truth—like why you're wandering around Los Angeles with a group of elves. Is Sauron in town or something?"

"Much worse," Beth said, very quietly. She glanced at Eric. "Banyon, why don't you go get us some more donuts or something, while I talk to these ladies?"

"Sure," Eric said. He waited at the counter behind two of the other elves, each of whom produced a fifty-dollar bill to pay for their breakfast.

There sure are lots of those fifties floating around in this elven community. I just hope this guy doesn't look at the serial numbers—

"What's a bearclaw?" Eldenor asked another elf behind him, in a low voice.

The second shrugged. "I don't know. Does sound familiar though, doesn't it?"

Donuts in hand, Eric sat at the edge of the one of tables, where two of the High Court, as brightly colored as tropical fish, were catching up on gossip for the last ten years. They smiled at Eric as he sat down with them, but continued with their conversation.

Eric glanced down at his donut, and wondered for the thousandth time what he was doing here.

It never changes. Even now, when I'm probably about to get myself toasted for these people, I'm not really a part of their group.

He bit into the donut, liberally dusting himself with powdered sugar. *It's just like Faire, all over again; I'm on the outside, looking in.*

Then Korendil sat down across from him, an eclair in his hand. "Bard—Eric, rather—have you tried one of these? The proprietor says they are quite fine, in truth—"

"No, thanks." *Chocolate eclairs really aren't my scene, I'm more into powdered sugar, really . . . Hey, wait a second—ohmigod—chocolate!*

Eric swatted the confection out of Kory's hand, just as he was about to bite into it. The eclair skidded across the floor, as Kory stared at him.

"That was a chocolate eclair,' Eric explained quickly, hoping that Kory would wait for the explanation before swatting *him.* "Chocolate has some caffeine in it. I don't know if it's enough to affect you or not, but I didn't want to take the chance."

Kory just looked at him for a moment, then he reached across the table, squeezing Eric's sugar-dusted hand gently. "Again, you are guarding me from harm, Eric. I must learn more of the ways of this human world, or you will have to spend all of your time protecting this foolish, headstrong elf."

"That's okay," Eric said, past the lump in his throat. "You've saved my ass more than a few times, yourself. We'll just have to keep looking out for each other, that's all."

They both looked up as Beth, a Styrofoam cup of coffee in her hand, slid in next to them. Eric leaned past her to look at the empty table where the two women had been seated. "Is everything all right?" he asked.

Like, are those two going directly to the cops to tell them about the loons in the donut shop, or what?

"Everything's fine," Beth said, adding some extra sugar to her coffee. "Turns out those two are the same kind of people as you are, Eric. Well, sort of. They're Healers. I let them know that we're heading into some rough stuff, and Elizabet promised to keep her ears open in case we need her help. Which, with any luck, we won't."

"That little punkette was a *Healer?*" Eric tried to reconcile the two images in his mind, and came up with a complete blank.

"Kayla is Elizabet's apprentice," Beth said. "And pretty damn good at the trade, from the sound of it. She's a nice kid."

A nice kid? Are we talking about the same girl? The one with the pins in her ears?

Then again, Beth does tend towards the black studded leather herself—

What the hell. If things turn out bad, we'll need their help, in a big way.

But it is one hell of a coincidence that they just happened to be in here eating donuts this morning—

"Beth!"

The other three members of Spiral Dance entered the shop, starting towards them.

Eric felt a tight fist closing around his gut. *Everybody's here. This means we're going to head over to Griffith Park and actually do this thing.*

And Ria and Perenor may try to stop us. Or, if we're lucky, they won't.

Personally, I'm not betting on that kind of luck.

He glanced at Beth, talking animatedly with Allie and Jim; and at Kory, sitting so close beside her.

At this point, I don't really care if she dumps me for him. Not now. I just want all of us to live through this. That's all I care about right now.

I'll worry about the rest of that later.

Afterwards.

· 19 ·

Twa Magicians

Eric tried to relax; tried to pretend that it was just another gig. After all, the *setting* wasn't that different from Fairesite—

Hell, I've even played a couple of weddings out here. Not with the Dance, though; with a pickup band—

Beth was tuning that exquisite twelve she was so proud of, fussing over it as if the least little discordance would throw everything out of whack.

And how do I know it wouldn't?

Allie had a little battery-powered Casio synth; state-of-the-art, and capable of producing anything but an omelet. She was giving Beth her pitches; she'd tuned Eric just a couple of minutes ago. The girl looked sleepy and uncertain.

Like maybe wondering about our sanity?

Like maybe I'm wondering about our sanity.

Dan had his bouzouki and was noodling bass runs; he was the only one of the Dance who didn't look nervous. But then again, Uncle Dan was probably stoned to the gills. Jim kept running his finger around the rim of his bodhran, trying *not* to stare at the elves.

Which was pretty hard even for Eric, who was kind of used to them by now.

The little valley-meadow they'd chosen for the new nexus-point cupped the sunlight and held it, and the bright colors of the elves' costumes and armor shone with ironic festiveness in the golden light. They'd made a circle around the band, Val casting it once, Beth once, and a third elf (in

313

brilliant purple- and copper-trimmed robes) the third and
final time.

Now the elf-mages had stationed themselves on the
perimeter, facing outward; the elf-warriors just outside the
perimeter, swords drawn and alert. Kory was right in front
of them, his back to Eric, his blue and gold armor shining
with a faint, gilding aura of light, a haze that made him
look a little unreal, even to Eric, who had given him the
magic that made him glow—

*He looks like a special effect. Even with that bit of blond
fur escaping from under the edge of his helm.*

As if the thought had reached him, Kory turned and
looked over his shoulder at Eric. And smiled.

That smile is enough to stop anybody's *heart.* Eric managed a faltering grin in return, and Kory turned back to his
watch; scanning, Eric was somehow certain, with more
senses than just five.

He realized that Beth had finally stopped tuning, and
turned to her, his flute suddenly weighing in his hands
like a pipe of lead. He swallowed. "Ready?" he asked.

She nodded, and the other three members of the band
gathered around her. "How about you?"

He couldn't read her dark eyes this time. "About as
ready as I'll ever be, I guess . . ."

He closed his eyes and brought the flute up to his lips.

*Better start it fast, Banyon, before you lose whatever
courage you've got left—*

"Banish Misfortune"—it was the first thing that came to
his fingers. Just like diving into water, he slid into the
starting descant, tossing in his usual trill on the B, landing
solid on the F sharp. He tried to concentrate on the
melody, on feeling the power, and on finding a way for it
to come to him—

Nothing.

Oh, the magic was *there*, he could feel it, he could even
pull it to him—but the source was still Ria's. He couldn't
seem to make it come to him *here.*

Maybe a different tune.

He tried "Tamlin's Reel," "Smash the Windows," "Kid
on the Mountain," "O'Carolan's Farewell," all with the

same complete lack of success. The band followed him faithfully, taking the changes with him like they'd been playing together for decades, like they could read his mind. And the magic was *there*—

But just out of his reach.

"Sheebeg Sheemore," "Tom O'Bedlam," "Rocky Road to Dublin"—song after song, jigs, reels, everything.

Nothing.

Eric began to feel angry and frustrated, and his anger increased, until he could scarcely hear what he was playing, scarcely sense the magic through the red haze of emotion.

But a gentle touch on his arm startled him, cooled the rage, broke him out of the downward spiral of trial and failure. He jumped, and ended on a squeak, and the band faltered to a halt behind him.

"Eric?" Kory's green eyes graced him with concern. "Eric, you are not reaching the magic."

"I *know*," he muttered. "I'm trying, but—"

"You try with that which is already created, already old—but you are a Bard, Eric. Master of the creative magics. Try what you Called me with." As Eric tried to figure out what the elf was getting at, Kory smiled again. "In the Grove, Bard. What you used to reach me, and break the spells of Lock and Ward."

"You mean 'Sheebeg Sheemore'? Kory, I *tried* that already— "

"No." The elf shook his head, his eyes bright under the shadowing helm. "No, that was what you played that awakened me. Play what you *Called* me with, what you used to unravel the spellbindings."

"I—"

I sort of segued into something else, something original. God, I was more than half drunk—

More like three-quarters drunk, now that I think about it—

I remember it—I think. But what if I remember wrong?

"Kory," he faltered, "I—"

The elf laid one armor-clad finger across his lips. "No, don't say it. You *will* succeed, Eric. I know this."

Korendil's eyes seemed to be seeing right into his mind,

just as they had this afternoon. Gazing into his heart, so open, understanding him, *trusting* him in a way that no one ever had before.

:—*Eric, my friend*—:

Kory smiled, and took his hand away. Still smiling, he backed up, one slow, careful step at a time, never taking his eyes from Eric's. Eric raised the flute to his lips as Kory reached the perimeter of the circle—

—never taking his eyes from Kory's.

He was shaking so hard that his teeth rattled against the mouthpiece; and the first three notes he produced were so aimless that he barely held back a sob of profound despair.

He saw Kory's lips move, soundlessly.

:*You can, Eric. I* know *this, as I know you.*:

And Eric's fingers found the melody.

He closed his eyes then, overwhelmed, as it began to flow without any real thought or planning on his part. In moments he was lost to it, within it, more completely than he had ever been in his life.

He could *see* the spell he was weaving now, just as he had seen the one that brought Kory back from the brink of death, lost to Dreaming. Saw it begin to build a lattice-work of power, an anchoring-point for the new nexus, a framework to stabilize the rift in the curtain between the Worlds, a patterning that would hold it open forever.

When that framework was complete, his music would pierce that wall, and let the magic flow through. And he knew from the fragility of the net he wove that if his concentration wavered the slightest bit, it would all collapse—and there would be no second attempt. Eric knew he'd never manage to achieve this level of concentration, of power, ever again.

But already the magic he was calling from Ria's stronghold was fading, weakening.

Terrific. I'm running out of juice—

Running out, like a stream trickling away to nothing, drying up.

He wavered—and the memory of Kory sprawled unconscious in the dust of the ruined Grove rose up in his mind. His throat closed, and he braced his shoulders, and poured forth a defiant, liquid run. *No! I won't let them—him—die!*

So he played with all his heart, forsook the fading stream of power, and spun the shining strands of his spell out of the fabric of his soul.

As the world faded from around him—except for the music, the spell, and his own fierce determination.

The Porsche accelerated past the open metal gate, past the park rangers standing beside their pickup truck, a pair of young men who eyed the crazy lady driver, her blond hair flying with the wind through the open window, with appreciative glances.

But Ria scarcely noticed. Her thoughts were far away, with a particularly scruffy minstrel. Eric, who even now was standing in the knee-high grass, intent upon his music, as the first stirrings of Power swirled around him in scintillating light.

Even without trying, I can see him, touch him, feel his thoughts. Feel the bond between us, living Power calling to Power. How could Eric ever have left me, knowing that there is this between us?

A silent voice interrupted her thoughts. :*Ria?*:

Concentrating on the twisting road, and on the presence of the Bard, in the hills far above her, Ria bespoke a wordless reply. :*I'm tracking them, Father. They're in the park, away from the main road.*: She spun an image of the valley, the gathered elves surrounding the Bard, and sent it swiftly to Perenor. :*If we park on the other side, their steeds will not detect our approach.*:

:*Good.*: Perenor's mental voice was tinged with satisfaction. :*I will meet you there.*:

Her lips tightened as his voice faded. *I still don't trust him, even if he promised not to hurt Eric. I know how much his promises are worth.*

If I can just have enough time to speak, before the elves try anything stupid—

Eric will listen to me. And he'll understand. It'll be easier this way; I'll just send the Old Blood back under the hill, to the Faerie Lands. If they weren't such fools, they'd have fled as soon as they realized they'd lost, instead of lingering here to die.

Her hands were clenched tight on the steering wheel. *Before now I didn't care whether they lived or died. I wouldn't have deliberately tried to harm them, even though the temptation is definitely there, especially after so many years of living with their contempt for me, the half-breed. But now it's not worth it. I'll help them, even Korendil, if only so that I'll never have to deal with them again.*

So they'll never interfere in Eric's and my lives, ever again.

Ria carefully eased the Porsche off the winding road and parked on a barren, flat strip overlooking a small valley. She stood on the rough gravel, gazing down at the grassy vale, as a white limo stopped beside her.

Perenor stepped from the car and leaned back through the open passenger door to say something to his driver. He closed the door, and the limo pulled away, heading back in the direction of the city.

Ria's father was dressed in a business suit, immaculately tailored as always. As she watched, his outline shimmered briefly. A moment later, he stood in full armor; armor that shone dully, like blue glass or blued steel. He had his sword sheathed at his side.

"You won't need that, Father," Ria said slowly. "Remember your promise to me? You agreed not to harm any of them, not unless my plan doesn't work."

Perenor chuckled dryly. "You forget, my dear, how thick-headed your full-blooded cousins are. If nothing else, this may impress them a little. I expect they look rather shabby—it has been several lean months for them since the nexus was destroyed. If they see how much Power I can command at this moment, they may listen to reason. I can sense all of them, including your Bard, down there." He gestured at the valley below them. "Shall we join them?"

Ria nodded, following her father down the grassy hillside.

I don't think I can trust him. I think he's going to try something, as soon as we're close to the elves.

And he's going to expect me to help him. Because the elves will attack me, as well as him, and he probably thinks that I'll have to fight, if only to keep myself alive.

Except—I won't.

She stumbled a little and cursed her high-heeled pumps—
then, recklessly, changed them to flat, glove-leather boots.

*It'll be a risk, because the elves won't know that I don't
intend to fight them. And I might get hurt. Or killed. But
if I raise Power against them, I've lost. Because Eric will
never trust me again.*

*Yes, it's dangerous. But I can't risk losing Eric, not
after everything that's happened between us, not the way I
feel about him.*

Her father strode along ahead of her, the heavy armor
encumbering him not at all. She picked her way through
the weeds carefully, and noticed how he looked neither to
the right nor the left; simply trod over everything in his
path.

*And after I've sent the elves across the veil, back to the
Faerie Lands, when there's nothing more that can stand
between us, Eric will make a choice. And if he wants to
walk away from me again, I won't stop him. Or coerce him.
I want him to choose to stay with me of his own free will.*

*And he will choose me. He has to. How can he deny
what is between us, the way his Power is reaching out to
mine, even now?*

Through the sparse trees she saw the circle of elves, the
human musicians, and the young man with the flute. Even
at this distance she could feel the power of his music; a
melody that resonated through her, a power that made her
hands tingle and her heart ache.

*He's so beautiful, with the magic shining through him
like a beacon. I'll never let him go again—*

As Ria paused on the hillside, gazing at the Bard, Perenor
strode forward impatiently. She caught up with him at the
edge of the trees. The elves saw them, and moved closer
together, forming a living barrier between them and the
musicians.

"Eric!" Ria called, but the Bard did not move or even
look at her. He seemed entranced, lost in his music, oblivious to everything around him.

One of the elves drew her sword in a swift, fluid movement. Ria set her hand over her father's sword arm as his
hand reached for the sheathed blade.

:*No. You promised me, Father.*:

Perenor gave her an askance look. :*Of course, daughter. But I doubt you'll be able to convince these fools of anything.*:

:*But let me try, at least.*:

He nodded cursorily, and stepped back a pace. Ria took a deep breath, the narrowed eyes of the elves intent upon her.

"We don't have to fight," she said, pitching her voice loud to be heard over the music of the band. "There's no need for bloodshed. I'll help you, transport all of you back to the Faerie Lands. It won't matter anymore that we control the nexus, you'll be safe. All I want is Eric."

An elf in blue and gold armor stepped between her and the young Bard.

"Touch him, sorceress, and I'll kill you," Korendil said quietly.

Ria restrained the impulse to summon the lightnings and burn that insolent look from the elf's face. "There's no need for that. I won't hurt him. He'll be happy with me, I can assure you. And all of you will be safe, far from this place."

Another, in green and silver, raised his visor and looked at her with an expression full of irony. "What makes you believe that is what we want?" Eldenor asked calmly. "Why should we flee this land that has been our home for so many years? What right do you have to demand this of us?"

Perenor spoke, very softly, before Ria could answer. "The right of the strong over the weak, Eldenor. Of the master over the slave." His voice grew in strength, filled with hatred and madness. "The right of the one who was unjustly banished, cast from his place among you, and has dreamed of the moment when all of you shall lie lifeless in pools of your blood—"

An invisible fist reached out and gripped Ria, ripping through all of her carefully-constructed defenses, through the layers of *self*, to the wellspring of her powers, her innermost being. She screamed, caught helplessly in the whirlwind, as her life and magic drained away.

She fell to her knees, controlled by forces beyond her imagination. A last thread of coherent thought battled through the waves of pain, the maelstrom of power surrounding her.

He—he planned this for years. When I was a child, too young to stop him, he set this up. Knowing that he could do this to me at any moment he chose—

And he's mad. Completely insane.

He's going to use everything against them, and kill me, to destroy the elves.

And then he'll murder Eric—

NO!

Beth focused on her fingerings like a mantra; kept her eyes squeezed shut to keep her attention on one thing.

The music.

Caught up in the melody, Beth could feel the currents of power dancing around her; tendrils of magic like a living creature, weaving and darting in strange patterns.

This—this is almost better than sex. Witchcraft never felt anything *like this.*

She smiled. Her eyes were still closed, and she concentrated on the music. Her hand moved lightly upon the guitar, fingerpicking a quick-running counterpoint to complement Eric's melodic line.

Lovely work, Banyon. For a while, I wasn't certain if this was going to play, but this sounds—feels—just right. Like everything is coming together, fusing, creating something new and wonderful—something truly enchanted.

Then she heard something else, a distant noise like pieces of metal clanging together. Beth opened her eyes, looking past Allie and Jim, towards the edge of the circle.

And her heart stopped beating.

The sunlit meadow had been transformed into something from one of her nightmares: a shadowy glen surrounded by billowing black fog, from which half-glimpsed creatures appeared, attacking the elven warriors, then fading away.

Beyond the elves she could see another figure in bluish-silver armor, battling sword against sword with Eldenor; and a blonde woman, kneeling motionless on the ground.

Somehow, in a way she didn't quite understand, Beth could sense the flow of power between Perenor and Ria, as the elf-lord drew strength and will from the sorceress.

Perenor. And his bitch daughter. They've found us—

And the bodies, littering the ground: Val, the lovely silver-haired elven woman, with claw marks across her face and throat; an armored swordsman, his turquoise breastplate nearly buckled in two, as if some immense force had crushed him like an insect in its grip.

They're working their way past the defenders, trying to get at us—at Eric—

She realized that she had stopped playing, and forced her fingers to continue, even as Perenor's sword bit deeply into Eldenor's side. The purple-mohawked warrior staggered back, into the murky depths of the unnatural fog.

Something, a creature that Beth's mind refused to admit could exist, reached out and dragged Eldenor back into the darkness.

Not even the music could mask his screaming.

Oh God—please, no—this can't be happening—

Her hands were shaking so much she could barely hold on to the guitar, much less play the chords. As Eldenor's screams faded, Perenor looked across the meadow at the band.

His jade-green eyes met Beth's through the slits of his helm. He moved toward her.

Then Korendil was between them, sword raised, forcing Perenor back with a wild flurry of blows.

For a moment Beth thought that Kory had a chance, that he could defeat the elf-lord. Then Perenor recovered his balance and counterattacked.

She could barely hear the music over the clashing of blades, the combatants' harsh breathing, the distant howling of the mist-creatures and the war cries of the elves; as Perenor forced Kory back a step, then another, and another, all the time moving closer to the band.

Edged steel clattered in strike after strike as Korendil fought grimly. From his stance, and his desperation—and from the strange magic that seemed to bind her, the elf, and Eric together—Beth *knew* that he knew he had no chance, but he refused to give up or falter—

Perenor feinted high, then came in at Kory's side.

Kory swung low, trying to shove Perenor's blade to the side, but not fast enough, recovering a split second too slowly.

Beth saw the opening, even before Perenor pivoted and brought his sword around in a fierce, whirling arc—

Oh God—he's going to kill him!

—and the blade sliced through Kory's armor.

Kory made a strange sound, a choked gasp, as the sword cut halfway across his torso. Beth saw him slip to one knee, then fall silently to the damp grass.

No—please, God, no—

The sounds of the battle, the horrific snarling of the monsters, all were nothing compared to the noiseless screaming in Beth's mind, the convulsive pain that gripped her heart.

Oh Goddess, no—Kory—he can't be dead—he can't be.

Perenor braced his foot against Kory's chest and yanked his weapon free.

Sobs tore her chest; her throat ached from holding back a scream. *No—please, no, anything but this—*

Perenor looked up; looked straight *at* her—

And smiled; a smile that froze the scream in her throat, turned the tears on her face to ice.

He took one slow, deliberate step toward her, smile widening as she backed up a pace.

You sadistic bastard—you won't take me without a fight!

She stopped playing; reversed the guitar and took its neck in both hands, her tears now as much of anger as sorrow.

You got Kory—but you'll have to go through me to get Eric!

He licked his lips slowly, sensuously. And with a start, she heard a low, ironic voice in the back of her mind.

:That can easily be arranged, mortal child. Especially if you propose to fight me with nothing but that foolish piece of wood—:

"Indeed?"

The new voice rang out over the sound of the fighting like a trumpet-call, startling Beth so much she nearly dropped the guitar.

The fog parted—and through the rift came another armored figure. Gold armor, with touches of brilliant scarlet, so brightly polished it hurt to look at it. The stranger raised his visor—

Beth gasped. *Terenil? But*—

"So, High Lord Perenor has taken to slaughtering children, has he?" Terenil said contemptuously. He glided confidently through the tangled knots of fighting, around the fallen bodies, with no sign of his *ever* having been the wreck Beth had seen after Eric vanished—

—except for the sad and haunted look in his eyes; the look of someone who has seen himself in the mirror and found only self-condemnation for what was there.

He stopped, just for a moment, beside Beth; caught up her hand and pressed it to his lips.

:Forgive me, child.:

Before she could react to that, he gave her an odd half-smile, turned on his heel and took Kory's place between Perenor and the band, pulling his visor down as he did so.

Suddenly a golden blaze of light flared up around him as he brought his sword up to guard position.

Perenor snapped his own visor down and his blade up—and an answering glow of cold blue sprang up about him.

Beth couldn't tell which of them moved first; they seemed to spring at each other simultaneously, blades and magic clashing in an exchange of lightning-quick strokes.

Unlike Kory's fight, or Eldenor's, this one involved both sword *and* Power. Which, since Ria was channeling magic to her father, made it two against one.

By the gods, if I can't do anything else, I'll see if I can't fix those odds!

There didn't seem to be anything but fallen bodies off to her left. Beth edged slowly past the band, out of the circle, never taking her eyes off the sorceress. All of *her* attention seemed to be on her father.

Funny, if I didn't know better, I'd swear she was fighting against him. That strained expression on her face—

Whatever she was doing, Ria was *not* watching the puny

mortal witch making her way toward her, guitar neck still
in both hands.

Just a few more steps—

The fighters were evenly matched; even Beth could tell
that. Neither one drove the other back for more than a
step or two, and always ground lost was regained in the
next exchange of blows. Terenil gave Perenor no openings
at all; Terenil could find none in Perenor's defenses—

Which means if I deep-six that bastard's magic source—
She was almost within reach. Then she *was* within reach.
The sorceress stared blankly ahead, apparently oblivious
to Beth's presence, or anything else happening around her.

Oh my beautiful guitar—you're all I've got left—

Gods. She raised the instrument over her head. *This is
for Kory, you—*

Ria turned suddenly, and stared *right* at her.

Beth froze.

There was a flicker of something unreadable in the
blonde woman's eyes before she closed them.

:Damn you, witch, DO IT!:

Beth brought the guitar squarely down on Ria's head
with a splintering crash and a jangle of strings. The woman
folded soundlessly.

Beth whirled, expecting that now, *now* she would see
Terenil take the upper hand—

—only to watch in horror as Perenor snaked his blade
around Terenil's guard, and ran him through.

Beth screamed.

Terenil went to one knee, Perenor's blade embedded in
his chest—and looked up into his enemy's face. As Perenor
stood, seemingly frozen, Terenil reached for Perenor's
sword arm—

*And pulled himself toward the dark elf, impaling him-
self still further on the blade lodged in his chest.*

And while Beth watched, he grabbed Perenor's shoulder, hauled his enemy within reach of his own blade, and
drove his sword into Perenor's side.

Terenil cried out something—a word Beth didn't recognize, a war-cry, perhaps—and the last of his sorcerous
power surged up his blade and into the body of his enemy.

At Beth's feet, Ria began to stir, rising to her feet—
Oh shit—
Perenor's body jerked, convulsing impossibly—and the
energy lashed from him in a visible arc into the body of his
daughter.

Ria shrieked, clutched her head with both hands, and
fell.

Terenil folded around the blade lodged in his chest, the
light fading from him, as Perenor toppled to the ground
beside him.

Christ!

Beth shook off her shock; ran to Terenil's side and knelt
there—but as she opened his visor, she could see that the
Prince had gone far beyond anyone's reach.

But—but he's smiling.

*He's smiling—as if he's having a peaceful dream. Oh
gods, Terenil—*

Terenil—what about Eric?

She lifted dazed eyes toward the band—but her eyes
fell on Kory instead.

KORY!

Before she realized she had moved, Beth was on the
blood-soaked ground beside him. His skin was as cold as
the metal of his armor as she cradled his face in her hands,
silently begging for him to live, but knowing, *knowing* . . .

She heard his voice through her tears, a last dying
whisper in her mind.

:Beth—my love—:

Then silence, like the emptiness within her soul.

*No—God, no—it can't end like this—please, I love
him, I can't live without him—*

· 20 ·

Banish Misfortune

God. Eric felt like he was about to float away. There didn't seem to be much of *him* left—it was mostly part of the delicate weaving of the spell, threads of luminous gold, emerald-green, sapphire-blue. What there was of him had become a wispy and transparent ghost in the heart of the structure.

Hang in there, Banyon. You're almost through. You can't let them down now, not when you're so close—

Spiral Dance's music wove around and around the outside of the spell, making it stronger, turning the threads into cables with a greater tensile strength than braided steel—but their efforts weren't what created it in the first place. And their efforts wouldn't be what created the new nexus.

He was so tired—

Don't think about being tired. It's not that much more. Just reach out—touch the veil—and call the magic—

The melody had long since slowed; not a lament, not quite. This had too much hope and promise to be a lament. It was a longing, though, a heart-song of yearning. And it lacked only a handful of notes to complete it.

Only Eric could play those notes, the key that would complete the spell and bring the magic.

I can't. There's . . . nothing left . . .

Oh God. I . . . have . . . to—

From somewhere he found a last little drop of strength, a last breath. And played.

327

At the first note, the veil thinned beneath him. At the second, the spell-structure suddenly *focused* on him, on the thinning spot he touched.

And at the third—

He hadn't been quite sure what to expect—a fountain, a river, a waterfall? It was like none of these things. Instead, it was like opening a window to the sun into a blacked-out room. For a moment all he could do was feel the warmth and life flooding back into him, replacing everything he'd spent in the spell. Like one sun-blinded, he stood in the pressureless flood of power and gasped, unable to sense *anything* beyond the light.

Then, as he felt more and more solid, he began to see things, somehow; or sense them in some other fashion. He could *hear*, all over the city, the minds of all the Lesser Court elves; he heard them waking out of Dreaming, heard them calling to one another in incredulous joy. Voice after voice in his mind, all joining with the song-spell he'd created, elaborating on it and making it stronger.

My God, he thought in wonder. *We did it—we really did it!*

Then he felt the pain. Not his—but around him. Close. *Very* close.

God! It doubled him up. *Death. There's somebody dead. Lots of somebodies. And lots of dying. I have to wake up out of here.*

Please—not Beth. Don't let it be Beth—

He began pulling his way up out of the spell; it was hard—and he was exhausted. Power was all around him, a glowing mist, and it would be so easy just to stay—

No!

He broke through, finally; felt the real world settle around him; forced his eyes to open.

And his heart just about stopped.

There was blood *everywhere*. Spattering the grass, sprayed across the clothes of the shocked musicians—

Oh shit—

Splattered on *him*.

And bodies. Graceful, attenuated elf bodies, sprawled around the perimeter of the circle, so much dark blood

soaking their slashed and singed costumes and armor that
they *couldn't* be alive.

There were a few of them moving; one or two still
standing. None in blue-and-gold armor.

Oh shit. Kory!

The strangled sob told him where to look: just on the
periphery of his vision, to his right. Beth, cradling a
red-streaked blond head in her lap, crying like her heart
was broken.

Oh God, Kory! No!

He took one step—and inadvertently reached out with
the magic that still surrounded him, even as he stretched
his hand out toward them. And as his sixth sense touched
them, he knew that, appearances to the contrary, Kory
was *still* alive.

But he wouldn't be for long. Not without a miracle.

Or magic—

*And if I do nothing, he'll die. My rival. I don't have to
do a damn thing.*

And how could I ever compete with him?

He could *feel* Kory slipping away; *see* the elf losing his
fragile hold on life.

No! Dammit, NO!

It was like grabbing the trailing hem of a garment that
was sliding over a cliff-edge; he caught and held the tenuous essence that was "Kory," and hung on to it with his
teeth gritting at the pain it caused him. Recklessly he
gathered the magic around himself; recklessly he flung it
at his . . . his friend. Without pausing to wonder how
much this was going to cost him, Eric wrapped himself in
the healing spell, with a touch of the "Simple Gifts" magic
he'd worked to such good effect before. Hoping that some
of this would spill over, touch and help the others—but
focusing the power on Kory.

*Live, you frizzy-haired sonuvabitch! Goddamn you any-
way, live, you idiot elf!*

He was jarred out of the spell when his knees gave, and
he found himself panting on the blood-speckled grass,
hands clutching his flute so hard they hurt. He looked up,
quickly, his heart in his throat, afraid he would see failure.

And Kory, lifeless on the blood-stained grass—

Beth was still sobbing, her face buried in her hands, but Kory's chest was moving, slowly rising and falling.

The elf opened his eyes just as Beth seemed to notice his movement. Their eyes met. Kory's expression was one of confusion, Beth's of disbelief.

"Kory?" she whispered.

Then they were embracing, crying and laughing, kissing one another, and holding each other as if they'd never let go.

Eric felt like crying too, but for a far different reason.

Okay, Banyon, you knew this was going to happen. So, how much do you care for them, anyhow?

Enough to give them each other, to get out of their way and let them love each other in peace?

His hands shook; his throat knotted.

Yeah. Yeah, I guess I do. Shit, what could I give her? I haven't got anything but the clothes on my back and the flute. And Kory—maybe this'll pay him back for when I ran out on him before.

Hot tears splashed on his hands as he quickly took the flute apart and stowed it in its case. His stomach tightened as he lurched to his feet and shoved the case away in the gig bag still slung over his shoulder.

Okay. This is where the hero's best friend saddles up and rides off into the east—so the hero and his girl can ride off into the sunset.

But it hurts so much, dammit, it hurts—

No one seemed to notice as he walked to the edge of the clearing. Eric glanced back once over his shoulder, wanting a last glimpse of Beth.

They were still kissing, so lost in each other that if the big earthquake hit right then they probably wouldn't even notice.

'Bye, guys. Be good to each other, okay?

Someday, maybe, I'll . . get in touch.

Maybe.

A delicate cough jarred Beth and Kory out of their clinch. She looked up, startled, to see two people standing over her—the Healer who had been at the donut shop—

Elizabet? Yeah—Jesus Cluny Frog, what is she doing here?

—and her young protégée (looking *very* green and nowhere near as tough as her would-be image).

"Elizabet?" Beth faltered.

"You weren't exactly inconspicuous," the woman said serenely. "If my instincts are right, you have roughly twenty minutes before the reports of fireworks going off in this area bring in the police. I think you need a little help cleaning up—unless you don't *mind* doing your explaining from the inside of a jail cell. In which case, I hope you have a good lawyer. You'll need one."

"Oh Christ—" Beth got to her knees, and ran a blood-smeared hand through her hair. She looked around, bewildered.

The monsters were dissolving, exactly the same way Eric had described the "dragon" disintegrating: falling to bits, becoming heaps of dead leaves, old trash, and thin, noxious liquids. But the elves—

"Beth?"

"Yeah, Allie?" she replied, distractedly.

"Beth, I can't—I can't look at this anymore—"

"Lady, I'm blowin' this taco stand," Jim said abruptly from next to Allie. "Color me history."

Beth stared at her two band members, both of whom were wide-eyed with shellshock, and visibly shaking.

We all look like—like we've been through a war. Which, I guess, we have.

Allie moved towards Beth, as though she was going to hug her, then glanced down at her hands, wet with blood. She looked up and her eyes met Beth's, tremulous and afraid. "I've—I've got to get out of here, Beth."

Beth saw Dan across the glen, bouzouki in hand, already making tracks toward the park entrance without a single glance backward.

"Yeah, sure, you'd better get going—" Beth said slowly.

It occurred to Beth, as Allie and Jim hurried away, that the unity she'd always felt with the rest of Dance, even when they were all arguing over something, was completely gone. She felt nothing as they hurried away, not even a ghost of regret.

I think the band just died. Requiescat in pace.

Maybe they saw a little more magic than they were ready for. Talking about going out there and saving the world, no problem. But watching people die for it—

Big problem.

Not that I blame them. I don't know how I'm able to deal with this. This place looks like a slaughterhouse. At least . . . at least, it's over.

She looked around, quickly, searching for Kory, and saw him kneeling beside a body in golden armor—armor whose scarlet trimmings matched the scarlet blood smeared over it.

Oh God—he doesn't know about Terenil—

She stumbled across the grass toward him, and went to her knees in the blood-sodden weeds. Kory looked up at her, his green eyes brighter for the tears in them.

"Beth?" he whispered. "Why—why is he smiling?"

She took Kory's hand in hers, and told him.

Korendil concentrated for a moment, and his armor blurred and softened—and in a moment more he was clad again and in the blue trews and shirt he had "borrowed" from Eric. After a moment's consideration, he sent his sword after the armor.

Surely there will be no more fighting now. And this is far less conspicuous.

He knelt next to Elizabet, watching as the woman rested her hands against Narya's shield-arm. He could sense the bones knitting together beneath Elizabet's gentle hands. Beside her, Kayla was tracing a fingertip down a razor-thin cut along the warrior's cheek, the wound visibly closing behind her touch.

These two are truly amazing, truly gifted. If they hadn't found their way to us, I think we would have lost even more people. As it was—

He swallowed, looking at the once-peaceful meadow. *As it was, too many of our people died. And I was almost among them.*

If it had not been for Eric—

He was all that I dreamed he could be, and more. Even now I can feel the strength of his nexus; the limitless pool of magic welling up, like water from a mountain spring.

And he saved my life.

"I wish there was some way we could repay you," Kory said quietly, as the Healer helped Narya to her feet.

"We don't accept money," Elizabet said simply.

Kory looked up as someone rested a hand on his shoulder, and saw Beth gazing down at him. *:Beloved?:*

She answered aloud, her voice thin with weariness. "We'll need your help to . . . take care of the bodies, Kory."

He nodded, rising to his feet.

It was a simple spell, one that the youngest child-mage learned: to Call fire. There were no words for this moment, as he, the surviving elves, and the three human women watched each lifeless elven body dissolve into smoke and ash.

At last he stood, gazing down at Perenor and Terenil, still locked together in death.

Perenor, I can consign to the flames, easily enough. But my Prince—

A low moan distracted him; he saw the Sorceress stirring weakly, trying to move. He began to reach for his sword with his magic, but the dusky Healer spoke first. "No. Let me see her."

It was long moments (Kory's fingers aching to clench onto the hilt of his blade, wanting to summon the weapon into existence and quickly finish off the evil creature) before the Healer spoke again. "She's no danger now. That backlash nearly killed her—as it is, her mind is like a child's." She looked up; ebon-dark eyes met his. "You want to repay me—then give me this woman's life. Kayla and I will take care of her, and I'll try to mend her shattered mind."

Kory hesitated, his hand still twitching restlessly. From behind him, he heard Beth's voice, silently pleading with him.

:There's been enough blood here for one day, Korendil. Let them take her.:

Grudgingly, he glanced down at the semi-conscious blonde woman, half-curled on the ground.

Indeed, Beth speaks truth. Perenor is dead, and the nexus is restored. There is no need for this woman's death, other than my desire for vengeance.

And that is not enough reason to kill her.

"Very well. Though Eric, who has lost more than any of us to this sorceress, may wish differently—"

Eric—

Kory suddenly realized that he had not seen Eric for the last hour.

Where is he? What has happened to the Bard?

He saw that Beth had had the same realization.

"Goddammit," she said, looking around frantically. "What could have happened to him? He was here, I know he was all right, Perenor didn't even touch him—"

"He Healed the blond hunkola here," Kayla said. "I could feel it; it was right when we were driving up the road."

"And now he's gone." Beth slammed her fist into her palm. "Dammit, Banyon never thinks before he does anything! Come on, we've got to find him!"

"And how do you know he wants to be found?"

Kory and Beth both looked at Elizabet. "What?" Beth asked obviously puzzled.

Elizabet shrugged. "From what I saw in the donut shop this morning, I'd say the young man is in love with you, Beth. But you care for Korendil. That's obvious as well. Perhaps you should just let him leave, if this is what he wants."

"But I don't want him to go! I love him too, that stupid whistler! And he knows that!"

The Healer shook her head. "I think you have to make a choice, Beth."

Kory watched Beth waver; then her mouth tightened with resolve.

Is she choosing between us? Or, is it as the Bard assumed, and the decision is already made?

My heart is caught by this mortal woman, but how can she choose one of the Faerie over another of her own kind? And when the other is a Bard? There is no comparison between us: I, a lowly warrior with some paltry skill at magery, and Eric, a human Bard whose power shines through him like sunlight through the leaves!

She will choose to love him, of that I am certain. And I will be alone again.

But I love them both, my dark-eyed human witch, and the Bard who saved my people.

I love them.

But I have done enough harm to them, embroiling them in this war. If I leave now, perhaps they can return to what their lives were before. In time, I do not doubt they will forget me—

Kory's dark thoughts were interrupted by Beth grabbing his arm and dragging him to the parked jeep on the far side of the meadow.

He could not bring himself to break her agitated silence until they were both in the vehicle and he had shielded himself against the jeep's Cold Iron shell. "Beth?" he ventured from the passenger seat, as she started the engine. "Beth, perhaps I shouldn't go with you. I'm not certain that is wise. Perhaps you should talk with Eric alone—"

She didn't answer, just floored the accelerator. Kory sat in silence, wanting to ask her that final, unspoken question, but not daring to speak.

Not until he saw the bright metal gate of the park, firmly locked against all traffic, and the peculiar black-and-white car parked beside it.

"Beth, stop!"

The brakes squealed noisily as the jeep screeched to a halt. A mortal, garbed in dark blue, walked swiftly towards them. Kory recognized the pistol in the man's hand from the many television shows he had seen through the windows of the electronics store near the Elfhame Grove.

"You, in the jeep! Neither of you move an inch."

The man's voice seemed strained, as he circled to Beth's side of the jeep, holding the tiny weapon at ready.

We must look somewhat unusual, compared to this man's bland clothing. Beth is still dressed in High Court finery, and I in Eric's garb, and both of our persons are thoroughly stained with blood.

The sight of blood does seem to unnerve many of these humans.

"You're Eliza Kentraine?"

"Yes," Beth replied carefully. "But—"

"Miss, just step out of the car, slowly. We want to ask you some questions about the disappearance of Philip Osborn and an explosion this morning in Tarzana. You there, just stay where you are, no fast moves. Miss Kentraine, you have the right to remain si—"

Kory was uncertain what was happening; but the look on Beth's face, that he understood instantly.

She is very frightened. But she will not do anything against this man, for reasons that I cannot understand.

But the power of the new nexus is still flowing strongly through me—it is scarcely an effort to reach out lightly and—

The policeman froze, one arm still raised in midair.

Beth turned and stared at Kory.

Kory shrugged. "I think we can leave now," he said, breaking the awkward silence.

"I think you're right," Beth said at last. She got out of the jeep, walked around the frozen policeman, and opened the park gate.

She climbed back into the jeep and sat there for a moment. "I guess—I guess I can't go back now. You know, it's kinda funny—I just thought that we'd save your people, stop Perenor and Ria, and then—then I'd go back home to my apartment, and in another couple weeks the show would come off hiatus and I'd be back at work again—"

"I'm sorry," Kory said softly. "I never meant to ruin your life, Beth. I never even meant to change it."

Beth sighed. "No, it's okay. It's just . . . a shock, that's all." She turned the key in the ignition. "Doesn't matter. Besides, we have a Bard to find. God only knows what trouble he's in already—"

*   *   *

A lock of hair flopped into Eric's eyes. When he pushed it out of the way, his fingers came away sticky and wet.

He stopped, halfway down the hillside, and stared at them.

Red. Blood. Christ, I'm covered with blood.

Nausea hit him, and he rubbed his hand frantically on the burgundy-red silk of his breeches.

Funny, I don't feel tired. Just sick.

He realized in another moment why—the invisible, but omnipresent flow of *magic* all around him, radiating out of the new nexus. It was restoring some of what he'd put into its creation, a little more with every moment that passed. And if he closed his eyes and listened with his "inner" ear, he could hear the elves, more and more of them Waking again . . .

Well, that's one good thing you've done with your life, Banyon. He sighed. *I sure's hell don't need the cops stopping me for looking like a Faire loonie who just slaughtered half his troupe.*

Okay, disguise time. Then I can stop at the restroom by the gate and get— he swallowed his nausea—*cleaned up.*

A moment of concentration, and he was, to all outward appearances, just another skinny guy in red T-shirt and jeans. He continued his scramble down the hillside, practically stumbling down onto the hiker's path that would take him to the entrance.

For such a bright, clear day the park seemed completely deserted. He didn't see anyone until he was nearly at the entrance—but when he got within shouting distance of the cement-block restroom building, he was suddenly *very* glad he'd done his little disguise trick. Because there were an *awful* lot of cops in the park, all of a sudden.

He concentrated very hard on being inconspicuous. It must have worked, because although they were stopping anyone over the age of consent, and even a few kids, they didn't stop him.

Once inside the restroom, suddenly the most important thing in the world was to get the blood off—

He threw up a couple of times too.

He was still needlessly, neurotically sloshing icy-cold water from the sink over his head and arms when Dan staggered in the door, bounced off a stall support, and came to rest clutching the sink next to him.

"Oh God," the musician moaned. "Bummer, bummer. Not again. Not ever again. Blood. All that blood. Oh God . . ."

"Dan?" Eric whispered.

The other began to babble.

Eventually Eric made out some of what had happened, and a partial roster of the dead. Val and Eldenor.

And Terenil; Eric recognized him from Dan's description —and Dan was coherent enough at that point that Eric got a fairly good idea of just *how* the Prince had met his end.

That was when *he* began to cry.

Dan didn't seem to notice.

"Just before then one of those *things* got past the guy in black—just about reached us. *Got* my coat." He turned enough so that Eric could see the rent torn in the sleeve of his jacket. "Allie broke her Casio over its head. Man, that was too close. No more."

He finally faced Eric, and the flautist could see that Dan's eyes were white-rimmed, his pupils dilated. Dan, unflappable Dan, was half-mad with fear.

Christ. If he goes out there like that, the cops'll be on his ass and they'll throw him where the sun don't shine.

Maybe I can do something about that.

Eric concentrated, calling out of memory the soft notes of "October Winds," an old Irish lullaby. And when he thought he was ready, he reached out with the soothing notes and wrapped Dan in them.

When he opened his eyes again, Dan was standing there with a silly little smile on his face, a glazed expression like he'd just done some of his own best weed. When Eric moved a little, he seemed to snap out of it, although his expression still seemed more than a bit glazed.

"Hey, Banyon, long time, no see—you gonna—oh, that's right."

"What's right, Dan?" Eric asked quietly.

"We broke the band up." Dan shook his shaggy head.

"Allie's job, Beth's—not enough time, man. Not enough t' get us outa the Dive, anyway."

Eric shrugged, feeling his heart contract at the sound of Beth's name. "You know how it is."

"Yeah. Glad I ran into you, anyway. Well, later!" The bassist strolled out as if he hadn't a care in the world.

Yeah, Dan. Later. Couple years, maybe. Eric sighed, and slicked back his wet hair. *Now if I could just self-administer some of that oblivion I just gave you—*

He had just enough change in his pockets to get him to the Greyhound station on Riverside.

If I had a choice, where would I go? he asked himself, staring at the weekday crowd hustling past him in the bright sunlight. *San Fran, I guess. That's about fifty bucks. Plus some eating money, some clothes, a toothbrush. Make it an even hundred. And only one way I know of to get it—*

Hell, why not.

He opened his case at his feet, got himself positioned right there on the street corner so that the cops couldn't hassle him for blocking traffic, and fitted the pieces of his flute together.

Okay, world. Bard Eric needs a hundred bucks. Let's see if you'll oblige him.

The magic was still there, after all—still flowing freely around him. Potent magic—

But I won't play games with their minds. I'll just give them the most beautiful music they've ever heard.

Only . . . nothing Celtic.

So he closed his eyes and started in on an Andean tune, one Simon and Garfunkel had popularized: "El Condor Pasa." The minor air suited his unhappiness, his loneliness—

From there he went to classical; Tchaikovsky, Liadov, all the melancholy Russians. He could feel a crowd gathering; sensed their appreciation. After playing for about half an hour straight, he ended the session with the "Frog Galliard."

> Now, oh now, I needs must part;
> Parting though I absent mourn.

Absence can no joy impart;
Love once fled can ne'er return.

His eyes filled; he held the tears back with an effort.

And although your sight I leave,
Sight wherein my joys do lie,
If that death doth sense bereave,
Never shall affection die.

When he finished, and wiped his eyes, and looked down—there was fifty dollars in bills and assorted change in the flute case.

Okay. One more try.

Maybe—maybe just one Celtic tune—

He closed his eyes again, and began "O'Carolan's Farewell to Music."

The tune that old Turlough played for his patroness, Mrs. McDermott Roe, when he returned home to die.

When the last note had died away, he opened his eyes just in time to see a man in a dark business suit standing up after setting something in his case. The man's eyes were bright—and as he averted his face and hurried away, Eric saw tears escaping from them to trickle down his cheek.

And lying on top of the rest of the money was a fifty-dollar bill.

Eric stared at it, then stared after the man's retreating back. *I wonder if I should check the serial—*

No. Let it be. Thanks, friend; whoever, or whatever you are.

An hour later, and he was sitting on the bench of the station, a ticket in his pocket, backpack on his back. Now he was *really* dressed in khaki jeans and a clean T-shirt (thanks to the army surplus store); the fancy outfit was carefully folded away in the bottom of the pack with his change of underwear, towel and toothbrush. The only things he was still wearing were the boots. Somehow he couldn't bear to take them off.

Terenil—I'm sorry. I wish I hadn't thought so badly of you. You were a hell of a lot better man than I am.

Even if you weren't human.

The waiting room was more than half empty.

His life felt entirely empty.

So now what? he asked himself dully. *Go off to San Fran and busk, I guess. Work the run of Northern Faire. I could probably busk up there until it's time for Texas Faire. After all this time they'll probably have forgotten what an idiot I made of myself . . .*

He closed his eyes, shutting out the dreary, plastic waiting room, and hunched a little farther down on the bench.

Funny, the stories don't ever say what happened to the hero's best friend. The Prince and Princess were married and lived happily ever after—and Sir Joe went off to . . . open an inn or something?

His eyes burned.

Probably went off to die in a ditch someplace. Of a broken heart, no doubt.

So far he'd been doing okay on the strength of feeling self-sacrificing and kind of noble—but it was beginning to wear thin.

Oh God, I miss them. If this isn't a broken heart—

—if it isn't, it's a damned good imitation.

What in hell am I supposed to do with my life now?

Something warm and wet trickled out from under his left eyelid, and he wiped it away with the back of his hand before anyone could notice.

I can keep from messing their lives up, that's what I can do. I can get far enough away so that they won't be able to find me; so they can concentrate on each other.

His other eye leaked, and he sniffed; and covered both up by rubbing at eyes and nose as if he was having a hay-fever attack.

Dammit, Banyon, act like an adult for once.

Suddenly he felt weights settle on the bench on either side of him. Which was *usually* a prelude to a bus-station mugging.

He gave up feeling martyred in favor of survival, and

cracked his eyes open surreptitiously so he could size up his presumptive attackers. *Oh shit, that's just what I—*

"Eric?" Kory said softly, his eyes mirroring care and concern.

Eric went numb. All that he could think was, *Shit, he's still wearing my clothes—*

"Hey, Clint," said a voice behind him; he turned to his left, quickly. Sure enough, it was Beth.

"You figuring on riding off into the sunset?" she asked quietly.

"Y-yeah," he said, after a long moment of silence. "I kind of figured that maybe it was better that way, you know?"

"I thought," Kory admonished, "that you were going to think about how your actions affected others before you did anything."

"Yeah, but—"

"Didn't you ever think about how *we* would feel when you vanished?"

"Well, I—"

"We felt," Kory told him, "abysmal. Bereft, in truth. Dreadfully, dreadfully lost and alone."

"Y-yeah," Eric stammered. "But—"

"We felt like hell, Banyon," Beth said. "We thought we'd finally gotten everything on the right track, and we looked around, and there was this Eric-shaped hole in the air. And no Eric."

"But—"

"Great conversationalist, isn't he?" she said in an aside to Kory.

"We haven't given him much chance to really say anything, beloved—"

Right, guy, leave me the odd man out, and make sure you remind me about it! Dammit, you frizzy-haired creep, why don't you rub it in a little more!

"*Damn* you, why don't you just leave me *alone*?" he cried, as heads turned all over the bus station. "You've got what you wanted! The magic's back, the elves are safe— you've got everything I promised you! And you've . . . got . . . each—"

He couldn't bear it any more. Eric lurched up off the bench and stood with his back to them, his arms crossed tightly across his chest to hold the misery in, fighting to keep the tears from coming again. "You've got places here, things to do. Beth's got her career. Kory, you're a hero, you could probably take the Prince's place if you wanted it. You've both got everything you could ever want."

"But we don't, Eric," Kory replied from right behind him, as gentle hands rested on his shoulders. "Truly, we don't. Not without you. Eric—we love you."

For a moment, Eric couldn't speak, or think.

What? Does he mean that?

"Me?" he faltered. "W-we?"

A second set of hands joined the first, and turned him so that he had to look into their eyes. As always he was caught—and held—by Kory's emerald gaze. "Eric—"

:Eric, look into my heart. I love you no less than I do Beth. And she loves you no less than she loves me. No more, and no less.:

With a last, valiant effort, Eric tried to make his mind work again.

"What Kory's saying is that he thinks it could work with us; that we'd make a pretty tight little trio." Beth gave him half a grin. "I agree."

He clenched both his hands into fists, trying to resolve the conflict inside him into an answer. He looked from Beth, to Kory, and back again.

I love her.

And—God—I can finally admit it to myself. I love him, too.

Like he said. No more, no less.

How in hell can I deal with that?

He opened his mouth to deny it all—but what came out was a hoarsely whispered question. "Can—can it really work?" he whispered.

Kory's eyes were very bright. "We'll never know if we do not try, will we?"

"We've all learned a few things lately," Beth added. "Including one of the hardest—how to admit you're wrong and take your lumps." Her expression remained deadly serious for about three more seconds, then she grinned. "Except you aren't allowed another apology for at *least* a month, Banyon. So—what do you say?"

He opened his mouth; closed it. Opened it again. Looked for an answer.

And found it in their eyes.

"I—I love you," he whispered to *both* of them.

And was caught up again in one of those magical three-way embraces.

Tears came, and this time he didn't try to stop them. *You don't fight tears when you're happy. And God, if I'm dreaming—don't let me wake up.*

Beth giggled finally, breaking the mood.

"What's so funny?" he asked, sniffling a little.

"This is *so* much nicer without all the armor."

Kory chuckled, and finally Eric joined him, freeing an arm long enough to wipe away his tears of joy.

"So, Banyon, where are *we* going?" She loosened her arms enough so that they could look each other in the face without going cross-eyed.

"I was heading for San Fran," he said slowly. "But—I thought—I mean you've got a job and all—"

She shook her head. "Not no more, babe. We damn near got arrested in the park. I think they want me on suspicion of being a drug-producer, or something like that. And they think I did for Phil—there's an APB out on me."

"They *what?*" Eric felt stunned. "Aren't you—don't you want to tell them the—oh."

"Exactly." She shrugged. "So, methinks the life of a footloose street busker may not be so bad for a while. I don't think I could deal with jail, really. I have this . . . problem with confined spaces . . ." She went a little quiet for a moment, then turned a faint smile back toward Kory. "So, Korendil, know anybody in San Fran?"

"A distant cousin—"

"Is he an elf or a faer—"

Kory interrupted her with a grin of his own. "Finish that sentence, Beth Kentraine, and you will surely regret it."

She feigned shock. "Gods be praised, the pillar of sobriety has developed a sense of humor!" She raised an eyebrow at him. "I was only going to ask if he was involved with humankind. If he is, he could be useful. I've *heard* the busking was good up there, but there's busking and there's busking."

Eric tried the idea of the three of them living and busking together on for size, and found it felt wonderful.

Perfect, in fact.

He held the other two closer—and they responded instantly.

No, I don't ever want to wake up.

"San Fran, then," he said. "If it's all right with you. Only . . . Kory?"

"Hm?" the elf replied contentedly.

"Could you *please* give me my clothes back?"